VICIOUS
FAE

AURORA ACADEMY

VICIOUS FAE

CAROLINE PECKHAM & SUSANNE VALENTI

WELCOME TO AURORA ACADEMY

Please take note of where The Lunar Brotherhood and Oscura Clan have claimed turf to ensure you don't cross into their territory unintentionally. Faculty will not be held responsible for gang maiming or disembowelment.

Have a great term!

Lake Tempest

Lunar Pit

The Capella Observatory

The Dead Shed

The Weeping Well

Rigel

The Cafaeteria

Kipling Emporium

The Acrux Courtyard

Altair Halls

Aurora Academy

ELISE

CHAPTER ONE

"I should hunt him down and tear him limb from limb," Dante growled as we stumbled along the street towards his SUV.

"Then who would drive me home?" I teased, wincing as pain shot through me from the wound in my stomach. I'd healed most of it before the magic I'd stolen from Felix had burned out, but there was still a deep cut bleeding steadily just to the left of my navel.

Dante wasn't in much better shape than me; the scent of his blood filled the air as the deep cut in his side continued to bleed and the injuries Felix had given him in their fight only made his condition worse.

The air was cold and my bare feet were frozen against the sidewalk as we hobbled on towards Dante's car. There wasn't a Fae in sight, no one I could bite and drain for the magic we so desperately needed. They'd all run far, far away the moment the gangs had collided and I didn't blame them. Anyone who'd grown up in Alestria knew to run when The Lunar Brotherhood and The Oscura Clan came to blows. It was all too easy to get caught in the crossfire.

We made it to the car and I practically fell inside it, groaning as I leaned back against the leather seat.

Dante started the engine and set a fast speed as we drove back to the academy.

We fell into silence, each of us in too much pain and too exhausted to say anything anyway. But we were alive. That was what counted.

I reached across the seats and took his hand, smiling as his fingers engulfed mine and neither of us let go.

By the time we made it back to the academy, the place was deserted. It was nearly five in the morning, the sun was rising and everyone was safely tucked up in their beds.

I drew in a deep breath as we reached the foot of the stairs in the Vega Dorms and grabbed Dante, shooting to the top floor with my enhanced speed and the final scraps of my energy just to get us there faster.

I dropped him with a hiss of pain and he fell back against the door to our dorm, dragging me into his arms.

I let out a shaky breath and let him draw me close to his chest, pressing my forehead against his shoulder as my heartbeat finally started to settle. We were back. We were safe.

I didn't know how the hell that was the case after everything we'd come up against tonight, but it was and I just wanted to bathe in the comfort of his arms for a moment to soak it all in.

"I'm sorry," he began, but I leaned back and pressed my fingers to his lips to silence him.

"How could you have predicted any of that?" I asked, sliding my fingers from his mouth and down his neck until they rested above his heart.

"I should have done something about Felix sooner," he growled. "But he's my father's brother…it's hard to see family clearly sometimes."

"You shouldn't beat yourself up for wanting to see the best in him," I replied sadly. I knew too well what it was like to hunt for the good in a member of your family. I'd excused every failure my mother had ever made. I'd turned a blind eye to the depression, the gambling, the neglect… I guess I just hadn't wanted to believe that she didn't love me like she should have, but I certainly had my proof as of late.

"I shouldn't have taken you there tonight, bella," Dante breathed, tucking a bloodstained strand of lilac hair behind my ear.

"No," I agreed. "Everyone knows that the best strippers perform on Thursdays."

Dante snorted a laugh and the mood lightened a fraction despite what we'd been through. He fumbled behind his back for the door handle and we spilled inside suddenly as it burst open. I almost fell and his strong arms wrapped around me as he drew me back towards his bed.

"I've got you, amore mio. And I'm not letting go."

I bit my lip as I righted myself, liking the way he said that a little too much.

I glanced around the room to see if we'd disturbed our roommates, but Gabriel's bunk was empty and the window was open a crack. The cover around Laini's bed was pulled back showing that it was empty too, so I guessed she'd gone to stay with her girlfriend. Which was lucky for her because if she'd been here, I would have bitten her, no question.

I couldn't remember the last time my magic had drained this low. It left me feeling hollow, like an empty vacuum. I needed something to fill the wells of my reserves so desperately it hurt.

Dante stripped down to his boxers and dropped onto his bed, lifting the corner of the mattress and pulling out a handful of gold chains which he proceeded to drop over his head so that he could refill his own reserves.

I cursed beneath my breath as I reached up and snagged my Atlas from my bed, tapping out a message to Leon to see if he would come and let me bite him. I was going to give him ten minutes to reply before I went banging on his door, because there was no way I'd be able to sleep with this injury and I needed magic to heal it.

I lifted my dress to get a look at the wound on my stomach, wincing at the huge slice in my skin. It was a wonder I hadn't bled out before I'd managed to heal myself a little.

"It will take a while for my reserves to fill enough for me to help you, amore mio," Dante murmured as I dropped my dress again, checking to see if Leon had received my message.

He hadn't.

I was itching to go and start banging on his door, but I didn't really want the whole school talking about me again which they would if anyone saw me like this.

Dante reached up to the base of my mattress and started pulling gold rings out of the space around the frame. He placed them on his fingers one after another and I watched him as I tried to convince myself that I wasn't trying to stop myself from dashing out of the room and breaking down Leon's door.

A gust of cold air blew over me and I looked around just as Gabriel stepped through the window.

His eyes widened as he dropped into the room and he paused, his huge black wings flexing wide so that they blotted out the view of the sun which had just finished rising into the pale blue sky.

"What the hell is going on?" he asked with his upper lip peeling back, looking down at Dante where he sat on the bed covered in bleeding wounds. "Is this some kind of Vampire blood fetish thing?"

"You think I get off on cutting people up?" I asked, raising an eyebrow at him.

My fangs were tingling with his proximity. My gaze slid to his throat where his pulse hammered like the greatest temptation I'd ever known and I had to force myself not to lunge at him. That wouldn't go so well for me. I was definitely outmatched when it came to Gabriel Nox, but that really just made him more tempting.

Gabriel's brow furrowed as he noticed the blood staining my black dress and he strode towards me.

"What the hell happened?" he demanded angrily, glaring at Dante like it must be all his fault.

"We got caught up in a gang war." I shrugged like that was just a normal occurrence, which in Alestria it actually was. "And we're both out of magic."

"What the fuck?!" Gabriel bellowed, lunging towards Dante like he intended to start laying into him.

I shot between them, cursing at the pain it caused me as I grabbed Gabriel's arm and used my enhanced strength to stop him.

"Don't you dare touch him," I snarled as Dante gazed up at Gabriel through narrowed eyes with his muscles tensing.

"Stupido stronzo. If you took me on I'd leave you bleeding in a puddle of your own piss," he muttered, reaching beneath his bed and tugging out a box of gold coins which he started scattering over his mattress.

"Didn't I warn you about hanging around with scum like him?" Gabriel demanded, reaching out with his free hand to press it to my stomach. The bite of pain was quickly followed by a wash of pure bliss as he healed every wound on my body and I sighed in relief. "If you keep behaving like this, you're going to get yourself killed."

I blinked up at the rage in his eyes with a flicker of unease. There had been no way that I possibly could have known what would happen in that club tonight, but I wasn't going to bite back at him over his anger. Because I could see that it was really just a mask. He was afraid for me. And I was more than a little surprised to see how much.

"I'm alright," I said gently, placing my hand over his where it lingered on my stomach. "Good as new again now."

Gabriel's scowl deepened at my words and he drew his hand back. "I don't hear you saying that you're going to keep away from this asshole or any of the others you waste your time with," he growled.

I pursed my lips. I might have been willing to let a bit of his anger slide, but if he started trying to tell me what to do or who to spend my time with again then he'd fast find his way to the sharp end of my temper.

"This *asshole* is one of the best people I know," I growled, my own words surprising me as they rang with honesty. "And you can't tell me what to do."

"Just ignore the stronzo, carina," Dante muttered as he reached down the side of his bed and pulled a big ass gold crown out of some hiding place before putting it on his head. "He'll fuck off back to his rooftop soon enough."

Gabriel growled a warning, his wings flexing and feathers ruffling as he glared down at Dante.

"Maybe it's time I reminded you who's the most powerful Fae in this school," Gabriel threatened.

"Enough!" I snapped before Dante could reply. "There's enough testosterone in here to drown a cat. You can have a dick measuring contest later when I've had a shower and some sleep. In the meantime, Gabriel can you please heal Dante's wounds so that we can both rest?"

"No," Gabriel replied darkly.

"No?" I balked.

Dante was still bleeding steadily and every movement he made was painted with the pain of his wounds.

"I don't want help from some half-plucked vulture anyway," Dante growled as he started pushing gold bangles over his wrists. He looked like some kind of giant, demented leprechaun sitting there counting his treasure, but I bit my lip on commenting.

"Just cut the macho bullshit and stop being a pair of assholes," I demanded. "You're not going to just lay there in agony for hours while you wait for your magic to replenish enough to heal yourself, Dante."

"I am," Dante countered, laying back on his bed, covered in gold and looking absolutely ridiculous.

"Gabriel?" I asked, fixing him in my gaze.

"No," he replied simply, like a fucking psycho.

Well if he wants to act like a psycho, then I will too.

I lunged forward in a blur of Vampire speed, slamming into Gabriel and knocking him back so that his ass hit the desk and his wings were pinned behind him.

His hands gripped my arms as he tried to force me back, but my fangs were in his neck before he could even try it.

Gabriel inhaled sharply as his blood slipped past my lips and the raw ecstasy of his power flooded my tastebuds. He was freedom and sweetness and something entirely exotic embodied.

Dante laughed behind us and a surge of triumph prickled along my spine. I'd just overpowered the most powerful Fae in the whole damn academy.

I moaned loudly as I drank from him, my body pressing flush to his as my hands moved over the hard lines of his chest.

Gabriel's grip on my arms tightened and he wasn't pushing me away any more, he was pulling me closer. His breaths were coming heavier and I could feel the hard length of his arousal driving into my hip. His pulse started pounding faster and I moaned again as I felt exactly how much he was enjoying this.

My hands slid lower and his breath caught as my fingertips traced his waistband.

Dante cleared his throat behind us and I flinched, pulling back suddenly as I remembered he was still there. In moments like this, I could almost buy into Gabriel's prediction about us. It was too easy for me to get caught up in him, for me to lose myself in his company and forget about the rest of the world.

I looked into Gabriel's dilated pupils as I licked his blood from my lips and he growled hungrily in response.

He didn't even say anything. In fact, I was fairly sure he didn't have words for that because he'd definitely been getting off on it despite the fact that he clearly hadn't expected to.

My gaze slid down to the huge swell in his pants for a moment before I forced myself to remember why I'd bitten him in the first place.

I shot back across the room and touched my hand to Dante's wound as I pressed healing magic beneath his skin.

He watched me in silence until I was done then reached out to catch my hand before I could withdraw it.

"I'm sorry for getting you involved in my family's business, bella," he breathed, the look in his eyes betraying just how bad things had gotten tonight. He almost died. Hell, *I* almost died. It was fucked up and insane and weirdly exhilarating too.

"I wanted to come out with you," I replied, shrugging off the guilt in his eyes. "I'm a big girl, Dante. I make my own decisions."

I looked over my shoulder at Gabriel who was watching us with a scowl in place.

"I'm gonna go have a shower," I announced suddenly. Now that I had some magic back in my system, I just wanted to wash the blood from my skin and get some rest. I didn't give either of them a chance to reply before I shot around the room, grabbing a change of clothes and my wash bag then sped away to cleanse myself in hot water.

GABRIEL

CHAPTER TWO

I was left in a room with a raging hard on which wasn't going away and Dante fucking Oscura under a pile of gold. *Great.*

I didn't know why I'd reacted that way over a bite, but I'd been taken by surprise. And then Elise's body had rubbed against mine and the sting of her teeth and the press of her lips had sent me haywire. I hadn't fucked anyone else since I'd had her and I sure as shit wasn't going to. I couldn't get her out of my head and that meant one touch from her was goddamn nuclear.

Dante leaned up, reaching for the edge of the sheet hanging from his bunk with a frustrated sigh. He couldn't quite reach, his fingers grazing it and I sat watching him from my bunk with my lips pressed tightly together.

Maybe I should go and join Elise in the shower? What are the chances her going there was an invitation for me to follow?

I checked my Atlas a little hopefully then scowled at myself. *Fucking idiot. She doesn't want you. You're the asshole who hurt her brother. Not that she knows that.*

I'd been awake early wondering if I should tell her the truth. Deep down, I knew it was what she deserved. But I also knew she'd never want to speak to me again once she found out that little nugget of shit. And while I was helping to find her brother's killer, I was at least being useful to her. Maybe I was a selfish prick though, because I couldn't deny being anything to her felt sinfully good.

Dante finally snagged the sheet, pulling it across and it wasn't long before his soft snores reached me from behind it.

I chewed on the inside of my cheek, knowing I should probably let Elise sleep when she returned from the bathroom, but I had too much to say to her. She needed to know what I'd found in the Kipling Cache. She needed solid reasons to stay away from the fuckers in this school who were putting her in danger at every turn. And now I had those reasons. Something she couldn't ignore, because apparently my word wasn't good enough.

When she returned from the shower wrapped in a towel, my eyes followed her across the room to where she dropped it without a thought. As Dante had passed out, I had the feeling this little display was just for me. Either that, or she didn't give a fuck about parading around naked. *Probably the latter.*

My eyes swept over the curve of her ass as she tugged on a pair of sweatpants then pulled a tank top on. She turned to climb up into her bunk and I jumped silently down from mine.

"We need to talk," I said in a low voice and she jolted, realising I was right behind her.

"By the stars, Gabriel! You need to wear a bell around your neck."

I smirked, holding out my hand. "Come with me to the roof."

"No, I'm going to bed."

I gave her a look that said this wasn't optional and she gave me one in return that said it was.

"It's important," I growled then lowered my tone, even though it was clear Dante was asleep. "It's about your Pegasus friend."

Her eyes widened and all stubbornness fled from her expression. She nodded quickly and I caught her hand, dragging her to the window and pulling her to my chest.

She squealed as I opened it and leapt from the ledge, flexing my wings and holding her against me as I soared through the air.

"I could have walked!" she yelled as I climbed higher toward the roof and a dark smile pulled at my mouth.

I landed lightly outside my tent and she lingered against me for a full second. I could feel the thrum of her heart against my chest and the wildness in her eyes made my own pulse rise.

I guided her into the tent and dropped down onto the furs at the heart of the space, looking up at her as I waited for her to join me. I'd already decided what I was going to do. At first, I'd wanted to keep the video of her brother from her, but now she was here in front of me the idea seemed impossible. She deserved to see it. She *needed* to see it.

She frowned then dropped down, her leg brushing against mine as she settled herself into the space beside me. I was keenly aware of the time I'd had her pinned beneath me right here, her body bending to my will as she gave into her desire for me. It was the best fucking night of my life if I was being totally honest. And the thought that we'd never have that again was majorly depressing.

"What did you want to tell me?" she asked, hope shining in her eyes like she was praying I'd found out who had killed her brother.

I reached into a fold at the edge of the tent, disbanding my concealment spell and taking out the flash drive and the photograph I'd found in the Oscura stash. I passed the photo to her first, my gut knotting with tension as I waited to see how she'd react. It pictured her brother with his hand clasped in Ryder's, a flare of magic sparking between them as they made some deal.

She stared at it for a long moment with her brow furrowed. "This doesn't mean anything," she sighed, looking to me.

I drew in a long breath. "I found it in Dante Oscura's belongings in the

Kipling Cache. So I'm guessing Dante thought this was important enough to keep. And I would imagine he would have seen this as a betrayal."

"A betrayal?" she frowned heavily. "My brother wasn't in with the Oscuras."

"I'm not so sure that's true…" I picked up my Atlas, plugging in the flash drive and Elise shifted closer, her expression taut as I brought up the long list of recordings kept on it. "Dante has all of these videos on people he knows, people he thinks could become threats to him one day I guess. The teachers at the academy, people close to him who he doesn't trust…" I clicked on the one entitled *Gareth Tempa* and Elise inhaled sharply as it began playing.

The Oscura Clan were beating up a bunch of Fae in a locker room and Gareth stood at the heart of them, punching a guy who lay on the ground beneath him again and again. Leon Night appeared, drawing him away and Elise clutched my arm, snatching the Atlas from my hand as she replayed the video. She watched it over and over, staring at everyone in it then brushing her fingers over Gareth's face.

My heart tugged and I instinctively wrapped my arm around her shoulders.

"I don't want your pity," she growled.

"This isn't pity," I murmured. "It's support."

She shrugged like that was the same difference, but she didn't remove my arm.

"So you think Gareth was friends with them? Leon…Dante. The Oscuras?"

"I don't know about friends," I said in a low tone. "Maybe they blackmailed him into this."

"My brother knew his own mind," she said firmly. "He did this because he wanted to do this."

"And what about Ryder?" I pressed. "How long do you think Dante would have stayed *friends* with your brother once he found out he was striking deals with his enemy?"

Elise's brows pinched together as she stared at the screen, then looked at the photograph once more.

"What were you doing, Gare bear?" she whispered to herself.

I held her closer, giving her time to accept this. To realise that the people Gareth had been hanging around with had most likely gotten him killed. He'd been right in the heart of some gang brawl for fuck's sake and anything he could have offered Ryder Draconis could only have been bad.

"So it's time you stopped letting them into your life, Elise," I said gently when I'd thought she'd had enough time to come to this conclusion herself.

"What?" she hissed, shrugging me off suddenly.

"They're dangerous-"

"I know what they are," she snapped. "And this proves nothing." She tossed the photo into my lap and I scowled.

"It proves everything," I said forcefully, leaning into her face. "You're going to end up like your brother if you continue spending time with them."

Her palm crashed into my cheek and I snarled in fury.

"You don't know anything," she growled. "This isn't proof. It's snapshots of the past. There's no context. Dante might have known my brother was talking to Ryder. Or maybe he was never friends with Gareth in the first place. Just because he was in some Oscura fight doesn't mean they were friends." She got to her feet and I shot up after her as she pocketed the flash drive.

I darted into her way before she could leave, even though I knew she could bolt with her Vampire speed at any second. "I'm just trying to protect you! This may not be proof of who Gareth's killer is, but it's proof of who he spent time with. Who knows what he got caught up in when he kept that kind of company?"

"Exactly," she hissed. "Who knows? Maybe only the stars and his killer."

"Who could be in that video or that photo," I snarled.

"Yeah maybe. Or maybe not."

"You need to trust me on this," I pressed.

She tsked, rolling her eyes at me. "Trust you? You could be lying to my face to cover your own ass for all I know. I don't see how you're more trustworthy than any of the men I spend time with."

I gaped at her, astonished that she could really still suspect me. "I know I haven't been entirely honest, but I swear to you-"

"Save it. I've heard it before, Gabriel. And I'm tired of empty promises. I've had enough of those to last me a lifetime. Gareth swore he'd always be around, Mom promised to love and look after me no matter what. But where are they now, huh?"

I caught her hand before she could shoot away, pressing my palm to her cheek to make her look at me. "My promises aren't empty, Elise."

She yanked her arm free of me with a glare. "Words don't mean anything. Anyone can promise me the moon, but I've never seen anyone pull it from the sky." She sped away and my heart crumbled as she left.

She was going back to the arms of men I couldn't save her from. I simply couldn't be there twenty four seven to watch over her. After last night, wasn't it more obvious than ever how dangerous it was to get tangled up with the Lunars and Oscuras? She could have died.

My stomach churned at the thought and the Libra tattoo on my chest itched like crazy. I dropped down to sit on my furs, resting my head in my hands as I tried to think of a way out of this. There was only one real option, and it wasn't even a possibility. If Elise was ever going to trust me, I had to open my flesh to her and bare my dirty soul. She had to hear the truth. Every blackened, ruined part of me.

But I wasn't ready. I wasn't brave enough. Because if she ever heard those words from my lips, she'd despise me. She'd take out her rage on me, and why shouldn't she? I'd hurt her brother. I was responsible for a terrible,

terrible thing.

By the stars, if I'd only taken a moment to wonder why he'd been so desperate for the money, if I'd asked him, made him tell me why he needed it before I'd acted so brashly, maybe we wouldn't be in this mess now.

The saddest thing of all, was that I'd never have met Elise if her brother hadn't died. It was a cruel twist of fate. But if I could undo what had been done, I'd take that fate instead. Because Elise would rather have her brother in her life than some fucked up Elysian Mate who didn't deserve a hair on her head, let alone her heart.

I'm sorry, Gareth. I am so, fucking sorry.

ELISE

CHAPTER THREE

"As Mr Draconis clearly isn't going to show up, will you please pair with Miss Callisto today?" Professor Titan's voice caught my attention and I turned to see who he was talking to.

My gaze snagged on Gabriel as he pushed himself up out of his seat at the back of the classroom where he was sitting alone. His lab partner had obviously decided to cut class too which meant I was about to be gifted an hour in his company. I turned away again as he walked towards me, glancing down at my morning horoscope and wondering what it meant for the hundredth time.

Good Morning Libra.
The stars have spoken about your day!
Today you may be tempted to tread the line between curiosity and
foolishness.
Beware of testing the bonds of a relationship for selfish gain, but if you find
yourself in stormy waters then honesty is always the best policy.

I glanced up at the clock, frowning at the time and wondering where the hell Ryder was. It was twenty past and I got the feeling Titan was right, he wasn't going to show.

I hadn't seen him since the club and I'd been more than a little concerned about coming face to face with him again for the first time. But now that he hadn't shown up, I was starting to worry.

I pushed out of my seat before Gabriel made it to Ryder's usual spot beside me and shot across the room towards Leon, coming to rest perched on the edge of his desk.

"Hey, little monster," he said with a grin, leaning forward so that he could brush his fingers along the side of my thigh. "Did you wanna ask Titan to pair you with me instead?"

"No," I replied with a shrug, glancing back at Gabriel as he dropped into Ryder's seat. He was frowning over at us, no doubt thinking up new things to say to try and keep me away from Leon, but he wasn't going to have any luck with that. Being with Leon felt like sitting in the rays of the sun on a summer's day and I had no intention of giving him up any time soon. If ever.

"So why do I get the pleasure of your company then?" Leon asked, sliding his hand up into my lap and taking my hand.

I smiled as he wound his fingers between mine and blew a bubble with my gum, the scent of cherries lingering on the air as it popped.

"Have you seen Ryder this morning?" I asked, running my thumb across the back of his hand.

"Don't tell me the only reason you came over here was to ask about that Pumbaa lover," Leon groaned, leaning back in his chair with a sigh.

"It's not the only reason," I replied, reaching out to run my fingers through his long hair with my free hand.

The Mindy beside him inhaled sharply and I couldn't help but look her way as she stared at me without blinking for way too long.

Leon purred like a cat as he leaned into my touch and I smiled as my attention moved back to him.

"But you still want my answer, right?" he asked with a knowing smile.

"I just need to talk to him about something," I replied.

"Fine." Leon leaned back and took his Atlas from his blazer pocket, quickly tapping out a message.

"I didn't know you and Ryder were on messaging terms," I teased.

"We're not. I just put the Mindys on high alert. If any of them have seen him today then they'll let me know."

His Atlas started pinging repeatedly until Titan walked past us and cleared his throat irritably. Leon silenced it as he looked down at the replies and shrugged before holding it out for me to see.

Oriane Steiner:

I'm going to hunt him down now!

Bethan Looms:

He wasn't at breakfast but I'll search every nook and cranny until I locate him!

Brandi Kneifel:

I can draw tattoos all over my body and do a good impression of him if that would help?

Abigail Cole:

I'm going to the roof of the Vega Dorms to scream his name to the clouds!

Jess Peters:

I'll leave class now and head down to the Lunar part of town to find him!

"So no one's seen him," I said, handing his Atlas back with an uncomfortable feeling writhing in the pit of my stomach.

"I'll let you know when they do," Leon offered.

"Thanks." I slipped off of his table but he didn't release my hand, tugging me down so that he could steal a kiss.

I sighed breathily as I leaned into him, pushing my free hand into his silky hair for a far too brief moment before I pulled away again.

"So is it my turn with you tonight?" he asked with a grin that had me biting my lip.

"Maybe," I replied before shooting away.

I dropped back into my usual chair and blew a lock of lilac hair out of my eyes as it settled from my speed. It fell straight back down onto my face and Gabriel leaned forward to tuck it behind my ear.

He pulled back again instantly and I narrowed my eyes at him. "Why do you do shit like that?"

Gabriel shrugged and I rolled my eyes at him.

"Of course you can't just be honest with me," I muttered as I flipped through my textbook, searching for the page on engorgement potions.

I could feel his eyes on me but I ignored him as I continued my hunt.

"Because it feels natural to look after you," he murmured, leaning close to my ear. "So natural that sometimes I forget you don't want me to."

I pursed my lips and looked around at him. "I only want you to be honest with me," I said as I looked into his dark eyes.

"Okay then. In my honest opinion, I think you need to stop hanging around douchebags like Leon Night and Dante Oscura," he said.

"Well, in *my* honest opinion, I think that as a person who has no friends, you shouldn't be giving me advice on how to make mine," I replied.

"Do you kiss all of your friends like that?" Gabriel growled like he seriously thought his Elysian Mate crap held some kind of sway over my actions.

"Yeah. But you wouldn't know, because I don't like you." I got to my feet and headed away to gather the ingredients we needed for the potion.

"Everything alright, Elise?" Titan called as I passed his desk.

"Nothing I can't handle," I replied and he gave me an encouraging smile.

"Let me help you with that, buddy!" Eugene cried enthusiastically as he practically ran towards me.

"Help with what?" I asked with a frown as I hooked a cauldron from the pile at the bottom of the supply cupboard ready to fill with the ingredients we needed for the potion.

"I can get your supplies for you!" he gushed, snatching things from the shelves and half throwing them into my cauldron for me.

"Erm…thanks," I said, not entirely sure why he was so keen to help me out, but I guessed I *had* agreed to be friends with him so maybe this was his way of being friendly. "So…how are you?"

"Me?" Eugene squeaked, looking up at me with wide eyes.

"Yeah, don't friends ask how friends are?"

"They do! And I'm doing okay, thanks. I've had a bit of an incident with my socks but the rash has mostly cleared up now and I have asked Ferdinand not to use them like that anymore."

"You've lost me, Eugene," I admitted. "Who's Ferdinand and what did he do to your socks?"

Eugene glanced around like he didn't want to be overheard before leaning close to explain. "He's my roommate and he's a Griffin. I kept getting these really sore, itchy rashes on my feet and I couldn't figure out why. But then one day I caught him in the act."

"What act?" I asked.

"He was…using my socks to wipe his ass. And you know how Griffin turd is super corrosive…"

I clamped my teeth shut as I tried not to laugh. I really fucking tried but I didn't quite manage to stop the snigger which found its way past my lips. "I hope you kicked his ass for that," I said as he blushed beetroot.

"Well…he apologised…kind of. I mean, what he actually said was that he was sorry my socks felt so good in his ass crack…"

I burst out laughing, slapping a hand over my mouth to try and stop myself. "I'm sorry Eugene but that's pretty fucking funny. You know, in a hideously disgusting way. But you need to teach that asshole a lesson or I think you're going to keep on having itchy feet and shitty socks."

Eugene twitched a smile too and even laughed a little. "Maybe I should challenge him over it…" he said, sounding pretty damn unsure about that.

"Hell yeah you should," I agreed. "You told me yourself, you're more powerful than everyone thinks. So Fae up and show that gross Griffin who's boss."

Eugene's smile widened a little and I could have sworn his spine straightened a bit too. This kid needed some serious attitude adjustments, but maybe with a confidence boost or two he'd be able to get past his self-doubt and learn to claim his place in society like every other Fae.

"Whoops, you've only got one swelling stone there, Dipper," Leon said loudly as he moved to join our conversation, tossing four extra stones into Eugene's cauldron. "You need more help engorging than the rest of us, so better add a few more."

"I don't need extra help engorging," Eugene squeaked, raising his chin as he looked up at Leon.

"Are you trying to say you've got a swollen dipper in your pants already?" Leon asked, slapping an arm around Eugene's shoulders. "Because I know you're hot for my girl but I really don't think you can handle her."

"Leon, don't be an ass," I warned as Eugene's blush spread right up to his white hairline.

"I'm not judging, little monster," he assured me. "It's been suggested that I spilled engorging potion on my lap too, due to the unbelievably enormous size of my dick. Do you wanna help me check?"

I snorted a laugh, pushing his arm off of Eugene so that the poor boy could escape.

"I have been wondering why the hell it was so hard all the time," I teased. "I just assumed you were *really* into learning."

"Nah, little monster. I'm *really* into *you*. But if you wanna play with this potion when it's done then maybe we could find out what happens when it gets poured over a pair of perfect tits?"

"If they're so perfect then why would you want them to be bigger?" I asked, arching an eyebrow at him.

"You can never have too much of a good thing," Leon replied with a grin.

"Is that so?"

Leon shifted closer to me and Eugene took the opportunity to escape, hurrying back to his desk.

I backed up, reaching behind me to dip my fingers into the pot of crushed pink whisper leaves on the shelf behind me as Leon prowled closer.

He caught my chin and pressed a kiss to my lips and as I gave in to his demand, I traced my stained fingers over his white shirt, painting a pair of full breasts onto it complete with really big nipples.

"I dunno, Leon," I breathed against his mouth, glancing down as I slipped away. "I think maybe they're a little *too* big now."

Leon's gaze dipped to his stained shirt and he barked a laugh as he spotted my artwork. I smirked at him then shot away before he could catch me.

By the time I'd made it back to my desk, Gabriel had clearly decided that he was done talking to me and was busily typing away on his Atlas.

I leaned back in my chair and glanced over to see what he was doing and frowned as I found him scrolling through a missing persons site.

"What are you looking at?" I asked curiously.

"Hunting for the boy who was killed in the woods. If someone's missing him then they might have listed him on this site."

Gabriel didn't look at me, but I found myself staring at him. I couldn't work out his angle. He insisted on lying to me about the thing I cared most about in the world. And yet he was still going out of his way to help me. Time and again. He didn't doubt anything I said and he seemed to be almost as invested in this investigation as I was.

I reached for the ingredients and started up the work on our potion. He may have been confusing as fuck. But I really did get the impression he was on my side.

By the time class ended, Leon still hadn't gotten word about Ryder from his Mindys. He didn't show up for Tarot class either and by lunchtime I was growing anxious.

It wasn't like him to skip class. He cared about his education, about learning to harness his powers and make sure he was the strongest Fae he could be.

Something was wrong. And in my gut I knew I wouldn't be able to sit through another lesson until I figured out what.

I pulled my Atlas from my bag and shot him a message as I walked down the corridor in Altair Halls. The gothic building was alive with the noise of students moving between their classes, but I zoned them out as I stared down at my screen.

Elise:

Hey...

It was pretty lame, but I didn't think I'd ever actually messaged him before. He just didn't really seem like the messaging kind. I could almost hear him asking why the hell people would bother doing something so normal.

The two ticks at the bottom of the screen didn't illuminate to let me know he'd read the message and I let out a huff of frustration.

If the snake doesn't want to come to the mouse, then maybe it's time I strapped on my war whiskers.

The rest of the students headed for the Cafaeteria to collect their lunch, but I headed straight out to the Acrux Courtyard.

I kept going until I reached the bleachers where the Lunar Brotherhood always congregated and paused as I found them entirely deserted.

I chewed on my lip, looking around in case any of them might have been headed this way, but there wasn't a single member in sight.

I didn't even know if he'd come back to the academy at all after last night, but there was one other obvious place to check out.

I shot toward the Vega Dorms before I could chicken out and pulled open the door, intending to head straight to Ryder's room on the ground floor. But just as I took a step into the hallway, the sound of a door opening caught my attention and I turned the other way instead.

Beyond the stairwell was a door which led down into the maintenance rooms beneath the building where the boilers were housed and I caught sight of Ryder just before he closed it behind him again. Relief spilled over me as I saw that he was clearly okay, but it was quickly followed by suspicion as I wondered what the hell was so important that he'd skipped classes and was now skulking off into deserted corridors beneath the school.

I hesitated, wondering what the hell he was doing down there and the sneaky stalker in me pricked her ears as I tried to listen in on anything that was going on beyond that door.

Even with my Vampire hearing, I couldn't detect a single sound beyond the door which was enough to let me know a silencing bubble had been cast.

It was probably a bad idea to follow Ryder Draconis down into the dark. But then I'd always been rather fond of a bad idea.

I shot forward and eased the door open just enough to slip inside. The heat of the pipes washed over me and I focused on my gifts and sharpened my eyesight so that I could descend the stone steps in the dark without needing to create a light with magic.

A soft amber glow drew me on and I placed a tight silencing bubble around myself to hide my movements as I sped towards it.

I kept going at the bottom of the stairs, through a long corridor lined with pipes and electrical wires before finally finding myself at the entrance to the boiler room. The light spilled out of the opening and I peeked around the corner at the wide space which housed the two enormous boilers.

It looked like every member of the Lunar Brotherhood was congregated inside, their attention fixed on Ryder who stood at the far side of the room talking to them.

I couldn't hear a word he was saying due to the silencing bubble that had been cast around the room and I cursed in frustration as I tried to figure out what to do.

One of the huge boilers sat close to the entrance, the ever burning flames beneath it flaring with the orange light which had led me here.

Behind it, where a nest of pipes were gathered, a shadowy corner sat forgotten. We'd been doing work on illusion spells in Cardinal Magic and I was confident that I could create a basic cloaking spell to hide myself in shadow. All I had to do was get into that spot and put it in place without one of the members of the most bloodthirsty gang in Alestria spotting me.

I must be fucking insane.

Everyone in the room had their gaze fixed on Ryder and their backs to me. If I stayed low, I'd be hidden by the crowd and my silencing bubble would conceal my passage.

I didn't overthink it beyond that and quickly sped into the room.

I moved as fast as I could before coming to a halt in the shadows behind the boiler and throwing my illusion up around me.

My heart was pounding with adrenaline and it took me a few moments to calm my breathing enough to focus on what was being said.

"If the Oscuras are descending into a civil war then why don't we just let them fight it out? Let them spill as much of their own blood as they like and once either Felix or Inferno emerges as the victor, we strike at them then," a girl suggested forcefully.

It was impossible for me to see most of the faces in the sea of Brothers but I could just see Ryder's face between the crowd.

He scowled, his lips pursing just enough to let me know that the speaker had pissed him off with her question.

"Because I don't want to wait. The Brotherhood don't need to hesitate while our enemies weaken themselves. I want to go after Felix myself and I didn't ask for your opinion on it," he snarled.

Muttering broke out around the room, but it was swiftly silenced as Ryder released a deep rattle from the base of his chest.

"If anyone here is questioning my decision then you must be questioning my leadership. So why don't you challenge me for my place if that's the case?" he asked in a low voice.

The muttering died a quick death and silence fell so thick and fast that my ears practically popped with it.

I frowned as I looked at the determined set of Ryder's jaw. He was willing to face down his own people over this, so it must have meant a hell of a lot to him. But why was he so hellbent on taking on Felix himself? I felt like I was missing a piece of information here and I itched to get my hands on it.

"No takers?" Ryder asked with a deadly hiss. "Why am I not surprised?"

Whatever Ryder's reasoning, one thing was clear. He was the leader of his people and his word was law. I just wished I knew why he was so determined to deal with Felix himself. Because I had the feeling the answer ran a lot deeper than pride or Clan superiority.

RYDER

CHAPTER FOUR

I cracked my neck as I waited for everyone to leave, running my tongue across my teeth. I'd put a subtle detection spell in place the moment I'd cast the silencing bubble. I didn't take chances on being spied on. I also knew exactly who had spied on me because I recognised the magical signature the spell had sent back to me.

I moved to block the exit then turned my head to where I knew Elise was hiding behind the boiler.

A dark smile pulled at my mouth. "Come out, come out wherever you are."

She shot forward in a blur and I lunged sideways, catching her arm and throwing her against the wall. I boxed her in against it, dipping my head as I stared down at my prey. And fuck I was already hot for her. My knuckles curled up and the word *pain* throbbed as keenly as *lust*. But I knew exactly which one I wanted to give to her most right then.

Her lips parted and her pupils were dilated. I didn't know if that was because I'd caught her or if it was because she was turned on by how close I was to her. Probably both.

"Spying on me for the Oscuras, little lamb?" I snarled. "I gave you a free pass at that shithole club the other night and this is how you repay me? You should be down on your knees begging to suck my cock in exchange for your life." *Now there's a sexy as fuck image.* Not that I'd get her to kneel for me with any real ease. But the look in her eyes was worth the comment.

She stood up straighter, gathering herself together like I wasn't affecting her, but it was too late for that. I'd seen the fear, the lust, the temptation.

"I'm gonna guess that's what you were hoping for with this little stunt," she said airily.

"My little stunt?" I scoffed. *"You're* the one who snuck down here to listen in on a private Lunar meeting, baby. Maybe you should remember who you're talking to."

"And yet you didn't call me out in front of your friends, oh mighty Lunar King." She twisted a lock of lilac hair around her finger and I had the urge to grab hold of it myself and tug. "If you knew I was here the whole time, then why not punish me in front of them and stop me from hearing your diabolical plans?"

"Maybe I want to punish you alone," I growled, crowding her in so her chest was crushed by mine. She licked her full lips and a groan almost escaped me as I imagined her tongue rolling around my dick.

"Or maybe you just hoped to keep up the pretence that you don't trust me," she continued. "Because let's be honest, you know I'm not Oscura aligned, Ryder."

"So why are you spying on me?" I demanded, pressing my hands flat to the wall either side of her.

"I saw you sneaking down here and got curious." She shrugged like it was so simple. But it was anything but that.

"Do you think your pretty face is safe from my fists, Elise?" I growled close to her mouth, because fuck I wanted to see her quiver. I wanted her to feel my power right down to her bones. "I'd beat you like I'd beat any other

Fae who betrays me."

"Who said anything about betrayal?" she asked sweetly, biting down on her lower lip.

Fuck, I swear she was doing it on purpose. She arched her back so her tits pressed against me and a groan of longing escaped me.

Her mouth twitched victoriously. *Shit, did I just show her my cards?*

"Want to know the truth?" she whispered, tip-toeing up to speak in my ear. Her breath on my neck might as well have been a handjob for how hard it got me. I was going to need my blue balls surgically removed soon if she didn't do something about them. *But oh wait, she can't fucking do shit about them, can she?* That deal with Inferno was fast becoming the bane of my life.

"Tell me," I commanded, only I didn't. It sounded softer, like a purr instead of a roar. It was unlike me at all.

"You didn't turn up to class and maybe I was one percent worried you'd gotten yourself buried in a ditch somewhere last night," she said, leaning back and letting me see the truth of those words in her eyes.

I battled the shit-eating grin that wanted to take my lips hostage. "I'm the one who does the burying."

Elise was worried about me. It made me feel warm. Too pissing warm. *What the fuck is wrong with me?*

I pulled at my collar, stepping back. "So you have a soft spot for me, do you? Do you have a wet spot for me too?"

"Fuck you," she laughed then she gave me a curious look. "So why do you even care about going after Felix so much? Isn't he the Oscuras' problem?"

I pressed my lips together, frightened of her hearing the truthful answer to that question. The fact that Felix had offered me Mariella made me certain he knew where she was. And rather than doing his dirty work to pay for her, I planned on hunting him down and torturing the answer from his lips.

I shrugged at Elise. "He's an Oscura. I want them all dead."

I stepped back but she caught my arm to stop me, a knowing look in her eyes. "Really? Because I owe you a thank you over an Oscura."

"Why?" I grunted.

"For Dante," she breathed, her eyes searching mine. "You spared him."

A hiss escaped my lips. "I wouldn't use those words."

"Then what words would you use?" She gave me a stern look and I ground my jaw.

"I was after Felix last night, not him," I said simply. But why *had* I spared fucking Inferno? I'd firmly decided not to think about it or deal with it since it had happened. Maybe it had been the desperate look in Elise's eyes. Or maybe I knew on some level that the only Oscura who deserved to be calling the shots in their clan was Dante. I wanted an equal opponent, not an underhanded piece of shit like Felix. I'd gutted men like him amongst my own people. They were worthless rats who lived for blood no matter whose it was they spilled.

"You could have gone after both," she pointed out.

"Drop it, Elise," I snapped and she rolled her eyes.

I turned my back on her and started walking out of the room. I wasn't going to punish her anyway. She was right, I'd let her listen in on the meeting. Because for someone unknown mindfuck of a reason, I trusted this girl.

"You coming?" I called.

"Oh is the mighty Lunar King inviting me somewhere?" She shot to my side with a taunting grin.

She might have been calling me that sarcastically, but fuck if I was going to make her stop.

"I need you for something," I said with a shrug.

"Well I'm gonna need a bit more information than that, Ryder."

"Your loss then." I upped my pace and she kept to my side with ease as I headed up the stairs. I threw the door open, marching across the foyer and causing a couple of freshmen to scatter like ants around me.

I headed along the ground floor corridor toward my room and was surprised when Elise followed me all the way there.

She leapt into my way before I could open the door, tilting her head to one side as she stretched her arms across the doorway.

"Tell me," she demanded playfully. "Or you're not getting in."

"I'll just force my way in," I said in a low tone, moving up into her personal space. "Or is that what you want?" I eyed her full lips with a hundred filthy thoughts racing through my brain.

She took my hand, drawing it to her mouth and grazing her fangs over my knuckles. The sensation daggered right down to my dick. She'd picked the word *lust* to toy with and I wondered if she'd done it on purpose. A groan of longing escaped me and I leaned in closer, part of me on the verge of forgetting this deal with Inferno and just taking what I wanted. What she clearly wanted too.

She lowered my hand, twisting away and pressing my palm to the door so the lock admitted me. Then she shot inside with her Vampire speed and I grunted in irritation before following her into my room.

"So what is it you want me to help you with?" she asked and I looked up to where she was lying on her back on the bunk above mine, her legs bent and her skirt having slid up her thighs.

"With my aching balls ideally, but that's not an option." I headed to my desk, opening the bottom drawer and taking out the kit I kept there.

"Maybe you should put them on ice?" Elise teased as I turned to her with the box in my hands. Her gaze fell to it and she sat up with an inquisitive look.

"Come here," I ordered, placing the box down on top of my desk and flipping it open.

She shot past me, looking into it while I pulled my shirt off behind her. I might not have been able to fuck Elise, but this was going to come pretty damn close in my books.

Elise gasped as she realised what was in the box. "You want me to-"

"Add a new tattoo to my collection, yeah," I said with a smirk.

"I'm not a tattoo artist," she laughed, turning to face me. Her eyes immediately fell to my naked chest and I swallowed as her gaze raked over the myriad of scars which covered my skin.

"Ryder..." She walked forward, lifting a hand and pressing her finger to one near my collar bone. She traced the crescent shape with a look of pain in her eyes. "How did you get these?"

I shrugged, my heart tearing open and weeping blood as the truth washed through me. But she didn't need that truth. It was in the past. Done. Forgotten.

Her lips twisted as she continued to brush her finger over my scars, the touch feather soft, but agony raced through me at the memory of each one. I drank it in, letting my magic reserves feed on it, but this wasn't the kind of pain I liked. Especially not when it came from me.

I took hold of her wrist, guiding it over my heart and using her outstretched finger to paint a cross there. She glanced up at me under her lashes, remembering the moment up on the hill overlooking the lake when she'd painted a cross on my heart in a promise that said she wanted the real me. Not just the venomous creature everyone else got.

"That's what I want the tattoo to be," I said.

Her eyes widened as she nodded in understanding. This tattoo was for her. It didn't need to be said. It was fucking obvious.

"I know it's just a cross, but I'm not gifted with art like my brother..." she trailed off, chewing on her lip. "I don't want to fuck it up."

"You won't," I growled firmly.

She shifted closer with a thoughtful look, her hand moving to my sternum where a jagged line marred my flesh. "I'll do it on one condition."

"What?"

"You have to tell me where you got these scars," she whispered

I tried to swallow my tongue and when that didn't fucking work, I nodded, giving in. Because fuck it, if she really wanted to know, she could. I just hoped she didn't see me as weak when I was done.

She spun away from me, moving to the tattoo kit and I stepped forward to help set it up. Once it was ready, I taught her how to hold the needle gun and figured that was good enough. I trusted Elise. And frankly, so long as she was causing me pain, a shitty tattoo was going to be worth it.

"Lie down then." She pointed to my bed and I fought a grin so hard I nearly popped a blood vessel.

I dropped down onto my bunk and Elise brought the tattoo gun with her, the canister swirling with black ink and the glitter of magic. I waited for her to decide how she was going to do this and when she swung her leg over me, straddling my hips, I just about came.

"Fuck, Elise," I breathed and she gave me a mischievous look. She leaned forward, using the cleansing wipes to clean the area of my chest she was going to brand.

Of all the marks I had, I wanted this one more than I wanted to breathe in that moment.

She held the needle over my heart and I inhaled as I awaited the kiss of pain.

"Start talking, Ryder," she purred, switching the tattoo gun on and skating the needle through the air, never letting it touch me. She dipped lower and the sweetness of her breath made me hungry for her mouth. A mouth I could never claim so long as the deal stood.

"You're a prick tease," I said.

"By the stars, was that a joke!?"

"No," I said immediately.

"Yes it was," she sang, grinning from ear to ear. Fuck, it felt good making her smile like that.

"Just get on with it," I demanded. The buzz of the needle set my skin alight with need. I wanted to bleed for Elise.

"Not until you start telling me about these scars," she insisted.

A hiss of frustration escaped me. *"Fine,"* I snarled. "An Oscura gave them to me."

"You're going to have to be more specific." She held the needle poised and a sharp pinch in my chest made me desperate for it.

"I need pain to talk about it," I said seriously and her brows stitched together.

She lowered her hand, pressing the needle to my skin and I sighed as it bit into my flesh and gave me the relief I needed.

"My father was murdered by the Oscuras," I said, watching her for her reaction but she kept her expression neutral and her eyes on the needle. "A few months after Inferno's father lay in pieces, the Oscuras set a trap to catch my father. They rounded up every woman and child amongst our people that they could and demanded my father come and give his life in exchange for theirs."

Elise's brow creased, but she didn't say a word. I guess she knew I didn't want her pity. And I was glad.

"He never told me the truth," I said darkly, my insides twisting. "I found out everything that had happened a long time after. Most of the Brotherhood walked with him to his death to support him. He sacrificed himself to save our people."

"The Oscuras let them go?" Elise asked, the needle slicing into me once more.

I nodded, but my jaw was tight. "They had another angle," I growled. "While the Lunars were away and I was left at home, Inferno's aunt, Mariella Oscura, came for me."

Elise remained quiet, waiting for me to go on.

"A group of Oscura assholes broke into my house and I fought for my fucking life against them. But my magic hadn't been Awakened, I didn't even have my Order." My skin prickled from the memory. Who I was today pivoted on that moment. If I'd been faster, if I'd escaped…maybe I wouldn't be so empty now, so broken. "I was thrown in a van and taken to Mariella's house on the outskirts of Alestria. And that's where I stayed for fourteen months."

"Ryder," Elise breathed in horror, her hand halting.

"Keep going," I demanded and she pressed the needle to my skin again, making me relax. These memories could only be relived through pain. I needed the outlet. I hadn't spoken about this since I'd told that bitch of a school counsellor, Miss Nightshade. And she'd never gotten the details, only what was necessary. I'd told her over months, giving her pieces here and there. But Elise would get it all at once. I had no fucking clue why, but telling her this didn't feel like being eaten alive by hungry ants. That was how it had felt telling Nightshade. She'd had no right to know my past, but it almost felt like Elise already owned it.

"I was put in a room with no windows…" I shuddered as I remembered it. It was a room I knew like no other. Every corner, every mark on the wall, every tile on the floor. "It was as if she'd made it for me. There was a slot in the door for food, a metal toilet and one blanket."

Elise pressed her free hand to my chest and the warmth of her palm spread into my icy blood. "Let me see," she breathed, placing the tattoo gun aside.

I flicked my eyes up to hers and showed her the room through a vision, letting her into that cold, nightmarish place for a few seconds. I felt her body stiffen and a growl left her throat. When I released her from it, her fangs had extended and there was a savage look in her gaze.

"Go on," she hissed, continuing the tattoo.

I cleared my throat, focusing on a spot over her shoulder as I continued. "She started torturing me daily. At first, I thought she wanted information on the Brotherhood, but it soon became clear she just wanted to break me." My heart cracked like aged stone and I ignored the sensation, hurrying on. "She'd burn me with fire crystals, freeze my cell and leave me in it for hours with no clothes on, she'd cut me with a blade made of sun steel then leave my skin to scar." It was one of the few metals in the world that could leave a permanent mark on Fae. The FIB were the only fuckers permitted to have blades made of it; it was created for killing Nymphs. But the Oscuras had always been able to get their hands on anything they wanted. "She never went far enough to kill me with any of it, and she healed me any time I got close."

Elise inhaled deeply, tracing her fingers over one of the scars on my chest. "Fuck, Ryder…"

I bit down on my tongue hard enough to draw blood and let the sweetness of the taste roll through my mouth. The needle wasn't enough. Nothing was enough.

"Eventually, she started letting me out of that room. But I had to behave. I was so fucked up by then, I was just happy to get out. She gave me better food when I was out of there, and she started…" I frowned, suddenly fearing what Elise would think of me when she knew all of this.

She cupped my cheek, making me meet her eye. "I won't judge you," she swore, painting a cross over her heart and the gesture meant everything to me. It was ours. It meant trust.

The rattle in my body buzzed in time with the needle. "She started being nice to me. She'd stroke my hair, kiss my cheek and embrace me when I was well behaved. But if I ever upset her, she'd put me in this wooden box in the garage. She'd fill it with water until I half drowned, let her car engine run until I almost choked. One time she put razor beetles in with me."

Elise sucked in air between her teeth. "How did you escape her?" she begged, her eyes glistening. A tear slid down her cheek and I frowned, reaching up to rub it away.

"Don't cry for me, Elise. I'm not worth your tears."

"You're worth every one of them," she insisted, pressing down harder with the needle and drawing a groan from me as pain scattered through my body. Her hair fell forward to caress her face and shadowed the agony in her eyes. "Keep going."

I took a heavy breath because this next part was probably the most fucked up of all. "You may judge me for this, but after a while Mariella became the centre of my life. She'd trained me like a fucking dog and I started begging for scraps from her. I craved her soft touches and gentle kisses. And after a while…her touches became sexual." I pressed my lips together, anger rising in me like a tide. Disgust. I'd only been fifteen for fuck's sake. "For a while I'd been so broken, I'd forgotten who I was. I forgot she held me captive."

"I don't judge you," she breathed. "I can't begin to understand what you went through."

"The day I escaped, I was lying in the box, waiting for her to start her torture. She started humming this tune-" I stopped, swallowing down the rage which was biting at the insides of my flesh like a hungry fire. The rage that had never left me since that day. "It was a lullaby my mother used to sing to me. The Mountain Boy."

Elise's eyes widened. "My Mom used to sing that to me too. On top of Fable, he lives alone, with only the mountain to call home," she spoke the words.

"But when the wind howls, he hears them call. His family waiting in the squall," I finished for her, darkness washing over me. "I snapped when I heard that. It was like a switch flipping in my head. Anger consumed me, clinging to every nerve in my body until it felt like my soul was burning its way out of my flesh. But it wasn't that. My Order Emerged. A ten ton snake ripped through that box, crushed Mariella's car and coiled her up in its scales. I had her. But I was disorientated as fuck. I couldn't get a handle on this new beast I had control of. I hissed at her and spat venom, pure fucking Basilisk venom. It burned into her skin, her face. It would have scarred her for life, but I wanted more than that. I wanted every bone in her body broken, I wanted her screaming until I drank in every drop of pain she had to offer. My Order needed it. I could sense it in me, this new dark desire. But she was a trained Fae. She cast a shield of ice and made her escape out the door. I knew if I didn't leave then, she'd capture me again. So I broke my way through the garage door and made it down the street before I managed to shift back into my Fae form. Then I ran until my feet were bleeding and I couldn't fucking breathe. I ran until I found my way home and discovered everyone there had thought I was dead." I took a deep breath, returning to the present. "Felix came to me recently and promised he'd give Mariella to me if I killed Dante."

Elise inhaled. "Holy shit, and what did you say?"

"I said yes," I growled then I barrelled on before she lost her shit over that bit of info. "But I don't like being told what to do. So I changed my mind. I'm going after Felix instead and when I catch him, I'm going to torture her location out of him."

Elise's lips parted and she turned the tattoo gun off. I eyed the black X across my chest with a swell of pride; I'd wear this mark for her.

"You definitely undersold yourself, this looks fucking perfect."

Her mouth pulled up at the corner and she tilted her head to admire it. "It does look pretty good actually."

I went to get up, but she shook her head, her eyes commanding I stay in place.

"Don't move," she whispered, leaning in so close I could count every freckle on her cheeks, see every fleck of tropical green in her eyes.

I couldn't fucking breathe.

She brushed her lips over mine and it took everything I had not to reciprocate that kiss. A kiss that would break my deal. But she'd never made any promise not to kiss *me*. The feather light softness of her mouth sent warmth into the deepest regions of my body.

It felt like healing.

"One day you'll kill her," she said as she drew away. "And I'll stand at your side while you do it."

GARETH

CHAPTER FIVE

ELEVEN MONTHS BEFORE THE SOLARID METEOR SHOWER…

I lay in bed, staring up at the mattress above, unable to sleep. Barely able to blink.

Ryder Draconis had murdered someone right in front of my eyes just hours ago. A traitor. Like me.

I had a video of Ryder screwing Professor King sitting on my Atlas, waiting for me to share it with Dante. He'd sent me a bunch of messages, asking where I was, what I'd gotten on his nemesis. But now…how could I give it to him after what I'd witnessed?

If I gave it to Dante and Ryder found out, I was going to be in a hole in the ground before anyone even realised I was missing. I couldn't help Ella from a grave. And more than that, I didn't want to fucking die.

I rolled onto my side, listening to Leon's soft snores. Amy still had the lamp on over his bed, straddling his back as she kneaded the kinks out of his muscles. The guy had been asleep for over an hour, it was ridiculous.

I let my eyes fall closed, willing sleep to come. Tomorrow held a world of problems, but right now, I needed to try and forget about watching Ryder murder someone in the woods. And I especially needed to stop picturing Micky's body as mine.

I woke to my Atlas buzzing with a message and groaned as I checked it, my eyes cracking open. I felt like I'd slept for half a second under a ten ton log.

Starhawk:
Meet me for breakfast, cavallo. No excuses.

I sighed, forcing myself out of bed and making my way out of the room to have a shower.

It wasn't long before I was dragging my heels down to the Cafaeteria, figuring I didn't have any choice but to show Dante this video. I'd already told him I had something on Ryder, so what else could I do? But I wasn't going to be stupid about it. I was going to make Dante swear on the stars that my involvement in this wouldn't get back to Ryder. That was pretty much all I could hope for. I had another payment due soon and I needed the money Dante was going to give me for this job. And he never paid me before completion.

The wind was whipping around me furiously as I passed through the Acrux Courtyard and I got it under my control with my air magic, pushing it away from me so it no longer battered my body.

I entered the Cafaeteria, the scent of sausages, eggs and bacon wafting under my nose. My stomach shrivelled in response. I couldn't eat. Not after what I'd seen last night. It was going to take me a long time to get over that.

I headed across the vast hall to join Dante where he was sitting with a table full of his Werewolves. He spread his arms as he spotted me, welcoming me like family. Maybe that was what he thought I was now.

"There you are, at last. Show me what you have." He snapped his fingers at Tabitha beside him and she jumped up to give me her seat. She eyed me with a scowl as she headed away, but didn't question her Alpha for a second.

I dropped down beside Dante and he slung his arm over my shoulders, his gold medallion swinging around his neck. "What have you got for me, cavallo?"

I frowned, shifting in my seat as anxiety gnawed at my insides. "Look, I wanna show you, but…"

Dante's arm tightened threateningly around me. "But what?"

I glanced at his Wolves and he raised his free hand, casting a silencing bubble around us so they could no longer hear what we were saying. Not that they seemed remotely interested. They were too busy messing around, tussling each other's hair and hand feeding each other their breakfasts.

I cleared my throat as Dante looked to me for an explanation. "I'm worried about Ryder finding out I was the one who got this on him. So…" I held my hand out to him, knowing it was a bold move, but I didn't have any weaker ones on offer. "I'll tell you if you promise you won't breathe a word to anyone that I was the one who made this recording."

Dante's brows arched and the look in his gaze said he was either mildly impressed with me or I was about to get a beat down. A tense moment passed between us where I expected to land on the ground beneath the wrath of his fists at any moment. Then he snatched my hand into his grip, shaking it firmly. "I swear." Magic sparked between us and my jaw fell slack.

I hadn't actually expected the King of the Oscura Clan to strike a deal with me. He was really covering for my ass. Which made me wonder again if we were becoming true friends. If it wasn't for the awkward as shit situation I was in with trying to get money for Old Sal, I might have started to enjoy Dante's company more. Apart from the odd psychotic moment, he seemed like a solid guy. And in Solaria, psychotic moments weren't exactly rare anyway.

"So what is it?" Dante asked excitedly, his dark eyes glittering.

I took out my Atlas, forwarding him the video before playing it for him to see.

He snatched it from my hand, a bark of laughter falling from his lips as he took in Ryder screwing the life out of Professor King.

"Fuck yes," he whooped. "This could get his ass kicked outta school. I knew that bitch was fucking with my results. He must have been getting her to screw with me." He tossed my Atlas back to me and I fumbled the catch as he took out his own. "Delete it, don't get involved with what happens next and act as surprised as the next person when it comes out today."

I swallowed hard as he removed the silencing bubble, taking out his own Atlas and tapping on it excitedly.

I felt that was my cue to leave and slipped from my seat, heading over to my usual table where Cindy Lou was waiting for me.

"Baby boo!" She jumped up, wrapping her arms around my neck and planting a wet kiss on my mouth. "You look so tired, were you out late last night? You didn't answer my messages."

Yeah I was off delivering a guy to Ryder Draconis to be murdered. No biggie.

"Just went home to see my family," I lied, giving her a fake smile.

She bought it, leaning up to kiss me again, but this time it was a dirtier display. I tried to get into it, but I was having trouble functioning this morning and I found myself pulling away and dropping down onto a seat.

Cindy glanced over at Dante's table, pushing her fingers into her hair with a pout. Then she dropped down beside me, resting a hand on my knee and leaning in close to my ear. "I missed you last night, baby."

"Yeah, I missed you too," I said hollowly.

I remained quiet while everyone fell into mindless chatter over breakfast. My eyes drifted to Lorenzo who was sitting alone across the room, looking *jittery as he watched the Oscuras like he wanted to go over there. I caught his eye, remembering my deal with Dante to help him out and beckoned him over.*

Lorenzo's face brightened as he got up, carrying his untouched breakfast over with him and dropping down beside me.

Cindy wrinkled her nose as she looked at him. "What are you doing sitting with us, Blazer?"

I elbowed her, throwing her a sharp scowl. "Lorenzo's my friend."

"I am?" he asked hopefully, his eyes glittering.

"Yeah, man." I shrugged and he started eating his food, his smile never going away.

I didn't miss the fact that he started moving closer and closer to me, rubbing his arm against mine in the way the Werewolves usually did with each other. He was obviously desperate for the intimate needs of his kind and my own Pegasus Herd was pretty similar in that sense, so I didn't mind. I just kinda pitied him.

When the bell rang, I headed out of the room with the others, trying to remember what lesson I had first.

Everyone's Atlases started pinging and tension gripped my chest as I watched Cindy take hers out of her bag. She clicked on FaeBook and my heart stuttered as I spotted Dante's post. It had only been up for one second and it already had a hundred shock reactions and fifty comments. He'd cut the video down to just five seconds, playing over and over again of Ryder screwing King on her desk while she screamed his name.

Everything inside me knotted up with fear. Because I might have struck that deal with Dante, but no deal in Solaria could save me from the wrath of the Lunar King if he ever found out I was responsible for this.

ELISE

CHAPTER SIX

My Atlas pinged as I stood looking over the breakfast options while hovering by an empty tray and I welcomed the distraction as I pulled it from my pocket to see who was messaging me.

Old Sal:

I've been caught up worrying about you ever since you came to visit me, baby girl. I tried calling your momma but the lady I spoke to said she isn't taking any calls, not even from you. I hate to think of you dealing with your grief all alone, you know I always thought of you kids as family. Any time you need anything, I'm here for you x

My first inclination was to delete the message. Old Sal may have been a part of my life for as long as I could remember, but she'd also been a constant source of problems for my mom. Although if I really considered that, I couldn't exactly blame Sal for Mom's gambling. Or for the fact that she'd been willing to sell me to pay her debts. But if none of that had happened then Gareth never would have offered to make those payments on her behalf…

I sighed, stuffing my Atlas back into my pocket without replying. Whether or not Sal was responsible for my mother's issues, she was right, she *had* been almost like family to me. And though she might not have been the most honest person I'd ever met, she had been there. Besides, decent people were pretty hard to come by in Alestria no matter where you looked, and she had at least kept my mother in work which meant we'd had a roof over our heads. Maybe she really did give a shit about me in some small way and there wasn't a whole lot of people I could say that about.

I turned my attention from the message, and focused on picking out something to eat instead. My feelings on Old Sal could wait.

I yawned as I filled up my breakfast tray with an apple and a few slices of toast, completing my meal with a steaming mug of coffee before turning back to select my chair in the Cafaeteria.

It was stupidly early, but my mind had been so full of theories and ideas last night that I'd barely slept. In the end, I'd given up on trying to force myself to sleep and just gotten up instead. Which meant that I was currently one of five people in the Cafaeteria and the only one of the other four who I recognised was a member of the Black Card called Adrian. Considering the last time we'd hung out, I'd given him a swirly and half beaten him to hell, I doubted he would be up for a bonding session over his bagel, so I headed towards an empty table instead.

Before I could make it to my seat, the door opened at the far end of the room and Dante strode in. He was dressed in his uniform but his tie was undone, several buttons loose at his throat so that his gold medallion showed against his bronze skin.

He seemed lost in his thoughts and didn't even notice me as he headed to collect his own breakfast.

As he turned back towards the room, aiming for his usual table by the far wall, I put two fingers in my mouth and wolf whistled him.

Dante lifted his head, looking my way and a smile pulled at the corner of his mouth as he changed direction and moved to join me instead.

"Eating alone, carina?" he asked in a low voice before dropping into the seat opposite mine.

"I happen to like my own company," I replied with a teasing smile. "But I won't complain about my favourite Dragon joining me."

"Do you know any other Dragons?" he asked.

"No. But I hear they're all assholes…besides, I bet none of them can dance as well as you."

He laughed, leaning back in his chair and shifting his legs beneath the table so that his knee grazed mine and a little jolt of excited energy raced beneath my skin.

"You could give me a run for my money though. Who taught you to dance like that, bella?" he asked, raising an eyebrow.

"I spent a lot of time in a strip club growing up," I replied with a shrug. I didn't really like talking about my past with him or the other Kings because I always felt like I had to lie, offer half-truths and conceal things. That shouldn't have made me feel uncomfortable, but for some reason it did.

"And there was me thinking my upbringing was unusual," Dante teased.

"Well there aren't very many Fae who are born to lead a clan of Werewolf gangsters, Dante, so I'd say you've still got me beat on the unusual thing."

Dante laughed and started shovelling porridge into his mouth as I ate my toast. Some of the Oscuras appeared while we ate and they approached us in confusion as they found Dante sitting in the middle of the room, away from their usual tables but he just waved them off without comment.

"Are you breaking the rules for me, Dante?" I asked in an undertone, my lips lifting at the corners with the idea of that.

"I seem to break all the rules for you one way or another, carina," he agreed. "But as I'm the Alpha, I get to make the rules anyway, so I won't be losing any sleep over it."

"So what *do* you lose sleep over?" I asked because I'd heard him tossing and turning in the bunk below me all night too.

Dante hesitated a moment before casting a silencing bubble around us and leaning closer to speak with me.

"Now that Felix has shown his true colours, I have to make sure my clan doesn't tear itself apart. He's trying to turn my family against me, claiming I'm too young to rule because my education isn't complete. He's spreading lies about me and trying to convince everyone that they should follow him instead."

"And you're worried they might?" I breathed, a shudder racing along my spine at the idea of the Oscura Clan being led by that bloodthirsty maniac.

Dante shook his head dismissively, but the look in his eyes gave away his concerns. "For the most part, no. My family love and respect me. They can also see that I'm a true Alpha. I haven't lost a pack brawl since I was fourteen and even Felix wouldn't dare challenge me head on like that. He only showed his cards at all the other night because he saw I was weakened, out of magic. È un patetico codardo."

"He's still dangerous though, isn't he?" I asked, chewing on my bottom lip.

"Yeah, he's dangerous. But so am I," Dante growled, a wave of static rolling off of him and making goosebumps prickle along my skin.

I inhaled sharply and his eyes lit with desire as he watched me.

"So what will you do about him?" I asked.

"For the moment, he's gone into hiding so it's hard for me to plan a strike against him. In the meantime, I'll be solidifying my hold on my family. I'm going home for a Clan meeting tonight and once that's been dealt with, I can focus on hunting him down."

Static crackled in the air in response to the rage he was clearly feeling and I reached across the table to take his hand.

Electricity tumbled from his skin into mine at the contact; it carved a path beneath my flesh, lighting up all the dark corners of my soul with an energy so potent I couldn't help but draw in a ragged breath.

Dante made a move to pull away like he thought he might be hurting me, but I tightened my hold on him as his energy made my heart pound. I was gripped with the desire to find out just what it might be like to feel that electricity pouring from every inch of his flesh as it was pressed against mine and I bit my lip against the moan which wanted to spill from my lips.

"Remind me again why you made that deal with Ryder," I asked, looking into Dante's dark eyes as his grip on me tightened and his gaze flared with heat.

"I've never known anyone to bathe in my power like you do, bella," he said in a low voice. "I feel like I don't have to hold back with you at all."

"You don't," I replied, because it was true. His electricity set my blood humming with the most incredible sense of intoxication and there was never a moment when I'd wanted him to hold back.

"Mi fai venire voglia di dimenticare l'affare che ho fatto, bella," he said in a tone that seriously tempted me to crawl across the table and climb into his lap.

"What does that mean?" I asked.

"That you make me want to forget the deal," he replied.

"And risk years of bad luck?" I teased.

"I'm beginning to think you'd be worth it."

"I would be," I agreed with a smirk before pulling my hand back.

As tempting as it was to allow Dante to curse himself with years of bad luck from the stars just for me, I'd feel like a bit of an asshole when his life went to crap because of it.

"Good morning, Elise," Kipling Junior's voice scared the shit out of me and I flinched as I spun to find him standing right behind me. Those dudes were weird as hell and sneaky too. I'd been pretty distracted with Dante, but it was still quite the feat to sneak up on a Vampire.

Dante waved a hand to disperse his silencing bubble so that Junior would be able to hear my reply.

"Holy shit, Kipling, you almost gave me a heart attack!" I cursed as I looked up at him. He didn't so much as blink in reaction to my words, just pushed a hand into his pocket and offered me a small paper bag.

"The payment for your latest job," he said dryly, offering it to me.

I'd almost forgotten that I still hadn't collected on my most recent efforts at distracting Professor Mars a few nights ago, but excitement built in my gut as I reached out to claim my payment.

"Thanks," I replied with a grin. "When's the next job?"

"We'll be in touch," he replied predictably. I got the same reply every time I asked them that, but I liked to try my luck at getting them to change it up.

"What about the items I asked for?" Dante asked before he could walk away.

"I'll call Senior now and find out," he replied before stepping away to make the call.

"Did he just call his own brother Senior? Surely they've got names?" I asked Dante in a low voice and he sniggered.

"Who knows? I can't tell them apart for shit anyway." He shrugged and I bit down on a laugh.

"Mr Oscura!" Kipling Junior's panicked voice had us both turning towards him again as he hurried back to join us, his face pale with horror. My eyebrows rose at the obvious show of emotion and Dante pushed to his feet as if he could tell this was important. "I don't understand how it happened, I'm so, so sorry, truly, but my brothers have just gone to the cache and...and..."

"Spit it out," Dante snarled and suddenly there was no doubting he was the King of the Oscura Clan. The easy going guy who'd just been joking with me had vanished to be replaced by a man whose aura clearly warned everyone in the general vicinity to back the fuck away. And a hell of a lot of them were doing just that. I caught sight of Eugene Dipper actually running for the exit from the corner of my eye and Dante's Wolf pack all stilled in their games and tensed like they were awaiting a command from their Alpha.

Electricity danced in the air and everyone in the room quieted, turning to look at him as it almost seemed like a storm could break loose inside the damn Cafaeteria.

"It's the cache…someone managed to break through the wards and get into your haul…" Kipling Junior looked damn close to pissing himself as a deep growl of utter rage left Dante's lips.

"Take me to it," Dante demanded. He strode forward, snatching Kipling Junior by the scruff of the neck and practically hauled him out of the room.

My lips parted as I watched them go and no one dared move a muscle until the door swung shut behind them again. The Oscura Wolves were all on their feet within a moment, whimpering and howling as they raced out after Dante and a small part of me was worried about what might rain down on the Kipling brothers because of this. But Dante was reasonable and fair even when he was enraged, I had to hope that he wouldn't blame them for the break in. No, his rage would be aimed at the actual culprit.

I chewed on my lip, wondering what the hell would happen to Gabriel if Dante figured out that he was the one who had broken into his cache.

I glanced around quickly, wondering if he might be here, but there was no sign of him.

As the room slowly returned to normal and people dared return to their conversations, I got up and shot outside. I circled Altair Halls until I came to rest against the rear wall where I pulled my Atlas from my pocket and sent Gabriel a quick message.

Elise:

Dante just found out that someone got into his stash and he's on the war path.

Gabriel:

That sounds suspiciously like you're worried about me...

I let out a long breath, trying to deny to myself that he had a point. The sense of swirling unease in my gut was undoubtedly concern for Gabriel. Not that he needed to know I gave a shit about him.

Elise:

I just don't want him to find out that you went there on my behalf.

Gabriel:

I'm not afraid of the big bad Wolf leader. Sticks and stones can break my bones but Storm Dragons don't scare me ;)

I snorted a laugh, a smile tugging at my lips as I sent him another reply.

Elise:

Okay. Shall I just tell him it was you then? Save him the effort of the hunt?

Gabriel:

I wouldn't mind the excuse to kick his ass for putting you in danger the other night, so go ahead.

Elise:

I'm not a princess in a tower who needs protecting, I can look after myself, thanks. X

Gabriel:

Did you just send me a kiss?

My heart leapt at that suggestion and I was about to reply with a firm *no* when I glanced back at my last message and realised I had. *Great, now I'm back to flirting with the Harpy. But now that I've started it, I guess I can't really back down…*

Elise:

Well I told you I like to kiss all of my friends…

Gabriel:

Are we friends now then?

Elise:

I'm still deciding. So for now you only get kisses via text.

Gabriel:

I'll have to work harder at being a better friend then so I can claim the real deal.

Elise:

Good luck with that. X

I pushed my Atlas back into my pocket and my fingers brushed against the paper bag Kipling Junior had given me. I pulled it out and looked at the little spy camera I'd requested. I still had forty five minutes until class which was more than enough time to carry out a little bit of work on my investigations against Nightshade.

I sped around the front of the building again and grinned as I spotted Ryder heading straight towards the Cafaeteria.

I shot behind him and leapt onto his back, locking my legs around his waist and placing my hands over his eyes. "Guess who?" I teased.

He laughed. Actually goddamn laughed as his hands caught my thighs to keep me in place. The touch of his cool hands against my bare skin felt stupidly good and I smirked as I leaned down close to his ear.

"Is it that giant spider I've heard people talking about out in The Iron Wood?" he asked as he stopped walking, holding me up easily.

"I don't have enough legs for that," I protested.

"Hmm, must be that Vampire who keeps stalking me then."

"Stalking?" I scoffed as my hands slid from his eyes and he turned his head to look at me. "I think you mean *hunting.*"

My fangs snapped out and Ryder tilted his neck obligingly, inviting me in.

That was more than enough encouragement and I sank my fangs into his neck with a moan of longing as I let my eyes fall closed.

His grip on my thighs tightened as he held me up and I slid my hands down the hard planes of his chest, exploring his body while using the excuse of the bite to do it.

When I'd finally had enough of his sin-filled blood, I pulled my teeth free of his flesh and ran my tongue over the wound to claim the last few drops.

Ryder released me and I slipped from his back, landing on my feet as he turned to look down at me.

"Are you trying to ruin my reputation on purpose?" he asked mildly, not really sounding like he gave a shit.

"Why? Are you afraid people might realise you're not quite as scary as you seem?" I taunted.

"I'm scarier than I seem," he assured me. "You just haven't been unlucky enough to find that out yet."

"Well that depends," I said slowly. "Perhaps I like being frightened every now and then."

Ryder looked at me for a long moment like he was trying to figure out how much truth there was to that statement before he turned and started walking towards the Cafaeteria again.

"Wait." I shot in front of him and his lips twitched with what was damn near to a smile. "Do you wanna come help me fuck with Nightshade?"

Ryder's eyes lit up with that suggestion, though he tried to act like he didn't give a shit either way. "I need to have my breakfast," he said.

I rolled my eyes at him, reaching into my satchel and offering him a bar of chocolate I'd stashed there for later. "I've got a better breakfast right here."

"The nutritional content of that lump of sugar doesn't really contain what my body needs to-"

"Fine. I'll do it on my own then." I flashed him a smile and shot away from him to Altair Halls, slipping through the door in a heartbeat and heading inside.

I sped straight to the teacher's offices and paused to listen for any sound of the faculty members close by. I could hear the soft tap tap tap of a keyboard coming from Titan's office, but aside from that, the corridor seemed empty. I cast a quick detection spell to give me a warning if anyone else appeared before heading on in silence.

At the far end of the hall was a copy room and I moved inside before connecting my Atlas to the copier and setting it to print.

The machine quickly started churning out a hundred copies and I took up position by the door where I listened out for any teachers who might approach. There was a window on the far side of the room and if I needed to make a quick exit, I planned on using it. Could I survive the jump from the first floor? Yeah. Was a broken leg preferable to Nightshade realising I was on to her? Definitely. The plan was fool proof. Mostly.

As the copier sped through its work, the sound of footsteps started to draw closer and I bit my lip as I waited to see who was coming. My detection spell was good enough to recognise the magical signature of whoever it was and I smirked as it was triggered.

The copier finished its work and I grabbed the stack of paper before moving back to the door as his footsteps drew near.

"I'm beginning to think you can't resist me," I teased as I stepped out of the copy room right in front of Ryder.

"I think that's pretty obvious by now," he replied seriously.

"I'm not complaining." I smiled at him before shooting around him to Nightshade's office.

Ryder followed me, his gaze moving to the pile of papers I had clutched in my fist, though he didn't ask about them.

He helped me open the door by picking it with a sliver of wood he created like last time and I ducked beneath his arm as I headed into the space inside.

"You wanna fill me in on the plan, baby?" Ryder asked me and I grinned at him as I pulled the mini camera from my pocket.

"I'm going to send her a message. And I'm also going to plant this little device somewhere she won't see it," I replied,

"I can help with that," Ryder said, smirking as he reached for the camera and I let him take it.

I watched as he moved to a potted plant she had perched on a shelf beside her desk. He used his earth magic to make the plant's leaves curl around the tiny device until it was completely concealed within it.

"I knew you were more than just a pretty face," I said as I moved closer to inspect his work. It was seamless, there wasn't any piece of the little camera on show anymore aside from the tiny lens which was almost impossible to spot. And I had Vampire vision so that was saying something.

"Give me your Atlas and I'll link it up to the feed from the camera," Ryder said, holding his hand out for it.

I took it from my pocket and unlocked it for him before turning my attention back to the other part of my plan. A wicked smile tugged at my lips as I readied the tube of meglusa I'd brought to complete my plan. This stuff was double strength and spelled to stick more firmly than cement. She'd have a real bitch of a time trying to take it all down again. I grinned to myself and took a deep breath as I prepared to channel my gifts.

I shot around the room at speed, plastering every single surface with pictures of the file Nightmare had kept on the boy I saw murdered in the woods. When I was finished, his face glared down at us from every wall, window and even the door. To finish it off, I snatched a red sharpie from my pocket and scrawled the words *I know* across the centre of them.

"Nightmare's gonna lose her shit when she sees this," Ryder commented, amusement lacing his tone.

"We should watch the footage together later," I said with a smile. "I'll bring some popcorn and we can make it a date."

"A date?" he asked, raising an eyebrow at me like I'd just spoken French or something.

"What's the matter, Ryder, don't you like me like that?" I joked, taking his hand and pulling him back towards the door.

"I don't do dates," he said like I was insane.

"You claim not to do a lot of things," I pointed out as I waited for him to lock the door again behind us.

"Well you make me act out of character," he replied.

I took the chocolate bar from my pocket and broke a square off as I waited for him to finish locking up.

As Ryder stood and turned towards me, I reached up and pressed the chocolate between his lips. He stilled as my thumb lingered against his mouth and I smiled as he gave in and started chewing.

"Is acting out of character really all that bad?" I asked as he swallowed.

"There's still no nutritional value to this," he protested, though it didn't really sound like a protest at all.

"Well it can be our little secret," I replied as we headed back down the corridor, escaping the scene of the crime.

"I'll add it to the list," Ryder deadpanned.

"What's one more?" I agreed. "Anyway, you didn't answer my question. Do we have a date or not?"

"I don't know how to date. Besides, I thought we were just friends," he said dryly.

I pouted at him but he didn't relent. "Fine," I sighed dramatically. "No date. Way to make a girl feel special Ryder."

He looked so damn confused by me that I couldn't help but laugh as I tossed him the rest of the chocolate bar and I shot away before he'd even caught it.

DANTE

CHAPTER SEVEN

I had ten Wolves going through every inch of my stash in the Kipling Cache to figure out what the little fucking stronzo had taken. And it soon dawned on me that someone wouldn't have broken in here, forcing their way through those magical barriers unless it was important to them. Really fucking important.

My obvious suspect was Ryder. That pezzo di merda would want to get his hands on plenty of items in here, no doubt. But what exactly? And how would I ever get evidence?

Electricity was rolling off of me in waves and my pack kept whimpering as it zapped them. I tried to rein it in, but it was impossible. A storm was brewing in my veins and it wouldn't be sated until I could set it loose in the sky.

"Everything's been accounted for, Alpha," Tabitha said with a frown. My beta had been unsettled since it had emerged that her father was a traitor, but she'd sworn her allegiance to me without hesitation when I'd asked her to confirm it and I wasn't going to make the mistake of blaming the pup for the dog's mistakes. Felix was my blood too after all. We didn't get a say in that, but we did get to make our own choices about what path we followed and she had proved that she was loyal to me time and again.

"Hm, not everything." I stormed forward, ripping aside the tapestry at the back of the cave, checking on the most valuable things I kept in here.

The stardust was practically priceless. It could only be made with Dragon Fire; even I couldn't make this stuff – not that I'd tried. But Dragon Fire was a key ingredient and as I could only produce lightning, I didn't think it would do the same job. This dust was made from melted fucking meteors. And it could let you travel across Solaria in the blink of an eye. It was a thief's wet dream, a murderer's getaway vehicle, a rich asshole's commute. And yet it was still here…untouched.

Attenzione all'ira di un drago – beware of a Dragon's wrath.

I pushed the stash aside, reaching for the other items I kept there and my heart twisted into a tight ball.

I roared in anger when I realised what was gone, throwing my fist into the wall so that my knuckles split open, spewing blood. Electricity exploded from my body and my Wolves yelped, gathering closer and brushing their hands over my back as they tried to soothe me.

"What is it? What's missing, Alpha?" Tabitha asked, her wide eyes searching mine.

"My collateral," I growled, my heart thundering a powerful beat. Every single recording I had of every single stronzo who could ever be a threat to me was on that flash drive. Why hadn't I made a fucking copy?!

The truth was bitter. I'd thought I could trust this place. As far as I knew, the cache had never been broken into before. It must have taken some powerful bastardo to do it. So at least that narrowed it down for me. And the culprit was likely to be in one of my videos, or one of their little friends were. Either that, or it was a paid job. It dawned on me that there was something else missing. The old photograph I'd had of Gareth and Ryder together.

I paused, mulling that over as I looked back around the cave to check for it. Why would anyone want to take that? Unless I'd thrown it away and forgotten about it. But I was sure I'd left it here…

I ground my jaw, then muscled my way past my Wolves, heading out of the cave. The second I reached the end of the tunnel, I started casting my own protection spell, pouring my magic into every inch of it. The Kiplings had done a good job of sealing this place, but I should have known to add my own magic to it too. I was one powerful motherfucking Dragon and no one would pass through this place again without me knowing about it. I added a detection spell into the mix and strode out of the cache, pulling off my clothes as I went.

I needed to fly, to flex my wings and bring a storm down on the world. I was going to make the sky bleed, tear the clouds apart and make it pour so that every stronzo in the academy would know I was angry. And I hoped someone, somewhere was quaking in their little thief boots, terrified of me finding out they'd stolen from me.

I was heading home for the night, driving onto my family's estate with a knot loosening in my chest. I needed to be around everyone tonight, even a storm and a fly hadn't been enough. I needed my mamma's food in my belly and my brothers and sisters and Rosalie huddled around me.

I loved my pack at the academy. They were family too, but nothing beat the bond I had with the Fae I'd grown up with under this roof.

I parked up beside the eastern vineyard, walking up the dusty drive and kicking my boots off on the porch. Mamma would clap me around the ear if I trailed mud across her floors.

I headed inside, a smirk pulling at my mouth when I heard the thundering of footfalls racing along the floorboards upstairs.

All of my brothers and sisters fought to be at the front as they tore down the staircase and I spotted Rosalie behind them with a glint in her gaze. She leapt over the bannister at the top of the stairs, landing in a crouch then racing toward me and beating them all to it. I crushed her in my arms a second before my siblings collided with us.

"You've gotten taller again, fratello!" Luca called, tip-toeing up and measuring himself against me.

"I've been working out, see?" Ivan flexed his muscles and I grinned at him.

"Looking good," I commented. "But you're not quite a Dragon yet."

Ivan howled mournfully and Rosalie elbowed him in the gut. "He's been farting non-stop since he went on the Faeto diet," she lamented. "Tell him to stop, Dante."

"Listen to Rosalie," I told Ivan with a grin. "Or you'll have to sleep in the yard."

"Come on now, dinner is ready," Mamma called, appearing from the dining room with an apron around her waist and her hair falling out of its braid. "Oh Dolce Drago, you've grown again!"

"Told you," Luca said, folding his arms and cocking his head at me.

"He's taller than Papa now," Cristina said.

"He's been taller than Papa for months." Gabriella rolled her eyes.

They all moved around me, nuzzling into me as I headed toward my mother. I pulled her into my arms, placing a kiss on each of her cheeks. "You look flustered, Mamma. Is there anything I can do to help?"

"There's nothing to be done. Everything is ready." She patted my arms, then took hold of my chin, searching my face as if looking for specks of dirt. I grinned at her as I got her approval and she let me go. "I missed you, mio ragazzo."

"I missed you more." I followed her through to the dining room and everyone fell over themselves to get a seat next to me. The table was full of food and I wanted a bite of everything. Mamma had outdone herself. There was every kind of pasta I could imagine, plus a huge margarita pizza and a massive bowl of salad.

Ivan dropped down to my right and Luca made it to my left half a second before Rosalie tipped his chair back so he fell to the floor. She rolled him out of it with a growl, righting it in a second and dropped down beside me with a wide smile.

"Causing much trouble lately, Rosa?" I asked and she grinned mischievously as Luca moved away, grumbling under his breath.

"None at all," she said sweetly.

Cristina bashed her fist on the table, laughing wildly. "Mamma caught her up the chimney just this morning. You were all covered in soot, Rosa." Everyone howled with laughter and Rosalie joined in, catching my eye.

"Good to know. If you start behaving, I'll be very disappointed," I said under my breath and she gave me a wild look which said I never had to worry about that happening.

"Sì, dalle stelle, Rosalie," Mamma said in exasperation as she dropped into the chair at the head of the table. It was meant to be for the Alpha, but I never let my mamma sit anywhere but there. I might have been the head of our pack, but she was the head of our family. "One of these days you'll give me a heart attack and then who will get you out of the chimney with magic?"

"I will when I'm Awakened," Gabriella said, grinning proudly. She was the smartest one of my siblings and I knew she'd get a place at Aurora. She was made for school. I didn't think she'd ever gotten anything lower than an A in class.

We tucked into the feast Mamma had laid out for us and my belly was soon swollen and my worries were far lessened. I knew tonight was about more than just family. We had to discuss the Clan. And most importantly, Felix. I just didn't want this moment of peace to be broken, but when we'd all had too much dessert and worked together to clean all the plates, it was almost time. The clock struck eight and it was only a few more minutes before the doorbell rang.

Mamma let in my aunties, uncles, cousins. Nearly all of the Oscura Clan filed into our dining room, laying kisses on everyone's cheeks and sharing hugs. I waited until the room was full and a silencing bubble was in place before I ruined everyone's mood with what had to be discussed.

There were several of us who weren't here. And their absence spoke loud and clear, ringing of their betrayal to us all.

I shared a look with Mamma as we all settled around the table once more. Luca and Ivan were wrestling on the floor and Rosalie was refereeing them.

"Come, sit down," I called and they immediately responded, jumping up to join everyone. I rose from my chair so everyone could see me and a hundred anxious eyes turned my way. "Several of us are missing today. There are two reasons for that." My heart weighed heavily and everyone's expressions became grave. "As you know, Felix has betrayed us and others have abandoned us to join him against us. The night the Lunars attacked, we also lost several of our Clan."

Many of my family started whining, their pain echoing through the room.

"Felix attempted to kill me that night, but that wasn't the only dance with death I had."

"What do you mean, Dolce Drago?" Mamma asked.

I dipped my head. I hadn't told any of them this because I hadn't been sure how to say it over the phone. I wanted to say it in person. I wanted them to see the truth in my eyes.

"Ryder Draconis had me at his feet, bloody and without a drop of magic left in my veins."

Collective inhales sounded around the room and my gaze locked with Rosalie's as she frowned in surprise.

"He spared me," I stated, looking between them to make sure they all believed me. "I don't know why, but I do know that he's also after Felix. So

80

may the better of us get to him first."

Howls sounded through the room then frantic chatter broke out as everyone discussed tactics.

"I wish to speak with each and every one of you in private!" I shouted over the noise and Mamma gave me a firm nod of approval.

"Use your Papa's office," she encouraged and I gave her a taut smile before heading for the door. "Rosalie – you first."

She scampered to my side, falling into step with me.

"Did Ryder really spare you, Drago? What happened?" she breathed in awe, seeming more fascinated than worried. That was what I loved about Rosalie, she was fearless. She would have gone after Felix at my side with not a drop of magic in her veins if I'd asked her to. She reminded me of myself at her age. And maybe I was protective of her because of what Felix had done to me back then. He'd turned me into a murderer, destroying innocent members of the Lunar Brotherhood when he told me they were responsible for my father's murder.

I knew Rosalie itched to be on the frontline in the same way I had at her age. And though that filled me with pride, it also concerned me. She and the other pups needed to be protected, no matter what. And sometimes that was from their own natures too.

"I don't know, Rosa. He had me at his mercy and he let me go. My friend Elise was with me, I think it may have been to do with her."

"Your girlfriend you mean," she said, jabbing me in the ribs.

I snorted a laugh. "She's not my girlfriend."

"So…she's Ryder's girlfriend?" she asked and a snarl ripped from my throat.

"No," I said firmly.

"Right…so why would he spare you because of her?"

I sighed. "You'd get it if you met her."

"So when am I meeting her?" she asked immediately.

I chuckled. "So many questions."

I couldn't imagine Elise would want to come and meet all of my family. Leon had told me how he'd tricked her into meeting his and I reckoned she'd be on high alert for anyone trying to make her into girlfriend material again any time soon. I quietly liked the idea of bringing her here though. But it was just another dream I had of her which I'd never get to fulfil thanks to the deal I'd made with Ryder.

I led Rosalie into the office and directed her into Papa's big chair beyond the desk. I'd feel like a stronzo sitting back there, so I remained on my feet while she fell into the giant wingback, swinging from side to side.

"How are things? Are you making friends at school?"

She threw her head back with a dramatic groan. "I hate school. I can't wait to be Awakened. All I ever learn about is how The Savage King started wars all over Solaria and blah blah blah."

My mouth hooked up at the corner. "Well it won't be long and you'll be pranking Mamma with your earth magic left, right and centre. You can help in the vineyards in the summer too."

She groaned again and I chuckled, having baited her for just that reaction.

"Alright, maybe I'll let you come out on a run or two with me." I winked.

Her eyes lit up and she threw her head back, howling to the ceiling. "Hell yes! I'm going to be the best Wolf you ever had in your pack."

"So long as you don't challenge me for the Alpha position," I taunted. We always joked back and forth about it, but if any of my younger relatives were Alpha material, it was her.

"I'll beat you with a rolling pin, Dolce Drago," she put on my mamma's voice and I laughed.

"You have to catch me in the clouds first, little Wolf." I rested my hands on the desk, baring my teeth at her and she bared hers right back.

"Can I ride with you while you're here?" she asked keenly.

"I have to talk to everyone in our family first, but if you're still awake by the time I'm done, I'll take you to see the moon."

She grinned broadly. "I'll be awake, even if you don't finish until dawn."

"We'll see about that." My gaze fell to a large white envelope on the desk which had our address on it in golden lettering. I snatched it up, tearing it open in irritation and finding the predictable follow up to Lionel Acrux's last letter. If he hadn't gotten the hint when I hadn't responded to that one, then he'd have to get the message this time.

I scanned the words on the page, sensing a slightly firmer undertone to this one.

Dear Mr Dante Marcello Oscura,

Your presence is required by the High Lord Lionel Acrux, Dragon Master and ruler of the Dragon Guild. It is proper and most mannerly for a Dragon such as yourself to take a vow to uphold the Dragon Laws long before graduation.

To refuse such an opportunity would be an insult to the High Lord himself. However, I am sure your delayed response is nothing more than a misunderstanding and we expect a letter from you soon explaining as such.

Upon receiving your response, we shall arrange your travel via Stardust to the Acrux Manor post-haste.

Secretary for High Lord Acrux,
Amelia Starfold

I rolled my eyes, tossing the letter into the trash can and Rosalie raised her brows.

"What's that?" she asked.

"Just a letter from an old Dragon trying to make me do what he wants." I shrugged.

"Well he clearly hasn't realised our Alpha doesn't do as he's told," she said with a grin and I shot her a wink.

"Right, onto business then." I gestured for her to stand and she did so, cocking her head to one side. "I need to be sure that everyone in this house is on our side against Felix. Will you make a star promise with me?" I asked. "If you break this vow, you will suffer, Rosalie, do you understand? This is more than just a Fae deal. If you break it, the stars will hurt you, make you burn from the inside out. And everyone will know you broke your word." My tone became serious and so did her expression. I'd already made everyone in my academy pack take this vow, and by the end of the night everyone else in my family would have taken it too.

"Whatever you want me to promise, Alpha, I will. I'd never break it," she said, nodding firmly.

"Then hold out your hand," I instructed and she did so.

I took the blue Lapis Lazuli Crystal from my pocket. I'd taken it from Titan's supplies. He'd seen me steal it and hadn't said a word to me. But that was pretty much what he did with all of the Kings in our school. Anyone powerful enough to put him on his ass got away with murder while he turned a blind eye.

I pressed the edge of the crystal to Rosalie's palm, painting the Taurus constellation on her skin. The crystal glowed, leaving a glimmering mark on her flesh. Then I turned my palm over and drew my own star sign onto myself.

When I was done, I took her hand in mine and the constellations pressed together. A tingle of heat rushed through my skin and her eyes widened as she felt it too.

"Do you promise never to assist Felix Oscura in hurting our family, the clan, the pack? Do you swear that you won't aid him in any way or contact him without my permission?"

I knew this was a big deal for her. Felix was her father by blood, but he'd never acted like one. She'd lived under my mamma's roof since she was a pup and though she never spoke about him much, in my heart I knew where her loyalties laid.

"I promise," she said firmly, lifting her chin.

Energy crackled against our palms and white light flared between them as the powerful pact was made. I released her hand and the marks on our skin faded away. But they'd live on beneath it, binding us by this vow.

I dismissed her and waited for the next Wolf to appear. When this was done, I would never be betrayed by my blood ever again without me knowing about it. And may the stars help anyone who dared.

ELISE

CHAPTER EIGHT

The storm that had thundered down over Aurora Academy last night had finally blown itself out, but the entire campus was still feeling the effects of it as little rivulets of water ran off of every surface and everything from trash cans to small trees lay scattered across the ground in the wake of the destruction.

It was Saturday morning and the birds were singing to the blue sky now that the rain had passed. I hadn't seen any sign of Dante this morning and I could only hope that he was alright despite the fact that he'd brought a mini tsunami down on Alestria for the fourth night in a row.

He'd been in a foul mood ever since he'd found out that someone had broken into his cache, but I wasn't sure if it was all about that or if his Clan's issues with Felix were compounding it too.

I'd tried to talk to him a few times, but he'd shrugged off my concern with kind words and an easy smile which had held a ring of falseness to it that I hadn't quite had the balls to point out. Yet. But if this went on much longer I was planning on holding an intervention. Dante's problem was that he wasn't used to leaning on anyone for support. He had his family all backing him, but as the Alpha, he took the burdens of leadership solely on his shoulders. And I didn't think that was the healthiest way to deal with things all of the time.

I headed down to Lake Tempest and shot him a message to come meet me at the boathouse. My Atlas buzzed a few moments later, but my heart dropped as I read his reply.

Dante:

Sorry, bella. I have to head home again for the weekend but I wish I could be alone with you instead. Maybe we can take a rain check?

Elise:

If we wait for good weather it might be years before we meet up. I hear a Storm Dragon has been wreaking havoc with the weather patterns and ruining picnics for everyone…

Dante:

I promise you one sun filled afternoon of my company entirely storm free just as soon as I can,

Elise:

I didn't say entirely storm free. I've developed a taste for lightning recently.

Dante:

Then I'll be sure not to disappoint.

I smiled to myself as I thought about that, biting my lip as my imagination got more than a little carried away. Dante and Ryder may have made their deal to stop themselves from coming to blows, but sometimes I was pretty damn pissed at the two of them for agreeing to it. They weren't just denying themselves by keeping to their ridiculous rules; they were keeping me away too. And a lot of the time, the two of them were just too tempting to resist.

I sighed as I reached the lake and I looked to my right in the direction of the boathouse. But I didn't want to go there without Dante somehow. It had become our place and I'd only be thinking about him if I went there.

"So you do spend time alone then?" Bryce Corvus stepped out of the trees beside me and I stilled as I looked at him, getting the strongest feeling that Ryder's number two had been following me.

"Of course I spend time alone," I replied casually. "You're a Vampire too so I'd have thought you know that much about me. We enjoy our own company. Though I have to say, my moment of solitude is being somewhat ruined now."

Bryce took a step closer to me, pushing a hand through his dark hair and flexing his bicep as he did so, making it bulge in a way I guessed was meant to remind me of just how much stronger he was than me. But with our gifts that didn't mean a whole hell of a lot. I may have been less than half his size, but I could pack a punch like a charging rhino if the need arose.

"You spend a lot of time lurking around people you shouldn't, too," he said in a low tone.

"Like you?" I asked. "Because I hate to burst your bubble, but the only time we ever interact is when you decide to hunt me down."

"If I was hunting you, you'd know about it," he snarled, baring his fangs in a clear threat.

Mine tingled in response, but I wasn't going to rise to the bait. I had no interest in fighting him for my position. As far as I was concerned I'd already established my dominance. I'd claimed two of the most powerful Fae in the academy as my Sources and I was biting Leon regularly too. With a bit of persuasion, I was convinced Gabriel would be begging me to bite him again soon as well, so I really had no need to fight a vulture like Bryce for anything.

"I'd be very careful if you start hunting creatures in the night, Bryce," I warned, narrowing my eyes at him. "You might find that some of them bite back twice as hard as you."

I made a move to leave and Bryce sidestepped to halt me. "I'm watching you," he warned. "And I know there's more to you than your cherry pie smile and your spellbinding pussy."

"What makes you think it's spellbinding?" I asked with a snort of amusement.

"It doesn't take a genius to figure out you've mastered the art of spreading your legs," Bryce hissed. "Ryder's interest in a girl has never lasted this long before. So maybe he'll keep fucking you for the rest of your days or maybe he'll decide to kill you for letting that Lion asshole fuck you too. But whatever reason you've got for working your way into his life and his pants, just know that I'm watching. And I'm waiting. And the day you fuck up and do something to betray the Brotherhood, I'll throw you at Ryder's mercy and laugh as he tears you apart."

I rolled my eyes at him, blowing a bubble with my gum. "The problem is, I can't betray the Brotherhood because I'm not one of you. So keep watching if you want to. But you might want to keep your little hobby quiet. Because if Ryder realises you're doubting his judgement then you'll have bigger issues than stalking me."

"Watch your back, Callisto," Bryce snarled, baring his teeth for a moment before shooting away.

"I always do, asshole," I muttered, listening to his footsteps until they faded away and I could be sure he was gone.

My gaze trailed to the far side of the lake where the hills rose up towards the sky and I smiled to myself as I decided to stretch my Order muscles.

I shot away from the water in a blur of speed and dove straight into the forest with the wind whipping my lilac hair away from my face.

I sped between trees and through the undergrowth with adrenaline flooding my veins before heading on up the huge hill which crested the far side of the lake. I hadn't been up here since the hike I'd taken with Ryder but the further I went, the better I felt. It was so peaceful out here, there was nothing but trees and sunshine and freedom. None of the pressures which snared me could hold any weight out here. It felt like I could just take a breath of fresh air and let it wash away my anxiety and stress for a little while.

I reached the clearing where Ryder and I had had our picnic and came to a halt looking out over the academy grounds far below. The lake sparkled in the morning sun and the little clearing was bathed in warm light which had me sighing in appreciation.

It was meant to be an unseasonably hot day and I could already feel the heat rising in the air. I'd dressed for the weather in a pair of denim shorts and I pulled off my sweater, letting the sun kiss more of my skin as I was left in a black crop top with the words *Lost Cause* printed across it. The slogan seemed pretty accurate today because I still didn't feel like I was making nearly enough progress with finding Gareth's murderer.

I closed my eyes for a moment, letting the sun sink into my skin as I tried to get the tangled web of my thoughts and theories to align into something new. I felt like I was getting so close with this Nightshade and Black Card stuff, but there were still way too many holes in my evidence.

I leaned into my gifts, listening for the sound of anyone close by, but the only heartbeats I detected were those of animals hiding in the trees around me.

My Atlas pinged and I pulled it from my pocket, smiling to myself as I looked at the selfie Leon had taken. He was lying on Devil's Hill, sunbathing shirtless and looking like Hercules on a beach vacation. He'd even captioned it *wish you were here* to tempt me further, but as much as I wanted to go to him, I really needed to look through the footage in Dante's flash drive.

I'd spent a bit of time looking at it, but it was damn hard to do so all the time I was worried about him walking in on me in our dorm. I needed to take this opportunity to go through it while I knew he was away.

I lifted my Atlas and took a photo for Leon in response, promising to come and find him later when I was back from my hike.

I laid my sweater down beside a huge tree in a patch of sunshine and sat back against it as I took the flash drive from my pocket, hooking it up to my Atlas.

My heart beat faster and I couldn't help but glance around before I hit play, despite the fact that I knew no one was out here.

I started working my way down the list, watching the clips of footage Dante had kept on everyone around him. He didn't have anything on members of his Clan, but he had various things on all of the teachers at our school plus a fair few students too. There were also names of Fae I didn't recognise and I clicked through them as well just to make sure there was nothing in the footage which might lead back to Gareth.

Some of the clips weren't evidence for blackmail, but were more like warnings. There were images that involved people's families or homes with members of the Oscura Clan lurking close in a way that could only be interpreted as a threat. It was all a bit menacing but it was pretty damn clever too. He could control all of these people with nothing more than this file and a promise.

I tapped on a clip titled *Ashleigh Fielder* and watched the footage roll of a party where a girl was wielding fire magic while looking pretty damn wasted. She tripped up and set a whole group of trees alight and the crowd around her all fell back screaming and laughing.

As the camera swung around, my heart leapt as I spotted Gareth amongst the onlookers. He was laughing while Cindy Lou draped herself over his lap in a skirt so short that I could see her underwear beneath it. A low hiss escaped me as I watched her nuzzling into him. What had she done to him? Why had they broken up? And why the hell hadn't he mentioned her to me?

The clip ended and I pouted irritably as I scowled off into the trees. I'd been watching the footage on the flash drive for over an hour and that was the only link I'd found to Gareth at all and it clearly wasn't relevant. I was beginning to think that this footage wouldn't hold anything that could tell me more than the file on Gareth himself.

Not that I could stop until I'd seen them all.

With a sigh of irritation, I moved on to the next file which was titled *Katherine King*. My eyebrows rose at that as I wondered for the hundredth time who the King I was searching for was. Why had Lorenzo given me such an obscure fucking answer about the person I was hunting? Why couldn't he have just given me the real goddamn name?

I let out a huff of annoyance and tapped the file.

The footage started up and my lips parted as I found myself watching a sex tape. Ryder stood over Professor King as he pinned her to a desk and her cries of pleasure came again and again as he pounded into her.

I should have switched it off, but it was like watching a train crash. I couldn't make myself look away, even as a tingle of heat ran down my spine and my fist clenched tightly in my lap. I had no valid reason to feel the way I was, but I couldn't help it. Jealousy warred with pure fucking rage inside my chest as I looked at the image of Professor King and imagined myself ripping her goddamn hair out and beating her stupid face in.

My grip tightened on my Atlas to the point where I was worried I might break it with my gifted strength, but if I let go I was pretty sure I'd punch something.

My gaze moved to Ryder, his expression was blank, dark, a hard mask of emptiness as he pinned her down. Hell, it didn't even look like he was enjoying it.

My jaw ticked and I knew that I should just switch the fucking thing off as I continued to get angrier, but for some fucked up reason I just sat watching it.

I flinched as something touched my shoulder and my heart leapt half way out of my skin as I found a black snake about the size of a python lowering itself out of the tree to join me.

I leapt up with a shriek of surprise, dropping my Atlas and somehow knocking the volume up so that the sound of Professor King begging for more and panting Ryder's name filled the air.

The snake made it to the forest floor and I watched as it began to swell and grow before me.

My heart was still pounding but I remained still as Ryder grew into the largest version of his Order form and raised his head up like a cobra poised to strike. He was the width of a car and so long that I couldn't even see the end of his reptilian body within the clearing. The slow heartbeat of his Order form hadn't alerted me to his presence and I cursed myself for not considering the fact that someone could have been out here disguised this way. His scales were perfectly black but shone with a deep kind of glimmer which spoke of his power. His body was thick and muscular, a perfect killing machine, a true predator.

He lowered his head, his forked tongue flicking in and out as he drew closer to me and I looked into his dark green eyes, feeling the urge to stay utterly still as his Order power washed over me. He could eat me as easily as breathing, swallow me up in one bite. But I wasn't afraid he'd do that. I reached out and pushed my hand straight up the centre of his nose, feeling the smoothness of his scales beneath my palm.

He leaned closer, his tongue darting out again to taste the air surrounding us as Professor King's screams of pleasure grew even louder.

Ryder shifted so suddenly that I gasped in shock as I found myself touching a man instead of a snake, my hand pressed to his cheek as he stood naked before me.

"What are you watching?" he purred with a dirty as fuck look on his face. My lips parted and a goddamn blush just had to choose that moment to force its way onto my cheeks.

I struggled for a reply just as Professor King cried out with what was most definitely an orgasm and I cleared my throat uncomfortably.

"I don't think I've ever seen you flustered like this, baby," Ryder said, shifting closer to me and tilting his head as he watched me fumble for an excuse. It didn't help that he was naked. I kept my gaze on his face, but I couldn't deny that I was more than a little tempted to look down.

The footage finally ended and I licked my lips as I continued to hunt down an answer. Ryder watched the motion hungrily and I slowly slid my hand from his cheek until I'd retrieved it.

"I'm doing…research," I said lamely, not even knowing where the hell I was going with this.

"Research? If you wanted to know how big my dick is you only had to ask to see it…"

"That's not what I meant," I gasped, but my eyes instantly dropped down his body to take in the impressive length of him complete with a piercing that had my imagination running wild before I forced them back up to meet his again.

"So you just wanted to research what it might be like to fuck me?" he pushed, clearly finding this whole thing amusing as hell.

"No," I snapped.

"Were you getting off on it, baby?" he asked, dipping his mouth to my ear and sending a shiver of longing down my spine.

"No," I growled more forcefully. "Why would I want to watch a video of that…*woman* with you?"

I tried to step back, but Ryder caught my wrist. "Are you *jealous?*" he asked, his eyes sparkling in a way that told me he didn't hate the idea of that.

I raised my chin as I looked up at him, forcing myself to hold his gaze. I was here hunting down a goddamn murderer for fuck's sake. I wasn't going to run from a naked douchebag.

"What if I am?" I challenged, holding his eye. "What if I want you like that? What if I hate seeing you with her and I hated the look on your face while you were?"

"What look on my face?" Ryder asked with a frown.

"The look that said you were just going through the motions. The look that said you didn't feel anything while you were with her."

"You want me to feel for you?" Ryder asked, reaching out to brush his knuckles lined with the word *lust* across my cheek.

"Yes," I replied because it was true and I was so done with the lies that haunted me. I just wanted to be honest with him, at least as much as I could be.

"Well I do," he said in a rough voice. "I feel more for you than I've felt for anything in so long that I can't even remember."

I reached out to him and painted my finger over the tattoo which crossed his heart. The one I'd given him. The one he'd gotten for me.

We stood there for a long moment, both of us frozen by the deal he'd struck with Dante. And despite the desperate beating of my heart, I didn't make any move to push him into breaking it.

"I'm going to put some clothes on before I rip yours off," Ryder grunted, stepping back suddenly and striding away from me.

I let out a long breath as I watched him leave, my gaze lingering on his ass as he headed off into the trees to find his clothes.

He returned wearing a pair of sweatpants and I moved to retrieve my Atlas from the ground before dropping back down into my spot at the foot of the tree.

"So are you going to explain why you're sitting out here watching that video?" Ryder asked as he sat down beside me, his arm brushing mine.

I cleared my throat, wondering what the hell I was supposed to say to that. "Maybe I was just curious…after the rumours and all…"

"No. I don't think so," he disagreed. "If you were curious about King you could have asked me."

"I *am* curious," I said quickly, wondering if he'd really tell me about her that easily. "I mean…were the two of you like, a couple or something?"

Ryder snorted a laugh. "No. It was just sex. And I had her working for me against Inferno too."

I nodded thoughtfully. "So you don't…keep in touch or anything?"

Ryder's lips twitched with amusement. "You want to know if I kept in contact with her after she lost her job and was power shamed?"

I shrugged like I didn't care, but I did. Her name alone meant I had to look into her even if I didn't particularly want anything to do with a woman who had abused her position to screw him.

"She messages me every now and then," Ryder said dismissively. "Not that I ever reply. What use is she to me now? She wasn't even a good fuck. But I think she misses the taste of me so she keeps asking me to come visit her where she's living up in Tucana." He pulled his Atlas from his pocket and showed me a bunch of unanswered messages from her. My fingers itched to take it from him, to get her number and track her down, but Ryder just locked his Atlas again before shoving it back into his pocket.

"Good riddance," I said, taking Ryder's hand and lacing my fingers through his. I shifted my thumb back and forth over the L on his forefinger and he leaned his head back on the tree behind us, letting his eyes fall closed.

"Are you gonna give me the truth now then?" he asked after a few minutes.

"Truth?" I asked innocently.

"I was up in the branches above you for nearly an hour before we got to the clip of me and King. So don't try and bullshit me that you were just looking up that old video because you wanted something to get yourself off over."

I scoffed at him, trying to buy time as I figured out what I could say to explain myself.

"So you were just sitting in the branches above my head the whole time?" I asked to divert his attention.

"I had a pretty fucking perfect view right down the front of that tiny crop top you're wearing so I didn't see any reason to move."

I couldn't help but laugh at that and I pulled a stick of cherry gum from my pocket before pushing it between my teeth.

"No bullshit, Elise. I want the truth."

I turned to meet his gaze and my gut stirred with the desire to open up to him. I didn't want to lie anyway.

"Some of the truth," I agreed hesitantly. "As much as I can give you right now."

"Deal."

I bit my lip, wondering how much I should say before deciding he might as well just have my answer. He might have been one of the most dangerous people I'd ever met but somehow, I felt sure he was worthy of my trust. There was something between the two of us which defied logic and reason. Something which bound us and elevated us beyond the laws which might apply to our behaviour with anyone else. *My* Ryder wasn't the same man as the one the rest of the world got. My Ryder was just for me. And I knew that I didn't have to fear him using anything I said against me.

"I don't know if you've heard the rumours about someone getting into Dante's cache in the Kiplings' cave?" I asked slowly.

Ryder's eyes lit with excitement. "That was you?" he barked a laugh. "Inferno's been blaming The Brotherhood for that shit and it was you all along?"

I bit my lip guiltily, but I didn't say any more about how I'd actually gotten hold of the flash drive. I didn't want to tell him about Gabriel's part in it if I didn't have to.

"So that's what he's been looking for so desperately?" Ryder asked.

"I guess it's collateral on people," I agreed with a shrug.

"And what made you so eager to get your hands on that?" he asked darkly, his eyes sparking with excitement.

"I thought maybe there would be something on here that might answer a few questions for me..."

"And there isn't?" Ryder pressed.

"No. It's all sex tapes, outright threats and sordid secrets. The one of Principal Greyshine is going to give me nightmares for life." I shuddered and Ryder chuckled.

"So you don't really want it anymore then?" he confirmed, his gaze sliding to my Atlas where it sat in my lap.

"No…I guess I'll just give it back to him."

"Or, you could give it to me." Ryder gave me a hungry look and I squealed as he lunged for my Atlas.

I fell onto my back and his weight landed on me a second later. I whipped my Atlas up above my head and fought to keep it away from him as he crawled over me to claim it.

"Ryder, don't," I gasped as his hips pinned me down and he reached over my head to catch my wrists.

"He already thinks I've got it anyway," Ryder reasoned, his dark green eyes dancing playfully as he looked down at me. "I'm actually helping you out by taking it. I'm covering your ass."

"My ass is just fine, thanks," I replied, wriggling wildly to try and escape him.

"Are you sure about that?" Ryder grabbed my hips and flipped me over so suddenly that I hardly realised what was happening before he had me bent over on my knees before him.

His left hand gripped my hip tightly for half a second before he lifted his right to spank me.

"*Fuck,*" I gasped as pleasure skittered through me from the light strike of his hand against my ass. It didn't hurt at all, it just felt all kinds of good and I had to bite down on the desire to ask him to do it again.

"Yeah, your ass is all good," Ryder agreed with a dark laugh before he flipped me onto my back again where I lay panting in the dirt beneath him.

"You're an asshole," I said, but there wasn't an ounce of bite to my voice.

"I am," he agreed, no longer trying to wrangle my Atlas from me. "Though I'm considerably less of one around you for some reason."

I didn't fight my smile as he admitted that.

"Good."

"If I let you keep Inferno's little book of bargaining chips, will you stop trying to escape?" Ryder asked seriously.

"Yes," I agreed because I didn't want to escape him anyway and as he slowly moved off of me, offering a hand to help me up, I got the impression he knew that.

LEON

CHAPTER NINE

I sat in the auditorium before Astrology class with my eyes closed. Mindy was on her knees in front of me and I groaned as she put her back into pleasing me. "Yes Mindy," I sighed. "Right there."

A heavy book slammed into my lap and I yelped as it crushed my fucking dick. My eyes flew open and I found Elise dropping into the seat beside me.

"Whoopsie," she said innocently.

Holy asstarts, I'd nearly kicked Mindy right in the face. She didn't comment though, going straight back to giving me the best foot massage of my life.

"By the fucking stars, little monster."

"Sorry Leo," she teased, reaching out to pick the book up and pushing her other hand beneath it for a moment to caress my aching junk.

A smile hooked up the corner of my mouth and I grinned stupidly at her for a long moment.

Maybe she's going to give me a handjob right here in class.

Elise sat back in her seat, looking at Mindy with her nose wrinkling.

"Go back to your seat," I instructed the redhead and she nodded quickly, gathering up her lotions and pedicure kit before hurrying away.

My grin widened until I looked like the fucking Joker and I stared at Elise until she had to acknowledge me.

"What?" she asked, arching a brow as she turned to me.

"You're jealous."

"Of someone rubbing your feet? No thanks." She tsked and I leaned in closer. Because I'd seen her look at Mindy with those green glowy eyes.

"You wanna be down on your knees rubbing me one way or another, little monster," I taunted, leaning in and brushing my mouth over her ear.

I loved being in the back row of this class. The auditorium was so dark, I could probably have made Elise come ten times in a silencing bubble and no one would have noticed. *I'll put a pin in that idea.*

Elise's Atlas pinged and she took it out. I wasn't trying to look, but I totally did. The name Old Sal appeared at the top of a text and I leaned closer to my little monster.

"Who's that?" I asked. "Your silver haired bit on the side?"

Elise laughed. "No, she's my mom's old boss and pretty much the only family I have left."

I frowned but before I could ask her more Dante appeared, strolling into the classroom and making a beeline for us. He leapt over the back of the seat beside Elise and dropped into it.

"Morning amicos." He dropped his arm around her chair and I sucked on my lower lip as I was reminded of him watching me and Elise together.

I dropped my arm behind her too, resting it over Dante's, wondering if he'd blink.

He didn't.

"I'm sorry, am I in the way of you guys getting it on?" Elise smirked, swivelling to get a look at my arm resting over his.

"No, carina," Dante purred. "You're right where we want you…in the middle."

"Oh really?" she asked with a taunting smile. "And what are you gonna do now you've got me here?"

"I have a few suggestions…" My dick twitched and I was genuinely starting to consider the silencing bubble idea. But a full on threesome in the back row probably wouldn't have gone unnoticed. I was like eighty five percent certain of that. Which meant there was a fifteen percent window where all my dreams could come true. *Worth it…?*

"Bing bong," Principle Greyshine's voice sounded over the tannoy. "I have an announcementeroo to make this morning which is going to knock your socks off. The prestigious Zodiac Academy has requested to do a student exchange programme with our fantabulous school! More informationio to come soon! Have a groovalicious day."

I glanced at the others with a grin. "Fuck, I'd love to go and check out their Pitball pitch. It's second only to the Skylark's training grounds. If we beat Sunrise Academy in the match next week, we'll face Zodiac in the final." Excitement thrummed through my veins at that. We'd never been this close to the final and the idea of really making it there would be a dream come true.

"Maybe you'll get picked." Elise shrugged and a smile took over my face. *Maybe I will. Or maybe I'll punch Greyshine's face until he lets me go.*

I pulled out my Atlas, checking my morning Horoscope. Mindy had read it to me over breakfast in bed, but I'd been too focused on a daydream about Elise playing Pitball naked to concentrate on it. But now I had reason to. Because I needed to see if the stars were going to work in my favour. I needed lucky Jupiter to start moving into my chart in time for the Sunrise game.

Good morning Leo.
The stars have spoken about your day!
Your mood is at an all-time high. And with Venus in your chart, why wouldn't it be?
You're going to want to spoil the object of your affection today and you

might even find yourself behaving as wildly as your Order form as the
excitement of the sensual planet takes hold.
All in all, a good day ahead, but remember to tend to your own needs as
well. You don't want to burn out.

Well that didn't sound half bad at all…

Professor Rayburn walked into the room, clapping her hands to quiet the students and moving to take her position at the podium at the base of the seating area.

"Today, we'll be discussing the theories of Aisling Kismet who conducted the world's largest study of Star Bonds with a special focus on Elysian Mates. She collated data from around the globe to produce countless theories. Some of which have been flouted, while others remain popular in modern studies." She waved a hand and the seats began to recline as the ceiling lit up, the constellations spreading out above us.

Both Dante and I had to remove our arms from the back of Elise's chair and I pursed my lips in disappointment.

"Kismet was the first scientist to shine a clearer light on the Star Bond we know the least about. The Elysian Mate bond, whereby two soul mates find each other and are tested by the stars to show their devotion to one another. This seems to have little to no pattern. For example…" The Pisces constellation lit above us then Sagittarius followed.

I was already getting sleepy lying back in my chair and Elysian Mates didn't interest me all that much. It was like a one in gazillion chance that you'd find your mate *if* you even had one. Besides, I was more than happy with the girl right beside me. Mate or otherwise. She was perfect for me whether the stars decided it or not.

The two constellations dimmed above and another two lit up, then another two, the sky pulsing with light. "If two Fae are lucky enough to find their mate, how long before they must answer the question of fate varies vastly.

It can be anything from just hours up to several years. At first, Kismet believed the tests each couple faced were random in their extremeness and subtleties. But when speaking with the Mates who were still alive amongst the records she'd gathered, she began to realise there was one thing they all had in common."

The Leo sign lit up and Libra followed, making me smirk. I shot Elise a glance, but if she noticed our star signs were highlighted in the heavens, she clearly gave no shits. Not one quarter of a shit. Not even a mouse dropping of a shit.

The Professor continued, "Each couple were tested pertaining to their individual circumstances. For example, subject three one six and two eight four lived on opposite sides of the kingdom. After their chance meeting in the city of Viren, they decided to try and make their new relationship work long distance. The tests they faced were nearly all based around the journeys they tried to make towards one another. Storms would ground their planes, train workers would go on strike, they'd fall ill just before the day of travel. Through all of this they persevered until just over a year later, the stars asked them the question of whether they wanted to be bonded and they chose to be together."

"Psh, it's all bullshit," Elise muttered and I raised a brow, glancing over at her.

"You don't think I'm your Mate, little monster?" I teased in a whisper, leaning in to run my thumb across her lower lip.

Dante rolled onto his side, reaching out to tuck a lock of hair behind her ear. "Or you don't think the stars chose me for you?" he played along, throwing me a smirk.

Elise rolled her eyes, batting our hands away. "I think if I have an Elysian Mate it'll be a four kilo chocolate bar."

I snorted a laugh and Professor Rayburn stopped mid-sentence. "Minus two rank points, Mr Night!" she called and I pouted, looking back up at the stars.

"Now...what we have much less data on, is couples who chose to become Star Crossed instead of Mates," she continued and the Libra and Leo constellations above us turned black. "There are only three known cases in history of when either party in a couple chose not to be bonded with their Elysian Mate. Of course, the repercussions of this are rather dire. A black ring around your irises would mark you as Star Crossed and the stars would thwart you from ever trying to bridge the gap between you and your Elysian Mate again. Though the couple would pine for each other for the rest of their lives and be unable to love any other. Does anyone know the most famous example of why a woman from Fortuna chose to be Star Crossed instead of accepting her Elysian Mate?"

My ears perked up because I was a scrap more interested now we were talking doom and gloom. Call it morbid fascination. But from what I knew of Elysian Mates, if they showed up in your life and the stars tested you, you'd tear the world down to be with them. So who would choose not to?

"Her mate had murdered her father the previous year," Gabriel answered from across the room and my eyes snapped to him. His gaze was fixed on Elise and I wondered what he was thinking for a moment. It almost looked like he was jealous. Did Mr Blackbird want to catch the Elise worm too?

"Yes, Mr Nox," Professor Rayburn said. "A feud between their families was settled in blood, and the woman in question decided she would rather be Star Crossed to her father's murderer than Mated to him. Kismet theorised that this was one of the star's tests which her Mate failed. Most Mates, upon meeting, are drawn to each other irrevocably and tend not to fight these feelings. However, if they do, Kismet suggests the path is rockier and could lead to a decision of being Star Crossed if one or both sides of the couple continue to fail their tests. Despite this, she believed that this still had no bearing on *when* the question of fate would come from the stars."

Eugene Dipper cleared his throat, sitting up in his seat. "So, um, would you say that those who were Star Crossed were a bad match for each other? Like er, like the stars made a mistake?"

"Good questions, Dipper," Professor Rayburn said. "Take a rank point."

Eugene looked like he'd just come in his pants as he dropped back down into his seat and gazed up at the sky like he was dreaming of finding his one true love. *Good luck with that, rat boy.*

"Kismet concluded that each Mate were equally matched to one another. She did personality analysis for as many of the Mates as she could, including those who were Star Crossed and all of them possessed extremely complimentary traits which would make them a perfect match. So the stars made no mistake."

"And what if your Elysian Mate dies?" Ryder asked with a smirk.

Trust him to bring the mood down ten notches.

"Tough shit," Professor Rayburn said brightly and the class laughed.

"What if you choose your Elysian Mate, but then you don't want them anymore because some fine piece of ass comes along?" Bryce Corvus asked, receiving a high five from his Lunar pal beside him. *Twat monkeys.*

"Stupid question," Rayburn answered. "You would never want anyone else once you were bonded with your Mate. It's unheard of."

"What if you were Star Crossed but then changed your mind about it?" Mindy asked, biting her lip and throwing me a look over her shoulder.

"You cannot change your mind, your fate is sealed," Professor Rayburn said firmly.

"But you have so little data on being Star Crossed, how do you know?" Gabriel chimed in with a taut frown like this was an actual problem in his life. The guy was the definition of a loner, so if his Mate showed up it was going to be an empty room.

"Fair point, Mr Nox," Rayburn replied. "Kismet tried to answer just that by comparing other Star Bonds to the Elysian Mate bond. For example, Astral Adversaries – who are mortal enemies driven together by the stars to clash over and over – have been known to be asked a question of fate too."

I frowned, my attention firmly grabbed. Chatter broke out in the room because everyone knew this was some juicy shit. I'd only ever heard of Elysian

Mates answering a question of fate.

"Yes, on occasion, *very* rarely, there have been Astral Adversaries brought together under the stars. Not to be bonded, but to be *un*bonded. To break the powerful urge to destroy one another that feasts on them day in and day out. It seems these Adversaries must undergo their own tests to reach this destination, acting out in kindness to each other instead of cruelty, despite their natures driving them against one another. Kismet theorised the rarity of this happening was because hate is such a potent emotion that it can taint one's being. It can corrupt even the most kind-hearted of Fae. So for two Adversaries to overcome their bond, they would have to want to do so very powerfully indeed."

I glanced at Dante who'd fallen still. Everyone knew the rumour that he and Ryder were Astral Adversaries just like their fathers had been. Putting their hatred aside for one another was practically laughable.

My gaze dropped to Dante and Elise's hands which were intertwined and my heart tugged. The deal he'd made with Ryder must have been eating him alive. And there really was no fucking way around it unless the two of them agreed to end it. Which was as sad as Sally the snail in a snowstorm because I was more than willing to share my girl to keep her happy. So we were all losing out.

Elise looked over at Ryder, unthreading her fingers from Dante's and pushing her hand into her hair with a sigh. I frowned as I watched, seeing a thousand fucking things before me. Elise wanted *all* of us. The asshole Lunar leader as well. Which I'd known because of that deal, but I hadn't realised until just right now how much she liked him. Maybe because I was hashtag team Dante, but I couldn't refute the burning look she'd thrown Ryder. She might have hidden her emotions well, but I was starting to become a master at reading them. I mean, I sure as hell could share her three-ways, but I couldn't even fully share her two-ways with Dante. So how was I supposed to make Elise happy?

When the class came to an end, Dante got up followed by Elise who lingered close to him. His hand skated over her arm for a moment then he headed away. Elise was about to follow him when I grabbed her bag and upended it, tipping her shit fucking everywhere. And I mean *everywhere*. Between the chairs, under the seats, on the seats, rolling down the aisles.

"Leo!" she scolded in annoyance, diving on some of her things and stuffing them back in her bag. I could see she was about to go full Vamp on that shit and pick it all up in a flash, so I caught her arm.

"I'd better stay behind and help you pick that up, huh?" I gave her a dark smile and her pupils dilated as she realised what I was implying.

She fought a grin, nodding as she continued gathering things but at a slower pace.

"Turn the light off when you leave please," the Professor called as she headed out of the room with the last of the students.

"Will do," I answered, getting to my feet with a grin.

While Elise continued to hunt for her things, I reached into my pocket and took out the bunch of shit I'd stolen from Dante when I'd rested my arm over his. Four gold rings, a bangle – who wears a bangle dude?? – and his prized medallion.

I scraped my hair up into a bun, putting on the jewellery and waited for Elise to notice.

"Are you gonna help or-" She looked up at me, her brows pinching together as she took in my new look.

"What's the matter, carina?" I purred in the way Dante did. "Have you never seen a Storm Dragon before?"

She snorted a laugh, getting to her feet. "I've never seen one who's so ruggedly…blonde."

She wasn't going to be laughing in a second.

I caught her waist, dragging her against me with a growl. "Don't take that tone with the leader of the Oscura Clan."

"Are we seriously roleplaying right now?" she giggled and I caught her chin, giving her a firm look.

"Yes, bella, and if you don't start playing along I'm going to have to punish you." Yeah, I was awesome at this.

Her smile dropped away, her eyes becoming hooded as she leaned forward, pushing her hand down between us towards my waistband. "How do you want me then, Dante?"

Heat spread through my chest and my cock swelled. It's. On.

I caught her hand, guiding her along the aisle and hurrying down the stairs towards the podium at the heart of the room. I moved to the front row seat, taking out my Atlas and pressing my tongue into my cheek. Was my little monster going to be into this idea? Or was I about to push her past her limits at last?

She moved to my side and I dropped character, lowering my mouth to her ear. "How do you feel about making a little video for our Dragon friend, little monster?"

She glanced up at me, biting on her lower lip as she nodded keenly. I pushed her down into a seat, lifting my Atlas and pressing record as she gazed up at me in surprise. Her expression quickly melted to lust and she took hold of her skirt, pulling it up as she widened her legs.

"Dante," she said softly and a groan of need escaped me.

"Take your panties off, carina," I commanded and she did as I asked, sliding the little red thong down her legs and tossing it on the floor.

She moved to touch herself but I got there first, dropping to my knees and pushing my hand between her thighs. She gasped as I teased her, rubbing my knuckles up and down the centre of her so she felt the metallic bite of Dante's rings.

"*Fuck*, more," she begged, widening her thighs and I pushed two fingers into her, so deep I lost sight of his rings.

She started panting as I slowly worked her pussy, watching her face the whole time and making sure the camera recorded every inch of perfection which sat before me.

When I'd tortured her enough, I withdrew my hand and stood back, sucking on my lower lip as I watched her. "Stand up and turn around, carina," I purred in my best impression of Dante – which was pretty damn excellent thank you very much.

She did as I said, smirking at me before turning and bending over without direction, clutching on to the back of the seat.

I wanted to toss my Atlas aside and take her with both hands, but I was going to do this for my friend. And fuck if I wasn't getting off on it.

I moved forward, standing behind her and pushing her skirt up, running my palm over her ass. I dropped my fly, freeing my aching dick one-handed then I positioned myself between her thighs, needing her so bad it was seriously fucking hard to stay in character.

"Do you want me, amore mio?" I asked.

"Yes," she gasped. "Please Le-Dante."

I smirked, splaying my hand on her back and taking her with one powerful thrust. She cried out and her voice echoed around the auditorium. I should have put a silencing bubble up, but I didn't give a shit right then and clearly she didn't either.

I liked the rush. My heart was thrashing like a wild cat as I pounded into her, angling my Atlas down as I knotted my fingers in her lilac locks.

She pushed back against me with every thrust and the divine squeeze of her body around me made me groan. She was pleasure embodied. A fucking witch sent here to charm me under her spell. And I never wanted to break free of it.

"You're so wet for me, carina," I said through gritted teeth, telling Dante more than her. Dude was gonna jerk off over this a hundred times before it got old. That should've been weird for two friends, but hell if I gave a shit. I wanted him to be a part of this. She was ours. And I was gonna work my way around that stupid-ass deal he'd struck with Ryder as best I could.

I moved my hand onto her stomach, running my fingers down until I found her clit and started toying with her until she was coming undone.

"Dan-te," she gasped like she really was fucking him.

I growled, getting off on that so much, I started driving into her mercilessly, absorbing every wave of her orgasm. She clutched the edge of the seat harder as I reared over her with a groan. I came hard, my world tipping as pleasure invaded me and I grasped onto Elise's hip as I held her still, filling her with every inch of me.

"Shit," I breathed, a deep purr starting up in my chest.

"Dragons don't purr," she laughed as I drew myself out of her.

I tucked myself away as she turned to me and I tossed my Atlas onto the seat, grabbing the back of her neck and pulling her in for a messy kiss. "You can forget the Dragon now," I said against her mouth. "I'm all Lion."

She ran her hand up my chest to feel my haywire heartbeat. "Forgotten," she whispered. "But let's go find him and watch his face when we send it to him."

"Oh hell fucking yes."

ELISE

CHAPTER TEN

I strode across campus to the Empyrean Fields where Elemental Combat class was about to begin and Professor Mars was setting up for the lesson.

We hadn't been able to find Dante during lunch which must have meant he was off on Oscura business somewhere so Leon had held off on sending him the sex tape we'd made until now.

Leon caught my eye as I approached, grinning widely as he held his Atlas ready and I moved into a position where I could see Dante's face as he hit send.

I trained my heightened sense of hearing onto my Storm Dragon just as his Atlas pinged and waited in anticipation for him to react.

Dante was giving half of his attention to some of his pack mates as they engaged in a tussle, but he pulled his Atlas from his pocket lazily and looked at it as the video started playing on the screen.

My breathy voice came from the speakers a moment later as I moaned Dante's name and his eyebrows shot up as he quickly flicked the volume off, looking around to make sure no one had noticed what he was watching.

"Dalle stelle," he breathed, his gaze glued to the video for a long moment before he cleared his throat and quickly shut it down.

His gaze found mine across the crowd of students and I bit my lip against a smile as his eyes burned with desire.

"Are you trying to give me a heart attack, bella?" he murmured, realising I was listening in on him.

I shrugged innocently, like I had no idea what he was talking about and his gaze darkened with a promise I wished he could fulfil.

"Did you like your gift?" Leon asked excitedly as he bounded over to join him and I laughed as he handed over Dante's stolen jewellery with a grin. "I did a fucking awesome impression of you, admit it."

"Yeah. But my dick's bigger than yours," Dante teased and Leon scoffed in return.

"You wish."

I laughed to myself as I made myself move to join the class. Despite the fact that I spent so much of my time trying to catch a murderer and flirting with the Kings of this academy, I was actually supposed to be here to learn...

"Hey Elise!" Eugene called, waving enthusiastically and beckoning me over as he practically bounced on the balls of his feet.

I smiled lightly and gave him a salute in return as I moved into the crowd of students and took up position at the edge of the group away from him. Of course that wasn't the end of the interaction and after a round of *'scuse me, coming through, pardon me,* Eugene appeared beside me with a bright smile.

"Did you have a nice lunch?" he asked, smiling as I blew a bubble with my gum and let it pop loudly.

"Sure. Sandwiches are great," I joked.

"Oh yeah, I love a good sandwich. With all the bread and fillings and the other piece of bread to hold the fillings and...crusts..."

I snorted a laugh. "Gotta love the crusts."

His smile grew. "So I was wondering if, this weekend, you might like to come out with me to see a movie that's playing in town?"

"Erm-"

"There's a few good ones on. There's this unlikely romance about an almost powerless Fae falling in love with an Heir to the throne..."

"I'm not much of a romance fan," I said slowly.

"Okay, well there's an action movie that's just been imported from the mortal realm. Something about car heists and shooting and-"

"Fuck off Dipper," Leon's voice interrupted us and I turned to find him striding towards us, pushing a hand through his long, blonde hair and drawing my attention to the way his bicep made his shirt stretch to contain it.

"I was just...me *and* Elise were just discussing our plans for the weekend," Eugene squeaked, sounding decidedly more rat like.

"Elise's plans for the weekend mostly include being pinned beneath me and though I'm all up for an audience, I really had a Fae with a more *predatory* Order in mind."

Eugene blushed so hard it looked like he might be in danger of shifting into a radish.

"Stop it," I chastised Leon, batting his chest lightly to tell him off. "Eugene's my friend."

"*Best* friends," Eugene added firmly.

May the stars have mercy.

Leon laughed loudly, nuzzling against my ear and kissing my cheek.

"Then it must be your lucky day, Dipper. If my girl says you're cool then it has to be so. So now you're *my* best friend too," he announced.

Eugene looked like he was trying to work out if Leon meant that or not and I decided to save him from having to answer.

"Maybe we can rain check the movie?" I asked Eugene, though I didn't really have any intention of rearranging it.

He hesitated, clearly not wanting to leave while obviously seeming terrified of Leon too.

Leon draped an arm around my shoulders in a way that felt suspiciously like being pissed on and looked at Eugene for a long moment.

"Boo!" he said suddenly, lurching forward a step and Eugene squeaked loudly as he shifted in fright. His clothes fell into a crumpled heap on the ground and a little Tiberian Rat poked his nose up out of the neck of his shirt a moment later.

A snort of laughter drew my attention and I looked up to find Ryder biting down on a smirk. Leon noticed too and his smile widened. "Do you think I'm funny, ssssnake boy?"

"Maybe funny looking, Simba," Ryder replied flatly.

"You really do love The Lion King, don't you?" Leon asked thoughtfully. "Maybe we should watch it together some time."

"In your dreams, Mufasshole," Ryder scoffed.

"Elise can come too," Leon added. "I'm sure she won't mind sitting between us, will you, little monster?"

"I can think of worse things," I teased, looking at Ryder as his gaze skimmed over Leon's arm where it rested around my shoulders.

"I'll leave that little portion of hell to the two of you," he said dismissively before striding away from us.

I pouted dramatically and looked up at Leon. "You're scaring everyone away today."

"I can't help it if they can't handle the competition," he replied, tugging me closer again so that he could speak into my ear. "Besides, I've been daydreaming about that noise you made when I got you alone in the auditorium earlier."

"Which noise?"

"You know. The one you made when I took my dick and put it-"

Eugene suddenly shifted back into a very naked, very pasty boy again beside us and I flinched in surprise.

"Way to kill the mood, Dipper," Leon grumbled, shielding his eyes dramatically.

I tiptoed up to press a kiss to his lips while he couldn't see and he growled appreciatively, catching my waist and dragging me closer.

"I've been thinking about tonight," I breathed as I slid my hands across his waist. "After Pitball practice. Maybe you, me and Dante should-"

"You read my mind, little monster!" Leon replied enthusiastically. "We should go over all of our plays for the Sunrise match next week. Everyone knows the three of us are the star players and if we can perfect our three pronged attack then I just *know* we'll smash it out of the park in the game. And then we'll be in the finals where we'll face *Zodiac Academy*."

"You want to stay and practice late?" I asked, raising an eyebrow at him. "I was thinking we could do something with less clothes involved..."

Leon smiled widely, gripping my ass as he pulled me against him. "That would be very distracting, little monster," he purred. "I need to focus on my game…but maybe we could have some kind of reward system in place for good plays…"

"Oh yeah?" I asked with a laugh.

"Yeah. You can earn a kiss for every pit you score and if you can make it past both me and Dante at once, I'll bend you over the firehole and put my-"

"Callisto!" Mars barked and I broke away from Leon with a laugh. "Less canoodling more fighting. Let's see how you do against Galaxa."

The laughter died on my lips as I looked over to Cindy Lou and my face fell into a scowl instead.

"Seriously?" I asked, hoping that Mars might realise that it was a terrible idea to pair us and let me off.

"Now!" he demanded and I sloped away from Leon with a sigh.

Cindy Lou pouted as I approached her, looking far less than pleased about the arrangement too.

"I don't see why I have to be paired with the gutter whore," she said in a voice loud enough to carry.

"And I don't see why I have to be paired with someone so far beneath me on the power scale that it's embarrassing to even face off with you. But here we are."

"I'll make you eat your words, you piece of trash," she growled.

"Let's see if I can make you lose control of your Order form again, shall we?" I taunted.

Cindy Lou threw a fistful of fire at me so quickly that I almost didn't have time to suck the oxygen from it before it hit me. She snarled as she followed it up with another series of blows, one after another, shooting them at me at speed so that I couldn't aim my power at them fast enough to put them out individually.

I leapt aside, throwing my hands out and sending a huge gust of wind barrelling straight at her. The fireballs were blasted off course and the weight of my power slammed into her a moment later, knocking her off of her feet.

I increased the pressure of the air holding her down and pinned her into the mud, immobilising her hands to stop her from casting again as I kept running to avoid the fireballs.

Once I had her contained, I drew in a deep breath then threw my hand up to suck the oxygen from the space surrounding me.

The largest fireball didn't stutter out entirely before it reached me and the kiss of the flames burning through the left side of my shirt sent pain blazing across my flesh before it went out.

Irritation flashed through me that she'd landed a hit, but I'd won and that was all that really counted.

I returned the air to normal around me so that I could breathe again and clenched my teeth against the pain of the burn.

"Plus five rank points, Callisto," Mars said casually as he passed us. "Change partners when you're ready."

I released the magic pinning Cindy Lou to the mud and turned away from her to find myself a new partner without bothering to speak to her again. She started coughing dramatically behind me, sounding like she might just heave her guts up at any moment but I ignored her.

Dante caught my eye as he climbed off of a guy who looked half dead and he jogged over to join me with a warm smile.

"Winning again, carina?" he purred, reaching out to touch my side and heal the burn Cindy Lou had given me.

"Like always," I joked.

"She tried to kill me!" Cindy Lou sobbed dramatically behind me and I turned to look over my shoulder at her where she was still sitting in the mud, panting desperately as she clutched her throat. "She almost strangled me to death!"

Dante's fingers slid from my waist as he looked down at her too and Cindy Lou pulled her hand away from her neck to show a ring of red finger marks pressed into her skin which she'd clearly given herself.

"What's going on?" Mars called as he circled back through the class to see what the commotion was about.

"That psychopath just tried to kill me!" Cindy Lou wailed, pointing at me in accusation.

"Are you insane?" I asked in disbelief. "I didn't even touch you physically!"

"She cast her air magic into a hand shape and tried to squeeze the life out of me while covering it with the attack which held me down!" Cindy accused.

A crowd was gathering around us as people stopped their fights to see what was happening.

"As much as I might like to wring your scrawny neck, I wouldn't risk a sentence in Darkmore Penitentiary for *you*," I sneered.

Cindy Lou scrambled to her feet and threw herself against Dante's chest as she sobbed.

He looked half disgusted as he tried to peel her off of him again, but he glanced at me with a frown all the same.

"Maybe you shouldn't go so hard at her if you're paired together again, carina," he suggested in a low tone. "She clearly can't match you, so it seems a little unnecessary."

"Did I just speak a foreign language?" I snarled. "I said I didn't do it!"

"Alright, alright. Let's just put this down to a little bit of over excitement from both parties and move on," Mars suggested, waving everyone away. "And let's not have anyone carted off to Darkmore on my watch, eh?"

Cindy sobbed even louder as Dante finally managed to peel her off of him and she turned and fled away back towards the Vega Dorms.

"She's obviously a little more fragile than you, amore mio," Dante said with a shrug. "Best to just leave her be."

"Leave her be?" I asked, arching an eyebrow at him. "She's a fucking liar and a shady bitch and I'm not going to put up with her shit anymore."

"What are you going to do about it then?" Ryder's voice came from behind me and I turned to him as his eyes danced with a dare. "Beat her up in the bathroom and push her head down the toilet?"

"Don't tempt me," I said darkly, not feeling remotely inclined to laugh in that moment.

My Atlas pinged in my pocket and I pulled it out to find I'd been tagged in a FaeBook post.

Cindy Lou Galaxa:

I've just fallen prey to the gutter whore's psycho attacks once again. Beware of @EliseCallisto – she's a straight up nut case. #whoevenletherinhere #gobacktothegutter

Dante let out a low whistle as he read the post over my shoulder and I snarled angrily.

"Show her who she's fucking with, baby," Ryder encouraged.

"That's it," I snapped. I was so fucking done with her shit. I already knew she'd hurt my brother anyway so I didn't really need much of an excuse to go after her.

I shot away from the others, not giving a fuck that I was cutting class as I raced back to the Vega Dorms.

Cindy Lou's dorm was on the floor beneath mine and as I reached it, I spotted her opening the door.

I sped forward and made it inside before she could close the door, snarling at her as I came to a halt.

Cindy Lou screamed as she spotted me, stumbling away and raising her hands like she thought she might fight me off.

I snatched the air from her end of the room before she could cast a single flame and my fangs tingled with the urge to snap out as I took a step towards her.

"What's your problem with me?" I demanded. "No bullshit, no theatrics. There's no one here but you and me, so I just want it straight. Between the two of us. What the fuck is it?"

Cindy Lou glared at me, her eyes full of hate and her jaw locked tight.

I shifted my grip on the air, creating ropes from it which I used to bind her hands at her sides so that she couldn't cast any magic in retaliation before I let her breathe again.

"I spoke to my momma about you," she snarled in accusation. "And I'm pretty sure I've got you all figured out."

"Oh yeah?" I asked, folding my arms as I waited to hear the rest of it.

"She said she's met girls like you before. Girls who turn up out of nowhere, batting their lashes and parting their thighs and getting guys to fall all over themselves for you despite the fact that you're so *average.*"

"Coming from the most basic bitch I've ever met, I'm hardly offended," I replied with a sneer.

"People go to prison for what you're doing," she hissed, tossing her long black hair like she expected that statement to frighten me.

"And what's that exactly?" I asked, my heart pattering as I wondered if she really did know anything incriminating about me. There was plenty of shit that I'd done outside the confines of the law recently, but I had been careful to keep my tracks hidden. At least, I thought I had...

"*Bedazzlement*," Cindy Lou announced, her eyes flashing with triumph like she'd caught me out.

Relief spilled through me at the ridiculous claim and I blew out a laugh. "You think I'm Bedazzling someone?" I'd known strippers who did a little bit of that back at Old Sal's, but it wasn't exactly easy. First off you needed to be damn powerful to manage it – which I was, but that wasn't the point - then you had to slip past the mental shields of your target and let your magic infect them and cause an addiction. Done right they'd ache for you, lust for you, do everything and anything they could to please you. There were cases of Fae who were so good at it that they'd gotten other Fae to commit crimes for them all in the name of a love they'd been tricked into feeling. It was a pretty serious crime and it came with a hefty prison sentence if you were caught. Of course, you had to be caught first. And it could be pretty hard to prove that it had been used at all if the Fae in question truly believed they were in love and not under an enchantment.

"Not some*one*. *Three* someones. Why else would three of the Kings of this school be so damn obsessed with a nothing little nobody like you?" Cindy Lou hissed.

A real laugh left me that time. "So you're jealous?" I asked incredulously. "Is it that you want all of them or one in particular?"

Cindy Lou ground her jaw but didn't reply.

"I can take a wild guess," I said. "And I'm sorry to burst your bubble, but I haven't laid any spells on anyone to make them fall for me. If Dante just doesn't want a piece of your trashy ass then that's not on me."

Cindy Lou shrieked in rage and launched herself at me, charging me down like a rhino while her arms remained tethered to her sides.

I leapt out of the way, knocking into one of the bunks before righting myself, but I lost my hold on the spell controlling her as I fell.

Cindy Lou didn't even try and launch fire at me, she just leapt on me, tearing at my face with her nails and snatching hold of a fistful of my hair as she threw me back against the wall.

My fangs snapped free and I launched my fist into her gut, fighting off the urge to bite her. I didn't want a single drop of her nasty bitch blood in my veins.

I hit her again and she stumbled back, releasing her hold on me with a shriek of anger.

I threw a blast of air at her to push her even further away and she smacked into the wall behind her, knocking the large mirror off of it as she fell.

Cindy Lou gasped in horror as the mirror crashed to the ground but I didn't even look down to see it smash as all of my attention fell on what had been concealed behind it.

There was a wide hole carved into the wall and inside it was what I could only describe as a shrine. There were little candles which were lit and burning with tiny everflames lining the base of it and hundreds of photographs were illuminated by the glow of the orange fire. Photos of Dragons in shifted form and not. And a hell of a lot of photos of one Dragon in particular. *My* Dragon.

"What are you, some kind of crazy stalker?" I gasped as I stepped closer, forgetting our fight as I stared at the little models of Dragons which sat all over the space. There were sketches too. They weren't done by anyone with a great deal of talent, but it was hard to miss the giant cocks scrawled everywhere even if they did look a bit like badly wrapped sausages.

"I'm not a stalker!" Cindy Lou protested, scrambling forward to try and block my view of her creepy collection, but I knocked her aside with air magic again, wrapping it around her to hold her down.

"Holy shit – is that...*hair?*" I grimaced as I spotted the lock of short black hair which lay in a heart shaped silver box on a shelf in the middle of the shrine.

There were so many photos of Dante that I couldn't count them, but I could tell that almost all of them had been taken without his knowledge. There were shots of him with his clan, practicing Pitball, sitting in class and walking down corridors. There were blurry photos of him in his Storm Dragon form, flying through the sky and wielding lightning. There were even a few which had been taken by someone hiding while he showered in the locker rooms.

What the actual fuck? And she called me *a psychopath??*

Cindy Lou started cursing me, struggling against my magic in desperation as I continued to stare in fascination at her collection. I was equal parts fascinated and horrified, especially when I spotted a sketch of a shifted Dragon with a cock the size of a car standing over a naked girl with long black hair.

Does she fantasise about him fucking her in his Order form? I'd seen a lot of weird and wonderful things growing up around strippers and whores, but that took the fucking biscuit.

A gold ring lay on a red cushion beneath a plastic model of a navy blue Dragon and I spotted the Oscura Clan symbol of a Wolf howling at the moon etched into it beneath the initials M.O.

"Let's see which one of us Dante thinks is insane when he sees this," I suggested as I plucked the ring from the cushion and pushed it onto my thumb.

"No!" Cindy Lou shrieked. "I'm begging you! I *need* that!"

What the fuck for?? I was suddenly struck with the desire to wash my hands and scrub the ring clean in a vat of bleach.

I grimaced at her as I backed up towards the door. "Well I'm guessing Dante didn't give you this. But if you want it back, you can ask him for it."

I pulled the door open and turned to leave, but I came face to face with Dante and Leon instead.

"What's going on, little monster?" Leon asked, raising his eyebrows as he spotted Cindy Lou still immobilised on the floor.

"It looks like Cindy Poo has a little crush on Dante," I said, looking up at him as I offered him the ring from my finger.

Dante's gaze had fallen on the creepy ass shrine as Cindy Lou started sobbing, but he looked down as I pressed the ring into his hand.

A deep growl resonated in his chest and static rolled through the air so thickly that Cindy Lou yelped.

"My papa left me this ring when he died," he growled. "I spent weeks searching for it when it went missing. I mourned it like I'd lost him all over again."

"I'm sorry," Cindy Lou whimpered. "I only wanted it so that I could be close to you. I love you!"

Dante growled again, stepping forward like he meant to teach her a lesson of his own and I placed a hand on his chest to try and hold him back.

"She's not worth it," I breathed, drawing his gaze down to meet mine.

The tension coiling in his body was so rigid that I could feel it resonating right down to the base of my spine. My hair was standing on end as electricity rolled off of him but he slowly managed to rein in his anger enough to step back.

"Per me sei morto," he snarled at Cindy Lou, spitting on the floor before striding away from her room and back towards the stairwell.

Leon pulled his Atlas from his pocket and took a picture of the shrine with a mocking smile. "Hashtag desperate for the Dragon dick," he said with a mocking smile as he posted it to FaeBook before flicking his fingers at the shrine lazily and setting the whole thing alight.

Cindy Lou wailed as if she was in actual agony as her collection went up in flames and I followed Leon out of her room as he caught my hand.

129

"I never liked that girl," he muttered as we headed after Dante and I couldn't help but laugh as he pulled me close.

"Me either."

GARETH

CHAPTER ELEVEN

ELEVEN MONTHS BEFORE THE SOLARIS METEOR SHOWER...

*T*he swell of students washed me out into the Acrux Courtyard where the chatter was utterly consumed with one, single topic of conversation. Ryder Draconis was fucking a teacher.

My heart pounded to an unsteady rhythm as I tried to act shocked, shaking my head again and again as people kept asking whether or not I could believe it.

Yes I can believe it! *I was in that fucking cupboard for over half an hour watching it happen and the sound quality on that little slice of hell was way sharper than the repeated orgasmic screams of our Professor coming out of a thousand tinny Atlas speakers!*

Cindy Lou waved her Atlas in my face, pointing out the fact that he seemed to be half choking King at the same time as he was slamming his dick into her. Thanks for reminding me.

"Do you think he could have forced her into it?" she asked in a voice

intended to carry. "Maybe he threatened her with the might of the Brotherhood to make her-"

"Every other girl in this school is begging to suck some Basilisk cock, Cindy," Harvey said happily as he zoomed in on King's face in a freeze frame. "And that look on her face, that look that says he just blew her fucking mind as well as his load is exactly why. He didn't force her to do shit. She wanted that, plain and simple."

"But he's a student!" she gasped in horror as she began to turn the idea around in her head. "Do you think she forced him to-"

"Do you seriously think some washed up Professor could force Ryder Draconis to do anything?" Harvey scoffed. "Hell, I doubt the Savage King himself could make that guy do anything he didn't want to if he was still alive."

I forced a laugh a little too hard and the two of them looked at me like I was mad so I switched it into a fake coughing fit which I wasn't entirely sure made it any better.

"I can't believe Draconis stuck it to a teacher!" Lorenzo howled excitedly as he bounded towards us. "Do you think they bonded over the fact that they both have fangs or because neither of them has a soul?"

I almost laughed at that assessment of their relationship but I was too damn terrified to manage it.

"Probably both," I replied and he grinned in triumph.

The tannoy buzzed overhead as the sound of Principal Greyshine clearing his throat drew our attention to him. "Professor King and Ryder Draconis report to my office. Now!" The announcement cut off abruptly and my mouth dried out. I didn't think I'd ever heard Greyshine use the tannoy without so much as a bing bong before.

The tide of students all swarmed towards Altair Halls as if we might be allowed to listen in on their meeting too and I followed, doing my best to seem as intrigued as everyone else. So long as no one noticed I was trying my hardest not to crap myself, I was good.

I could see Dante leading the swarm of students ahead of me. His Wolf pack were howling their excitement for their victory over the Lunar King and I just had to hope to hell that no one ever discovered the part I'd played in it.

We made it into Altair Halls and I stayed between Cindy Lou and Harvey as they discussed more and more theories about the clip. They came up with a thousand scenarios for how Ryder had come to start screwing our Elemental Magic Professor and I laughed along, half-heartedly suggesting that maybe they had a real connection just to make sure I'd had an input. The two of them stared at me for a long moment when I said that though and eventually Harvey scoffed.

"Ryder would be more likely to form a real connection with a blunt hacksaw than a woman. That guy's blood runs cold in every way. He's a stone. Cold. Killer. Nothing more. Nothing less. And I sure as shit don't ever want to get on his good side let alone his bad side. Only Dante Oscura has balls big enough to face off against him like this and even so, I bet he'll be rewarded with a mortal wound or two before the day is out."

My racing heart almost gave out at that suggestion. I'd never even considered the implications to Dante now that Ryder would hold him accountable for this. What if I'd just signed his death warrant? Though as Dante's booming laughter broke over the crowd, I could at least admit that he certainly wasn't worried about whatever retaliation came his way.

A chill crept along my spine a moment before a cold hand slammed into my shoulder, knocking me aside as Ryder carved a path into existence through the crowd.

I forgot how to fucking breathe as I watched him go. He didn't look back, didn't seem to have registered me amongst the masses at all. Which was good. Really good. I was nothing and no one and so long as he remembered to forget me then he'd never even think of me at all. I certainly wasn't someone who would have gone up against him. I was all for fighting for my position, but I was also realistic and my power didn't even tickle his in a straight contest.

No way I'd ever be looking to challenge him for anything. And that was just fine by me.

No one dared to step back into the path he'd carved for a long moment then Cindy Lou snatched my hand and dragged me down it. I was taken off-guard before I could resist and I suddenly found myself mingling with Dante's pack at the front of the crowd as we made it to the corridor outside Greyshine's office.

Lorenzo hung back, keeping his distance from his old clan leader and making me wish I had an excuse to stay out of the middle of this too.

Ryder pulled the door open and a moment before he managed to step inside, a blur of motion caught my eye, announcing Professor King's arrival too.

Greyshine blanched at the sight of the crowd who had turned up for the show and he tried to throw the door closed to block us out. Dante lifted a hand and knocked the door back open with a sharp blast of wind.

"I don't think the pervertita should be shut in a room with the student she molested again, do you?" Dante called loudly and Greyshine dabbed at his bald patch nervously.

"Erm, I suppose that perhaps you have a point, Mr Oscura…" he said, looking absolutely terrified of my gang leader friend.

Dante caught my eye and grinned at me, fucking winking as Greyshine backed up and started stumbling over various questions which he aimed at King and Ryder.

Ryder looked about as entertained as he would be at a funeral. His jaw was locked tight and his muscles straining against his school shirt as he folded his arms, but he didn't utter a single word. Professor King on the other hand looked like she might pass out, she kept stammering excuses and half apologies that I couldn't hear over the baying Wolfpack.

Dante yawned like he was bored and pulled his Atlas from his pocket. My gaze was drawn to it as he opened up the file which I'd given him and he

forwarded the entire thing to someone saved in his contacts as FIB Barry no
balls.

*Greyshine was pacing, shaking his head, pointing fingers and not really
saying anything at all. It was pretty obvious he had no idea how to deal with
this, but that didn't really matter because all of a sudden, eight FIB agents
materialised out of thin air.*

*Professor King screamed as she tried to shoot away, but one of them
threw a canister against the wall and a cloud of Order Suppressant filled the
office, spilling out into the hallway.*

*I shivered as my Pegasus retreated deep within me, blocked off by the
gas instantly.*

*"Katherine King, you are hereby detained by the Fae Investigation
Bureau for the unlawful influencing of a student in your care and engaging
in a sexual relationship with said student. You are stripped of your position,
pending investigation and your Order and Power are hereby restrained until
further notice."*

*Professor King tried to struggle but the officer holding her threw a
pinch of stardust over them and they disappeared, her scream echoing over
the now silent crowd even after she'd gone.*

*"We need to take you in for questioning too, son," another officer said
kindly to Ryder, approaching him with a soft smile like he thought he was some
poor victim. Either the guy had no fucking idea who he was talking to or he
had a death wish.*

*"I'm not your son and if you speak to me in that patronising tone again,
I'll kill every fucking member of your family in ways so fucking torturous they
won't even be able to release the details to the press. You'll be burying the
pieces of them in a hessian sack because you won't be able to put them back
together well enough to fill a coffin," Ryder hissed.*

*The FIB officer flinched and backed away, looking to his colleagues
like he didn't know what the hell to do. Maybe he was new, and I'd guess*

not from Alestria either if he didn't instantly recognise the King of the Lunar Brotherhood when he saw him.

"I'm not talking to the police," Ryder continued. "I've got Potions in ten minutes and I'm not missing class. You've got a video of me fucking her so go ahead and convict her using that, because I have nothing to say."

The FIB officers all stared at him as he turned and strode toward the exit. Law enforcement rarely mixed it with the high up gang members in Alestria and I doubted they'd push the issue with Ryder. It wasn't worth the body count.

"Err, Mr Draconis," Greyshine piped up, sounding as authoritative as a bagel in a bag of donuts. "I don't think you should speak to the officers like-"

Ryder hissed at him, baring fangs which had transformed into his Basilisk form and dripped acidic green venom to the floor where it instantly burned holes through the plush white carpet.

He walked from the room and everyone backed the fuck away to let him go. Everyone aside from Dante.

The two of them stood eye to eye in the centre of the corridor for a long moment, neither of them willing to move aside for the other.

"Nice work trying to sabotage me by screwing an old slut," Dante purred. "Did you catch Faemydia from her or does your dick always look so enflamed?"

"Watch your back, Inferno," Ryder hissed. "There's a storm coming which even you won't be able to ride."

They glared at each other for another long moment with the promise of death hanging between them before they both turned away and strode in opposite directions down the corridor.

I released a shaky breath and surreptitiously brushed my hand over my junk to make sure that I definitely hadn't pissed myself. Luckily I was bone dry, but I was also half sure that my balls had crawled right up inside me to hide. I was going to go and sit in my room and spend the rest of my day trying to coax

138

them back out again because I sure as shit wasn't going to risk running into Ryder while he was in this mood.

I made my excuses to Harvey and Cindy Lou and half ran back to the Vega Dorms. My heart rate didn't even begin to slow until I arrived back at my bunk and I sank down on it with a sigh of relief.

The moment barely lasted a second before my Atlas pinged.

The message there made my heart stop beating altogether.

Ryder:

You're going to find out who made that recording for Inferno. And when you've located them, we're going to see just how much pain a Fae can take before their heart gives out.

I was going to die. Shit on it.

GABRIEL

CHAPTER TWELVE

"Hey kid," Bill said as I dropped down onto the bench beside him in New Moon Park in the south of Alestria.

"Hey." I put up a silencing bubble around us, folding my wings behind me.

A group of Werewolf pups raced past us chasing their mom and dad in their large canine forms, howling together as if practising for the night. A herd of Pegasus were playing in the lake, kicking water at each other and sprinkling glitter everywhere. The sense of peace in this place was unlike any other part of the city I knew. I wondered if Elise had ever come here.

"Got anything good for me?" I asked hopefully. I'd practically put everything about my investigations into my past on hold in favour of getting Bill to help Elise instead.

"Well it was a pain in the fucking asshole, but I got that file you wanted from the FIB." He lit up a cigarette, taking his sweet time before pulling out the file and handing it to me. I flipped it open, eyeing Lorenzo Oscura's face staring back at me.

I shut it again, placing it on my lap as I soaked in the sun, the feel of summer whispering to me on the breeze. "You got anything else?" I asked curiously.

"Nope, that's it. But er...there is something I wanted to say." He scratched his large moustache, fixing his gaze on a Minotaur who had a little boy riding on his shoulders while gripping onto his horns.

"Oh yeah?" I frowned curiously.

"Look, don't take this the wrong way, kid, but are you sure you know what you're doing getting involved with Gareth Tempa's sister?"

"I wouldn't say involved," I muttered. "I'm just helping her."

"Right, sure. And what's gonna happen if she finds out what you did? How's she gonna feel about you *helping* her then?" He air-quoted the word and I scowled, my chest tightening.

"I'm just trying to do what's right."

He turned to me with a frown lining his forehead. "Because you care about her," he said frankly and I clenched my jaw, refusing to answer. It was irrelevant anyway.

"Maybe the best thing you could do for her would be to tell her the truth," Bill said earnestly and rage rushed up inside me.

I snatched the cigarette from his hand, scrunching it in my fist and throwing it on the ground. It was childish and pointless and he immediately took another one out and lit it up. But I'd shown him how I felt about that.

"Kid-" he started again.

"Enough, Bill. I'm not your kid. I'm no one's kid," I said slightly bitterly, turning away from him. I should have left, but I didn't. I sat there hurting.

"Not true," Bill grunted, shifting half a centimetre closer on the bench. I eyed the foot of space between us then looked up at him, waiting for him to elaborate. "I'm shit with children, always was. But if I did have one, I'd hope he'd be like you." He didn't meet my eye, inhaling his cigarette smoke and tarring his lungs. With those few words, he'd given me more than my foster family ever had.

"Fuck, Bill," I breathed, lowering my right wing so it brushed against his back. It was about as emotional as I knew he'd want me to be and I wasn't exactly the hugging type anyway. "You mean that?"

"I mean that," he said, nodding as he glanced over at me. "And if you care about this girl, then I care about her too, alright? So do what's right by her."

"She'll hate me," I choked out, my brows pulling tightly together.

"Maybe," he said darkly. "But it's still the right thing to do."

I bowed my head, releasing a heavy sigh. "Thanks for the file."

"No worries. See you around, kid." He got up, heading off down the path without looking back. I hadn't even paid him.

I stretched my wings, releasing the silencing bubble before taking off into the sky. The afternoon sun poured across my back, feeling divine as I made my way to Aurora Academy with the file clutched in my hand.

As I flew, that familiar tugging sensation filled my mind which always preceded a vision. I blinked as a series of images flashed before my eyes. A guy around my age with raven hair and dark eyes was kneeling in a cave, a shining dagger in his hand. He ran the blade up his arm to split the skin and tipped his head back as he fell under some spell.

I jolted out of the vision with a frown, unsure who I'd just seen. But what I did know, was that whoever it was had been performing dark magic. And that made my gut squirm uncomfortably. It was illegal and downright dangerous. But I didn't often get visions about strangers, so I wondered what the stars were trying to show me. With my abilities blocked, I couldn't call on the vision again and soon had to give up trying to reach it. If the heavens wanted me to know something, I just had to have faith that they'd find a way past the block again to let me see it.

It wasn't long before I was landing on the roof of the Vega Dorms, dropping down to sit on the wall which looked out over Devil's Hill. I opened the file, reading through it slowly to take in every detail, hunting for clues.

The FIB had concluded the Killblaze Lorenzo had taken the night he'd died had driven him to suicidal thoughts. He'd been found in an alley with a puncture wound in his chest they believed he'd inflicted on himself with a blade of ice. Whether he'd intended it or not, it had ended his life. But the rest of it didn't add up to me as I looked through the post-mortem images. He was covered in bruises and there were marks on his side which looked like they'd been put there with the heel of a woman's shoe.

The FIB had clearly wanted to write this off as just some junkie Oscura lost to Killblaze, but they'd had clear evidence here that suggested otherwise. I checked the notes, finding that most of the post-mortem records had been redacted. At the bottom was a conclusion stating that Lorenzo had inflicted the wounds on himself before his death.

I took out my Atlas, relieved that I finally had something to go on. If Lorenzo *had* been murdered, then maybe the person who'd killed Gareth was responsible. And maybe there was something in these images that could give us a clue to who it was. It certainly didn't look like a regular Lunar killing. They were known for leaving bodies in ten pieces. But I guessed the FIB had wanted to write it off as a suicide rather than suggesting foul play without firm evidence. They never wanted to mix it with the gangs so there were plenty of unsolved murders in this city. But something about this one smelled off to me.

I shot Elise a text, wondering what she might be up to this afternoon. She normally spent Sundays in the library, but as it was a particularly nice day maybe she was outside somewhere. I pictured her tucked under a tree with a book in her arms, her long legs stretched out beneath a pair of shor-*concentrate motherfucker.*

Gabriel:

I've got something that might help with you know what.

Elise:

Be right there X

I grinned stupidly at that kiss for way too long. Long enough for her to arrive with her Vampire speed. She hadn't even asked where I was, so I guessed that made me a predictable bastard.

"What is it?" Elise asked, dropping down beside me on the wall. She wasn't wearing shorts like I'd pictured, she was wearing a tiny black skirt and a lilac cami which matched her hair.

I cleared my throat, passing her the file. She flipped it open, her lips parting as she stared at Lorenzo's picture.

"I think he was attacked before he died," I said, forcing my mind away from how good she looked. "So I thought maybe whoever attacked him could have killed Gareth."

"I did this," Elise blurted, handing the file back to me and staring straight ahead.

"You – what?" I balked.

"He wasn't supposed to die," she said, a crease forming on her brow. "I needed information. He was high as fuck and he garbled some stuff about the killer being a King at this school and then he just…killed himself." She swallowed, turning to me as I tried to absorb this. Her hands began to shake and I reached out, lacing my fingers with hers. I didn't care what she'd done, I was here for her. In her corner. Always. "I really didn't mean for him to die."

"Fuck, I'm sorry." I stared down at the file, disappointment rolling through me.

"You're sorry?" she questioned in confusion. "Sorry he's dead, or sorry I had a hand in it?" Her tone was sharp like she expected me to have a go at her for this, to tell her she was in the wrong, that she shouldn't have hurt this guy. But who was I to fucking judge? And hell, if it had been my sibling who'd died, I sure as shit would have acted the same way. Not that I knew what having a brother or sister felt like. But I could imagine I'd tried to protect them in any way I possibly could.

"No, Elise," I said, squeezing her hand before she could pull away. "I'm sorry because this file is fucking pointless." I tossed it behind me onto the roof and I felt her eyes burning into the side of my head.

"You don't care that I did that?" she whispered.

"No," I said, my throat too tight. "Because I've been that person too."

I thought of what Bill had said to me and could feel the truth pushing at the base of my tongue. I was terrified of her reaction, but maybe he was right. I owed her this. And maybe she deserved the chance to hate me for it too.

"What do you mean?" she asked, tension spanning between us.

I released her hand, scraping my fingers through my hair as anxiety ate me alive. "Elise I…I don't want to lie to you anymore."

She inhaled, saying nothing, waiting. I could feel how desperate she was to hear the next words that came out of my mouth. But she should have been terrified. She should have been ready to destroy me for it.

"Your brother was blackmailing me for money as you know," I forced out and she nodded in my periphery. "The night of the Solarid Meteor Shower, my private investigator contacted me with Gareth's information."

"And then what?" Her voice was cold. I sensed her retreating. She was going to want to hurt me and I'd let her do what she needed to in penance for this. It was time I faced my fate.

I hung my head, pushing my fingers into my eyelids. "I hunted him down in the Acrux Courtyard. There was no one there. It was late. It wasn't long before the shower was about to start."

"What did you do?" she asked in a low growl, sounding heartbroken and furious.

"I hurt him," I breathed, unable to say it louder. "I held him down with magic and beat the living hell out of him. My fists were bloody, his face fucking pulverised. Then I told him he was nothing and-"

"And?" Elise demanded, a snarl ripping from her throat.

"And I left him there, tied down and bleeding. And hurting. That was barely an hour before he was found dead. It was one of the last things in the world he ever experienced. And it was *my* fucking hands which dealt him all that pain." My heart cracked up the middle and I rose to my feet, walking away from Elise. How could I look at her now?

I waited for her to attack, the bite of her fangs, the clash of her magic. But nothing came.

"You stupid idiot," she gasped and it took me a second to realise she was crying.

I turned, finding her standing up on the wall glaring down at me. "How could you keep this from me?"

"I'm sorry, I'm so fucking sorry Elise. I was terrified of what you'd think."

"What I'd think?!" She leapt off the wall in a blur, rushing over and slamming into me. I expected claws and fangs but she cupped the back of my neck and dragged me down so my forehead hit hers. "I thought you murdered him, you asshole. I was terrified of it. But you beat him up because he blackmailed you. So what? He would have healed! He was Fae. And a strong fucking Fae too. We all take beatings every day. That's life. And after what he did to you, why would he expect anything else?"

"You're not angry?" I asked in astonishment.

"No I'm fucking *relieved*, Gabriel." She clung onto me like her life depended on it, sniffing as her tears stopped falling. "Because *finally* I can rule you out. I can stop fighting this." Her mouth met mine and I froze, unsure what to do for a whole eternity. Because surely the stars were not this kind?

I broke the kiss, shaking my head as I stepped back. "You're not thinking straight."

"Don't tell me what I think," she said, prowling forward and I continued to back up.

"Elise…"

"Stop running. You're making me hungry." Her eyes blazed as her fangs snapped out.

My heart pounded and darkness washed through me at the carnal look in her eyes. "You must be angry with me at least a little."

She lunged for me and I took flight, her fingers grazing my shoe as I flew over her head and landed behind her. She shot forward and I darted sideways to evade her.

"A little," she agreed, rushing at me again.

I dropped low, flipping her legs out from under her so she slammed onto her back. "A little more now?" I gazed down at her with my eyebrow arched.

She sprang upright with a growl and I jumped back as she swiped at me once more.

I couldn't help a smirk, wanting to rile her up into a tempest. I wanted her angry with me, fucking raging. It was what I deserved.

"I'm going to have your blood," she said determinedly, her eyes locking on me. The instincts of the hunt were rising in her keenly and I could see the beast of her Order form taking control of her completely.

"Come and get it then," I challenged.

She ran at me once more in a blur of speed and I ran too, diving off the edge of the roof and circling back over her with two powerful wing flaps. She leapt at me, catching my ankle and dragging me back towards the roof. I let her pull me down and she crashed to her knees as I landed gracefully in front of her. She still had hold of my leg and she jerked forward to try and sink her teeth into me. I moved in a flash, catching a handful of her hair and forcing her to look up at me.

"I'm not prey, I'm the hunter," I warned.

"Wrong. You're a bird, I'm the cat," she hissed.

"Then prove it." I yanked her head back hard enough to make her yelp then released her so she hit the ground on her ass.

She swung her legs out to knock me over but I hovered over them lightly, landing beside her once more. "Come on kitty."

She remained on the ground and I waited for her to attack, but instead she arched her back and pulled her top off. A lump rose in my throat as I found she had no bra on and my cock swelled for her immediately.

"Gabriel," she said breathily.

"Mm," I grunted. *Fuck. Me.*

She lunged in a blur and I was too distracted to react as she collided with me, knocking me to the ground. My back impacted with the concrete and I growled as she sank her fangs into my throat. My hands fell to her hips as she ground herself against the solid ridge of my hard-on, making me swear between my teeth.

"Be angry with me," I demanded.

She wrenched her fangs free and slapped me hard across the face. "I am fucking angry." She rolled her hips and pleasure resounded through my dick.

"Oh fuck…be more angry," I groaned.

She shoved my head to one side, digging her fangs into the opposite side of my neck. She was rough as hell and I could feel her drinking in my magic with every bob of her throat. And it felt so fucking good.

She reached between us, unzipping my fly and lifting her hips as she pushed her panties aside.

"Elise," I said in the weakest protest ever to pass my fucking lips. Then she slid onto me and I lost myself to her.

"Screw it, I'm done trying to fight this," I growled and I pushed her hips down as she rode me, drinking from my throat with greedy mouthfuls. Her knees scraped against the concrete, grazing as they rubbed the ground.

I let her take and take and take until I'd had enough, my own instincts rising up and demanding I put her in her place.

I snatched her thighs, rolling us over and slamming her down onto her back. She huffed as her fangs were forced free from my neck and I plunged my tongue into her mouth before she had a second to recover. She tasted like blood and cherries, mixed into a perfect sinful cocktail.

I thrust into her again and again, forcing her thighs wider and making her take every inch of me.

She caught a fistful of my hair, biting into my lower lip to spill more of my blood onto her tongue. I tugged her hands free from me, pinning them to the ground above her head and breaking our vicious kiss.

"You're mine," I growled as she gazed at me through hooded eyes. Eyes which were the colour of a fucking tropical sea. I could have swum in them all day.

She opened her mouth to protest and I drove into her harder, refusing to let her. If she wasn't going to hate me, then she was damn well going to be mine. Simple as.

"*Mine*," I reiterated as I felt her coming apart, her body constricting around me as she cried out to the sky. Her back arched and I slid a hand beneath her, driving into her body as my knuckles split against the hard ground.

"Oh - fuck - stars," she slurred as she came, her thighs clamping around me, gripping me tight.

I finished with one final thrust, growling her name as pleasure coiled up at the base of my spine then burned through me like a wildfire.

I released her wrists, breathless as I laid over her, resting my forehead to the cool concrete beside her head.

Her arms closed around me and she brushed her fingers tenderly across my feathers. I shivered as pleasure chased everywhere she touched. Then I kissed her neck, her jaw, her mouth. She was my gift from the stars. My one good thing in this world.

"So you're not mad?" I asked with a smirk when I'd caught my breath.

She laughed, the sound lighter than air. "No Gabriel." She caressed my wings again and the sensation seemed to fix some deeply broken thing inside me. "I'm not mad."

ELISE

CHAPTER THIRTEEN

I walked along the corridor to Professor Titan's office in Altair Halls on my way to my Liaison session with a pout on my lips and a scowl on my face. My gaze fell on Nightshade's office at the end of the corridor and I huffed as I turned my back on it to face the door.

Weeks of watching mind numbing footage of her in there had resulted in nothing and I was done waiting around and just hoping she'd slip up. She clearly didn't conduct business with my mystery murderer from in there and so far I hadn't come up with a way to gain access to her phone either. I mean sure, I could just steal it but that wouldn't really help me. She'd have a passcode and even if I got past that, I was pretty sure that the asshole she'd met in her downtown office would have damn stringent security measures in place, meaning that I couldn't glean anything from any messages or calls anyway. They clearly went to a lot of effort to hide their identity and I knew there weren't going to be any shortcuts to finding them like that. But she was my way in. I knew it. I just hadn't figured out how to make that come together yet.

I knocked on Titan's door and he called me inside.

"Good evening. Elise." he said through a yawn as he covered his mouth. "I apologise for my sleepiness – I had to run the labyrinth last night to recharge my magic and I got a little carried away. I barely got back in time for dawn and had a class at eight so I missed out on sleep."

"That sounds intense," I teased. I didn't know a huge deal about Minotaurs aside from the fact that if you got them in a maze they practically came in their pants over it and it was damn near impossible to get them out again once they started running about. Stubborn as a bull and all that. So when they went to run in their labyrinths, it was easier to let them be until they tuckered themselves out than to try and convince them to leave. And despite the fact that Titan looked knackered, he did also seem to be fighting a grin so I was guessing all that charging about had been fun.

"There were a herd of us there last night," he said enthusiastically. "And we had a few volunteer runners – you should think about doing it actually! It's great fun and as a Vampire you'd pose a real challenge because you're so fast!"

"Err, sure, I'll consider it," I said with a laugh.

I wasn't sure how much I'd enjoy being chased around in circles, trying to escape a maze with a bunch of half bull men charging after me, but I guessed it could be fun.

Titan cleared his throat a little self-consciously as he seemed to realise he'd been gushing and he fought against a blush that rose in his cheeks. "Yes. Well, anyway, back to business. So, erm…you've been making progress as far as friends go?"

I shrugged because I'd actually kinda forgotten about that little task he'd set me. "Well…I like hanging out with a few guys," I hedged.

"Guys who are friends or guys you're dating?" he asked like he could see right through me.

"I'm not *officially* dating any of them."

"Right. But the interest you have in them goes beyond platonic?" he pushed.

"Yeah, you could say that."

Titan sighed like I'd disappointed him. "I do think you should spend some more time trying to make *friends,*" he said in a total dad voice which had me raising an eyebrow at him. "I just think that the emotional support you get from pure friendships can be supremely important."

"Yeah, I know. I guess I've just had a lot going on and stuff and the socialising thing kinda falls through the cracks. Eugene Dipper wants to be my friend though," I added with as much enthusiasm as I could muster.

"Don't go wetting yourself with excitement there, Elise," Titan teased. "How about a few girlfriends? Anyone you like to chat to?"

The way he said *chat* genuinely made me cringe, but I forced myself to consider his question.

"My roommate Laini is cool. I haven't spent a whole lot of time with her since she got together with her girlfriend, but I could definitely make more effort," I suggested.

"Perfect. Laini and Jessica would be a great fit for you. They're both smart, sweet girls, who-"

"Who the hell is Jessica?" I asked with a frown.

"Laini's girlfriend…"

"Shit, I didn't know that. I've definitely called her Tanya more than once. To her face." I groaned and fell back into my chair. "See? I'm horrible at making friends."

Titan chuckled and waved off my objections. "I'm sure she won't hold it against you. You've had a lot of names to learn since coming here. Perhaps you could suggest a little get together with the two of them for a bit of old fashioned bonding?"

I sighed, nodding my agreement because it was clear he wasn't going to let this go.

"Are you excited for the game against Sunrise Academy tomorrow?" he asked, changing the subject and I offered him a genuine smile at that.

"Yeah," I replied enthusiastically. "We've been training really hard and I'm actually starting to think we can win it."

"Oh boy, I don't think Aurora Academy has been in a semi-final match for years," Titan said with a dreamy look. "I'll be there in the front row to cheer you on."

"Thanks," I replied with a laugh. It wasn't horrible to know I'd have a supporter in the crowd though as I would definitely be the only team player who had no family coming to watch.

"Well, we won't let this meeting go on too long. We'll finish up quickly and you can get a good night's sleep."

"Sounds good to me," I agreed.

"Then let's move on to assessing your studies," Titan suggested cheerfully, pushing a Numerology book my way.

The sound of the crowd cheering outside the Pitball locker rooms had my gut turning over with a mixture of anxiety and pure, honest to the stars exhilaration. I was so pumped for this game that I couldn't put my feelings into words. It was half time and we were already eight points up. The extra practice Leon had been forcing on me and Dante had definitely paid off and the three of us were fucking unstoppable out there.

The moment I got my hands on the ball, none of the opposition could get to me. With the two of them flanking me and working tirelessly at defensive and tackling moves, I was left with the clear target of the Pit.

I swear to the moon, the Sunrise Pit Keepers were actually afraid of us now. They saw us coming and their faces paled as Leon and Dante bombarded them with combination attacks of air and fire magic and I used a shot of air propulsion to guide each and every ball straight into the Pit while they fought their hardest not to get burnt to a crisp.

I'd been late for practice last week and Professor Mars had decided to punish me by making me practice tackles with Leon and Dante for the first half of the session. I couldn't really say I minded rolling around in the dirt with the two of them so it hadn't been so bad, and on the plus side it had really upped my game when it came to fighting my way out of a tackle.

There was a big ass Manticore playing as their Waterguard and he'd made it his mission to take me out of the game as often as possible. He was damn fast too. But when he caught me, he had to keep me pinned to the ground for five whole seconds to knock me out of the round and my expert escape skills meant that he'd only managed it twice so far. I wasn't above headbutting, kidney strikes and even taking a shot at a knee to the balls if I had to. There were no rules about how you could fight in Pitball, and that meant I was free to get as dirty as I liked in aid of the game. In all honesty, it was the best outlet for my rage that I'd found in a long time.

Leon was finishing up his half time pep talk as the team got ready to head back out and I bounced on my heels as the excitement out on the pitch bled into my veins.

We were playing a home game on our own turf which meant that the Sunrise team didn't have a whole lot of supporters in attendance. Most parents and students didn't want to risk a visit to Alestria and I couldn't entirely blame them, but it just meant that almost the entire crowd was out there screaming for *us*. I'd even seen a few banners with my name on them, one of which was being waved by a way too enthusiastic Professor Titan. It was kind of mortifying but I was secretly pleased that he'd turned out for me like that. The other players all had their families watching and cheering them on and I was obviously light on the family figures. It wasn't like I needed a parent cheering me on from the sidelines but having *one* Fae who thought enough of me to show up and cheer my name made me feel just a touch better about being the odd one out.

Dante and Leon's families had come to watch the game and I was trying not to feel the pang of longing that gave me too sharply. It wasn't their fault that they were so loved while I was so alone. And I liked to think that Gareth was here anyway. He'd adored this game. I was playing for him and I'd win for him too.

The whistle sounded the start of the second half and I took up my position as Airstriker in my quarter of the pitch with excitement. I was full of energy, waiting for the first ball to shoot out of one of the holes when a shadow shifted overhead.

I glanced up in surprise as Gabriel flew past before he dropped down to take a seat at the back of the bleachers. I couldn't help but stare a little as he sat there shirtless with the sun haloing behind him over his black wings. He looked like an angel fallen from heaven and placed here as a perfect temptation just for me. The memory of what we'd gotten up to on the roof the other day had a tingle of energy running through my core and as his gaze fixed on me, I couldn't help but grin.

The group of girls who made up our school cheerleading squad all started whispering and pointing at him excitedly but he just ignored them, his gaze zeroing in on me.

I offered him a confused smile as I wondered what he was doing here, but he didn't beckon me over or look in any way concerned so I had no reason to suspect his presence had anything to do with our investigations. He just leaned forward with his forearms on his knees and watched.

Has he seriously come out here to watch me play?

I tried not to grin like an idiot at that thought and a moment later I was distracted by the fwump of the hole in my quarter of the pitch ejecting an airball.

I leapt up to snatch it and started running as fast as I could as I fought to outpace the players from the Sunrise team.

Dante ran beside me, charging forward to tackle a player who tried to make a run for me. They hit the ground with a thump that shook the earth at my feet and I swung around them, making a beeline for the pit.

I threw out a hand as more players ran for me, sending a huge gust of air magic towards their legs and sending them scattering like a bunch of bowling pins. The Pit Keepers were the last obstacles in my way but as I charged towards them, Leon ran forward to tackle them, leaving my shot clear.

I slammed the ball down into the Pit with a whoop of triumph and clamouring applause assaulted my ears from the stands. The Oscura Wolves all howled and leapt up and down as Dante ran a victory lap past them before circling back to his starting position in the air quarter.

Gabriel grinned at me as he clapped enthusiastically and I smirked, a light feeling growing in my chest. I offered him a salute as thanks before jogging back to take up my position again for the next round.

We played out the entire second half with the stars on our side and so many balls in the Pit that I almost couldn't keep count. But the final score was clear. Aurora Academy thirty seven. Sunrise Academy nineteen. We hadn't just won, we'd fucking smashed them.

Leon roared so loudly that I could have sworn he'd shifted.

"We're going to play Zodiac Academy!" he cried in triumph, dropping to his knees in the mud like he couldn't believe it was really happening.

I shot forward and dove on him in celebration. He wrapped his arms around me tightly as he fell back into the mud and I squealed as I was dragged down on top of him.

Dante cried out in victory and I shrieked in panic half a second before he dove on top of the two of us, flattening us and making sure that I was totally smothered in mud as I was squashed between them.

I laughed as a pure lightness filled my chest. This was something I could give myself to entirely without having to lie or hide; on the Pitball pitch I was free. And better than that, I'd just lived out one of Gareth's dreams for him.

Leon scrambled beneath the combined weight of me and Dante as he tried to buck the Storm Dragon off of us and I managed to wriggle my way out from between them.

They started play fighting in the mud and I laughed as I got to my feet, leaning forward on my knees to catch my breath. Most of the other players and cheerleaders were celebrating with their friends and families or heading for the locker rooms.

Dante and Leon started wrestling more aggressively as they got too into the game as usual and I moved forward to take my place as referee. It was our unofficial post-play tradition and I kinda loved it.

I bit my lip as I watched them throwing punches and trying to get the upper hand as they scrambled about. I was pretty sure they knew how much I liked it when they fooled around like that, but I wasn't against them putting on a show for me.

The soft rustle of feathers came a moment before Gabriel landed behind me and I turned to look up at him in surprise.

"Did you come here just to watch me play?" I teased, my gaze slipping over the myriad of tattoos which covered his bare chest.

"I love Pitball," he said. "Though I usually just watch the League games. But I was definitely more motivated to attend this match. Sorry I missed the first half though, I got caught up in a vision and lost track of the time."

"Anything interesting?" I asked.

"Nothing I could make any real sense of," he replied in frustration.

Gabriel reached out to take my hand and I gasped as water magic slipped over me, washing all of the mud, blood and sweat from my body before he drew it all away again, leaving me as clean and dry as if I'd just had a twenty minute shower and been wrapped in a fluffy towel.

"Thanks," I said with a grin that just wouldn't quit. Winning at Pitball might have been the best feeling in the entire world.

"You were brilliant out there. Maybe you should think about going pro after you graduate?" he suggested.

I scoffed at his blatant flattery and smacked his arm playfully. "What are you after?"

"You," he replied simply.

Before I could respond to that, he caught my waist and pulled me flush against him as he kissed me.

My heart leapt in surprise. He'd always been so secretive about his feelings for me before, like letting anyone know how he felt might put me in danger, but it seemed like he'd really meant what he'd said the other night. He was done trying to fight it.

My lips parted for his tongue as I wrapped my arms around his neck and I moaned in pleasure as he deepened the kiss. Everywhere that our bodies met came alive with goosebumps and I couldn't help but push up on my tiptoes as I tried to press even more of my flesh to his.

"What the fuck is happening right now?" Dante demanded loudly and I broke away from Gabriel like I'd just had freezing cold water dumped over my head.

"I think I just woke up in some kind of crazy alternative universe," Leon added, staring at the two of us like he couldn't work out what the hell he'd just seen.

I looked between the two of them as they stared at me in shock and I struggled for the right words to say. I mean, I'd always made it clear that I wasn't going to be committing to any one of them alone, but perhaps making out with Gabriel right in front of them hadn't been the most thoughtful way to let them know that there was another guy in the mix. I'd just put that moment of madness down to a post win high.

"Both of you have just seen the way things are now and you need to get over it," Gabriel replied darkly before I could. "Elise is *mine*. I've seen it and we've both decided that that's what we want. So you might as well get over it, because you can't fight the stars."

"What?" I demanded just as Dante and Leon asked the same question.

Gabriel still had hold of me and as I tried to step back, he fought against releasing me.

I jerked out of his grip and took a firm step away from him as I pointed a finger directly at him.

"Firstly, I might have agreed to start seeing you again, but there was absolutely zero mention of that being exclusive because believe me – it isn't."

Gabriel frowned at me like I was speaking another language, but I barrelled on before he could interrupt.

"I'm not a prize to be won or a bone to be fought over," I said plainly. "I like you. *All of you.* So if you want to keep seeing me then great. But you need to accept that this is who I am. I'm not going to make the mistakes my mother made. I'm not going to limit myself to loving one person. So either you want me like this or you don't want me at all. It's simple."

"You're my Elysian Mate, Elise," Gabriel said angrily. "I don't even understand how you can spare any attention for these assholes now, but once we're bonded you'll hardly even remember they exist."

"What the fuck are you talking about, stronzo?" Dante demanded. "I don't see any silver in her eyes. Are you just imagining up bullshit now as well as spouting it all of the damn time?"

"You really don't want to try and fight me on this," Gabriel growled, stepping in front of me as water swirled between his fingers. "I'm the strongest Fae in this school and you'd do well not to forget it."

"You wanna put that to the test?" Dante demanded as electricity crackled all around us.

"If I have to fight for her then I'll happily take you both down," Gabriel snarled, flexing his wings.

Dante growled, squaring his shoulders as he strode towards Gabriel, looking like he might just rip him in two. Leon bared his teeth at the challenge too, the Alpha in him rising to the fight out of instinct.

"Stop it!" I demanded, moving around Gabriel in a blur of motion and putting myself between them before they could come to blows in front of a whole crowd of Pitball fans.

A bolt of lightning slammed into the ground beside us and I flinched as Dante's power crackled through the air and a storm built.

"I'm not going to let the three of you get into a fight because of my choices. I've always been upfront with you about the fact that I don't want to be tied to one man. This really shouldn't be surprising anyone!" I snapped.

"Fuck, little monster, how many of us are there?" Leon asked, almost sounding amused though he mainly looked shocked.

"Just four," I said, realising as I said it that it did sound a little insane, but whatever. I felt what I felt and each of my Kings gave me something I needed. The way I felt about each of them didn't detract from how I felt about the others and they would just have to accept that if they wanted me the way they claimed to.

"What do you mean, *four?*" Gabriel demanded and suddenly the three of them were all staring at me with the storm clouds circling darkly in the sky above. It was pretty damn intimidating and my heart started racing.

"Well…you three, obviously. And Ryder," I said defiantly.

"Draconis? Are you fucking kidding me?!" Gabriel shouted and Dante growled darkly, suddenly in agreement with him.

"I don't have to justify myself to you!" I snapped back. "This is how it is. I like you. *All* of you. And if I'm choosing what *I* want then that's what it is. All or nothing. Take it or leave it."

They stared at me like I was insane or maybe like they were seeing me clearly for the first time. Leon had a smile playing around his lips and I really wanted to kiss him for it. But with the tension that was still hanging in the air following my last kiss, I decided that might not be the best idea.

"*Elise,*" Gabriel started in a tone which said he seriously thought this might be up for discussion, but he needed to get his head out of his ass because I'd spoken clearly enough.

"I think you might all need a bit of time to think this over, so I'll catch you later," I said, taking a step back.

"Wait," Dante tried, but I was done. I tossed them a salute and shot away before I had to hear any more of it.

I'd made my feelings clear. They could figure out the rest between themselves.

RYDER

CHAPTER FOURTEEN

I held a pipette over the cauldron on my desk in my room, biting down on my tongue as I concentrated. One millilitre of Icebain more than was necessary would not only fuck the whole potion, it would leave a crater in my desk as big as me. But it was such a small quantity as it was, I always risked squeezing the right amount out of a pipette.

"Ryder!" Knock. BOOM.

"Fuck!"

I leapt back from the explosion, looking to the window where Elise was standing, her hand pressed to the glass and a guilty-ass expression on her face as she eyed my destroyed desk.

I brushed the ash off my legs, casting a web of Baruvian Ivy around the remains to absorb any toxins in the air.

I moved to the window, unlocking it and wrenching it open with a snarl. My anger dissolved in an instant because it was her. And her being here was worth the destruction of a potion it took six weeks to brew.

"Elise," I hissed her name, letting her believe I was pissed as all hell.

"Sorry. Can I come in?" Her forehead crinkled and I immediately realised something was wrong.

I dropped the act, nodding and moving aside. She leapt into my room, pushing the window closed behind her. Then she rushed forward, wrapping her arms around me and resting her cheek against my bare chest. I stilled, slowly closing my arms around her as I got used to being hugged. Motherfucking *hugged*.

"Did someone do something to you?" I growled, ready to rip out their throat as soon as I had a name.

She sighed, going slack in my arms, her body so warm against my cold skin. "No, it's nothing like that."

"What's it like?" I frowned, wishing I could help. But I didn't have much of an emotional range no matter what Nightmare liked to say. And if Elise was hurting, I was probably the last person who could help. But she was here, she hadn't gone to someone else, so I'd do what I was capable of doing. Even if that just meant drinking away her pain.

"It's Dante."

"*Dante*," I echoed in a snarl, my hands curling into fists.

"And Gabriel."

"Gabriel?" What the fuck had Nox done?

"And Leon…well not really Leon. But he's involved too."

"I'll snap all of their necks if that's what you want," I said seriously.

She breathed a laugh, looking up at me. "That's the exact opposite of what I want."

"You want me to fix their necks?" I suggested with a smirk and she broke a sad sort of smile, pulling away from me.

I instantly missed the contact and took a step after her as she headed across the room to my bed. I scrubbed my knuckles down the back of my neck, frowning as I tried to work out what to do.

Elise slumped down onto my bed. "Gabriel kissed me in front of Dante and Leon then they freaked out because apparently sharing me between the two of them is fine, but add a fourth guy into the mix and-"

"Back the fuck up," I snapped. "You and Gabriel?" *I knew it.*

"Well…" She shrugged innocently.

"And what the fuck is this about Inferno sharing you? What about the deal?" I stood completely still, my Order form rearing up inside me like a cobra about to strike. Had Dante figured out a way around it? I hadn't felt it break, but had I been a total fucking fool sticking to it while he'd been sticking it to my girl?

I was about to lose my fucking shit when Elise shot in front of me in a blur, cupping my cheek to make me look at her. "He didn't break the deal. He's just been…working around it. Like we have."

She tip-toed up, brushing her mouth over mine in a kiss she gave but I couldn't participate in. It was the sweetest fucking thing and it was hardly even a thing. It soothed my frantic heart and my shoulders dropped slightly.

"You do this with him?" I grunted.

"No actually. But he has watched me with Leon." She shrugged innocently and my right eye twitched with rage.

I needed to kill someone. Most likely that piece of shit Mufasa. Then Inferno. Then the peacock.

"You can watch me with him too if you like?" Elise raised a brow and I grunted, trying to pull away, the idea searing into my mind.

"No. Fuck no. I want you. I don't want to see you with some fucking Simba-loving Pride Cock."

She clenched her jaw, heading to the window. "Great. You can't handle this either, can you? Why do none of you understand I'm never gonna be with one guy? It doesn't mean I care for any of you any less." She reached the window and the idea of her leaving physically pained me for a hundred reasons. My magic reserves swelled, but it didn't feel good. It wasn't the pain I wanted. I wanted *hers*.

"Stay," I said in a low voice. I wasn't going to beg like some whipped bitch. If she really wanted me like she wanted them, she'd stay. And she'd take what it was she liked from me. Because that was the point wasn't it? If I was going to even try to understand this – which I really didn't fucking want to – then I guessed she wanted me for who I was. Which was a dark Fae with an even darker soul.

She turned to me, biting down on her lip as her eyes sparkled with hope. "So you understand?"

"I get that this is who you are. But who *I* am is possessive. And I want to possess you. Not as an object, Elise, like a demon. So does that factor in to your little arrangement, or am I meant to agree to your terms only? Because it seems like everyone else in this arrangement is getting what they want from you. Do I not get the same courtesy?"

She swallowed firmly, moving toward me with a look of trepidation in her eyes. "Show me."

"What?" I questioned flatly.

"Show me what you want from me. Work around the rules." She stood before me, her shoulders heaving as she panted, waiting for me to act.

On the one hand, she was giving me everything I'd dreamed of within the terms of the deal, but on the other, I had to accept that three other guys in this school had touched her already. At least one of them had fucked her, had her in ways I wasn't allowed to. But…there were ways she could be touched that only I could give her. And there were ways within the deal I could do it too. I'd had plenty of fucking time to think about that.

Elise inched closer, waiting, but I gave nothing away, my expression steely. I rolled my tongue piercing between my teeth, mulling over what to do.

"Ryder?" she breathed, her voice quiet and fraught with tension. Or was it excitement?

"You'll do everything I say," I commanded and her eyes widened. "Or this doesn't happen."

She contemplated that for a long moment. I knew it went against her nature, but I wasn't asking her to bow to my will outside of this room. But in here and for her pleasure, she fucking would. Or it wasn't going to work for me.

Slowly, she nodded and blood instantly rushed to my dick.

"Do you remember the rules of the deal?" I asked, moving forward and surveying her closely as I circled her like a wolf.

"No kissing me, no fucking me, no touching me beneath my underwear, no overnight bed sharing, no handjobs or blowjobs, no jerking off over me while you're in the same room and no hurting me for pleasure." She gave me a pointed look on the last one and I smirked.

"Good girl." I moved behind her, brushing her hair away from her neck. "So what am I going to do with you, baby?"

I ran my thumb down her spine, feeling every rivet as she arched into my touch, a violent shiver rolling through her. "I don't really care what you'd do with a good girl, Ryder, but I'd like to know what you'd do with a bad one."

A deep laugh escaped me. She had no idea how glad I was that she fought back against me. It was so fucking refreshing. But that was my little secret. And it only applied to her.

"I can't do what I want to do," I growled, a deep need dragging at me to make her hurt and scream with pleasure all at once. I moved in front of her, dropping my head to meet her gaze. "But I can show you."

"No visions," she said quickly, reaching out to press a hand to my chest. "I want you in the flesh, right here."

My throat tightened and I looked away, unable to meet the intensity of her gaze. It undid me, cutting into a lump of flesh deep inside me and making it bleed. She wanted *me*, nothing else. I didn't think any girl had ever wanted that.

"Arms up," I instructed and she did as I said. I took hold of her Pitball shirt, drawing it over her head and tossing it to the floor. She was wearing a black sports bra which pushed her tits together and begged for the rake of my

171

tongue. I couldn't touch her beneath her underwear, but if skin was on show then that seemed like fair game to me.

She dropped her arms and I shook my head. "Did I tell you to drop them yet?"

A smile played at the corner of her mouth as she lifted them again. I rested my hands on her waist, skimming my thumbs over her velvet soft flesh. Then I hounded forward, making her back up towards my bed. I shoved her back against the strut at the far end, raising my hands to lock around her wrists and hold them against the rail of the bunk above.

Her breathing hitched as my bare chest pressed to hers and my hard-on drove into her hip. I used my earth magic to create two thick vines, binding her hands to the rail, tight enough so she couldn't move, then I dropped my hands with a smirk, admiring her.

"Do you have any idea how many times I've fantasised about having you tied up in my room, Elise?"

"You need a hobby, Ryder." She tilted her head and a lock of lilac hair fell into her eyes. I caught it, pushing it back behind her ear as she grinned at me.

"*You're* my hobby," I growled, running my fingers down to her jaw, her neck. I brushed them over her breasts and down to her stomach, making goosebumps rise everywhere I touched. I didn't think I'd ever been so tender with any woman. And I had to admit that part of it wasn't because of the deal.

I reached the edge of her shorts and gripped onto them, dropping to my knees as I pulled them down. She stepped out of them and I looked up at her with need clawing at my insides. I had plenty of restraint, but this was testing my will to its limits.

How fucked would I be if I claimed her for my own and waited for the stars to rain down hell on me? Not to mention Inferno.

I traced my fingers up the backs of her legs and she bit down on her lip as she watched me.

No, I couldn't take her. But I could give to her.

"Shut your eyes," I ordered and she did as I said.

I dropped my hands, reaching under the bed to the sports bag I kept there. Everything in there was new. Since I'd met Elise, I'd been buying all kinds of fucking shit every time I had a new fantasy about her. I took out a metal vibrator and rose to my feet with a smirk, switching it on and brushing the cold device against her stomach.

She gasped, her eyes flying open as she took in what I had. I didn't give her any time to prepare as I kicked her legs apart and pressed it straight down on her little black panties.

She moaned, tipping her head back and my cock throbbed in response. I might not have been able to hurt her for pleasure, but I could still torture her.

I lowered the vibrator to her inner thigh and she gave me a pleading look.

"Do you really think I'd make it that easy on you?" I taunted.

"Fuck you," she laughed.

I pressed myself against her body, hooking her thigh over my hip and driving the vibrator against her panties once more. She gasped, breathing heavily as I held it there then rolled it slowly up onto her clit through the material.

The most delicious moan left her lips and I had to forcefully stop myself from swallowing it with a filthy kiss. That mouth belonged to me and yet I wasn't allowed to devour it. Frustration burrowed through me and I lowered the vibrator once again, making her groan in annoyance.

"This is how I feel around you every day. I want you so much it drives me insane," I said in a low tone, grinding myself against her so she could see how hard she made me. "Do you want me too?"

"I don't want you," she said breathlessly and a growl escaped me. I drove the vibrator onto her clit hard enough to make her jerk against her binds. "I *need* you."

A grin tugged at my mouth, but I fought it away. I slid my free hand around her slim neck, squeezing gently and angling her chin up to make her look at me. I pushed the vibrator beneath her panties, careful not to touch her with my hand as I pressed it down on the centre of her.

Her eyes almost closed and I squeezed her throat to keep her attention. "Look at me."

She fought to keep her gaze locked on mine and I watched her lips part and her body begin to tremble. I could sense how close she was. Her skin was burning and her back arching.

I pulled the vibrator free from her panties and she yanked against the vines in rage.

The urge to spank her for it rose in me and a hiss slid through my teeth. "I'll find a way to punish you if you don't keep still."

Her eyes lit with the challenge and she struggled harder. She used her Vampire strength to snap the vines and I barked a laugh as I caught her around the waist and threw her onto my bed face first. I fell onto her before she could get up, pinning her down with my weight and grinding my aching hard-on against her ass. I captured her wrists in one hand, pushing her thighs apart with my knees.

"Ryder," she begged, sounding desperate. "Fuck this fucking deal, why did you have to make it?"

I released a heavy breath, dropping my mouth to her ear. "Because I'm never going to let you fuck *him*." I tightened my grip on her wrists then pushed the vibrator between her thighs, keeping her legs wide so I was in total control of her pleasure.

She moaned into the pillow as I held her still, caging her body as I brought her to the edge of climax, then drawing her back from the brink again. Over and over until she was shaking beneath me.

"This is nothing in comparison to the way you make me feel, Elise." I brushed my tongue piercing over the shell of her ear and she shivered all the way down to her toes. "But I'll endure it because I'd rather this than know Inferno had you."

"You can have me too," she moaned as I brought her close again. "Isn't that better than this torture?"

I grunted, holding the toy down on her clit as anger rolled through me. She tried to lean into it, but I controlled her body, making her take this as uncomfortably as possible. I pulled it away at the last second and she wriggled beneath me in frustration.

"Ryder!" she demanded.

I held her down, not giving her anything, clenching my teeth as I thought of Inferno and her together. I couldn't get it out of my fucking head.

"I need you," she said breathlessly and I frowned.

Suddenly I felt like a complete idiot. I had my fucking girl beneath me and I was ruining it because of that Oscura scum.

I flipped her over, dropping onto her and resting the vibrator between us. I released her hands, clutching her hips instead and grinding into her. The buzz of the toy resounded right through my dick, but I wasn't going to come like this. I needed pain to experience pleasure. But that wasn't what she needed.

She clutched onto my shoulders and I surrounded her, pressing my forehead to hers and rolling my hips. She locked her legs around me and we were so close to fucking it had my head spinning with lust. I fisted one hand in the pillow above her as she raked her nails down my back.

She arched into me, coming apart and it was like watching the best fucking fireworks display of my life. She moaned my name over and over and I pressed my fingers to her lips to feel it.

I tugged the vibrator out from between us, switching it off and tossing it to the floor. I went to move, but she held me tighter, drawing me close again and a lump rose in my throat. I'd never spent a single minute with a girl once we'd finished fucking and this felt terrifyingly intimate and yet really fucking good.

Elise leaned up with a playful smile, pressing her mouth to mine and I swear for a second, I didn't need pain or lust or any-fucking-thing anymore. I just needed her.

I sat on the bleachers, watching Elise as she walked toward Devil's Hill with The Lion King during lunch hour. My right fist flexed and unflexed as I watched them smiling, laughing.

Someone snapped their finger and thumb in front of my face and a hiss passed between my teeth as I turned toward the Fae responsible. Bryce.

He pushed a hand into his unruly dark hair, sitting forward and resting his elbows on his knees. He wore one of his usual tank tops, displaying his biceps which were partially inked.

"What?" I growled, pissed off for being disturbed.

"We got some new Lunar sign ups this morning," he revealed, then pointed to them further down the bleachers.

Two girls in crop tops and tiny skirts glanced our way eagerly and one of them even spread her legs to give me a shot to her panties.

I turned away again, hunting for Elise on the hill, but apparently Bryce wasn't done boring me.

"The one with the come-fuck-me eyes, Bokanie Sakala, says she's up for anything. And the one with the dirty smile, Stephanie Gomez, says she doesn't have a pain threshold," he said quietly, a smirk on his face. "I think these two might really suit your tastes."

"I don't care what they're up for," I muttered, clenching my right hand and eyeing the word *pain*.

"You don't act on lust so much these days," he commented, like I could give a fuck what he thought of that. "There's plenty of girls who-"

"Drop it," I hissed.

"I'm just saying…you're the Lunar King, why not enjoy the girls throwing themselves at you?"

"Because there's only one girl I want," I snarled at him, surprised I'd even bothered to tell him that much. But he needed to back the fuck off. He was my second in command when I was on the academy grounds, not my fucking wingman.

"Elise," he tsked her name like it meant nothing and my Order form rose its head, fury slicing away at my core like a knife through an apple. "That girl's trouble. She won't even align herself with the Lunars. How can you let her make a fool of you, boss? She's obviously spreading her legs for that Lion asshole-"

I rounded on him, snatching the collar of his shirt in my fist and yanking him forward so he was nose to nose with me. "Mention her name again and I'll rip your tongue from your throat and make you watch me swallow it whole. She is not your concern. And who I fuck or don't fuck is none of your business."

I shoved him away from me and he cringed back, bowing his head a little. He said nothing more, but I could almost feel the words burning at the back of his throat. He wasn't done thinking shit about Elise, but he was done saying it. I'd make sure of that, even if I had to hold fights for a new second.

I got up from the bleachers and leapt down to the ground with a thump, stalking away from the Brotherhood and heading toward the Vega Dorms where I could be alone.

My hand moved to my chest and I found myself tracing the tattoo Elise had painted there, the movement soothing my rage as I walked.

It didn't matter what Bryce or anyone else thought. Some part of me owned Elise, and I planned on conquering every inch of her until the rest of her was mine too. No Fae in the world could stop me.

ELISE

CHAPTER FIFTEEN

I sat in the windowsill at the end of the hallway outside my dorm and looked out over the academy grounds as I watched for Nightshade leaving her office, determined to follow her again tonight when she did.

Rain sheeted down over Aurora Academy as Dante let his rage over Felix taint the sky once again. I'd decided to watch for her in the warm and the dry rather than drawing attention to myself by hanging around out in the rain.

My breath fogged the glass and I reached out with a finger to paint a pattern against it. First I drew a little Storm Dragon wheeling through the sky then I added a Harpy soaring along beneath him. Next, I drew a Nemean Lion sitting to the right of the glass and then a Basilisk creeping along the base of it. There was a space left between the four of them and I painted a little stick Vampire girl into that position. After a moment's hesitation, I added a smile to her face with a snort of amusement. *A girl can dream, right?*

Not that it seemed all that likely that that outcome would ever come to pass. Gabriel was so possessive that it could be stifling at times and he clearly thought that whenever the stars called us together to become Elysian Mates, I'd forget all about the other Kings anyway.

I frowned at that thought. Would that really happen? It seemed ridiculous to even consider it. Dante, Ryder and Leon all meant so much to me that the idea of just waking up one day with silver rings around my irises and zero desire to be anywhere near them just didn't make sense. That wasn't who I was. Could answering fate's call seriously change the fundamental things that made me, *me?*

Screw that. I didn't believe in fate anyway and I still wasn't convinced on Gabriel's claims about our future, so I'd just have to forget about it unless it ever came to pass. I had more pressing issues anyway. I needed to find a killer. And when all was said and done, maybe I wouldn't survive long enough to find out what fate had had in mind for me anyway. Or I'd be locked away in Darkmore Penitentiary and it wouldn't matter if the stars did try to call me out to meet my Elysian Mate because I'd be locked in a cage and there would be absolutely no way I could get out to meet them. Although as I thought about that, an uncomfortable pull twisted in my gut and it took me a moment to realise that it was fear. Fear that I really would trade my life or my freedom for this and that I might never get to find out what my future could have held. Fate or not. Guilt followed that thought as I gave it a moment of my time because I had no right to be feeling like that now. I was trying to make right the fact that Gareth's future had been stolen from him, not worrying about my own. I banished my doubts with a growl of frustration and focused my mind on my mission once more. I wasn't a girl with dreams or ambitions, I was a missile primed to unleash hell on the guilty. That was all.

I swiped my hand across the glass, erasing the picture I'd drawn and looking back out over the dim grounds again.

Light was slipping from the sky, but I could still see well enough with the aid of my gifts.

Off in the distance, I was watching Altair Halls for any sign of movement. There were no students over there at this time of evening so anyone coming out would almost certainly be a member of staff.

The door opened and I smirked to myself as I spotted Nightshade's fuzzy brown hair and clipped stride.

She was wearing a red raincoat, but she hadn't raised the hood. I guessed being a Siren meant that you loved all water, even unseasonable storms.

She headed off at a fast pace, but instead of crossing the grounds and making her way around to the parking lot, she was heading towards the Cafaeteria.

I didn't hesitate another second, jumping from my perch and shooting out into the rain.

I sped across campus, throwing up an air shield to protect myself from the storm and racing towards the Cafaeteria to see what she was up to.

I paused as I made it to the doors, reaching out to grasp the handle and listen for any sound of her inside.

The building seemed quiet, but I turned my head as the sound of footsteps reached me from somewhere to my left.

I abandoned the Cafaeteria and turned left instead, slinking along as I moved towards the corner of the huge building. I peeked around the edge of the brickwork just in time to spot Nightshade heading into the restrooms.

A sigh of irritation left my lips. *Did I just follow her out here to take a shit?*

I leaned against the wall and waited for her to emerge so that I could follow her home like planned. She may not have kept anything incriminating or helpful for my investigations on campus, but her home was a different matter.

The minutes slowly ticked by and she didn't reappear. My frustration grew as I waited for her to take the world's longest shit but eventually, I began to grow suspicious. There were facilities for the staff inside Altair Halls. Why would she trudge all the way out to these student restrooms in the rain? Even if she was going to stink out the entire building, it didn't seem all that likely that she'd go to this amount of effort to avoid it.

I gritted my teeth and headed straight to the restrooms. It wouldn't matter if she spotted me anyway. What could she accuse me of? Needing a piss? There were no laws against that.

I made it to the restrooms, half holding my breath in case she really had just been in here taking a massive dump all this time and dropped my air shield as I pushed the door wide. The scent of some kind of pine disinfectant assaulted me as I moved into the peach coloured space.

There were sinks along the left wall and a row of five toilet cubicles along the right with the doors all closed over. Directly in front of me was a floor length mirror which gave me a look at the puzzled expression on my face. Because I was still focused on my enhanced senses and there wasn't a sound in this building aside from the dripping of a leaky tap. No shuffling of underwear or tapping of the keys on an Atlas and not even one lonely heartbeat. There was no one in here.

I moved to the row of toilet cubicles and knocked the doors open one by one just to be sure Nightshade hadn't had a heart attack and died mid-shit on the toilet, but she wasn't there.

"What the fuck?" I breathed, turning in a slow circle.

I'd seen her coming in here, there was no doubt in my mind. And I'd had my gaze firmly pinned on the door the whole time I'd been waiting outside too. The only windows in the room were tiny little things which ran along the wall by the roof and there was no way she'd squeezed through one of those.

She couldn't have left. Which meant I was missing something here. Some other way out of this room. But where?

I paced the walls, reaching out and knocking my fists against the brickwork. I even pushed the sense of my magic out to inspect everything around me, but the only thing I gained from that was a slight chill which ran down my spine as I brushed my power up against the floor length mirror beside the sinks.

I frowned at the reflective glass, moving forward to inspect it. I tried to pry it from the wall but it was bolted down. I pressed more magic against it to see if it held any secrets but it didn't reveal a damn thing to me, it only sent another shiver running down my spine.

I chewed on my bottom lip as I looked at it more carefully. It just seemed like a normal mirror to me. There was only one marking on it which was etched in the bottom right corner like a maker's mark, but I squatted down to inspect it all the same.

A diamond shaped symbol looked back at me with a kind of twisted Y in the centre of it.

I stilled. I'd seen that symbol before.

I shot back out of the toilet block in a blur of motion and sped all the way to my dorm at full speed.

I leapt up onto my bunk and the whole thing bounced as I landed on it.

"Hey, Elise," Laini's voice came from her bunk and I answered with a vague greeting as I grabbed my school bag from the foot of my bed and turned my back on the room so that I could tug Gareth's journal free.

"I've been meaning to ask if you wanna go clubbing in town on Saturday?" Laini asked.

"Errr..." I flicked through the pages, one after another, searching through garbled notes and sketch after sketch after sketch until- "Yes!" I exclaimed as I found the symbol I'd just seen in the restroom.

"Great!" Laini replied enthusiastically. "There's this cool new bar opened up called Enfae and its meant to be totally insane. It's Lunar run but it's fine for unaffiliated to go to too. I was thinking we could get ready together here and maybe grab a bite to eat before we hit the dance floor?"

The sketch sat in the centre of a page which held nothing else aside from the symbol for the water Element in the top corner. I flicked it back and forth, hunting for some other clue, a note, a suggestion, something, *anything*.

"C'mon," I growled in frustration. "I need more than that!"

"Oh, okay, well there's a fairly strict dress code and apparently they mark you with a Lunar fading tattoo which lasts twenty four hours when you go in. I heard they serve these crazy cocktails enhanced with magic that make you feel like you're on cloud nine and-"

"What?" I turned to Laini with a frown as she barrelled on.

"Yeah, I know. Sounds good right? So shall we meet here to get ready about seven on Saturday?"

"Saturday?"

"Yeah…" Laini frowned like she'd just realised I had no idea what she was talking about and I quickly flashed her a smile.

"Sounds good to me," I agreed brightly. "I've just gotta run, but we can figure out the final details nearer the time, yeah?" I offered.

"Great." Laini grinned and I jumped off of my bed, saluting her and heading back out the door with Gareth's notebook still in my hand. I may not have been any closer to an answer about that damn symbol, but I'd done what Professor Titan had asked and made progress with a friendship. Albeit unintentional, random luck driven progress, but I'd work harder to make good on that when I went out with Laini on Saturday…wherever the hell we were going.

I bit my lip and made a mental note to put in proper effort for Saturday as I jogged back down the stairs with no real destination in mind.

My brain was a mess of half formed ideas and general irritation with my brother. Which made me feel like a piece of shit, but there it was. Why hadn't he just confided in me? Why hadn't he been as honest with me as I'd always been with him? If he'd just told me what was going on here at the academy, let me visit, spoken to me about Old Sal, Mom… Hell, the only reason I hadn't applied to come to Aurora Academy myself was because I'd been worried about what Mom would do if we both left her to come here. If I'd known she'd been willing to sell me then I could have taken control of my own life. What good had sticking by her done me anyway? She'd abandoned me now that Gareth was gone. She didn't even take my calls. So why had I put my life on hold for her? If I'd just been here with Gareth instead of back home then maybe I could have done something, maybe things would be different…

Tears blurred my eyes as I stepped out into the storm and I didn't bother to cast a new air shield, letting the rain disguise my tears as they fell. I didn't try to fight them. Ryder had been right to tell me to embrace this pain, so that was what I tried to do. Hiding from it wouldn't help me or Gareth. This was a part of who I was now just as much as he'd been a part of who I was when he was alive.

I trailed down the path towards campus, unsure where to go or what to do. I still wanted to follow Nightshade but she'd vanished. And there was no way for me to know if she would reappear by the restrooms or if she'd gone somewhere else. Hell, she might have even escaped using stardust, though the stars only knew where she'd get her hands on something so expensive.

Gareth's journal was still gripped in my fist and I looked down at it, cursing as the rain soaked into the pages.

I quickly tossed an air shield up around myself and shook it out, removing some of the water from it in the process. My thumb was still jammed in the page where the symbol from the mirror had been drawn and I flipped it open to see what damage had been done.

My lips parted as I stared at the page which had suddenly been filled with writing which definitely hadn't been there before. I glanced at the symbol for water in the corner of the page again and laughed as I realised it had been a clue. Gareth had locked away some of the contents of his book so that it could only be read with the right key. He'd left clues. And I couldn't help but think that he must have left them for me.

"Sorry I doubted you, Gare bear," I muttered as I read the newly visible note.

The cost of entry is your magic. Only those with none may enter.

I chewed on my lip as I thought about that. Did I really want to go through some secret door without a drop of magic in my veins to protect me? But if I didn't then I wouldn't be able to find out what was down there. I wouldn't know what Nightshade was up to. This was what I'd been waiting for. A solid lead. I couldn't just turn away from it out of fear. Besides, I'd pay any price it cost to get the answers I needed, so putting myself in danger wasn't really a factor. And it wasn't like I had to worry about dying and leaving some poor family member bereft. I didn't have anyone left who cared about me like that now anyway.

My gut twisted uncomfortably as I thought that. It was like an old habit I couldn't snap out of; I told myself it was true so often that I refused to believe anything else. But when I thought about the men in my life, I had to wonder if that was really the case anymore. They certainly made me feel like they cared about me. But I couldn't dwell on that. I hadn't come to this academy to find anyone or anything apart from Gareth's killer. If I managed that and survived it unscathed, I could figure out what to do with my heart afterwards.

I used air magic to dry out Gareth's journal then shot back to the restrooms behind the Cafaeteria.

I hesitated outside them then threw my hands up above my head and aimed a huge blast of air magic up and away from me into the sky.

I turned my gaze to the clouds, watching them swirl beneath the might of my magic as raindrops peppered my cheeks.

Lightning flashed above me and I spotted Dante soaring through the clouds in his Dragon form, illuminated for a moment by the flare of light.

My heart lifted at the sight of him, but the rage and sorrow of this storm made me ache to soothe his worries too.

I didn't stop pouring magic from my body until it stuttered out. A hollow, empty sensation filled my chest as the last of my power slipped from me and my fangs immediately began to ache with the desire for blood to replenish my supplies.

I forced my mind away from that need and headed into the restroom.

I pushed Gareth's journal into the back pocket of my jeans and strode straight up to the mirror.

My breath fogged the glass before me as I hesitated and I reached out to press my palm to it.

For a moment the cool glass pressed firmly against my skin and then suddenly, it was gone.

I sucked in a breath as I found myself at the head of a staircase that led beneath the ground. A warm breeze drifted up to me, drying my cheeks and delivering a strong, chemical scent to my nostrils.

I listened with my gifts and stepped onto the stairs once I was sure no one was lurking nearby.

The glass reappeared behind me as soon as I stepped over the threshold and I glanced back at the darkened view of the bathroom for a moment before plunging on down the stairs.

The stone staircase curved as I walked and I kept my steps soft so as not to disturb the silence.

Beneath me, a bright light grew clearer and clearer until I finally found myself outside a modern, glass door.

It vanished at my touch just like the mirror had and I stepped forward into a huge, white laboratory. I stared around at the long work surfaces laid out with ingredients undergoing various processes. There were fire crystals, umbar toxins, canisters of Faesine and various herbs I couldn't easily name, Gamma Crystals and even pixie bones. At the furthest end of the room was a huge refrigerator with glass doors and as I drew close enough to inspect it, I spotted rows of test tubes laid out inside. I pulled a door open and lifted one of the little vials out as my heart pounded.

Bright blue crystals glimmered inside, twinkling innocently as I turned the tube over in my hand. Killblaze. This was where they made the stuff that had killed my brother.

Bile rose in my throat, quickly followed by a scream which ached to be set free of my lungs. Rage rose in me like a flood and it was all I could do not to rip this place apart.

But before I could consider what to do next, the sound of voices jolted me out of my momentarily frozen state.

I shoved the test tube back into the refrigerator and closed the door, shooting across the lab and ducking down beneath one of the long workbenches just before someone entered the room.

"-some really promising candidates for the next full moon, Card Master," Nightshade purred excitedly and my pounding heart damn near leapt out of my body as I spotted her shiny red high heels on the other side of the room. Someone else stood beside her, but I couldn't get a lock on any solid detail about them other than the fact that they were there. My mystery King.

"Good. It won't be much longer now. I can already feel the power in me aching to be used to the fullest extent of it. You'll all soon be rewarded for your devotion." The voice that replied was at once harsh then soft, masculine, feminine and goddamn canine for all the good it did me. They must have gotten here via another entrance because they were definitely using magic. Which put me at even more of a disadvantage if I was discovered.

I held my breath, cursing the fact that I couldn't even cast a silencing bubble to hide myself.

"Have you been having any more trouble with the Vampire?" Nightshade asked, lowering her tone as they crossed the room.

"Not since the incident. I've reinforced the magic though and I don't foresee any way that it could happen again."

What Vampire?

"Have you managed to locate your mystery wallpaper artist?" King demanded and I swallowed thickly against the lump in my throat as I realised they must have been referring to the posters I'd plastered all over her office.

"Not yet," Nightshade replied in a shaky voice. "But if I receive any more threats, you'll be the first to know."

"If you don't plug this leak quickly then I'll cut off the loose end. I'll gut you quicker than you can take a piss and never think of you again."

"Y-yes, Card Master," Nightshade stammered. "I'll find whoever did it. You have my word."

"Good."

Guess I'll be extra careful not to let any suspicions fall back on me then…

The Card Master moved to one of the long work surfaces and took something from it before turning and leaving the lab through a door on the far side of the room. They closed it behind them as they walked away and I remained frozen as I waited for them to leave. Thankfully they kept walking and their voices moved away from me until I couldn't even hear them despite the use of my gifts.

I pushed myself upright and crossed to the door they'd exited through. It was heavy, made of thick wood with strange carvings all over it. The hum of magic brushed against my hand as I touched it and I frowned, unable to use my own power to investigate it further.

I tried the handle and found it securely locked. It didn't budge at all.

I chewed my lip, straining my ears again as I stepped back. Once I felt confident that they were nowhere nearby, I called all of my gifted strength into my muscles and ran at the door.

I slammed into it and a huge rattle rang out, but it didn't budge an inch. I tried twice more before cursing as I gave up. Whatever held that door was strong enough to withstand a Vampire's strength and I had no other way to even attempt to get through it.

I turned my attention back to the lab and took my Atlas from my pocket, setting it to record as I walked up and down the benches, making sure I got a shot of everything. When I finally reached the refrigerators full of little vials of Killblaze, I paused.

That was the poison that had stolen my brother from me. The FIB may have been useless when it came to investigating Gareth's death, but they had been adamant about one thing: they were sure the Killblaze all came from a single source. Which could even mean that this was the only lab creating it in the whole of Solaria. The fridges could hold the only stock currently available. They could also be primed to kill another innocent victim like Gareth.

I shut off the recording and stuffed my Atlas into my pocket as I crossed back over the room to the canisters of Faesine. It was the most flammable substance in the world and there was enough here to burn down a small town.

With a surge of conviction or maybe madness, I twisted the lid from the canister and knocked the whole thing over. The ripe scent of Faesine filled the room, catching in the back of my throat and making me choke.

I sped away from it as it flooded out all over the lab, snatching a couple of fire crystals from the pile at the entrance to the room.

I hesitated in the doorway. With my gifts I was damn fast. But fast enough to escape an explosion with this much propellant involved? I wasn't sure about that.

My heart pounded out of rhythm as I hesitated. But this wasn't about me. It never had been. It was about Gareth and all the other Fae who could fall prey to the same monster as him. And though I couldn't strike directly at King, I sure as hell could cut off this limb. I'd cripple their operation. Without Killblaze making people suicidal, they wouldn't be able to get them to give up their power in that dark ritual. It could stop them in their tracks. Halt the amount of magic they were stealing.

"I love you, Gareth," I breathed, closing my eyes for a moment and remembering how it had felt to sleep nuzzled beneath the blankets in his arms when we were children. If this went to shit then maybe I'd get to feel that again in the afterlife.

My eyes snapped open and I struck the fire crystals together, tossing them away from me before the spark had even fully caught.

I turned and shot out of the room as fast as my gifts could take me. The whoomph of the fire igniting sounded behind me as I flew up the stairs, around and around until I made it to the mirror which flashed out of existence again at my touch but cost me a vital second.

Heat seared across my back as I burst out into the restroom and I shot towards the door as a huge explosion tore through the floor at my feet.

I leapt forward, the force of the explosion propelling me further as I slammed through the door and flew through the air outside where the storm still raged.

Pain raced across my back as the heat of the fire caught up to me, but a moment later I crashed into the cold, hard mud of the Empyrean Fields.

A fireball exploded into the sky as the restrooms were destroyed alongside the lab and a huge chunk of the Cafaeteria. I threw my hands over my head, jumping to my feet and shooting away into the trees as debris rained down from the sky. Lumps of masonry, plumbing and earth falling like missiles all around me.

My back screamed with the agony of my burns, but I didn't slow as I sped towards Lake Tempest.

I didn't even know where I was headed until I spilled into the boathouse, panting, aching, *burning.*

I released a pained cry as I stumbled to my knees and agony tore through me from my burns.

"Che diavolo è successo, amore mio?" Dante's panicked voice came to me in my fog of pain a moment before his hand met with the flesh of my back.

I cried out again as he pushed healing magic beneath my skin, and slowly the agony retreated until all I was left with was the scent of smoke and the aching emptiness within me where my magic should have been.

The back of my T-shirt had been half burned away, but it still held together enough to stay on.

I looked up into Dante's worried eyes as my fangs snapped out and his eyebrows rose half a second before I collided with him.

He fell back onto the wooden floor as I sank my teeth into his neck, moaning with pleasure as his blood slid over my tongue. My hands fisted in his hair and he drew me closer, giving me what I needed without complaint as the electric tang of his magic coursed through my veins.

I forced myself to release him before I really wanted to. And the moment I pulled back, I pressed my bloodstained lips to his mouth instead.

Dante stilled, his grip on me tightening as every muscle in his body seemed to tense up at once and he fought the desire to kiss me back.

I pulled away from him after a long moment lingering in the non-kiss, a sigh spilling from my lips as I looked down at him beneath me.

"I hate that I can't have all of you," I muttered as my gaze slid over his bare chest and my pounding heart slowly began to settle.

Dante laughed darkly. "One more second with your mouth on mine and I'd have forgotten about the damn deal and given you all you could want of me and more, bella."

"And be cursed with bad luck for years?"

"Maybe you're worth it."

"I am," I teased.

"Are you going to tell me why you just came running in here half burned to death?" Dante asked seriously.

"Maybe I was struck by lightning?" I suggested. "There was another unseasonable storm tonight. That makes seven this week."

"My lightning would never harm you, amore mio. Give me the truth."

I paused for a long moment then shrugged. "I found a Killblaze lab beneath the restrooms by the Cafaeteria, so I...blew it up."

Dante's lips parted for a long moment then he suddenly let out a laugh. "Why do I believe that?"

"Because it's true. Do you want to be my alibi?"

"Always. I'll say you were flying with me tonight and we came back here right after."

"We did," I agreed. "But where did we go?"

"I took you home to meet mia famiglia," he replied instantly. "They'll all back up the story if anyone asks."

"That must be nice," I said, painting my fingers in a slow trail across his chest.

"What?"

"Having so many people who love you like that."

Dante's brow creased and for a moment I felt like he could see right through me. I dropped my eyes from his, not wanting him to see the truth I was hiding: it would be nice to have *one* person love me like that. And I had. Once.

"La vita è stata cattiva con te, amore mio," Dante murmured, reaching out to catch my chin and tilt my gaze back to his again.

"What does that mean?" I asked.

"That life has been unkind to you. I wish I could change it."

"I guess the stars must not think much of me to turn their backs on me so often, right?" I tried to joke, but I was pretty sure the pain in my voice wasn't hidden.

"Quindi sono sciocchi… But I have an idea."

"Oh?"

"Come to my birthday party," Dante said with a grin.

I snorted a laugh. "Wow, I'm officially so pathetic that I just got a pity invite to a birthday party."

"You should see what a big, Faetalian party is like. You can meet my mamma, my siblings, my cousins and aunts and uncles and…well you get the picture, there's a lot of us. But at least it means the cake is enormous."

My lips curved into a smile at the thought of seeing him surrounded by his family and I found myself warming to the idea.

"Are you asking me on a date?" I teased.

Dante sighed, resting his hands on my knees. "I think for your safety, I can't do that, amore mio," he said and he looked so disappointed by that fact that I had to believe him. I knew that the amount of time I spent with the Kings of the two rival gangs could cause issues for both of them if it became too public. "But my family and the Nights go back years. I'll invite them too and Leon can bring you as his date - but you'll secretly be mine as well. What do you say?"

A warmth built inside me at the thought of being asked to join in with something so special, so private and I found myself nodding.

"Okay," I agreed and the smile he gave me in return was enough to give me butterflies.

I leaned down and pressed a kiss to his cheek before clambering off of him and offering him a hand up.

Dante let me tug him upright and my gaze slid over the firm muscles of his chest and stomach with a pang of longing.

"So…does this mean you've gotten over the whole me and Gabriel issue?" I asked hopefully, looking up at him from beneath my lashes.

Dante growled at the mention of my dark angel's name and a jolt of electricity flared from his skin.

"Tell me why," he demanded suddenly, catching my gaze and holding it. "If you want me to accept it then make me understand."

My lips parted on the reasons I'd always had for not wanting to tie myself to a single man and I almost gave them to him. I didn't want to make my mother's mistakes, I didn't want one person to be the sole keeper of my heart, because if I only offered up small pieces at a time then it couldn't be shattered by any single person. But that wasn't the truth. I wasn't giving the Kings fractured pieces of my heart and keeping the rest of myself back. I was offering it all to all of them, though I still didn't believe I was able to give them everything they deserved. I was a broken soul housed in a fractured shell.

"The truth," I said slowly. "Is that I always wanted to guard myself from heartbreak by never allowing one person to take sole ownership of my heart. But…"

"But?" Dante's soft tone had me coming undone. He was listening to me, *really* listening and for that I could give him the honesty he needed from me.

"But I'm not the same girl as I was before my brother died," I breathed, a thickness building in the back of my throat at that admission. "And his death did something to me, took something, *broke* something in me so profoundly that I feel like I've been torn into all of these pieces which just don't fit back together properly anymore. But when I'm with you, when I'm with any of you, I don't feel like that…I feel like each of you really sees me. But each in such different ways. And I need all of you. I need the light and the dark and the joy and pain. I can't pick between you any more than I could reach inside myself and choose a piece of my soul to keep and others to destroy."

Dante reached for me, taking my face between his hands as he looked deep into my eyes.

"Posso accettarlo. I don't want to cage you, amore mio. If this is who you are then this is who I want you to be. So long as you're all in with me then I can be all in with you too, on whatever terms you need."

Something fragile shattered inside me at his words as a euphoric kind of relief spilled through me and I pushed up onto my tiptoes to lay a kiss against his lips once more. Dante groaned as he fought the desire to return my kiss and I smiled against his mouth.

"I'm all in," I swore before shifting back again.

"Ci sto," he agreed fiercely.

He took my hand and led me through the huge room to the little rowing boat he kept filled with blankets just for us.

I followed him down into it willingly and he drew me close to him, pulling a blanket over us as I laid my head down on his chest. His fingers slid back and forth where my T-shirt had burned away across my back as we lay together and listened to the rain slowly dwindling outside as it beat down on the wooden roof.

"Do you want to talk about it?" I asked as we listened to the sorrowful tune of the storm which had sprung from his feelings.

Dante let out a long sigh. "I don't know that there's much I can say. Felix has gone into hiding and whenever he pops up it's just to spill blood. Too many of my people have chosen to follow him too, but there's nothing I can do about that."

"I suppose you could look at it as a chance to rid yourself of the members of your clan who weren't loyal enough in the first place," I suggested.

A crackle of electricity ran from Dante's body into mine as his irritation flared at the idea of his people betraying him and I arched my back as it ran riot through my flesh.

"Sorry," he muttered, his fingers stilling against my skin.

"I like it," I reminded him and he smiled, letting static trickle from his fingertips again.

"I suppose I just need to deal with it. This rage won't aid me in anything I have to do. But to know that someone around here broke into my stash too…I can't easily replace what they took from me and it could cause me all manner of issues if anyone realises I no longer possess it. Plus, now I have to worry about someone working against me inside the academy. I can't even find any evidence to say this was Ryder or one of his followers which makes it so much worse. Because if it's not them, then who else is out to get me?"

I stilled, pursing my lips as I realised this was something I really could help him with. The flash drive didn't have anything on it that was of any use to me and I'd already decided to give it back to him anyway.

I twisted around until I was leaning on his chest, looking down into his eyes.

"Don't be mad at me," I said slowly. "But…" I reached into my back pocket and pulled the flash drive from my jeans. Luckily my ass had avoided too much heat from the fire and I had to hope that the flash drive was still okay.

I offered it to him and he reached out slowly, his fingers brushing mine as he took it.

"How…"

"I didn't mean to cause you any problems," I swore. "I just wanted to see something on there for myself."

Dante's brow pinched and it took me a moment to realise he wasn't angry, he was hurt. "If you'd asked me, I would have just shown you."

"I'm sorry," I said honestly, reaching out to cup his jaw in my hand. "I should have trusted you enough to ask, I just... Ever since my brother died and my mom abandoned me, I haven't exactly found it easy to trust anyone. It's a shit excuse, I know, but-"

"Ti amo, Elise," Dante said in a low voice, interrupting me. "You can trust me. I'd sooner die than hurt you."

My lips parted and I could only stare at him. "But...I...did you just say you *love* me?"

He took the flash drive from me with a smile playing around his lips, not admitting to what he'd just said. But I knew what that meant. I might not have been fluent in his language, but that one was pretty clear.

"Stay here with me tonight," Dante asked in a low voice, catching my hand and tugging me back down to lay beside him again.

"That's it?" I asked, raising an eyebrow. "You're not pissed about the flash drive?"

"Did you have a good reason for taking it?"

"Yes."

"Well, you may not trust me, bella. But I trust you. You gave it back. Godiamoci questa pace finché dura," Dante said, his fingers resuming their trail across my skin.

I wasn't sure what that meant, but I wasn't going to argue either. I let my eyes fall shut as I listened to the steady thump of his heartbeat beneath my ear.

Had Dante Oscura seriously just told me he loved me? And why the hell didn't that feel as terrifying as it should have?

LEON

CHAPTER SIXTEEN

Professor Titan was moaning on and on in Potions Class about the gas explosion which had destroyed a toilet block and a lump of the Cafaeteria yesterday. I tried to zone him out and get some sleep, but he kept on nattering away like anyone cared that the ground was unstable, or that Eugene Dipper had already fallen into a hole this morning on his way to class, or that he was thinking of starting a fundraiser to help recoup the money spent on builders so the school didn't go bust. I mean, what did he want us to do? Give him a medal?

Greyshine had already called us to an assembly about it at the asscrack of dawn, did we really need to hear it again? The most annoying thing was that everyone had had to eat their breakfast out on Devil's Hill this morning. Well, everyone except me because a couple of Mindys had brought me poached eggs and avocado on toast in my dorm.

Titan finally shut up and I rested my cheek on my textbook as I had a little snooze. Mindy started making notes about how to make a metal dissolving potion as Titan finally started the class, but I knew exactly how to make one of those. I'd been using them to melt locks since I had a two inch mane. By the time everyone was starting their potions, I'd had a pretty decent power nap.

My head was angled towards Elise and Ryder's desk and I watched them through my lashes, the cogs in my brain whirring. She laughed at something he said and his mouth pulled up into an honest-to-the-stars smile. He covered it as fast as a Vampire with a hot poker up its ass, but I'd caught it. The only smile I'd ever seen on his face previous to that had been when he'd been beating the living daylights out of some poor fucker.

But if Elise needed Ryder to keep her happy, how was I supposed to help with that? Would Ryder be up for watching me with Elise like Dante had?

He threw a glance my way while Elise was writing something on her notepad and that infinitesimal look was full of pure envy. So no, watching me with her was probably not up there on his to do list. Murdering me in my bed was more likely topping it right now.

"Ah!" Eugene wailed and my eyes whipped to him, his cauldron overturned and spilling everywhere. Bryce Corvus shot past him back to his desk with his Vampire speed, his ass hitting his seat a second before Titan whirled around in front of the board.

"For the love of the moon!" he gasped, rushing forward to help as Eugene continued to shriek, hugging his hand to his chest. "What happened?" He reached for Dipper's arm and Eugene squeaked like a mouse, curling tighter in on himself.

"Hey now, let me help," Titan said softly. "If you're injured, I can heal it."

Eugene lifted his hand and my stomach churned as I spotted the silver ring there which had melted into his flesh. There wasn't a star's chance of Titan healing that shit. It was messed up. With a capital M.

Bryce was falling apart in silent laughter, his little pal beside him grunting away like a pig. Dipper might have been a weakling with a stalker tendency who I'd been more than happy to beat into a pulp not so long ago, but that shit was cold blooded.

"Alright, Mr Dipper," Titan sighed. "You'd best head off to see the nurse. There'll be some rather painful um…removal she'll need to do."

Eugene squeaked again, rising to his feet and hurrying toward the door. "I hate this place," I heard him choke out before he made it out the door.

Sad, that was what it was. But hey-ho, life goes on. I flicked my fingers at Bryce and his wayward black hair – which I'd always hated- went up in a flash fire. He screamed like a girl, diving out of his seat and smacking his head with his textbook, completely forgetting to use magic.

"Don't panic!" his Lunar friend cried beside him, twisting toward him and raising his hands. Water cascaded over Bryce, and the idiot fell still, his arms falling to his sides as he was left absolutely soaked and completely bald at the back so only his curtains at the front remained.

The whole class roared with laughter and I joined the hell in, clutching my side as I nearly sobbed with how fucking stupid he looked. Even Ryder looked tempted to laugh.

I lifted my Atlas, snapping a picture as Bryce rounded on me with a snarl, resembling an angry old man in a rainstorm.

"You did this!" he accused and I held a hand to my heart with an overly innocent expression.

"*Me?*" I elbowed Mindy beside me. "Would I do such a thing?"

"Of course not," she said, instantly coming to my aid.

"Sir!" Bryce rounded on Professor Titan in fury. "You're not going to let him get away with this, are you?"

"I er- I-," Titan stammered, looking between us nervously.

"Sit down, Bryce," Ryder's commanding voice filled the room. "We all saw what you did to Dipper. You can dish it out, but you can't take it."

Bryce glowered, staring at his boss in disbelief and a snort of laughter escaped me as he dropped back down into his seat, rubbing the back of his head as he healed the blisters away.

The class settled back into excited chatter, continuing their work and replaying what had happened. I promptly uploaded the photo to FaeBook with the caption: *a bald eagle swooped into class today #notsoregalinreallife #bowlingballshinerwanted.*

When it was posted, I swivelled around in my seat to face Dante behind me, giving him a mischievous smile.

"Hey," I said in a low voice, watching as he scraped some pickled water sprouts into his and Cindy Lou's cauldron. "Psst."

He glanced up at me with a smirk and Cindy rolled her eyes.

"We're busy," she said, moving closer to Dante as if I was a vulture circling her prized carcass. He growled furiously at her and she immediately leaned away again.

"I'm booored," I said to my friend, ignoring her. "Wanna have some fun with Elise?"

Dante chuckled. "What do you have in mind?"

Cindy tsked under her breath and I turned my attention to her with pursed lips.

"Did you have something to say?" I asked lightly.

"I just don't know why you're so obsessed with that purple haired bloodsucker," she said, flipping a dark lock of hair over her shoulder.

"Well you just named two of the reasons I'm hot for her so…" I shrugged, turning my attention back to Dante and he grinned.

I pulled my chair toward their desk, scooting myself along without getting up and sitting opposite Dante. Cindy Lou's lips became as thin as a paperclip, but she said nothing more.

I grabbed Dante's notepad, tearing a page from it and snatching up a pen. I couldn't draw that well, but what I had in mind didn't need much artistic skill. The dirty picture I sketched featured a Dragon, a Lion and one very naked Elise with a speech bubble saying *Oh my stars! Twelve orgasms?? You guys are the best I've ever had!*

Dante grabbed the page from me, stifling his laughter as he read the words. Then he took the pen from my hand and added to the end of the speech with, *and your dicks are HUGE!*

"Nice touch," I commented with a satisfied nod.

Cindy Lou glanced at it and her upper lip peeled back. "That's disgusting."

"Psh, says the girl who had a dirty Dragon shrine hidden in her wall," Dante said in a low growl.

"Not anymore she doesn't," I added in amusement and Cindy Lou shot me daggers, but I didn't miss the tears that watered in her eyes too. I couldn't find it in me to feel bad though. That girl was a sour grape right down to her core and that Dragon shit was creepy as fuck.

Cindy's hate-filled gaze moved to Elise across the room and my hackles rose. "That girl's got it coming," she muttered under her breath.

"What's that?" I snarled and she cowered under my punishing gaze.

"Nothing," she breathed, shaking her head.

"Better not be," Dante said in a deadly tone.

I glared at her until she returned to making the potion then forgot all about her and folded my picture into a paper airplane.

I aimed it at Elise, reaching my arm back and throwing it. Elise dropped her head at the last second to read something in her textbook and the plane collided with the side of Ryder's face and landed on his shoulder. *Whoops.*

He slowly lifted a hand, grabbing the plane with a snarl. He unfolded the page and a furious noise left him as he scrunched it up in his fist. I whipped up Dante's textbook, opening it and standing it on its side before Ryder looked this way. I ducked my head behind the book as I fell apart with laughter and Dante joined me behind it, laughing loudly.

"Did you see his face?" I snorted.

"Stupido serpente," he laughed.

My gaze snagged on Gabriel as he walked past us up to the store cupboard, not sparing us a glance. I slipped out of my seat and headed after him, pretending I needed some stuff too as I moved up next to him and started humming.

He growled under his breath as he began counting leven pods from a jar.

"Hey dude," I said lightly, but he didn't acknowledge me. "So look… no hard feelings about Elise, right? I mean it's better now that it's all out in the open. You know what she wants."

His jaw started to tick and he still didn't respond.

"Anyway…" I painted on one of my winning smiles, leaning forward to try and catch his gaze. He finished counting the pods and turned around, stalking back toward his desk.

Dammit.

I hounded after him and Elise gave me a confused frown as I passed her. I blew her a kiss and kept walking, following the happy Harpy all the way back to his seat. The moment he sat down, I rested my hands on his desk, standing in front of him so he couldn't ignore me.

"So how about me, you and Elise hang out later? We could come to you up in your little roof nest – I know how you like being all up high and shit. We could crack open some beers, talk it out, maybe see if Elise is in the mood for a little fun…"

Gabriel moved out of his seat in a flash, grabbing my hair in his fist and cracking my head down on the table.

"Argh!" I yelled, throwing him off as flames roared to life in my hands.

"Don't ever suggest sharing her with me again," he snarled and I glared at him, tempted to retaliate. But I could see that that wasn't the answer here.

I extinguished the flames then rubbed my head, releasing a shot of healing magic into my aching skull. I could take a hit or two if that was what was necessary. I knew Elise needed him, so hell if I was giving up yet.

I pointed at Gabriel as he lowered into his seat and resumed ignoring me. "You need to get your head outta your ass and realise what she needs or you're gonna lose her entirely."

His lips twitched, but he still said nothing. Stubborn much?

"Back to your seat, Mr Night," Titan called and I sighed dramatically before turning and heading back to my desk.

I nearly fell asleep again as I settled into watching Mindy brew the most dull potion in the world. *Why can't we make something that blows up for once? Just* one *time I wanna watch something explode, is that really so much to ask?*

"Bing bong," Greyshine's voice sounded over the tannoy and I lifted my head, yawning broadly. "First things first, I'm delighted to inform you that work has already started on rebuilding the damaged parts of the Cafaeteria. We have the finest earth builders in Alestria making sure everything is tickety boo and up to scratch, and no doubt you'll be able to eat your meals in there again within the day! On a sunnier note, I have some splendiferous news! Zodiac Academy has requested we send our top five ranking students to exchange with five of their students in just two weeks' time. So drumroll... those who currently hold the top five positions are..." The sound of plastic cutlery tapping together made it over the line and I would have found it funny if I wasn't crushing my pen in my hand so hard it snapped. I wasn't in the top fucking five. The last time I'd checked, I'd been sitting at number thirteen. Even if I worked my ass off in class until the trip, I'd have to perform a miracle to get the rank points I needed to take fifth place. I wanted to go to Zodiac more than any asshole in this academy. It wasn't fair. "As our top performer, Gabriel Nox will likely be shipping off to Zodiac to represent our school."

Gabriel groaned like he was having heart failure and I clenched my jaw. *I'd take your place in a second, assbird.*

"Then Ryder Draconis and Dante Oscura hold second and third places currently," Greyshine's voice quavered as he said the two clan leaders' names. They constantly switched between second and third position on the board, the two of them evenly matched. That trip was going to be about as happy as a trip to a graveyard on a rainy Monday morning. And I knew if it had been up to Greyshine, he wouldn't have sent the two of them together. But as Zodiac was the biggest baddest school in Solaria, what choice did he have? Neither Dante or Ryder would let their rank drop for the sake of not going. They were too damn stubborn. And I doubted they'd be allowed to refuse. The Celestial Councillors who ran the whole of Solaria pissed money into that academy and they'd come down on Aurora like a ton of bricks if we didn't do what they said. But why couldn't it have been the top thirteen dammit?

Ryder and Dante shared a glare across the room, their eyes narrowed. But if they even tried to refuse something like this, it would no doubt be worse than docked rank points, they'd be answering to the school board. And neither of them would want the board nosing in at Aurora, because they might figure out that the two gangs ran this school instead of the faculty.

"Bryana Jack and Lisa Webb are currently holding fourth and fifth place," Greyshine finished brightly. "So if you all hang onto your ranks for the next two weeks, you'll be readying your fanny packs and whizzing off to Zodiac Academy via stardust and spending a full week there. Have a groovy day!"

"Stardust?" Mindy breathed beside me.

I blew out a low whistle. No doubt Zodiac had sent that here just for this occasion. Aurora Academy didn't get stardust stipends. It wasn't in the budget. If we had a few relations to the Celestial Councillors preparing to attend our school, maybe we would have gotten more funding. But nope. They didn't want to send their fancy little Heirs to Alestria for their education. Go figure.

"For fuck's sake," I said overly loudly and Titan shot me a look.

"Language, Mr Night," he said sternly, then motioned for the class to continue working.

But I wasn't done. I was pissed as all hell. Because at the very least I knew Gabriel and Ryder wouldn't give a shit about going to Zodiac Academy.

And it had been a dream of mine for years. I'd worked my ass off in Pitball for this and we'd clawed our way into the final, damn well earning our place there. Now we were due to play their asses the week of the exchange and I wanted more than just a day visiting their beautiful dreamboat of a Pitball pitch. I wanted time to caress their field, brush my fingers over their lockers, run my tongue over their waterhole. A whole week on an exchange would have given me time to meet all of their team, get inside tactics, improve my fucking game. I could have grilled their star player, Lance Orion, over brunch. *Brunch* dammit! We didn't do brunch in Alestria, unless you counted a hobo licking an old breakfast burrito wrapper at eleven thirty in the morning on the corner of Altair Street. And let's be honest, no one fucking did count that.

"Fuck the system." I slammed my palm down on the table and everyone turned to look at me.

"Mr Night-" Titan warned, but I cut over him, rising to my feet so my seat crashed to the floor.

"I could beat Bryana Whatsherface and Lisa Whofuckingcares in a Fae on Fae fight any day. This is bullshit." I swept all of my things onto the floor with a roar and Mindy jumped to her feet, immediately gathering them up. I tossed her shit onto the floor too for good measure, upending her pencil case so her pens scattered everywhere.

"Leon!" Elise scolded me across the room.

"It's my fucking *dream*!" I snapped, a snarl ripping from my throat.

"Chill dude." Dante said from behind me.

"I'd happily give you my place," Gabriel said and I twisted around to glare at him at the back of the room.

"That's the problem, isn't it? None of you even want to fucking go!"

"Mr Night!" Titan tried harder.

I grabbed Cindy Lou's notes from beside Dante and tossed them at the wall, sending them flying everywhere. Cindy shrieked in annoyance and the class started laughing.

Dante rose an eyebrow at me, cocking his head. "I can fix it, fratello," he said in a low tone with a meaningful look.

I knew he had sway on Greyshine, but this decision wasn't coming from big old shiner. It was coming from Zodiac. And how was I supposed to fight that?

"Calm down, Mufasa, you can have my fucking place," Ryder said and I glanced over at him, finding Elise had slipped out of her seat, looking at me intently.

"I can't just take your place, asshole. Didn't you hear what he said? Zodiac Academy have decided-"

"No one decides shit for me," Ryder hissed and I rolled my eyes.

"Yeah yeah, you're the Lunar King and blah blah blah. Well guess what, Ryder? There's no Lunar Brotherhood at Zodiac Academy. And it's run by the most powerful assholes in the kingdom. So if you think you're not going, think a-fucking-gain." I punctuated my sentence by knocking everything out of Mindy's hands and storming out of the room.

I was too hot as I marched down the corridor, my fire Element raging inside me and my Order form begging to be released.

Stupid snake-faced bitch. He didn't know what he was saying. He might have been a King in this school, this city even, but that was where it ended. We all lived our lives inside a tiny fucking box that everyone else in the kingdom ignored. But there was a whole world out there and rules we had to fucking abide to when they *did* pay us attention. And if they started shining a light this way, they were going to start noticing Fae who were getting too big for their grubby little boots. Because the Councillors weren't going to let a threat crawl in their back door.

The fact that a double Elemental like Gabriel, a rare-ass Basilisk and an even rarer-ass Storm Dragon were sitting comfortably in this city without anyone trying to assassinate them or turn them into a candidate for the Council's scheming was nothing short of a miracle. Except, the fun truth was, no matter how powerful anyone was in this part of the kingdom, they weren't going to get backing. The kingdom could be taken by force by a strong enough Fae, but it sure helped if you were a popular posh pure blood with money coming out of your asshole.

Besides, the four Councillors equally ran the country, that was what made their alliance so iron clad. One Fae couldn't easily take them all on individually. It was also why they were grooming their most powerful offspring to take their places when they were gone. They had literally controlled every aspect of their kids' conception to plan their star signs, Orders and power levels. They had created four little replicas of themselves, each as powerful as each other so they'd never turn against one another. It was messed up if you asked me. And my guess was those kids were fucked in the head.

But I still wanted to go taste the life they were going to live. Breathe in their beautiful academy, roll across their Pitball pitch naked, eat their food and drink their filtered-through-a-Pegasus's butthole water, to just experience what that might have been like.

I ground my jaw, storming out of the building and tugging off my clothes as I went. I needed to run free in my Order form. I wanted the wind in my mane and my heart pounding with heated blood.

"Leon!" Elise shot in front of me, planting a hand to my bare chest.

I couldn't find it in me to smile, even though the sight of her always made me smile. But not right then.

"I can't believe you just threw a temper tantrum," she said, snorting a laugh, her eyes all light and happiness. She didn't always look like that. Sometimes she looked so sad it made me want to carve out my heart and swap it with hers so I could bear her pain for her. But never around me.

"It wasn't a tantrum," I said moodily, unbuckling my jeans. I noticed a Mindy had appeared, gathering up my shirt, tie and blazer and carefully folding them for me. No doubt they'd be washed and ironed and hanging in my closet perfectly by the end of the day. "I care about this, Elise. And it's bullshit."

"I know you do." She stopped smiling, reaching out to cup my cheek, but I jerked away and headed past her. "Leon, maybe we can talk to Greyshine. Maybe he'll be able to fix this."

I dropped my pants and glanced back over my shoulder. "Maybe. Maybe not. Right now, I wanna go for a run. So are you coming?"

Her eyes brightened and I leapt forward, shifting into my huge Nemean Lion form. I shook my head as my golden mane tumbled around me and the wind sent a ripple all the way through my fur.

Elise shot to my side again, threading her fingers into my mane and it felt so damn good, I leaned into it to nuzzle her.

I bowed my head, offering her my back if she wanted it and her lips parted in surprise. If she was going to skip class with me, she might as well do it in style.

Before she got on, she pressed a hand to my nose, running it up to the spot between my eyes. "You're a King, Leo. You can have anything you want."

A low purr rumbled through me and she leapt up onto my back, settling herself between my shoulder blades.

I tipped my head back, releasing an almighty roar then took off across the grounds, racing towards the Empyrean Fields. I'd run as hard and as fast as I could, letting my rage loose in the form of pure energy powering through my muscles. And when I was calm, I'd find a way to go to Zodiac Academy, because Elise was right. I *was* a King. But even if I had to go as the fucking porter carrying everyone else's bags, then I'd be the best damn porter Zodiac had ever seen.

I lay on my bunk while Mindy massaged my back, the lights low and the scent of burning oils filling the air. Whale music rolled into my ears and helped loosen every knot in my body.

"Mmm," I sighed, finally feeling relaxed after the bad news I'd received that morning. I'd skipped the rest of classes and the last bell had rung not long ago. I'd put out an SOS on FaeBook and fifty Mindys had responded. But this one gave the best massages. She was a Siren and she fed on my dark emotions as she massaged me with her silky soft hands, taking away all of my pain.

A knock came at the door. "Come in!" I called, not lifting my head from the pillow.

"This is getting ridiculous now," Elise's voice sounded and my heart sang. "Can you give us a minute, Amy?" she spoke to Mindy.

"Go on," I encouraged and Mindy slipped off of me, her footsteps sounding out of the room.

"I brought Dante," Elise announced and I lifted my head, finding him leaning against the doorframe with a smirk.

"Dalle stelle." He shook his head at me. "Get up, you're coming with me."

"Can't," I grunted.

Elise shot forward, snatching my hand and pulling. She gasped as her hands slipped off of my oiled up skin and she slammed down onto her ass. I broke a grin as I got a view up her skirt.

"Maybe you should both stay and make me happy," I suggested with a hungry growl.

Elise rose to her knees with a firm look. "Go with Dante or you can keep your oily paws to yourself."

I reached for her and she swatted my hand away. Then she darted back to Dante's side and pressed herself against him, locking her fingers behind his neck. "Actually, maybe me and Dante will just go hang out in our room together…" She bit down on her lower lip and even though I knew she couldn't actually do shit with him, I still pouted at being left out.

Dante started grinning like a school kid, winding his hands around her and steering her through the door. "Yeah…let's go, carina."

"Wait!" I got up. "I'll come."

I grabbed a towel, rubbing off the worst of the oil before dragging on some sweatpants and a shirt. I pushed my feet into my sneakers and headed after them.

"I'll catch you later then," Elise said, slipping out of Dante's arms. I caught her hand before she could escape, throwing her back against Dante's chest and pressing my lips to hers.

She gasped into my mouth as I forced her harder back against him, wedging her between us. Dante groaned, pushing his fingers into her hair as I devoured her mouth with a torturously slow kiss. I rested my hands on her hips and Dante's hand skimmed mine as he held her in place.

"Catch you later," I said, releasing her with a smirk at the same time as Dante did. She eyed us greedily as we headed away down the corridor and the taste of cherries lingered in my mouth.

Dante moved to my side as we walked downstairs and we shared a grin.

"So what's the plan?" I asked him.

"I'm gonna tell Greyshine to let you come with us." He shrugged.

"But Zodiac made the rules, not him."

"Just trust me, fratello." He clapped a hand to my shoulder and I let it drop, following him all the way to Greyshine's office in Altair Halls.

Dante knocked on the door loudly and threw me a wink.

"Who is it? I'm quite busy!" Greyshine called. The guy was as present as a ghost in this school. In fact, the ghost of The Weeping Well made more appearances around campus than he did.

"It's me," Dante said in a growl.

"Oh my," Greyshine replied then a bunch of locks sounded a moment later before the door swung open. "Forgive me, Mr Oscura…Mr Night." He ran a hand over his sweaty bald patch on top of his head then ushered us inside.

"Sit down," Dante directed and I fought a laugh as Greyshine weaved through stacks of books and practically fell into his chair. "We have a problem." Dante moved forward and splayed his hands flat on Greyshine's desk.

"P-problem?" Greyshine squeaked. "Is this is about the p-poptarts?"

"No," Dante growled while I covered my laughter with a cough. "This is about my friend here being left out of the Zodiac trip even though he's in the top five rank of the class."

I frowned as Greyshine's eyes whipped to me. "But M-Mr Night is not in the top five."

"Are you calling me a liar?" Dante demanded and static rolled off of him, making my skin prickle.

"N-no, Mr Oscura," Greyshine stammered, his eyes wide with desperation.

"Then I must have misheard you," Dante said as lightning flashed beyond the window and thunder grumbled in the clouds.

Fuck me, this is awesome.

"Mr Night would need one hundred and twenty eight rank points to take fifth place," Greyshine said in as steady of a voice as he could manage. "He would have to do something quite wonderific to shoot up the leaderboard so fast."

"Like saving the principal from a rogue lightning strike?"

I flinched as the window exploded and Dante twisted his hand, snatching Greyshine full bodily over the desk with a whip of air just before his chair burst alight. He slumped to the floor with a whimper of fear, catching my arm to pull himself upright.

"Oh my stars!" Greyshine cried.

I took hold of the flames roaring in the room, putting them out with a wave of my hand.

"Aren't you going to thank Leon for saving you?" Dante asked, his storm dissipating as quickly as it had appeared.

"Oh y-yes. Thank you, Mr Night." He turned to me, still clutching my arm and I kinda pitied the guy for a second. But only one second, then it was gone because holy shit, I loved being friends with a Storm Dragon.

"You'd better make an announcement," Dante said casually, moving toward the door. "And make sure you thank Elise Callisto too. You really would have been fucked if she hadn't used her Vampire speed to get you out of that seat so fast."

I raised a brow at Dante with a shit-eating grin biting into my cheeks.

"C-Callisto?" Greyshine frowned.

"Yeah, she'll be sitting in fourth place now I suppose." Dante shrugged then flipped the door open, exiting into the hall.

I gave Greyshine a thumbs up and followed him out of the room, the two of us bursting into laughter the second the door closed behind us.

"Elise?" I questioned, throwing my shoulder into his.

"Yeah, you, me, her and a hotel room. *Perfetto.*" He gave me a mischievous look and my excitement grew. I slung my arm around him as we headed back to the Vega Dorms to tell her.

"Ryder and Gabriel will be there too," I said with a frown.

By the stars, was she going to be room hopping between us all week? Or maybe I could convince everyone to hug it out and share a bed. I grinned at the thought, even though I knew it was hopeless. The chances of getting Ryder and Dante to share a lasagne would be impossible, let alone a girl.

"Pfft, we can keep her away from them if we work together. She'll be too damn satisfied by us to even think about anyone else," Dante said cockily and I shrugged vaguely in agreement, not really caring either way. But I knew he wouldn't be able to handle seeing her with the other guys. I just might have had another hot date to stick it to while I was there anyway. She had five holes and kept her grass nice and trimmed. That Pitball pitch was gonna get it.

We arrived back at Dante's dorm and I bobbed on my heels as I waited for him to open the door.

Elise was wrapped in a towel, her hair damp from a recent shower as we entered. There was no one else in the room and I grinned as my eyes slid down to her bare legs.

"We have some news," I said.

"Did you get a spot on the Zodiac trip?" she asked hopefully.

"Yep," I said, sharing a look with Dante. "And so did you."

Her lips popped open as she looked between us, hunting for the joke. "You got *me* a spot?"

"Yeah, we couldn't go without you, carina." Dante moved toward her, energy crackling around him as he closed the distance between them.

"I have stuff to do here," she said anxiously and I frowned, hoping she wasn't going to try and refuse coming. Besides, what stuff was more important than a trip of a lifetime?

"It's only a week, little monster," I said. "The academy is amazing and you being there would make it a thousand times better than my wettest wet dream."

"Plus it's right near the town of Tucana and apparently there's a restaurant called the Dragon Bowl and the whole place is made of solid gold," Dante said excitedly. "They serve everything on gold plates and there's even gold napkin rings and-"

"Why would Elise care about that?" I cut over him and Elise giggled.

"Well...there's also a Vampire blood club where you can try every Order of blood! You can buy anything from Siren to Manticore, bella."

"Bleh, I'll pass on the Siren. But Manticore sounds interesting...and I did kinda wanna visit Tucana anyway." She slowly unfolded her towel, dropping it to the floor to pool at her feet. I took in every naked inch of her with a groan of desire. "So maybe you can find some way to convince me," she said with a grin as she glanced between us. And I was more than fucking up for the challenge.

GARETH

CHAPTER SEVENTEEN

ELEVEN MONTHS BEFORE THE SOLARID METEOR SHOWER…

*T*he Iron Wood was loud. Well the music was loud. And I was in the wood. So…

"Dude!" *Leon slapped an arm over my shoulders and I swear I sank an inch into the mud.* "Are you gonna do a hanging fiery whiplash?"

"No fucking way." *I drank from my beer bottle but it was empty. The Oscuras seriously knew how to throw a party and Leon had directed his Mindys to keep alcohol in my hand at all times.* Current status: waaaasted.

"Cindy's watching," *Leon said, turning me around to where students were being dangled over the fire by air Elementals and fed beer through a bubble over their mouth and nose by water Elementals. The guy who was currently doing it looked like he was about to catch fire.*

"Still no." *My gaze dropped onto Cindy Lou who was looking up at the guy dangling over the flames with moon eyes. He was lowered to his feet and Dante strode forward, pulling his shirt off and puffing his chest out.*

"Hang me," he commanded and Cindy Lou practically swooned.

"Oh hell no." I stumbled out of Leon's hold, marching around the fire and planting my hand on Dante's bare chest. "Me first, bella," I mocked him and his brows lifted in surprise. Oh shit on it, did I just call the leader of the Oscura Clan pretty??

"You sure, cavallo?" he asked with a smirk. "You look a little unsteady on your hooves."

"Psh." I waved him off, turning to the fire and throwing a cocky look at Cindy Lou.

She clapped her hands excitedly and I lifted my chin with pride. A whip of air snared my legs and I whinnied as I was flipped upside down and suspended above the fire.

Holy crap it was hot. I almost cried out again, but a bubble of beer was slapped over my face and I spluttered. All I could do was drink it, the beer sliding down my nose and throat, burning, choking me. I started jerking against the air holding my legs, my arms flapping wildly around me. I'm gonna drown. I'm gonna fucking drown.

Somehow, I swallowed the last of the beer away and a cheer reached me.

"Cavallo, cavallo, cavallo!"

I beamed from ear to ear as I was lowered to the ground, stumbling so my ass hit the floor. Cindy Lou launched herself on top of me – gah she was heavy. I was weighed down as I fisted my hand in her long hair and pressed my mouth to hers. Mmm it was so warm and stubbly. Wait.

"Sorry, dude. You're not my type." Leon started laughing, jumping to his feet and yanking me after him.

My gaze fell on the actual Cindy Lou as I wiped my mouth, wondering how I could have mistaken a six foot Lion for my petite little pony. She was watching Dante as he was hung above the fire, not even flinching as he crossed his arms over his broad chest.

Cindy Lou and her friends were awestruck as he started spinning himself in circles with his own air magic and I scowled.

I slapped a hand onto Leon's arm. "I wanna do something big tonight. Something seriously big. Something no one's ever done."

"Well you could take my whole cock in your mouth?" Leon offered. "That's big and something no one's ever managed to do before. But like I said, you're not really my type." He snorted and I scowled.

"I mean it, man. I wanna do *something."*

Leon swigged his beer thoughtfully then grinned at me. "I have an idea!" He took off into the trees and I jogged after him, stumbling over roots as I headed into the dark.

I cast a light orb above me, spotting Leon moving ahead through the shadows. I caught him up just as he headed out of the wood onto the Empyrean Fields.

"Where are we going?" I asked.

"You'll see," he chuckled, picking up his pace.

We soon reached the Rigel Library, heading around it to where The Weeping Well stood under the light of the full moon. I slowed my pace as Leon strode up to it, my gut knotting at the rumours that surrounded that well. Years ago, bullies had supposedly pushed a boy in there covered in Faesine, then he'd ended up killing himself when he lit a flame with his Element so he could see.

Leon took out his Atlas with a smirk. "Climb down there, right to the bottom and take a photo of the dead kid's remains."

I paused, frowning at him. I might have been drunk, but was I that *drunk? "Er…"*

"Are you scared, wittle horse?" He leaned over the well, sticking his head down it and yelling, "Hello creepy dead kid? Can you heeeear me?"

I moved to the edge, resting my hands on the stone and glancing down into the pitch black depths. I urged my light orb forward, letting it sail down into the darkness, lower and lower until it was just a distant orange glow in the thick black.

Leon jerked upright and I lurched backwards in alarm. "Boo," he laughed then threw his arm over my shoulders. "Come on then, forget it."

He tried to steer me away and I shrugged him off, setting my jaw. If this went around the school, I'd be a fucking king. Cindy Lou would be all over me. And she wouldn't look at Dante like that ever again. Like he was the best damn thing. A whinny escaped me in annoyance and glitter tumbled around my shoulders.

Leon lifted his Atlas hopefully and a ding sounded as he started recording.

"I'm going down there." I faced him, determination pouring through me in waves alongside the alcohol which was definitely dulling my fear. "I'm gonna see if the rumour is true."

Leon bobbed excitedly on his heels as I climbed up onto the edge of the well, swinging my legs over it and sitting on the wall. My throat thickened as I stared down into the abyss.

"Here, take this." Leon planted his Atlas in my hand and my heart ticked a little harder.

It's just a rumour. There's not actually a dead kid down there.

I steeled myself, conjuring air into my palm and guiding it beneath my feet. I lowered myself onto it, glancing back at Leon as I stood with my head poking over the top of the well, fear and excitement tangling inside me.

"Shit, you're really doing it," he said in awe and I couldn't deny how good it felt to have him look at me that way. Like I was cool.

I smirked as if I wasn't bothered about being neck deep in this creepy ass death pit and eased the air beneath me to lower me down further.

I took in a steady breath, keeping the camera angled at my feet as I descended. A shiver raced up my spine as I was engulfed by darkness, the light below seeming impossibly far away.

I gazed up at Leon as he leaned over the edge to watch me, the full moon haloing his golden hair.

Fear rattled my heart as I continued deeper and deeper, a chill driving right into my bones. The air was cold, damp and the smell of something vile rose under my nostrils. I hoped it was stagnant water and not a rotting body, but my mind was conjuring horrible images of decaying flesh and greasy bones.

My Faelight flickered down below and my heart rate ratcheted up as I felt some magical energy sweeping around the base of the well. The light stuttered out and I gasped, forcing my efforts into recasting a new one above me. It did nothing to ease my nerves, the light flickering again like something was affecting it. But what?

Water came into view below and I held myself over the dark pool. It was so still, it looked like ink and I couldn't be sure if it was a mile deep or an inch. I pressed my air magic into it, stirring the water and it churned like mud, a horrid stench rising from it.

Bile rose in my throat and I looked around at the glistening walls under the bluish light of my orb, searching for anything of interest as I made sure the camera recorded the whole thing.

"Gareth?" Leon's voice reached me from far, far above, his voice distorted and making me flinch. "Are you alright?" Anxiety laced his tone.

"All good – there's nothing down here!" I called back and my voice rang off the walls.

A forceful energy blew over me and horror ripped through me as my magic stuttered out. I screamed as I plunged into the mud, sinking into a foot of sludge. My hands slipped and slid and I lost sight of everything as my head dipped under. I kicked and flailed, blinded and gagging on the rotten scent in my nose as I tried to fight my way out.

My fingers brushed something hard and long and cold, so like a bone I immediately released it.

Fuck! I'm going to die!

I fought and clawed my way through the thickness, feeling like it was pressing in on me from all sides. I couldn't breathe, couldn't fight, couldn't cast.

My hands met a ledge and I clawed my way up, heaving myself out, Leon's Atlas lost to the bog.

I found myself in a doorway which definitely hadn't been there before. A long tunnel stretched out before me and the sound of heavy footfalls were pounding this way.

"Leon!" I roared in fear, throwing my hands out as my magic flared back to life.

"What's happening!?" he yelled.

I forced air magic into my hands, but in my panic, I cast it too hard and knocked myself onto my ass. "Fuck fuck fuck."

A horrible grunting, groaning sounded from the darkness as the footsteps pounded ever nearer.

I stumbled upright, clinging to the doorway and throwing out a hand to cast air beneath my feet. I rose upwards just as a snarling beast appeared. Haggard hair and wide, glaring eyes. He was pale and terrifying, his hand outstretched, coated in blood.

I cast air under my feet, rising up as fast as I possibly could.

What the fuck? What the hell was that?!

I soared out of the well, crashing into Leon full force and knocking him to the ground. He threw me off of him with a shout of alarm.

"Die you fucking well monster!" he yelled, throwing a fireball at me and I shielded myself from it at the last second.

"It's me!" I shouted as his fireball ricocheted off of my shield.

"Gareth?" he gasped, reaching down to help me up.

I backed away from the well, pushing him back with me. "There's someone down there. Or some – thing."

"By the moon, what the hell did you see?" Leon held my shoulders then a horrible wailing came from down in the well.

"Run!" I gasped and we raced away as hard and as fast as we could in the direction of the Vega Dorms. I wanted to be behind ten locked doors with Leon Night at my side before I was going to feel remotely safe again. Whatever the hell had been down there needed to stay down there for good.

There was no cool evidence of me going into the well, no nothing, but I didn't care. Because I didn't want anything to do with that place ever again.

ELISE

CHAPTER EIGHTEEN

I lay in my bunk, swinging my legs over the end of it as I stared up at the faded white ceiling and chewed on a piece of gum. It was after dinner and I didn't have anything to do. In moments like this, I could see a valid point to Titan's nagging about the whole friends issue I had. Aside from the Kings, I didn't really have anyone else to hang out with.

I'd had a brilliant night out with Laini when we'd gone clubbing together, but I hadn't made nearly enough time to hang out with her since. Sometimes I just got so caught up in my investigations that I guessed I just forgot to actually live my own life. And sometimes I didn't really feel like I deserved to have one anyway. Not yet. Not while Gareth's murder still went unanswered.

Dante had gone home to deal with more Felix stuff and Gabriel had hardly even spoken to me since the Pitball match while he brooded over our situation. Leon had gone home to visit his family for the evening too and Ryder hadn't answered my text, so I was left hanging.

It was pretty pathetic actually. The more I thought about it, the more I realised that this wasn't some new, strange thing that had happened to me since Gareth's death; I'd never really had friends. There were people I talked to at school, but no one who I ever sought out in particular. I'd thought of myself as having a fairly busy social life, but more often than not that had just involved me hanging out with the strippers at Old Sal's. Sure, I'd turned up to parties whenever they were hosted and I'd had my fair share of flings with guys here and there, but I was more like that additional invite. *You too, Elise.* Just noticeable enough to warrant the invitation, but not quite approachable enough to build anything solid with.

I guessed I just hadn't noticed because I'd had Gareth. He'd been there if I ever needed to talk to someone or confide in them. I had him for in jokes and TV nights watching trashy movies. Or at least I had before he came to Aurora Academy.

Maybe I was broken. Or maybe this was just the way Vampires were. It wasn't like I felt lonely...was it?

I flicked through some of the messages I'd been sending to Old Sal. She wanted me to come back and work for her over the summer and though I'd sworn never to return to that place the last time I'd been there, I had to admit I was a little tempted. She'd only give me an apartment if I danced on the stage though and that definitely wasn't happening. But with the jobs the Kiplings were giving me, I was setting aside a good little stock pile of money which I intended to use to rent somewhere and I could work the bar with my clothes firmly in place.

In Sal's last message she'd asked how my classes were going and I shot one back to her detailing a few of my favourite lessons from the last week with a strange feeling stirring in my chest. It was *nice* to have someone give a shit about what I was getting up to outside of this place. Almost like having a parent... I shook off that crazy idea and shoved my Atlas back into my pocket. Was I really going to sit here and start feeling sorry for myself over the fact that both of my parents had now chosen to walk out on me?

Probably. Especially if you stay here on your own.

I rolled my eyes at myself as I indulged in this pity party and decided to do something about it. Laini had headed off to the library earlier with a stack of books and though it probably wasn't the best idea to try and disturb a Sphinx while they were reading, I could at least offer myself up as a study buddy. Besides, we needed to finalise our plans for another night out. And this time I'd give her my full attention.

I hopped up and stripped out of my uniform. It had been a beautiful day today, the sun blazing down and the true feeling of summer hanging in the air, warming me through to my soul. I took a red sundress from my closet and pulled it on before grabbing a few of my books and shooting from the room.

I arrived at the library in less than a minute and slowed my speed as I pushed the door open.

Instead of the near perfect silence that usually greeted me when I entered the huge building, the sound of angry shouting filled the air.

I paused as I recognised Laini's voice raised in anger then hurried through the stacks in the direction of the noise.

"Sometimes I think you love these dusty old books more than me!" Tanya's voice rang out loudly. *It's not Tanya, it's Jessica! Dammit.*

"This is who I *am*," Laini snarled in response. "I don't just want to read, I *need* to. Don't you understand anything about my Order? If you seriously think you can win a competition for my attention with books then you're deluded. But you knew that when you committed to me!"

"I guess I just didn't realise how often I'd be snubbed for some dusty old pages," Jessica sobbed. "That's why I did it – I was *lonely*."

I rounded a corner and found the two of them facing off across a table stacked with books as other students all circled closer to watch the show. Harvey Bloom was cackling to himself as he watched, looking like he was off his face on Killblaze as usual.

"Why you did *what*?" Laini demanded and a prickle of apprehension ran down my spine as Jessica stilled.

"Nothing," she breathed. "It doesn't matter. This isn't about that anyway, I just-"

"Did you cheat on me?" Laini asked in a voice dripping with acid. Fire sparked to life in her fingertips and the gathered students sucked in a collective breath in alarm. It was strictly forbidden to use Elemental magic inside the library, *especially* fire magic, for obvious reasons.

"I...we...I *begged* you to come out with me that night," Jessica gushed, suddenly moving forward to reach for Laini, but she just stepped back to avoid her.

"Who was it?"

"It's not like that," Jessica insisted. "It was just a pack thing. The other Wolves could tell I was sad and they were just trying to cheer me up-"

Laini shrieked with pure rage and fire blazed in her hands. Before she could do anything to get herself expelled, I threw my hands up too, snatching the oxygen from the space around her and extinguishing them.

"Get the fuck out of here," I snarled at Jessica, my fangs snapping out in warning.

Jessica threw her hands over her face and fled the room sobbing, the crowd parting for her like a tide.

"Are you okay?" I asked Laini, moving forward quickly and pulling her into my arms.

"Thank you," she breathed, squeezing me tightly as the wetness of her tears fell against my neck. "I don't know what I was thinking casting in here..."

"It's alright," I said. "If we'd been anywhere else I'd have enjoyed watching you burn that bitch's perm off."

Laini released a half laugh, half sob but before she could reply, the harsh tone of the librarian reached us.

"One month's library ban!" she shrieked as she headed our way through the stacks. "And detention for whoever it is who is disturbing the sanctity of the library with this hullabaloo!"

I released Laini and looked around to find the crowd of gathered students had run for it.

Laini's lips parted with horror; banning a Sphinx from the library was like banning a Vampire from blood.

"Run," I hissed, shoving her towards the far end of the aisle, away from the sound of the approaching librarian.

"But-"

"Just go," I insisted, pushing her again before I hopped up onto the table.

I tipped my head back and started singing Wrecking Ball by Miley Cyrus at the top of my lungs.

Laini gaped at me for a long moment then turned and ran for it.

The librarian made it to our aisle a moment later, her eyes flashing with pure fire as she pointed a gnarled finger at me.

"Detention! No library for a month!" she shrieked as she lunged towards me.

"Sorry," I said, offering her a taunting grin before I leapt from the table and shot out of the room.

I could have just run for it with Laini, but the librarian wouldn't have quit hunting for a culprit so I'd had to take the fall. A library ban would be annoying, but I couldn't let Laini pay that price right after finding out that her girlfriend had gone all pack whore on her. Fucking Tanya.

I made it outside and into the light of the setting sun where I kept going until I reached the old well which sat around the side of the Rigel Library.

I came to a rest perching on the edge of it and blew a strand of lilac hair out of my eyes.

My Atlas pinged in my bag and I pulled it out to read the message.

Professor Mars:

Your detention is scheduled with me for 8:30pm on Wednesday. Failure to attend could lead to expulsion. Don't be late.

Peachy. I groaned at the idea of that. Mars's detentions were notoriously horrendous and I knew there was zero chance of him going easy on me just because I was on the Pitball team either.

My Atlas pinged for the second time and I looked down at it again, smiling as I found a much more appealing message this time.

Ryder:

Nightmare just left for the night, you wanna go fuck up her counselling room?

I was just about to reply with a hell yes when the sound of my name made me look up. A girl I didn't recognise was hurrying towards me with a triumphant look in her eyes.

"I found you first!" she gushed excitedly.

"Why were you looking for me?" I asked in confusion.

"I'm Eri…Mindy. Leon needs you to meet him in the Altair Auditorium. He says you *have* to go and to tell you that it's time."

"What?" I asked in confusion. The only time I'd ever been to the auditorium in Altair Halls was to watch that god awful drugs awareness movie after Cindy Lou framed me.

"That's all I know. But he also said that if you try to resist then all the Mindys should gather to make sure you get there." She eyed me like she was trying to decide whether or not she was gonna have to pounce on me and I suppressed a groan.

"For the love of the moon," I muttered, rolling my eyes. "Fine."

I got up and started walking while sending a quick message to Ryder letting him know that Leon had summoned me for something important and that I'd take him up on his offer later.

I had no idea what this was about, but if Leon had decided to set the Mindys on the case then it wasn't worth the effort to try and avoid it. Besides, I had to admit that I was pretty damn curious, not least because he'd made a whole production out of saying he'd be off at his parents' house tonight which had clearly been a lie.

Mindy fell into step with me, but I decided to cut her a break and save her from the escort duties so I offered her a word of thanks then shot away to the Altair Auditorium myself.

The door was closed when I arrived so I reached out to knock tentatively, but there was no response.

I eased the door open and found the space inside filled with a thousand tiny everflames which hung suspended all around the walls. It was pretty impressive magic and the effect meant that the dark room looked like it was lit by a sea of stars.

The huge projector screen was illuminated with a faint grey glow to let me know it was switched on, but I had no idea what Leon intended to play on it.

"Hello?" I called out tentatively, though with my enhanced eyesight I could see that there was no one here.

A huge grey couch had been moved into the room and it sat before the front row of chairs with a scattering of blankets tossed on it. The sweet smell of popcorn reached me and as I moved further into the room, I spotted a table on the far side of the couch which held a big bucket of it plus a cooler full of beers.

"This had better be important, Simba, or I'll break your legs for wasting my time," Ryder's voice came to me from out in the corridor and I turned to look back at the door as I heard Leon's reply.

"It is. Life or death. And you'll totally be thanking me for it too."

Ryder snorted derisively just before Leon pushed the door open.

He smiled widely as he spotted me and strode straight into the room, practically bouncing with excitement. He was wearing a pair of jeans and a white T-shirt which strained across his muscular frame and he'd tied his mane of blonde hair back into a messy bun.

Ryder stilled as he stepped into the space, his eyes landing on me as he folded his arms. He was wearing a black tank top which showed off his arms and my heart skipped a beat as his gaze slid over my light summer dress hungrily.

"What's the emergency?" Ryder asked, pulling his gaze from me to skim over the room which was so obviously laid out for a date that it might as well have had a flashing sign announcing it.

"I've decided to give you what you've been begging for, Scar," Leon teased. "We are *all* going to watch The Lion King."

"For fuck's sake," Ryder muttered and I couldn't help but laugh.

"C'mon, you know you love it. No one could reference it as much as you do without having it committed to memory," Leon teased as he moved to grab a couple of beers.

He tossed one to Ryder but he made no move to catch it and the bottle bounced off of his chest before falling to the floor and rolling away.

"No," Ryder said simply, turning to leave.

Leon's face fell and I shot forward, getting in Ryder's way before he could go anywhere.

"Stay," I asked, reaching out to catch his hand.

"Why would I sit around watching a fucking kid's movie?" Ryder asked with a glower.

"Because Leon went to all this effort. It would be rude to walk out now," I urged, tightening my grip on his fingers.

"I don't give a shit about offending the little lion cub."

"Less of the little," Leon said from behind us but his tone was joking.

"Do you care about offending *me*?" I asked, twisting my fingers between Ryder's.

"No," Ryder replied, but the corner of his mouth twitched with amusement.

"What if I sweeten the deal?" I offered, turning him around as I stepped back into the room and tugged him along with me.

"How?" he asked, his gaze sliding over me slowly.

I smiled as I reached around him to knock the door closed then lifted his hand to my lips. I kissed each of the letters which spelled out *pain* across his knuckles then slit his thumb open on my fangs before drawing it into my mouth and sucking the blood from the wound.

Ryder watched me with a dark promise dancing in his eyes and I pulled his thumb back out of my mouth before licking my lips.

"Stay," I urged.

When I released his hand, his gaze slid from me to Leon with a faint frown but he didn't make any more attempts to leave.

"Just admit you're not going anywhere and sit your ass down," Leon commanded.

Ryder sighed like he couldn't think of anything much worse than staying in this room with us, but he let me draw him towards the couch all the same.

Leon smiled broadly and headed off to the back of the room to start the projector running and Ryder hesitated before the sofa.

"I still don't understand the point of this," he muttered.

"When people like each other, they do shit like this," I pointed out.

"Well I might have admitted to liking *you,* but the Lion is a different matter."

"The Lion has exceptionally good hearing," Leon called from the back of the room. "And if you care about our girl as much as you should then you should want to make her happy. Which means becoming the Nala to my Simba."

"Nala ends up married to Simba. I don't know what kind of fantasies you've been having about me, but I can assure you that outcome is not in your future," Ryder said.

"I knew you loved this movie," Leon called triumphantly. "Do you need a tissue for when Mufasa dies or do you just let the tears flow free?"

Ryder growled low in the back of his throat and took a step away from the couch again. I stepped in front of him with a wicked grin and shoved him in the chest with the aid of my gifts. He fell back onto the couch with a hiss and I dropped onto his lap to keep him there.

"Stay," I insisted. "Play nice."

Ryder's hands landed on my thighs and shifted just beneath the hem of my dress. I gave him my best doe eyes and I could practically feel him caving.

"For you," he agreed finally.

I smirked at him and shifted out of his lap to drop into the seat beside him as Leon moved to the door and set a magical lock on it. A moment later, he leapt over the back of the couch and dropped onto my other side, throwing his arm around my shoulders as the movie started to play.

Ryder was watching me and Leon with his eyes narrowed and I slid my hand onto his thigh, high enough to make him shift in his seat.

Leon cut the tension by belting out the opening track at the top of his lungs, getting most of the words wrong aside from yelling the chorus so loud that we couldn't hear the movie.

I laughed as I leaned into him, slapping a hand over his mouth to quiet him again, but he only sang louder as he fought me off.

I scrambled to pin him down and he growled at me in a way that made a tingle run down my spine before catching my waist and tossing me into Ryder's lap.

"Bad, little monster," Leon scolded. "You can sit in the boring corner until you're ready to sing along with me."

I snorted a laugh and glanced up at Ryder as his arms slipped around my waist and he drew me closer.

"At least in the boring corner we can hear what's going on in the movie," he replied, his gaze on the screen.

Leon grinned. "I knew you loved it. I see you, Ryder. And I don't think you're as much of a blank page as you want everyone to believe you are."

"What's that supposed to mean?" Ryder muttered.

"That there's a soul lurking beneath the macho bullshit."

"I'm exactly who you always thought I was," Ryder growled.

"That's not all you are though, is it?" Leon asked, grinning as he swigged his beer.

Ryder hissed beneath his breath but before he could give some half assed denial, I reached out to cup his cheek, making him look at me.

"No. He's a lot more than that," I agreed, my eyes not straying from Ryder's.

The tension in his body eased as he looked back at me, his gaze skipping to Leon for a moment like he was surprised I'd say that in front of him too, but I'd never hidden how much I cared about any of my Kings from each other. If they wanted to know, they only had to ask.

"If you say so," Ryder muttered, his fingers sliding along my side until they reached the hem of my skirt again. He left them there, his cool skin raising goosebumps on mine as I shifted to get more comfortable in his lap.

Leon reached out to grab some more beers from the cooler, passing me one then offering Ryder one too.

"There's no point in me drinking alcohol," Ryder said, shaking his head. "It can't affect me anyway."

"Why?" Leon asked, raising an eyebrow as he took the cap from his then swapped it with mine so that he could open that too.

"Because Basilisks are immune to poison," Ryder said tersely.

"That's just an Order gift though, right?" Leon pushed. "Why don't you just switch that shit off and have a drink with us? You might even have fun if you let yourself."

"Switch it off?" Ryder asked, sounding like Leon had just suggested he put on a tutu and do a pirouette.

"Yeah. You know, like when I switch my Charisma off and the Mindys are a whole lot less obsessed with me…"

Ryder gave him a flat look.

"Or like how Elise doesn't just shoot all around the place at super speed twenty four seven…"

"You want me to switch off my gifts, so that I can get drunk with you?" Ryder asked.

"Have you ever done that before?" I asked him, a grin pulling at the corner of my mouth.

"No. Why would I?"

"For fun, Ryder!" I exclaimed. "C'mon. What's the worst that can happen? If you don't like it then you can just switch your gifts back on and burn right through the alcohol in the blink of an eye like you'd never even tried."

He gave me a flat look which was an obvious refusal and I pouted as I shifted in his lap, grinding my hips down on him so that I could feel the bulge in his pants swelling beneath me.

"Okay then, don't play with us," I said with a shrug, swigging my own drink.

Ryder sighed dramatically and reached out to take my bottle from me but I didn't release it, lifting my bottle and pressing the neck to his lips instead.

"Are you sure?" I asked, not really wanting to force him into something he was dead set against but I knew the drill with Ryder now. He was so set in his boring routines that he never even considered changing them up until he was tempted into it.

He stayed still for a long moment before rolling his eyes and parting his lips, letting me pour the beer into his mouth before he started swallowing.

Leon laughed in encouragement, passing me a second bottle as Ryder finished the first and I pressed that to his lips too. His grip on me tightened as he drank, his fingers hitching beneath the hem of my skirt and making my pulse race.

When he'd had two, he reached out to take the third bottle from Leon himself and slid me back off of his lap into the spot between the two of them.

They were both so big that I was squashed between them, their thighs pressing right up against mine. Leon tossed his arm around my shoulders again and Ryder's hand moved to rest on my leg.

We fell silent as we watched the movie and I couldn't help but keep casting furtive glances at Ryder beneath my lashes to see if he was reacting to it at all. He certainly never started singing along with Leon, but I was pretty damn sure I detected the hint of a smile from time to time.

By the time Timon and Pumbaa made an appearance, Ryder looked damn near relaxed which I was guessing wasn't hurt by the empty beer bottles that had gathered by his feet.

As Leon drank more, his fingers started twisting into the strands of my hair. I reached up to push a loose strand of his blonde mane back behind his ear and a deep purr came from him as my fingers lingered in his hair.

He caught my chin with his free hand, angling my mouth up to meet his as he planted a heated kiss on my lips. His stubble grazed against my jaw, sending shivers of goosebumps racing down my spine and I sighed as his tongue brushed against mine.

I leaned in to him for a long moment then pulled back again, feeling Ryder tensing beside me.

"Is that what this is?" Ryder asked Leon in a dark tone. "You just want me here to watch you stake your claim?"

"No," Leon said with an easy smile. "I only want Elise to be happy. And it seems like she needs you to be a part of her life to make that the case so I'm being open to that. If you care about her then you should be too."

Ryder hissed, his gaze narrowing.

"If watching us together doesn't turn you on then why don't you do something with her yourself?" Leon suggested, leaning back in his chair and swigging on his beer again.

"I can't," Ryder growled. "I made a deal with inferno."

"Psh." Leon waved him off. "If Dante is finding ways around those rules then I know that you sure as shit are too."

Ryder's gaze slid from Leon to me and he took a long drink from his bottle as he settled his gaze on me.

"You don't have to do anything you're uncomfortable with," I said, taking his hand in mine and running my fingers over the word *lust* on his knuckles.

Ryder shifted in his seat and pulled his hand from mine before leaning down to set his beer aside. As he sat upright again, his hand landed on my knee and he began to trail it up my inner thigh.

Goosebumps chased the progress of his fingers and I inhaled sharply as I leaned back into my seat and waited for him to make it further up my leg.

My heart pounded as his hand slid beneath my skirt and my back arched against the cushions behind me.

My thighs were still locked between the two of theirs, pressed together so that Ryder's progress was halted and I was left panting and wanting.

"Do you want more, little monster?" Leon purred in my ear and I turned from watching Ryder to looking at him, my eyes snaring in the golden depths of his.

Leon smirked at me, reaching out to catch my knee and pulling my leg over his, parting my thighs so that Ryder could keep going.

"Eyes on me, baby," Ryder growled and I turned to look at him again as his fingers slid over the lace of my panties.

I gasped as his thumb sought out that perfect spot at the apex of my thighs and he slowly started circling. I gasped as the rough material of my panties chafed against me in the most delicious way.

"Fuck," I hissed, my head falling back against the couch as I lifted my hips into his movements.

Leon's fingers twisted in my hair again and he purred louder as he watched me panting beneath Ryder's hand.

Ryder leaned forward, running the pad of his tongue straight up the side of my neck so that his stud grazed my skin and I couldn't help but imagine just how fucking good that would feel on other parts of my body.

"Look at you, little monster," Leon growled, reaching out to catch the hem of my dress in his grip and easing it up until it slid over my head, leaving me in my white underwear before them. "You're fucking perfection."

"You are," Ryder agreed. "My fucked up little fallen angel." His tongue drew a line along my ribs, tracing my tattoo and the words which sat there, branded onto my skin forever in memory of my brother.

Even angels fall…

And if I was going to fall then I couldn't think of many better men to catch me than the two of them.

Ryder shifted his fingers into a different rhythm against my panties and I moaned hungrily for more as I pushed into his movements, riding his hand.

"More," I gasped and Ryder hissed as he continued to push me towards the edge.

"Bite me," he offered, leaning in so that his muscular frame was all I could see.

My fangs snapped out and I lunged towards him, driving my teeth into his shoulder with a moan of need as I began to fall apart.

Leon's hand fell on my thigh, the heat of his skin so different to Ryder's cold blood that it sent my nerve endings haywire. He pushed his hand lower than Ryder's before nudging my underwear aside and pushing two fingers straight inside me.

I cried out as he started pumping them in and out, finding a perfect rhythm with Ryder's movements over my panties.

My hand fell on Leon's bicep as my nails bit into the skin and my other clutched Ryder's neck as I continued to feed from him.

Leon murmured my name and Ryder growled hungrily as the two of them both drove me towards a climax so fast that I could hardly catch my breath.

I came so hard that I reared back, my fangs falling from Ryder's neck as I arched against the couch and cried out. They guided my body through it as my nails bit in hard enough to draw blood from both of them and Ryder groaned with longing as he fed on the pain.

"Holy shit, Ryon," I mumbled, muddling their names together in my bliss.

Leon laughed darkly, dropping back into his seat as he drew his fingers back out of me.

Ryder reached out to wipe a bead of his blood from the corner of my mouth before pushing his thumb between my lips so that I could suck it off.

I held his gaze for a long moment as my heart pounded out of rhythm and the corner of his mouth twitched before he dropped back into his seat too.

"Fucking perfection," he growled in my ear, echoing Leon's words and drawing a blush to my cheeks.

I found my dress on the floor and tugged it back on before settling between the two of them again. Leon grabbed the popcorn and kept offering it around until Ryder finally gave in and snatched a handful of it to shut him up.

None of us said anything about what they'd just done, but it felt like we'd crossed some line, broken down some barrier and as my body tingled with satisfaction, I couldn't help but be excited about that idea.

We watched the rest of the movie in silence, but it felt so different to the tension that had sat between us before. And when Leon sang along to the credits, Ryder didn't even complain.

I lay in bed with my mind twisting over and over as I fought the battle for sleep and finally decided that I'd lost. The sun was just beginning to rise through the window and I'd been tossing and turning all night. I hated feeling like I was in a fight with Gabriel again, especially so soon after it had seemed like we were getting on track. Why couldn't he just accept me for who I was like the others were? Even Ryder was trying...

I got up with a huff of frustration. Gabriel wasn't in his bed which meant he was up in his brooding tent on the roof - *again*.

I was wearing a shorts and cami combo which I'd slept in, but I didn't see any point in getting dressed so I just ran a brush through my short hair and moved to hop out of the window.

I shot up the fire escape stairs and darted straight over the roof to Gabriel's tent.

I paused as I found him sleeping in the nest of blankets which took up most of the tent, unsure if I should wake him.

The sun crested the horizon and spilled over his bare chest, bathing his tattoo covered skin in golden light and I couldn't help but stare a little at the perfection of his features. He really did look like a fallen angel even without his wings.

His brow pinched and he murmured something in his sleep as his fist clenched on air.

"Wait," he hissed. "Please, don't leave me..."

My heart pounded unevenly as the nightmare gripped him and I dropped down, taking his hand in mine.

"Gabriel?" I breathed, brushing my fingers along his jaw as I tried to comfort him. "I'm here, it's okay. It's not real..."

Gabriel woke with a gasp, his grip tightening on my hand and his eyes wild for a moment before they fixed on me.

He yanked me closer on instinct and I fell over him as his lips captured mine and he kissed me with a desperate kind of urgency which I couldn't resist.

He groaned with need, his hands shifting over my body as he tried to push my pyjamas off and I pulled back with half a laugh, catching his wrist.

"I thought you were angry with me?" I asked.

Gabriel frowned like he had no idea what I was talking about then sighed as he seemed to remember, his hands stilling against my skin.

"I don't want to argue with you anymore, Elise," he said in a low voice.

"So don't," I replied. "Just accept who I am and what I need and then we can just carry on…" I trailed my fingertips down his chest and he groaned as he knocked his head back against his pillow.

"*Who* you need, you mean," he muttered and the tone of his voice let me know that he still didn't accept it at all.

I sighed, stilling my movements as I looked down at him. "Are we arguing again then?"

"No," he replied firmly. "We're just…not *not* arguing."

My lips twitched with amusement and I cocked my head at him. "So how does that play out?"

"Basically, we both know that we're in a disagreement but I don't want to fight about it. And I know that if I try and push you on the issue of the others right now, you're only gonna push right back. So can we just…not." He looked up at me hopefully and I nodded as I accepted his terms.

"Okay," I agreed, pressing my forehead to his. "But what does that mean for us?"

Gabriel sighed like he'd been defeated and he gripped my waist, flipping me over so that I laid on my back beneath him and his wings could burst from his spine. He spread them wide as the rays of the sunrise spilled over his black feathers, filling his power reserves and bathing him in orange light which made him look more angelic than ever.

"I'm not going anywhere," he said seriously. "I'm going to be right here, waiting for you to decide that you want me."

"I do want you," I replied forcefully, pushing up to kiss him again and show him how much.

Gabriel gave in for a moment then pulled away with a groan of frustration which told me just how much he wanted to stop holding back. "I know you do. But I want all of you. Every last piece. I want to be yours and for you to be mine. *All mine.*"

"But-"

"I'm not asking you to do anything now. I can see that you need the others for the moment, but our fate has been cast in the stars. Everyone knows that Elysian Mates face tests before they're given their Divine Moment and I won't fail at this one. We're destined to be together, my little angel. And I can wait for fate to make it so."

I released a slow breath, reaching up to paint the lines of his strong features with my fingertips.

"Okay," I agreed. Not because I had any intention of ever agreeing to belong to him solely, but because this had to be his choice. "I can wait too. If we're meant to be together then you'll come to understand who I am, even the bits you don't think you like. And then when you're ready to accept the fact that I'm going to keep seeing the others, I'll be waiting."

Gabriel's lips twitched with amusement. "Well at least we've agreed we want each other."

"I've wanted you from the first moment I laid eyes on you," I admitted.

Gabriel smiled widely at that and moved to lay beside me, withdrawing his wings as he fell down into the blankets.

"Is this the part where you run off?" he teased.

"It's usually the part where you're a jackass first," I quipped in return.

"How about you just stay this time then?" he asked, a flicker of vulnerability showing in his eyes like he thought I might not want to.

"Okay." I shifted closer to him and laid my head on his chest as I trailed my fingertips over the tattoos on his bronze skin. I lingered on the Libra symbol as always. "Well if we're not going to be hooking up then why don't we work on getting to know each other better?"

"What do you want to know?"

"You said that your tattoos all have meanings. Will you tell me about them?" My fingers moved to kiss a pair of flaming Phoenixes who were flying together with a Harpy over his hip.

"I have over a hundred tattoos," he replied with a laugh. "And each of them came alongside visions which held great importance, but were also shrouded in mystery. I still have to figure out what most of them mean."

"So tell me about them," I pushed. "And maybe we can figure some of it out together."

Gabriel hesitated as his fingers twisted through my hair and I waited to see if he was ready to trust me with this. He'd spent his whole life hiding and keeping people away from him, never letting anyone really *know* him and I wasn't sure if he was ready to let me in or not.

"Alright," he said eventually, pressing a kiss to the top of my head and making my whole body buzz with pleasure at the idea of him trusting me. "I guess we might as well start with those Phoenixes. I've had hundreds of visions about them."

I smiled as he started talking me through all of the things he'd *seen* and the information he'd guessed at or couldn't grasp and I took it all in with a warmth building in my heart.

He may not have been ready to accept sharing me, but if he thought for one moment that I cared for him any less than the others then he was wrong. My heart was beating harder just because I was close to him and the fact that he was baring his secrets to me meant more than I could easily put into words.

He thought that he had to wait for me to be his, but he was wrong. I already belonged to him heart and soul, and I was going to wait right here until he realised it.

DANTE

CHAPTER NINETEEN

"**H**e can't get into the school, Mamma," I said for the thousandth time as I lay on my bunk with the sheet hanging around it and a silencing bubble in place.

"That pezzo di merda can do anything. Don't underestimate him," Mamma said firmly.

We'd been chewing over Felix for the past hour. He'd killed my second cousin, Liletta, last night. She'd been found face down in the dirt outside the gates of my family home. I had every magical protection in the book on that house, plus I was paying ten extra guards to patrol the property at all times. But Mamma was more worried about Felix strolling into Aurora Academy and gutting me than herself.

"Mamma, he's not going to attack me here. The FIB have to get involved with deaths on school grounds. He wouldn't want the headache."

"Okay, Dolce Drago," she sighed. "I just worry about you. If anything happened to you…"

"Nothing will happen," I growled firmly. "Everyone in our clan is hunting for him. We'll get him, Mamma. Just hang in there."

"Che le stelle ti proteggano," she said with a sniff.

"May the stars protect you too, Mamma." I hung up with a sigh and found my Horoscope waiting for me on the screen of my Atlas.

Good morning Gemini.
The stars have spoken about your day!
With a dark shadow hanging over you, it's hard to see the light. So it may be the right time to look for the good in all things bad, and the bad in all things good. With a storm coming your way, you will have to call on the pull of the sun in your chart to have the strength to see the rays beyond the clouds. But if you manage to do so, salvation awaits.

I contemplated that for a while, picking it apart as I ran my thumb up and down my medallion. There were always clues hidden within Horoscopes and I knew it was a good idea to take their advice onboard, but I felt too angry right then to come to any clear conclusions.

I gave up trying to deduce it, releasing the silencing bubble and shoving the sheet aside. It was a Saturday and it looked like everyone had vacated the dorm already.

I moved to the window, shoving it open as a furious energy raced through my blood. I'd been shifting more than usual lately, but there was only two ways I knew which could relieve the tension in my body. And as I wasn't getting laid any time soon, flying was my only option.

"Are you okay?" Elise's voice startled me and I whipped around, spotting her up on her bunk. She'd been so quiet, I hadn't even thought to check if she was here.

"Sto bene," I muttered, pushing the window open. "I'm fine," I translated.

"Your tone says you're not fine," she pointed out, swinging her bare legs over the side of the bunk as she sat up. She was wearing denim shorts and a white tank top with the words *Faetal Attraction* scrawled across it in pink lettering.

"It's Felix," I growled and she jumped down from the bed, moving toward me with a frown.

"Has something happened?"

I shook my head then caught her waist and dragged her in for a hug. I was used to having my pack around me for support, but there was nothing quite like taking it from her. Wolves chose their mates based on their power level, eternally searching for their equal in every way. Once they did, they didn't rely on the rest of their pack anymore for emotional support; their mate supplied exactly what they needed. And though I was a Dragon, my mother and father were pure Wolf, and their nature still ran hot in my blood.

I'd told Elise I'd loved her because I did. Mamma had taught me to 'non mentire mai con il tuo cuore'. *Never lie with your heart.* My emotions didn't make me any less of an Alpha or any less of a man. And it didn't matter to me whether Elise felt the same way. I loved her, and I was going to continue loving her so long as my heart deemed fit. So that was all there was to it.

"Come fly with me, amore mio," I purred, brushing my mouth over her ear.

Her fingers slid down to my waist and she pushed my sweatpants lower on my hips, bringing a grin to my mouth. "Okay, but you'd better not ruin these when you shift. They're my favourite."

I glanced down at the grey pants which had a dragon symbol on the hip. There was nothing particularly special about them so I arched a brow at her, pushing her hair behind one ear. "Is that so, huh? And why is that, carina?"

"Because…they're the ones you were wearing the first day I met you."

"Dalle stelle, Elise. The best day of my life." I tugged them off with my boxers and she smirked, brushing a finger up the centre of my chest to my chin while she continued to look down.

"What are you doing?" I taunted.

"Admiring the view," she laughed, twisting me around and leaping onto my back. "Fly me to the moon, Drago!"

I stepped up onto the sill, pushing the window wide. "Hold on tight little Vampira."

I leapt forward and released my Dragon, my huge navy wings bursting out either side of me and glinting in the afternoon sun.

Elise laughed in excitement as she clung to the spines running down my neck and I wheeled sharply around in the direction of the lake. Electricity crackled along my skin and she gasped as I kept it from hurting her, but gave her enough to get her heart pumping wildly.

It didn't take long to soar over Campus and swoop low over Lake Tempest, then I sailed around it in a huge circle as I gazed down at the reflection of us below. Elise leaned over my side, grinning at me in the water and a mischievous laugh rumbled through me as I dunked my head into the lake then whipped it backwards to spray her with water.

"Dante!" she laughed, clinging on tighter as I raced across the surface at high speed.

I came to land beside the boathouse, moving beneath the fronds of the huge willow tree which leaned over the roof. Elise jumped down and I shifted back into my Fae form, plucking a flower from the ground as I rose to my feet. I held the tiny daisy in front of my dick and she giggled.

"That's not covering anything!"

"I need help making a big daisy chain to cover it all," I teased and she blew out a laugh before shooting off into the boathouse.

My troubles were long forgotten as I followed her inside and grabbed a pair of sweatpants out of the stash I kept there.

I glanced up to see if she was watching me and was disappointed to find her looking at her Atlas.

"Something more interesting on there than me?" I teased and she lifted her head with a smile.

"It's just my mom's old boss checking to see how I am," she said.

"You mean the woman who wanted you to work for her as a stripper?" I growled, my mood changing sharply as electricity trickled into the air.

She sighed, tucking her Atlas away. "I know it's not ideal, but Sal has been there for me. She's all I have left."

"You have me," I said firmly, stepping closer.

Her mouth pulled up at one corner and she nodded. "I know, I mean Sal's all I have left of the life I had before. Mom won't talk to me and my brother's gone so…"

My heart weighed down in my chest and though I didn't trust that woman one bit, I couldn't find it in me to argue my point any further.

"Okay, amore mio," I said gently.

Elise dropped down on the edge of the walkway, slipping off her shoes and dipping her feet into the water. I moved to sit beside her, watching the sunlight dance in her hair as it shifted through the willow fronds beyond the entrance.

"Sei così fottutamente bello, Elise," I whispered and she turned to me with curiosity in her eyes.

"What does that mean?"

A smile tilted my lips as I leaned closer to skate my thumb along her jaw. "I said you are so fucking beautiful."

Her lips parted and my gaze immediately dropped to them, hunger rising in me so keenly I almost forgot everything just to steal the kiss I'd dreamed of a thousand times. She'd pressed her mouth to mine in here just days ago, but it infuriated me that I couldn't give her a real kiss. I could make her moan with nothing but my tongue tasting hers and she'd never want it to stop.

She broke my gaze, dropping her head to look down at the water, her lilac hair falling forward to conceal her face.

"Shy, bella?" I mocked.

"Turned on more like," she said lightly and my brows lifted.

"What would you have me do if I could give it to you?" I asked keenly, shifting nearer so my shoulder rubbed hers.

She pushed her hair back, looking at me with a wicked glint in her gaze. She leaned in close to my ear, lifting a hand to lightly rake her nails over my neck. I shivered under her touch as she caressed my pulse like it called to her. Her mouth pressed to my ear and she released a soft breath against me that had me hardening for her immediately.

"I'd have you shift back into your Dragon form, then I'd oil myself up and slide all over your scales naked. I'm really into Dragon dick..."

My brow pinch and I turned to look at her in surprise. "Well I guess er...I suppose maybe we could try-"

"Ha – your face!" She slapped me on the back then jumped to her feet and leapt into a rowing boat that was bobbing in the water. "I can't believe you bought that. I'm no Cindy Poo."

I barked a laugh, rising to my feet and sizing up the gap parting me from her. "Now you're in trouble, carina. No one plays me for a fool."

"Except me," she said with a daring grin. "Unless you can catch me and teach me a lesson."

"No Vampire speed," I warned, dropping my voice an octave.

Her eyes sparkled with the game as she nodded, then leapt to the next boat across. I jumped forward, landing in the one she'd vacated and it rocked wildly beneath my feet.

"Would you really have let me get off over you in your Dragon form?" Elise taunted, leaping onto the jetty at the centre of the boathouse.

"Of course not," I said defensively, diving into the next boat before pulling myself up onto the wooden boards behind her.

Elise danced away, running for the ladder that led to the platform above us. I raced after her as her laughter rang through the space, determined not to let her escape.

"Seems like you would have," she sang, jumping onto the ladder.

I leapt after her with a growl of excitement and caught her around the waist, dragging her off of the second rung. I tossed her onto the floor and grinned as she scrambled onto her knees. "You look good down there, bella."

She caught hold of my legs with a seductive expression and my eyes became hooded. She gripped the backs of my thighs then used her Vampire strength to flip me off my feet. I groaned as my back slammed into the hard wood and she jumped on top of me, straddling my hips and grinning down at me. "I look even better up here."

I took hold of her waist, throwing her back onto the floor and rolling so I pinned her down, pressing the hard plain of my chest to hers. She panted heavily, pushing back a loose lock of hair which had fallen into my eyes. My arousal rutted between us and she arched into me with a look that said she wanted me. But was that just for now, or was it always and forever? Because I knew exactly how long I wanted her for. I just had to hope Ryder would lose interest and let me out of this deal. But if I knew that snake like I thought I did, he would stubbornly hold onto her for the rest of time even if it was just to spite me.

I hissed in pain as something yanked deep in my chest and I spat air through my teeth as I felt someone break the vow of trust they'd made to me over Felix. I'd been betrayed and it only took a second longer to sense who it was. My second in command, my beta, his daughter, *Tabitha*.

"Fuck!" I gasped.

Elise's head whipped sideways suddenly, looking toward the exit with a frown that said she'd heard something.

"Dante!" she screamed, forcing me to roll again and falling over me as my back hit the floor. She cursed in pain and panic snared my heart. I shoved her hair away from her neck, finding a dart sticking out of it with a red feather on the end. I ripped it from her skin and a bead of blood ran down her throat alongside a blackish substance that could only be poison.

"Elise!" I cried.

I rolled sideways, lowering her to the ground as she groaned. A whistling noise caught my ear and I turned towards the exit, throwing up an air shield a second before another dart collided with it. My gaze slammed into Tabitha's and a snarl ripped from my throat.

"I'm coming for you!" I roared, my Dragon burning at the edges of my flesh.

Elise groaned again and her head lolled against my chest. I cupped her cheek and her eyes locked with mine, her lips moving with words I couldn't hear.

"Fuck – *no*." Sheer terror raced through me as her eyes fell closed and she went limp in my arms.

I leapt to my feet, cradling her against me as I tried to figure out what the fuck to do. Professor Titan might have been able to help her if he knew what the poison was. But I didn't know where he was and who knew how long she had before she succumbed to whatever the fuck it was? Hours, minutes, *seconds*?

My pulse thumped against my ear drums and a ragged breath made it out of my lungs as I realised what I had to do. I ran from the boathouse, stuffing the dart into Elise's pocket and searching the area for any sign of Tabitha.

"You're dead!" I bellowed at the trees. "Run as far and as fast as you can, Tabitha! A morte e ritorno – but you won't be coming back from death!"

I placed Elise on the grass and twisted sideways, my skin splitting apart to release the Dragon inside me. I carefully lifted Elise in my claws and took off into the sky with an almighty roar. Lightning daggered into the heavens then crashed back down to the ground, splitting the earth apart in a huge explosion of dirt.

I flew across campus, racing toward the Vega Dorms and praying for the stars to be on my side. And that the Fae I needed was going to be in his room.

I landed beside the dorms, placing Elise down and shifting back into my Fae form. I scooped her up, running to Ryder's window and hammering my fist on it. There was no way I could walk into a Lunar corridor without getting stopped, so this was my only chance.

"Ryder!" I demanded and the blind whipped up. I locked eyes with my enemy and his face contorted into a sneer a second before he spotted Elise in my arms. "I need your help."

He wrenched the window open, snatching her from me and I clambered in after her.

"What the fuck did you do to her?!" Ryder demanded, fear lacing his tone.

"I didn't fucking touch her." I stormed forward, snatching the dart out of her pocket and holding it under his nose. "She was poisoned." I stared at him as he laid her down on the floor, kneeling over her. "Help her," I rasped.

Ryder didn't respond, but took hold of her hand and guided her wrist to his mouth.

He opened his mouth to reveal sharpened snake teeth a moment before he sank them into her flesh, releasing the antivenom that lived in him. He could heal her from any poison, it was one of his Order gifts. I'd made sure to know every possible thing about Basilisks so that I could always be ready to face off against him. I just hoped it wasn't too late.

Ryder grabbed her other hand, biting into that wrist too and I eyed the puncture marks he'd left on her other arm with discomfort. "This had better fucking work," I snarled.

"It will," Ryder spat then pushed her legs wider, leaning down to bite into the soft flesh of her thigh. I realised he was biting all the main arteries in her body and my heart began to slow as she released a soft groan.

"It's okay, I'm here, carina," I said.

Ryder dropped over her, digging his teeth into her neck and her brow creased in pain.

"Be careful," I growled.

"Do you want me to be careful or do you want me to save her fucking life?" he snapped.

Rain pelted the window like bullets as my storm took hold of the sky. I needed to go after Tabitha, but I couldn't move until I was sure Elise was going to be okay.

Ryder continued to bite her and she stirred a little more, but her eyes never opened. Those sea-green gems evading me.

"It's done," Ryder growled at last, not looking at me. "She'll need to rest. The antivenom will keep her sedated until it's finished healing her."

"Are you sure?" I demanded, my hands balling into fists.

"Yes I'm fucking sure. I know my own Order, asshole," Ryder snapped.

I backed up to the window with a firm nod. "I'll be back, I have a traitor to deal with."

I leapt out the window, slamming it shut behind me and shifting back into my Dragon form. Claws hit the mud and my tail whipped out behind me as I released an almighty roar, delighting in the power of my Order form. I took off toward the sky, the rain hammering against my scales as I raced back toward the boathouse. Tabitha would be running for her fucking life right now, but I'd gain on her. There was no way I was going to let her escape my wrath. And a Werewolf couldn't outrun a Dragon.

I tore through the sky, lightning slicing the air apart around me and sending adrenaline surging through my blood. I roared a warning, wanting her terrified and shaking. Because I was coming. And when I found her, I would make her pay for hurting my girl. For betraying me. For picking her worthless father over her true Alpha.

I circled The Iron Wood and the glint of her grey fur caught my eye down below. I spotted her tearing through the trees at a ferocious pace, whimpers of fear escaping her with every footfall.

My heart ached with the depths of her betrayal. She'd been my number two, my beta, my most trusted pack member here at the academy. We'd shared countless runs beneath the moon and grown up together, played together, wrestling in pack brawls and eating at the same table. I had loved her with all of my heart. And this was the thanks I'd gotten for my devotion? Not even a challenge? A poisonous dart. A cowards choice of weapon.

I roared to let her knew she'd been found, flexing my wings as I dropped lower, hunting down my prey as the storm rattled the earth beneath her paws. My grief over losing the Wolf I thought she'd been was consumed by the fiery pits of my rage as I set my sights on her and prepared to unleash the full force of my Order form on her. I was her Alpha, the leader of her family, her kin and now, her end.

I let a tremendous flood of energy build at the base of my throat, the electricity rising and rising until my ears were buzzing and my jaw was vibrating.

I focused on the Wolf below who had dared to defy me. Who deserved the bitterest end I could give her. She wasn't the girl I'd thought I'd known. She was a sheep in wolf's clothing and she'd followed her pathetic coward of a father only to be cast into an early grave.

With a roar that sounded like a thunder clap, I unleashed a huge lightning strike on the traitor beneath me. The trees turned to ash before it even hit the ground and a single yelp of fear came before an echoing boom sounded the lightning hitting its target.

Mud sprayed into the air and trees tumbled to the ground in a wide arc, the crater left in its wake sizzling as rain splattered over the burning earth.

There was nothing left of Tabitha, not a single hair. No sign that she'd ever even walked in this world. That was what happened to those who crossed me. They weren't just killed. They were eradicated.

RYDER

CHAPTER TWENTY

I pulled Elise into my lap, checking her pulse from time to time to make sure she was recovering. The antivenom was doing its job on her, but the rage inside me wouldn't ease. How could Inferno have put her at risk like this? That piece of shit was going to answer to my fists if he really dared to return here. The only reason he hadn't been laid out bloody on my floor while I fed on his pain was because of Elise.

I didn't like to admit to the emotions I'd felt when I'd seen her in his arms, looking so still…

I didn't think there was anything in this world which could frighten me. But I'd just discovered my biggest fucking phobia ever. Losing her.

Maybe it should have been obvious before now, but the way I felt about her went beyond anything I'd ever experienced for anyone. I curled my fingers into fists, eyeing the words on my knuckles. I hated to admit that that bitch Nightmare was right, it literally cut me to the bone, but fuck, maybe I *could* feel more than pain and lust. Maybe there was at least one more four letter word I'd be needing a tattoo for in the future.

Elise moaned softly and I brushed my fingers into her hair. With no one here and with her completely out of it, I was able to stare at her as much as I liked. I slid my finger over every freckle on her cheeks and felt the soft curve of her mouth beneath my thumb. She seemed so fragile like this, as if her heart was laid in my palm and I needed to coil around it and protect it from the world.

A knock came at the window and I grunted in annoyance, looking up to find Inferno standing there naked as the fucking dawn. I turned my head away to ignore him and he bashed his hand against the window again.

"Open it or I'll break it," he threatened and a rattle started up deep in my body.

I placed Elise on the floor then stood, moving to the window and wrenching it open.

"I can take it from here," I snarled.

"If you think I'm going to leave her with you, serpente, you are sorely fucking mistaken." He hauled his bare ass inside and a hiss rushed through my teeth. I slammed my hands to his chest, knocking him off course as he tried to get around me to Elise.

"Get the fuck out of my room or you're dead, Inferno," I warned.

He shoved me back, throwing his muscles into the blow to force me back a step. I bared my teeth and he bared his right back.

"I'm staying," he snapped, throwing his shoulder into mine and heading past me to Elise. "If you wanna fight me and tear this whole room down around her, then go ahead. But how happy do you think she'll be about that when she wakes up, stronzo?"

I clenched my fists, biting down hard on my tongue as he approached her. I snatched a pair of sweatpants from my drawer and tossed them at him. "Keep your filthy Oscura cock away from her."

He tugged them on, shooting me a glower. "She'd rather an Oscura cock over a Lunar one any day, but thanks to your deal-"

"*My* deal?" I spat. "You were the one who decided we couldn't even kiss her."

"So my mouth is okay near her, but not my cock?"

"I don't want *any* of you near her, so how about we agree to dissolve the deal and you go and find some Wolf pussy to satisfy you? She's just a challenge to you anyway," I growled, dropping down on the other side of Elise and capturing his gaze. I tried to send him a vision, but his mental shields were powerful, keeping me from getting into his slimy mind.

"Bullshit. Elise actually likes me. She only wants you because she has some vague fascination with your BDSM bullshit, so once she realises you're just a boring asshole who likes to fuck girls while prodding them with forks or some shit, she'll pick me anyway."

I lunged for him, locking my hand around his throat. His eyes narrowed and he cast a gust of air into my chest to throw me off. We both crowded closer on either side of Elise and when he snarled at me, I hissed right back.

"You think your tiny cock could satisfy a girl like her?" I asked dryly.

"You just saw it, stronzo, so let's not play dumb." He sneered and I blew out a breath of laughter.

"As if I'd bother to look at your midget dick."

"You really wanna play who's got the bigger cock?" Dante asked in a challenge, reaching for his waistband. "Because I don't think you can handle it."

"Handle it?" I laughed hollowly. "I once got my dick out in front of a girl and she thought I'd shifted."

Dante's eyes widened and a laugh ripped from his throat. I bit down on the insides of my cheeks as some fucking insanity almost possessed me to join in.

He reined his amusement in fast, a challenge flaring in his eyes instead as he gripped his waistband. "Well let's see who's gonna eat their words."

I ground my jaw, trying not to rise to his goading. But it was fucking impossible. He was trying to make me back down, bow to his fucking bullshit.

But I didn't bow to anyone.

"Fine. *Let's*," I hissed, my eyes narrowing to slits.

My Order form was begging to come out and put this worthless asshole in his place, but I wasn't going to move an inch from where I was sitting beside Elise. So a dick measuring competition seemed like the next best move.

I gripped my waistband, kneeling opposite him and pressing my shoulders back.

"On three…," Dante said. "One…two…"

"Ryder," Elise murmured and my chest swelled to twice its size as I looked down at her. Her eyes were cracked open, looking up at us as we gripped our sweatpants. Just two fucking idiots about to get our cocks out…

I dropped down to her side, clutching her hand. "Yes baby?"

"Dante…" she sighed and he dropped down too, his shoulder ramming against mine as we leaned over her. Elise smiled dreamily then passed out again but neither of us moved, shoving harder against one another.

"She needs more rest," I said in a low tone. "She can stay here tonight. So you can fuck off now."

"I told you I'm not going anywhere," Dante growled, moving to lay beside Elise and taking her other hand.

I glared at him with anger eating away at my ribcage. "You're not staying here."

Dante lifted his free hand, pushing it under his head and shutting his eyes. "Shh, stronzo."

I was about to get up and throw him out of my room with my earth magic, but my gaze fell on Elise. She'd said both of our names. She wanted both of us here. And as fucking shit as that was, she *had* just nearly died. So wasn't this the least I could offer her?

I headed to the bed, ripping my covers off of it and dropping them over Elise, making sure Dante didn't get so much as a fucking corner. Then I dropped down beside her and took her hand, shifting under the comforter.

According to the rules, we couldn't share a bed together so we'd be stuck on the floor all night. But even if I could have brought Elise into my bed, I imagined Dante would have come crawling in too like a fucking leach.

I released a long breath in annoyance, silence stretching through the room.

I threaded my fingers through Elise's and vowed to do this for her sake.

"Did you get the asshole who poisoned her?" I broke the silence after a long time. I needed to know, because if he hadn't, I'd make it my own personal mission to destroy them myself tomorrow.

"Yeah she's dead."

"How?" I growled.

"Lightning strike," he said darkly and I released a huff of annoyance.

"You should have made her suffer."

"I made her afraid, I made her know who was coming for her," Dante hissed. "The Oscura family don't torture Fae like monsters. We're not *you*."

Venom poured into my blood at his words and pain sliced through my chest. "Fucking liar."

"Excuse me?" Dante snarled, half sitting up to glare at me.

"You heard me," I spat. "I called you a fucking liar." I dropped Elise's hand, sitting up and tearing my shirt off before gesturing to my scars. "Did I imagine up the Oscura who did this to me then, you piece of shit?"

Dante's eyes roamed over my scars then he lowered back down beside Elise, his features taut. He remained quiet and I figured I'd put him back in his fucking box so I dropped back down beside Elise, fixing my gaze on a blemish in the paintwork on the ceiling.

"I shouldn't have spoken for all Oscuras," Dante said after a long while. "There's bad blood amongst my people. Felix…Mariella. But I don't think of them as family. So it wasn't a lie."

At the mention of *her* name, my fingers flexed and I ached for her death once more. It was the only dream I'd had for myself for a long, long time.

Up until I'd met Elise, Mariella's pain had been the only thing I'd ached for, dreamed of, yearned for. There still wasn't a day that passed where I didn't think about it. But since Elise had come along, it wasn't all-consuming anymore. I didn't have to dwell in the darkness of my mind at all hours of the day, thinking up ways I'd like to torture Mariella. Not when I had something far sweeter to spend my time thinking about.

"Well I can't see why. Your Aunt Mariella has only done you favours as far as I can see," I ground out.

Dante cursed under his breath in Faetalian. "When I took over the pack, I banished her for what she did to you. No one even knew she had you until the news spread that you'd escaped. She told everyone you were dead-"

"Bullshit," I snarled.

"I might be your enemy, serpente, but I don't lie to anyone. And what Mariella did was an atrocity I wish my Clan weren't linked to. That's why she's gone."

I fell quiet, the dull thump of my heart pounding in my ears. I didn't want to believe him, but maybe some part of me did. Why would he bother to lie? He wouldn't try to spare my fucking feelings.

"Do you know where she is?" I asked in a dark tone, the threat in my voice clear.

"No," he said.

"If she's not your family anymore then why protect her?" I hissed.

"I don't know where she is," he growled.

A long beat of silence passed as I processed that. "You wouldn't tell me even if you did. That's why you banished her and didn't kill her, you still protected her in the end," I muttered. "The Lunars get bad blood too. But I deal with it fast, efficiently, violently. You can't wait for bad blood to out."

"Don't tell me you've never been betrayed before," Dante tsked.

"I've been betrayed," I growled. "That's how I learned not to give second chances."

"Some people deserve second chances," Dante argued.

"And that's why your clan is falling apart."

"It's not falling apart," Dante said fiercely. "My family is stronger than ever. For Wolves, banishment is worse than death. It means being cut off from the intimacy they need, severing the binds that tie them to their kin. It makes the core pack stronger as a unit too. So we'll rise together and wipe out the threat against us and come out of this war even stronger because of it. What will you have around you when all is said and done? I have family and people who love me. The people around you are terrified of you. You have no family and you have no one who loves you. Whether you die tomorrow or as an old man, it will be alone and unloved. And that's a choice *you* made."

My chest tightened and I firmed my grip on Elise. She was the one thing I'd ever wanted of my own, and now she wasn't allowed to be mine. I was forced to share with three other guys, one of whom was my Astral Adversary, chosen by the stars to oppose me for the rest of time.

"That's why you should give her to me," I said as barbed wire coiled around my heart. "She's the closest thing to family I've had in a long time." I was glad I didn't have to look at him when I said it. Maybe it was pathetic, but it was the truth. And my tongue would never weave lies like his did.

"Well I can't do that, Ryder, because she's my family too," Dante said possessively. "I've already fallen for her, even if I was stupid enough to give her up for your sake. It's too late for me to back out on this, so maybe you should find someone else to be your family if that's what you want."

I gritted my jaw, saying nothing. I wouldn't dare breathe a word of the feelings surfacing inside me, spilling into everything that I was. Because little did he know, it was too late for me too.

ELISE

CHAPTER TWENTY ONE

I woke with a pounding in my skull and a lightness in my heart as I stretched my back out where I lay on a hard floor. Both of my hands had been claimed by the men whose heavy breathing filled the room. I stilled as I recognised the cool touch of Ryder's cold blooded flesh and the faint tingling which always came from Dante's skin as the soft hum of electricity passed beneath it at all times.

I must have died.

Even my dreams wouldn't have been ambitious enough for me to think up this scenario but as I peeled my leaden eyelids open, I couldn't deny the truth of it. We were in Ryder's room and the darkness which surrounded us told me it was still night.

I focused on my gifts and sharpened my eyesight so that the dark wouldn't make any difference as I looked at the two men who lay sleeping either side of me. Two sworn enemies who shouldn't have even been able to bear standing in the same room as each other and yet they were actually sleeping here, neither of them worried what the other would do while they slept.

Their hold on my hands felt binding somehow. Like it was its own kind of promise. They were here for me and while that was still the case, there was a strange sense of almost peace hanging between them. Or maybe peace was too strong a word, but they'd certainly called a ceasefire.

My mouth was unbearably dry and my joints were all aching in a way that screamed for attention and as much as I wanted to linger in this unreal moment, I couldn't lie still for another second.

I tried to wriggle myself upright, but a hiss of pain escaped me the moment I moved.

Dante and Ryder woke instantly, the two of them pushing themselves up so that they could look at me.

"Stai bene, amore mio?" Dante asked, throwing an orb of light up into the air so that he could look at me.

"Stay still, I've got you," Ryder demanded, his pinched brow telling me that he could feel my pain.

His hand released mine and landed on my stomach instead as he shoved my shirt up out of his way before splaying his palm across my skin. The cool touch of his flesh was quickly followed by a rush of healing magic and I sighed as it flooded through me, seeking out all the places that ached inside my bones and soothing away my pain.

"What happened?" I asked with a frown, my gaze fixing on Dante's warm eyes as he looked down at me. "The last thing I remember was being in the boathouse playing chase with you…"

"Tabitha betrayed me. She tried to kill me for Felix but you threw me out of the way and-"

"And nearly died because this piece of shit can't control his people," Ryder snarled. "Please tell me you didn't seriously throw yourself between him and death?"

My gaze moved to Ryder and though his posture and the look in his eyes said he was mad as hell, there was something about him that screamed pain and fear too.

I reached out and took his hand again, holding his eye so that he couldn't look away from me.

"Well I'm not dead, am I?" I asked lightly.

"No thanks to him," Ryder growled.

"I'm the one who brought her to you," Dante snapped.

"Yeah. And without me she would have been dead within five more minutes!"

"But I'm not," I said firmly.

I released my grip on both of them and pushed myself up to sit.

They eyed me like I might break at any moment and I rolled my eyes at them. "You don't need to look at me like that," I said.

"Like we nearly lost you? That's because we did," Dante said in a low voice.

I pursed my lips and combed my fingers through my hair to remove the worst of the tangles from it.

"I'm still here." I shrugged.

I hunted in my shorts' pockets until I located a piece of cherry gum and pushed it between my teeth. It was no toothbrush substitute, but it was better than nothing.

Ryder muttered something beneath his breath and Dante reached out to cup my face in his hand, tilting my chin up until I looked at him.

"I'm sorry you paid that price for my company, amore mio," he breathed, his brow taut with concern.

I placed my hand over his and offered him a smile. "You're worth it."

Ryder snorted loudly, making it clear he absolutely didn't agree with that statement but his attention was on something in his hands. I watched as he moulded his earth magic to grow a thin vine of roses covered in thorns until they formed a chain with one fat rosebud blooming in the centre of it. He frowned in concentration as he shifted his focus, solidifying the vine so that it slowly changed form, the green leaves turning to darkest silver as he transformed them into metal. When only the rosebud was left green, he lifted it to his mouth and sank his tooth into it, releasing some of his venom. Once the flower was filled with the essence of his power, he exerted his magic onto that too, solidifying it until it turned palest white. The smallest hint of a smile tugged at the corner of his mouth before he turned his gaze up to meet mine.

"This flower holds my venom in it. If you're ever poisoned again, prick your finger on one of the thorns and it will transfer into your blood and save you," he commanded before leaning forward and hanging the chain around my neck.

"This is beautiful, Ryder," I breathed as he fastened it for me, turning my head to look at him as he lingered close to me.

"It's not beautiful, it's practical," he snapped, sitting back with a huff of irritation and half a glance at Dante.

"I'm surprised you didn't make it look like a dead rat or something," Dante muttered, eyeing the necklace like he wanted to rip it off of my neck.

"Thank you, Ryder," I said loudly, cutting them off before they could start bickering. Honestly, if I didn't know they were ruthless killers and mortal enemies I'd think they were a pair of old dears fighting over the weather forecast at times.

Silence fell again and I blew a bubble with my gum before letting it pop loudly.

"You don't seem nearly worried enough about what just happened to you," Ryder growled, some of his anger spilling over on to me.

I shrugged. "My own mortality hasn't meant all that much to me for some time," I replied flippantly and the two of them winced.

"How can you say that?" Dante demanded.

I almost didn't answer, but I guessed if they'd saved my sorry ass from death they deserved the truth from me.

"It's not like I *want* to die," I said slowly. "It's just that I don't exactly have much to live for now…" I trailed off as my thoughts turned to Gareth and my mom. My imperfectly perfect family which had turned out to be built on a foundation of lies and deceit. But one thing about it had been real and true and pure and that was my love for my brother. It had been the thing that grounded me, kept me sane, let me know who I was deep down in my heart. And now it was gone.

"You have *me,*" Ryder and Dante growled at the exact same time and my lips parted as I looked between them and they turned to glare at each other.

Electricity crackled through the room and Ryder hissed between his teeth.

"Well if I've got you *both* then maybe we should turn this little gathering into a three-way?" I suggested with a smirk, trying to lighten the mood. "You could just agree to end this stupid deal and do anything and everything you want with me."

They turned from each other to look at me with a mixture of horror and longing written on their faces.

Silence hung between us and for the strangest moment I wondered if they were actually considering it. My heart pounded at the thought of that as my gaze trailed over their bare chests and I shifted forward slowly until I was on my knees between them. The thought of being pinned between their powerful bodies was a fantasy too intoxicating not to indulge in, but was there really any kind of hope that the Kings of the two most powerful gangs in Alestria might actually come together over me?

I leaned forward and placed my hands on each of their thighs, slowly shifting my fingers up their legs as their eyes remained fixed on me.

It almost seemed like they were going to give in, but Ryder's gaze suddenly snapped from me to land on Dante.

"I'd sooner cut my own dick off than let him put his anywhere near you," he snarled, catching my arm and tugging me towards him so that my hand fell from Dante's thigh.

"I'll happily cut it off for you, if you even *think* about fucking her, stronzo," Dante bit back as he caught my other arm and yanked me back towards him.

"Guys," I began, but Ryder's grip only tightened on me as he tried to drag me out of Dante's hold.

"Well maybe that's how we should settle this. We fight it out, whichever one of us survives gets to keep her," Ryder suggested.

"Did you seriously just suggest fighting over me like I'm a prize to be won?" I demanded just as Dante tugged me back towards him.

"If you want to die then that's fine by me, stronzo," he growled, static sparking through the room.

"Stop it," I snapped, yanking my arms out of their hold with a surge of my enhanced strength and getting to my feet. "The two of you don't get to make a decision for me with some fucking death match. And obviously I'd never want to have anything to do with either of you if you killed the other."

They both stood too and suddenly they were towering over me, crowding in close with their macho bullshit still hanging in the air between them.

"Then put us out of our misery," Ryder said in a dark voice. "Pick now and we'll end the deal. You choose one of us and the other agrees to let you be with him. I can't take this anymore, never knowing who you want more, I don't want this kind of pain."

"Good idea. Put him out of his misery, carina," Dante said confidently.

I raised my chin and glared at them. "I've made myself perfectly clear from the start. I'm. Not. Choosing. It's not a choice. I like and want you both the exact same amount. One relationship has no bearing on the other. This is who I am. I've always been clear about that. You don't have to have any part of it if you don't want to. But if you *do* want me then you're going to have to get used to the idea of sharing me. And don't ever ask me to choose again."

I didn't bother waiting for their response as I could see that the two of them were still too hooked on their rivalry to overlook it, so I tipped them a salute and shot from the room instead, tossing Ryder's door closed behind me and speeding all the way up to my bed.

A week had passed since I'd almost died and both Ryder and Dante had been annoyingly careful around me during that time, like they thought I might break at any moment. I wasn't sure if they were expecting me to suddenly go into shock over the whole thing or something, but I'd finally had to tell them to get over it like I had, which seemed to have done the trick.

Tonight it was Dante's birthday party and I was determined to have a simple night without drama and filled with fun.

A knock came at my door just as I finished getting ready and I headed to open it with a smile playing around my cherry red lips.

I pushed the door open and found Leon leaning against my doorframe looking stupidly hot in a short sleeved shirt and a pair of grey jeans.

He groaned as his eyes roamed over me in the navy blue halter dress I was wearing. I'd bought it especially because it was the exact same shade as Dante's scales when he was in his Dragon form. It was backless and the skirt fell to my knees, the thin material hugging my figure.

"Fuck me all day, every way, you look good enough to eat, little monster," Leon said, reaching for me hungrily.

"So do you," I replied as my fangs tingled and my gaze roamed over his throat.

I ducked back into my room to strap on a pair of silver sandals and Leon waited for me, watching my movements with a look on his face that said he was forcing himself not to pounce.

Dante had been at home all day for his birthday and we would be arriving for the main celebrations which were taking place this evening. He'd assured me that that was a good thing as most of his relatives would be too drunk to notice if he slipped away for some time alone with us.

I grabbed my purse which contained Dante's gift and moved out to join Leon in the hallway.

He caught my waist and whirled me around until I was pinned against the wall, kissing me with a growl of longing as his hands slid over my breasts through the thin material of the dress.

"Fuck, I love it when you don't wear a bra," he said between kisses and I laughed, tiptoeing up to whisper in his ear.

"I'm not wearing any panties either."

"What?" Leon's hand shifted down over my ass as he tried to hunt for the truth and I laughed again as he failed to find anything beneath my dress.

"Meet you by the car," I said and I shot away from him at full speed with his groan of frustration sounding in the corridor behind me.

I didn't stop until I was out in the parking lot where a brand spanking new, bright red Faerarri convertible was parked up with the top down. I'd never seen it before and was flashy as fuck which meant it had to be Leon's latest conquest.

I hopped up onto the hood and leaned back, enjoying the feeling of the setting sun on my skin as I waited for him to catch up.

He soon appeared, panting a little as he ran to catch up and I grinned as he stalked toward me.

"Bad, little monster," he said, shaking a finger at me like I was a naughty school kid. "Am I going to have to get Ryder to punish you?"

Heat rose in my skin at that suggestion and I slid from the hood of the car, moving to meet him with a smile on my face. Leon was the only one of my Kings who not only accepted the way I felt about the others, but embraced it wholeheartedly too and the way that made me feel was hard to put into words.

"I haven't even begun being bad yet," I purred as I tiptoed up to kiss him again, running my hand over the front of his pants and stroking his dick where it strained against the material.

"If this isn't you being bad then I'm not sure I'm ready for when you are," Leon teased.

I pushed my tongue into his mouth and my fingers into his pocket at the same moment, hooking his car key into my grasp.

"I know what you're doing," Leon growled against my lips. "But you can rob me blind all the time you're stroking my cock like that."

I laughed as I stepped back, spinning his car key around my finger. "I want to take a quick detour. Is that okay?" I'd asked Old Sal to put the urn with Gareth's ashes in the safe at the club before I'd come to Aurora, not knowing what to do with them at the time. I felt guilty about that now. Gareth belonged with me. Not in some safe in a place he'd always dreamed of escaping. So it was time to get him back.

"Anything you want," Leon replied, walking around to drop into the passenger seat without any complaint.

I smirked to myself as I leapt in behind the wheel and started up the engine. "This might be a good moment to mention that I can't drive," I said as I put my foot on the accelerator and the car lurched forward a bit too quickly and with way too much jerking action.

Leon barked a laugh as I yelped in surprise and placed his hand on my thigh. "Let's teach you then."

My smile widened as he shifted his hand to place it beside mine on the wheel and helped me guide the car out of the parking lot.

I soon got the hang of the basics and my heart felt lighter as we headed down familiar streets until we slowly closed in on the place I used to call home.

Leon looked about curiously as we drove into one of the shittiest neighbourhoods in Alestria, but he didn't ask any questions until we pulled up in front of The Sparkling Uranus.

"Your mystery stop off is at a strip club in the asshole end of Alestria?" he teased as every Fae on the block turned to look at the flashy sports car with interest. The cars around here didn't tend to be clean, let alone expensive so Leon's latest ride stuck out like a sore thumb.

"This is kind of my home," I said, feeling a little self-conscious. He'd taken me to his family home and it had been like a fucking Barbie dream house on steroids.

Leon stayed quiet for a moment as his eyes trailed over the dirty streets and tiny apartments that surrounded us.

"So are we seeing your family or something?" he asked, giving nothing away about his feelings on the place.

"Well, no…I don't really have any family left. But the woman who runs this place is kinda like…I dunno… she's just been in my life a long time." I shrugged. "My mom used to work for her."

"Okay then, let's go." Leon unclipped his seatbelt and I smiled tentatively as I followed suit.

He locked the car and casually cast a wall of flames burning around it to keep the lingering Fae away from it while we were inside.

I led him around to the back door which was always wedged open and he followed me into the darkened hallways where the thump of music and the smell of sex and money waited for us.

The girls stripping on stage spotted me and called out hellos, not caring that they were interrupting their sets to greet me. I smiled warmly and led Leon to a seat by the central stage.

"I'll only be a few minutes," I said, pointing to get him to sit. "I just need to grab something I shouldn't have left behind."

"Okay," he replied, frowning faintly but not objecting as I left him there.

I shot away from him and headed through to Old Sal's office out back.

She was sitting behind her desk, puffing on a cigarette as usual but as she looked up to see who had interrupted her, her eyes widened with joy.

"Elise! Baby!" she cried, standing and opening her arms to me for a hug. I couldn't remember ever hugging her before, but I didn't object as I moved forward and let her pull me into an embrace.

As her arms wrapped around me, I was filled with a sense of homecoming and the feeling that I was where I belonged for the first time in a long time. I knew she was a Siren and she was probably projecting her own feelings onto me, but knowing that she felt that way unlocked something in my heart.

"Look at you," Sal cooed as she stepped back and assessed me in my party dress. "You look fit for centre stage! Punters would flock from all over Solaria to see you dance!"

I breathed a laugh and shook my head at the tired suggestion. I knew she'd pay me a small fortune to get me up on stage, but there was no way in hell that would ever happen. Although as I stood there, I found I didn't feel as strongly about my resolve to stay off of the stage as I had before.

I shook my head to clear it, trying to remember why I'd come in the first place as I was distracted by the strange feeling of being home and the general rightness this place held. I'd known that I was missing that sense of having a home, but I hadn't really expected to feel it so strongly here.

I narrowed my eyes on Sal, but I couldn't detect her power pushing at me. If she was manipulating me it was subtly done.

"I'm just popping by because I think it's time I took Gareth's ashes," I said, forcing myself to keep my jaw tight and chin high. I hadn't had anywhere to hide the urn when I'd first gone to the academy, but the Kings had all figured out that I was grieving by now and even if I hadn't been entirely honest with all of them about *who* I was grieving over, I felt safe enough to bring him with me at last.

Old Sal may have been almost like family but she wasn't. And he belonged with me until I could figure out where to scatter his ashes.

"Of course," Sal agreed, turning away from me to open up the safe.

I waited as she shoved stacks of aura notes aside and she finally pulled the small, black box from the back of the dark space.

I swallowed thickly as she passed it over to me. It was a wooden cube with a thin metal plate on the front of it bearing Gareth's name.

"I'll give you a moment," Sal said, pushing to her feet as tears pricked the backs of my eyes.

I hated this box. Hated that all that was left of my beautiful, funny, kind, loving, utterly hopelessly, noble brother was the contents of something so small. Because he wasn't small. He was big and bright and important and... gone.

Sal closed the door behind her, leaving me alone with my grief as it piled in on me. This place held so many memories of the two of us and I couldn't quite decide if I should come back here for the summer like Sal had offered or just leave it behind for good. I knew she wanted me dancing, but I wasn't going to be pushed into that no matter what I did.

Maybe I should just leave and never look back...

I sighed as I failed to make my mind up and levered the name plaque off of the urn before tossing it in the trash. I tucked the urn into my purse as I left, my fingers brushing over the wood before I closed it. It was impossible to know what I should do while this mystery hung over me. How could I make decisions about my life while I was still trapped in this bubble of grief? The only end to it would be in getting justice for him. Once I knew his killer had paid the price for taking him from me then I could figure out what to do with my life. And maybe in the meantime, coming back here for the summer wouldn't be the worst thing in the world.

When I made it back down to the bar, I found Leon leaning back in his chair as he spoke to Old Sal about something which didn't seem to be sitting too well with him if I was guessing right by the frown on his face.

I strained my ears to listen and Sal's voice came to me. "She could be a star, you know. Wouldn't you be thrilled to have a girl like that on your arm? A girl who was desired by every Fae for miles around, who was famous for-"

"I'd be thrilled to have Elise on my arm even if she spent her days rolling around in trash and eating onions," Leon said abruptly, pushing himself to his feet.

His Charisma rolled from him as his temper flared and every stripper in the joint stopped dancing and started to move towards him. He caught my eye and strode towards me purposefully, ignoring the tide of Mindys who were trying to grab his attention.

"Are you ready, little monster?" he asked me, his brows pulling together like he could see my grief written on my face.

"Yeah," I agreed, taking his hand as he offered it.

He tugged me towards the door with his shoulders tight and I threw a wave back at Old Sal as he guided me back out to the car.

Leon's fire magic fell away at his command and he led me straight to the passenger side, opening the door and ushering me in before getting in behind the wheel himself.

He started the engine and I frowned, wondering when he'd stolen the keys back from me but before I could ask, we tore away from The Sparkling Uranus so fast that I was pushed back into my seat.

"Are you okay, Elise?" he asked me seriously as we took a few turns before pulling out onto the freeway.

"Yeah," I replied, pushing my grief back into the little box where it lived within my heart. "There's just a lot of memories for me in that place."

"I don't like that woman," he said seriously, no sign of a smile around his lips for one of the first times ever.

"Sal? She's a bit odd but she's mostly harmless-"

"She's not harmless, little monster," he said seriously. "She was trying to manipulate me into getting you to go and work there for her. And I don't mean she was trying to talk me into it. She was pushing at me with one of the most subtle Siren spells I've ever felt."

"Don't worry about that," I replied dismissively. "She's always going on about that and it's never going to happen."

He relaxed slightly at my words and we both fell silent. I'd always hated the way Sal manipulated my mom so it wasn't like I was going to sit here defending her, but it wasn't easy to explain to Leon why I'd been feeling the draw to go back there all the same. If I spent the summer there then I could own my grief openly, honestly. And after months of hiding it and lying about it, I was beginning to think it might be good for me to be around people who knew exactly who I was and what I'd lost for a while. I'd never dance for her though. And I still planned on escaping Alestria as soon as I graduated if I managed to survive bringing down King.

I switched on the stereo as we drove and found a station playing I've Got A Feeling by the Black Eyed Peas. I cranked up the volume and tipped my head back to sing as the wind blew through my hair and Leon raced along the freeway way too fast. As expected, by the second chorus, Leon had forgotten his concerns and was singing along with me and I felt my grief sailing away on the wind as I bathed in the heat of his company yet again.

It took another twenty minutes to make it all the way out of the city and we climbed up into the mountains where vineyards peppered the landscape and made everything look like a shoot from a holiday brochure.

It was a beautifully warm evening and I watched the sun sinking towards the mountains with excitement buzzing through me at the idea of seeing the place that Dante called home.

We finally made it to a huge set of gates where a group of guards double checked who we were before we were admitted. We drove through more vineyards up a sloping drive to a beautiful cream house which stood at the peak of a long hill looking out over the view which surrounded us.

Leon parked his car up beside a flashy Hondusa and tsked beneath his breath as he cast his eyes over it.

"Roary's here," he explained as he got out of the car and moved around to open my door for me.

"Well maybe you can have some fun together," I suggested. "You shouldn't fight with the only brother you've got."

"Yeah, maybe," Leon agreed in a tone which said he didn't believe that for one moment and I sighed in disappointment.

He took my hand and led me towards the house where music was thumping and a huge archway of gold and navy balloons stood around the wooden double doors. But instead of heading up the steps to knock on the door, Leon tugged on my hand and led me to the right of the house instead where a long row of stables sat adjoining the property.

"Where are we going?" I asked.

"I had an idea a few weeks ago and I decided to save it for Dante's birthday," he said suggestively as he kept leading me towards the stables.

"What?" I asked in confusion.

"Another way that we can bend the rules, little monster. And I'm not waiting until the end of the party now that I know you're going commando," he growled and heat flooded through me at the idea of that.

Leon took his Atlas from his pocket and sent Dante a message asking him to meet us by the stables for his birthday present and I bit my lip as I tried to figure out what he had in mind.

We slipped around the back of the stables and I couldn't help but giggle as the sounds of the party reached us.

We made it to a sheltered spot behind the building where green grass peppered with wild flowers grew in a small space between the white wall and the first row of grape vines.

I snatched Leon's shirt in my fist and shoved him back against the wall with a growl of desire as I tried to figure out what he'd thought up.

"Tell me what you're planning," I demanded as I reached out to unhook his shirt buttons and reveal his golden skin.

"You'll have to wait and see," he teased, moving to touch me but I growled in frustration and knocked his arms back with a gust of air magic, locking them to his sides with a wicked smile.

"I don't like being kept in suspense," I warned.

"Tough. I'm not telling until Dante gets here and then the two of us are going to have you at our mercy." Leon smiled at me cockily and my lips twitched as I came up with a better idea.

"So you've thought about exactly how you're going to have me?" I asked, moving closer to him as I trailed my hands down his muscular chest, drawing a growl from his lips.

"Yeah. So just be a good girl and wait for Dante to get here."

"I don't think I want to be told what to do today," I replied wickedly, stepping closer and pushing my hand down to caress his fly. "So either you give up your secret or I'm going to force it from you."

Leon cleared his throat, struggling a little against the magic I was using to contain him.

"I'll take it to the grave," he joked.

I narrowed my eyes at him and undid his fly, pushing his jeans down and pulling the smooth, hard length of him free of his pants.

"Wait," he breathed but his eyes were already hooded and my smile widened as I started moving my hand up and down.

"Last chance to tell me," I warned. "Or I'm taking charge of this little fantasy once and for all and having you *my* way."

"I'm not telling," Leon replied firmly.

"Fine." I dropped to my knees before him and he gasped as I ran my tongue straight over the head of his dick.

"Elise," he growled, trying to fight off my magic one last time before I wrapped my lips around him.

Leon groaned as I drew him into my mouth and I couldn't help but release my own moan of desire as I felt just how much he wanted me.

I dug my fingernails into his thighs as I sucked and licked, pushing him closer to his climax with every movement of my lips and tongue.

He started cursing as he fell prey to my desire and I couldn't help but moan with need as I kept working at his body, tasting how much he wanted me and owning every inch of his pleasure for my own.

I released my hold on my magic and suddenly Leon's hands were in my hair as he clung to me, urging me on, forgetting that he'd been planning something else before I took charge.

I looked up at him as I felt him swelling in my mouth and he groaned and his fingers knotted in my hair.

I twisted my tongue around and drove my lips down his shaft one final time before he snarled my name and I tasted his orgasm filling my mouth.

A crackle of electricity ran up my spine as I heard Dante curse beneath his breath behind us.

"Merda santa. I thought it was *my* birthday," he joked and I pulled back as Leon groaned with satisfaction.

"Leon wouldn't tell me his plans for us, so I was ruining them for him," I explained as I ran my gaze over Dante hungrily.

"I'm less upset about that than I should be," Leon admitted with a laugh as he caught my hand and yanked me to my feet before tucking himself away.

"So what's this gift you have for me?" Dante purred as he moved closer and ran his fingers down my spine.

"In the deal you said that you can't jerk off in the same room as her," Leon explained finally. "But, out here, we aren't in a room."

My eyes widened as I turned to Dante with my teeth biting down on my bottom lip. In all the ways that we'd bent the rules, he'd always been left wanting at the end of it. If this was true then that meant that I could at least participate in his pleasure as much as he'd been able to participate in mine up until now.

Dante's gaze darkened with realisation. "He's right," he growled and I shot towards him, shoving him back against the stable wall as I grabbed his shirt and ripped it open in my excitement.

Dante laughed as I pressed my lips to his skin and ran kisses down his neck as I fisted my hand in his hair.

He growled in encouragement as my kisses moved lower and I tasted his skin, bathing in the feeling of his powerful muscles flexing beneath my touch.

Leon moved behind me, brushing my hair away from my neck as he kissed me too and I moaned as I found myself crushed between the two of them.

The heat of their bare chests pressing against my skin set my flesh alight with need and my heart leapt as I could feel the hard ridge of Dante's arousal driving against me urgently.

I ground my ass back against Leon as Dante's hand moved over the thin fabric of my dress, grazing my nipples in the most agonisingly delicious way.

I shifted my hand over his fly, rubbing my fingers around the swell of his dick as he growled against my cheek, pressing himself against me demandingly.

Electricity crackled around us and I moaned as it set every fibre of my of being alight.

Leon caught the edge of my skirt and started to hitch it up as I unbuckled Dante's belt, catching his hand and bringing it to his waistband as my heart thumped in anticipation.

"I can't quite work out if you're giving her to him as a birthday gift or if sharing her is something you do regularly," Roary's voice came from behind us suddenly and I damn near leapt out of my skin.

"Motherfucker," Leon snarled and I gasped as he dropped my dress and turned around to shield me from his brother.

Dante cleared his throat on a laugh as I buried my face against his chest and tried to banish the blush I could feel racing across my cheeks.

"Why the hell are you sneaking around out here, Roary?" Leon demanded. "Did you just sense me enjoying myself and come running to ruin it on purpose?"

"If I had that power I'd make use of it more often," Roary teased. "But

I'm actually out here because everyone is looking for the birthday boy."

"Well thanks to you, the birthday boy has blue balls now," Leon snapped.

I straightened my dress and forced myself to turn and look at Roary as Dante and Leon really fucking obviously buckled up their pants.

"I could tell you were a handful, sweetheart," Roary said to me with a dirty grin on his face.

"And I could tell you were an ass, so I guess we had each other pegged," I joked and his smile widened.

"Can't you just go and tell whoever is looking that Dante will be there in like twenty minutes?" Leon asked.

"I'd have guessed more like five at the pace you were all going at," Roary replied. "But as his mamma just told the pups to hunt him down, I'm guessing I've actually saved you a touch more embarrassment. I mean, I *know* what I just found you guys doing but imagine what little Fabrizio would say." He dipped his voice to imitate a small child as he continued. "*Mamma, mamma, I just found Dolce Drago by the stables playing with his friends. They were catching snakes and Elise won because she caught two!*"

I burst out laughing and Dante joined in.

"Thank you mio amico, it sounds like you just saved my poor mamma from a very awkward conversation over the birthday cake," Dante joked as he moved to follow Roary back to the house.

Leon still looked pissed as all hell with his brother and I offered him a smile as I moved to take his hand and follow the others in to the party.

Dante tried to make his torn shirt look vaguely presentable and I quickly brushed a few stalks of grass from my knees.

"C'mon then, put me out of my misery. What's the deal here?" Roary asked as we headed around to the front of the house.

"We're together," Leon snapped. "All of us. But no one can know about Dante being involved with us at the moment. So keep your fat mouth shut."

"Who am I going to tell? The girls at the next big sleepover while we're all braiding each other's hair?" Roary snorted a laugh at his own joke and I couldn't help but smile too.

Leon muttered something beneath his breath and I squeezed his fingers to cheer him up as we passed beneath the balloon arch.

"Get ready, bella," Dante purred as he turned to look back at me, his eyes dancing with mirth. "The Wolves are about to descend."

DANTE

CHAPTER TWENTY TWO

I led Elise and Leon through the house, my hard-on sinking fast as I followed Roary. Thank the stars he'd found us before a bunch of the pups had.

I threw a look at Elise over my shoulder, deciding to leave my shirt open considering there was no chance of buttoning it up again. "Do you make a habit of ripping people's shirts off at birthday parties, bella?" I murmured.

She smiled wickedly and I fought a groan, wishing we'd had a while longer. I didn't know when we were going to sneak away again, I just knew with an absolute certainty that we would be. But first, it was time to party.

We headed through to the conservatory and into the backyard where the raised garden overlooked the northern vineyard. A large table was set up to one side of the lawn, piled high with breads, cheeses, salad and cakes, cookies, sweets; every bowl and plate was practically overflowing. Mamma had cast an insect repellent spell around it and Uncle Hugo was currently frosting all the bowls with ice to keep everything fresh.

Some of my cousins were playing violins and hand-drums to a fast beat within the gazebo and half of my family were dancing already. More than half of them were drunk too. The lunch we'd had this afternoon was meant to be for immediate family only, but most of them had assumed that meant them and they'd turned up several hours before the party officially started to join us. And when my family gathered en masse like this, it was always carnage. And fun as hell.

"There you are, Dolce Drago!" Mamma appeared across the lawn, her fitted white dress covered in little blue flowers. Her dark hair was woven into a fishtail braid that Rosalie had done for her earlier and the only sign that she was flustered was the rosiness of her cheeks.

"I'll go call off the hunt," Roary said with a smirk, heading away across the grass toward a group of the pups who were howling to the moon and waving sticks like swords.

"Dalle stelle, Dante!" Mamma scolded. "What way are you wearing your shirt?" She frowned at the open buttons and I hoped she didn't notice half of them were missing.

"I popped a button." I shrugged. "I figured this looked better."

Mamma tutted. "Go upstairs and change, we're about to cut the cake." Her eyes slid to Leon and her face split into a grin. "Il mio leone bambino!" Mamma rushed forward and Leon wrapped his arms around her, her head barely tickling his shoulder. She stood back to admire him then swatted his arm. "Why are you late?"

"Sorry Aunt Bianca," he said with one of his mischievous smiles that always had my mamma melting.

Her smile became gooey again and she patted him on the cheek. "You missed the canapés but I saved some for you in the kitchen." She winked and Leon grinned broadly.

"Thank you. And don't you look as beautiful as the stars tonight?" he said and she blushed, waving her hand at him. *Suck up.*

He caught Elise's hand, pulling her forward and I stepped closer, my gut tightening as I waited for Mamma to greet her. Little did she know how much this moment meant to me. Even though the Wolves were known for being polyamorous, as soon as they found their mate, that ended. And it was unheard of for a Dragon to have multiple mates. Not that I'd ever done anything that stuck to the mould. So I was sure Mamma could accept the fact that Elise was shared. The problem was her ties to the Lunar bastardo.

"Hi, I'm Elise." She held out a hand with a polite smile that made me grin.

"She's my girl," Leon said proudly, his chest expanding and a pang of jealousy hit me that he could own her so publicly without consequence.

"Che meraviglia!" Mamma cried, lunging at Elise and wrapping her in her arms. "It's buono to meet you. And what a beautiful girl you are. I never thought I'd see mio bambino leone settling down."

She released Elise who had a deeper blush than I'd ever seen on her and her eyes sparkled with happiness. Mamma's eyes snapped to me. "What are you still doing here? Go change, Dolce Drago!"

"Sorry Mamma." I grinned, hurrying back inside and heading upstairs to my room. I soon had a fresh white shirt on and ran back down to join the party as quickly as I could.

The crowd had gathered in the gazebo and I headed inside, receiving claps on the shoulder and birthday wishes from all of my family. An enormous cake stood to one side of a table which was overflowing with presents. The cake was eight tiers high, the white layers of icing painted with black silhouettes of wolves howling to the moon and running together. At the very top, was a navy blue Dragon made entirely of icing, but it looked as real as if it was a small version of me. Its long tail draped down one side of the cake and lightning bolts had been painted around it. The words *Happy Birthday Alpha* ringed the top layer and a grin pulled at my mouth as Mamma ushered me toward it.

Elise and Leon stood amongst my family, chatting with Uncle Gino who was the size of a horse and had a plate of pastries in one hand and a glass of wine in the other.

I moved to Mamma's side and she handed me a large cake knife, hushing the crowd and the band.

"Today my little Drago is twenty years old," Mamma said, practically sobbing with pride already. Everyone started clapping and I smiled, dropping my arm over Mamma's shoulders.

"Speech!" Uncle Gino called, swaying as he sipped on his huge glass of wine.

Someone tossed me a microphone and I caught it at the last second to a round of cheers. I brought the mic to my lips, deciding to speak from the heart.

"It means everything to me to have you all here today," I started and a few whoops went up at the back of the crowd. "It's been a hard year. There are too many people who aren't here today. Some have left us, hurt us…but we won't speak of them today. Let's remember those who gave their lives for the Clan, for our home, our freedom, our family!"

Everyone raised their drinks and a couple of my cousins rushed forward to plant gold chalices of champagne in mine and Mamma's hands. I'd made Mamma one just like mine but hers had a ring of rubies around the base of it.

I tipped the champagne into my mouth, swallowing it as the bubbles fizzed along my tongue. When I lowered the cup, I found the Wolves were going wild, howling loudly and embracing one another.

Mamma started everyone off singing Happy Birthday to me and I smiled indulgently as the whole clan sang at the top of their lungs. They cheered and clapped as they finished and I gave a teasing bow before lifting the huge knife which was waiting for me to cut the cake.

"Let's eat!" I sliced out a huge chunk and put it on a plate for Mamma as the Wolves howled to moon and clamoured forward for a slice.

Tears swam in her eyes as she took it, then leaned in to kiss me on both cheeks. "Sono così orgoglioso di te, ragazzo mio. Your father is smiling down on you from the stars today."

My heart tugged at the mention of my father and I hugged Mamma tight, our broken hearts finding a whole between each other.

My cousin Angela soon stepped in to take over cutting the cake and I left her to it, carrying three plates over to Leon and Elise as the band started up again. Our cups were refilled constantly as wine bottles were passed around the gazebo and I was soon feeling high on life.

I hunted for Rosalie in the crowd. I hadn't seen her since lunch this afternoon. When Roary had arrived, she'd disappeared, but it wasn't like her to miss out on a party.

After we'd eaten our cake, I left Leon and Elise to dance, slipping out of the gazebo to go look for her. I spotted Roary beside the food table, surrounded by a bunch of my female cousins. He was trying to get to the food, but every time he moved, they tightened the circle around him, not letting him free.

"Cuginas!" I barked. "Get dancing, let the poor guy eat."

They giggled as they ran away, a few of them howling as they raced into the gazebo to join the party.

"Sorry, fratello," I said with a grin as Roary started filling a plate.

"I'm not using my Charisma on them," he swore.

"I trust you," I said with a smirk. My cousins had been trying to bag themselves a Lion husband for years and both he and Leon were always swamped by them at events like this.

A door sounded behind me and I turned to the conservatory, my brows arching as I spotted Rosalie there. She was in a stunning baby pink dress that swung around her thighs and her face was painted with subtle make-up and a soft lipstick to match the dress. Her long dark hair was half pulled up and her eyes held a hint of vulnerability in them which I'd never seen in her before. But more importantly than that, I'd never seen her in a dress before. Mamma had tried on countless occasions to get her to wear feminine clothes, buying her all kinds of fancy gowns, but Rosa had always refused. Even on baby Luca's cermonia delle stelle last month, her compromise had been a jumpsuit.

She looked more mature, like the Alpha she was becoming.

"Dal sole," I breathed. "You look beautiful, Rosa."

She moved across the lawn and I realised she was wearing wedges, making her taller than usual. She walked in them like she'd done so a thousand times.

"Well it is your birthday." She shrugged, but her eyes moved over my shoulder and I turned, finding Roary watching her with a smirk.

"Very pretty little pup," he teased before turning his attention back to his food.

I glanced at Rosalie as she practically glowed from the offhanded praise, raising a brow knowingly. She pressed her lips together, giving me an expression that said *if you say a word, I'll gut you.*

I said nothing, but couldn't fight a grin as I offered her my arm. "Come dance, cugina."

I leaned in close to her ear as we moved far enough away from Roary and whispered, "You're too young for that Leone, Rosa. He's ten years older than you."

She tsked, trying to pull her arm free of me, but I didn't let go. "I don't know what you're talking about."

I chuckled. "Okay, little lupo. Come and meet Elise."

"Oohh, your girlfriend?" she teased.

"No," I said offhandedly. "She's with Leon."

"*Sure* she is." She mimed zipping her lips, her eyes twinkling.

"I'm serious," I pressed but she just laughed.

I guided her into the gazebo to join Elise and Leon, finding them dancing wildly to the lively music filling the tent, surrounded by my family as they taught the two of them how to do the Oscura danza. It was a stupid routine where everyone patted themselves on the head while jumping on one foot, then did the do-si-do with a partner before grabbing hands in a group and running around in a circle. Every time they finished a round, they chugged a drink then started all over again.

I laughed, tugging Rosalie into the dance and grabbing Elise's hand as we joined in with a circle. Mio amore beamed at me, laughing wildly as more drinks were handed out again and I let Uncle Gino fill my chalice with wine before tossing it down my throat.

The Oscura danza started all over again and I was soon drunk as hell and laughing my head off. I grabbed Elise for the do-si-do this time then dragged her against me.

"Are you having a good time, bella?" I called over the music, delighted to see her looking so happy.

"Your family are so much fun!" she said, laughing again as Leon snatched her hand and I caught hold of Rosalie's as we started spinning in a circle once more.

The song finally ended and everyone clapped and howled.

A slow song started up and I panted, grinning at Elise as I tried to catch my breath. Rosalie snared Leon into a dance before he could catch hold of Elise and she shot me a wink as he twirled her around under his arm.

A grin bit into my cheeks as I offered Elise my hand. "Will you dance with me, carina?"

She smiled, stepping forward, placing one hand on my shoulder and the other in my palm. My heart thundered harder as we danced, her body inching closer and closer to mine until only a breath parted us. She gazed up at me under her lashes and my throat closed up. She was the sweetest, darkest thing I'd ever known. And I needed her like the sun needed to shine.

"I got you a gift," she said with a mischievous smile. "Shall I put it on the present table?"

"No," I said immediately. "Give it to me now."

She laughed, tipping her head back and it took everything I had not to kiss her in that moment. I was bound by a hundred reasons not to, but they stung more than ever right then.

She reached into her purse, taking out a smooth lump of rose quartz with a Dragon engraved on it. My heart rate rose as she pushed it into my pocket without a word before anyone could see. Because rose quartz meant belonging to someone. It was a promise and a pledge of its own. And though I'd hoped she was mine in some small way, to give me this meant it was true. And that set my veins on fire with electricity.

"Thank you, bella," I whispered and a shy grin pulled at her lips.

"Let's go outside," she said, then her fingers slipped through mine and she backed away into the crowd mouthing, *"Bring Leon."*

The song came to an end and I caught Leon's arm, tugging him away from Rosa and dragging him out of the gazebo without a word.

"Is it going down?" he asked excitedly and I nodded keenly.

"I think so, fratello."

He practically bounded along at my side as we raced after Elise and I hunted the yard for her. She stood at the far end of the garden by the steps that led down into the vineyard, turning back to face us so her dress swung around in the breeze.

She grinned then shot away down the steps and Leon and I rushed forward, our shoulders rubbing as we took chase.

I glanced back to make sure no one was watching, but my entire family were dancing in the gazebo, paying us no attention as we raced down the steep steps and into the vineyard.

"Little monster!" Leon called as we strode along beside the rows of vines, searching for the one she'd headed down.

I cupped my hands around my mouth and howled to the moon, letting her know we were hunting her.

Her laughter rang out from somewhere to my right and I caught Leon's shirt in my fist, tugging him down the nearest aisle. The vines ran all the way down to an orchard at the bottom of the hill and I grinned as I spotted her sitting up in an apple tree, swinging her legs as she watched us approaching.

We kicked up the dry earth as we raced down the narrow space side by side, charging into the orchard and gazing up at her in the tree. She was eating an apple, a wicked look in her eyes as she looked down at us. Her shoes were discarded by the foot of the tree and she flexed her bare toes as the wind whipped around her.

"Come down, amore mio," I purred.

"We'll make it worth your while," Leon added in a deep growl.

"I'm sure you will," she said, finishing the apple and tossing the core to the ground. "But I'd rather make it worth the birthday boy's while."

Her gaze slid to me and I sucked on my lower lip, half tempted to start climbing up there to get her. But with her Vampire speed, she could just run away if she didn't want to be caught.

"You're killing me, bella," I begged. "Come down."

"Tempt me," she said in a devilish tone and I groaned.

Leon moved toward me, reaching out to push his hand into my hair. "Come and get him, Elise."

He started unbuttoning my shirt and I swallowed a laugh, glancing at Elise to see if she was enjoying this. The light in her eyes said she was and I rolled my shoulders back as Leon pushed my shirt off, my gaze locked on her the whole time.

She bit down on her lip as Leon brushed his knuckles over my chest. "Are you coming down?" he called, shooting her a hopeful glance.

"Not yet," she whispered excitedly and I released a dark laugh.

"Do you like what you see, little Vampira?" I moved forward, wrapping my hand around the back of Leon's neck. I'd had enough to drink that I didn't give a shit what I had to do to get her down here. And if she wanted a show…

I pressed my mouth to Leon's and he clutched my hair tighter, pushing his tongue into my mouth. His stubble raked against mine and though I didn't feel anything sexually toward him, the moan that left Elise had me hardening for her instantly.

She was suddenly beside us, shoving us apart with a desperate need in her gaze. She moved between us, leaning back against Leon and reaching behind her to cup the back of his neck, turning her head towards him and drawing him down for a kiss.

I watched hungrily, stepping forward and brushing my hand over her breast, feeling her nipple pebbling beneath her dress. She gasped as I released a line of electricity into her body, breaking the kiss with Leon and he pushed her toward me. Her eyes became hooded as she knocked my hand away from her dress, approaching like a hungry animal.

"This is about you," she said and my cock swelled for her.

"Fuck yes," Leon agreed, walking up behind her and placing his hands on her waist.

Elise leaned in to my throat, scraping her fangs across my skin in the most exciting way. I grabbed hold of her hair as she moved lower, nipping and licking and driving me crazy as she bent forward and unbuckled my pants.

The sound of a zip being undone reached me and my gaze drifted to Leon as he undid her dress and she stood upright, letting it fall around her feet. She was completely naked, her perfect body just inches away from me and begging to be claimed.

"Elise," I groaned breathily, eyeing the swell of her tits as I freed myself from my pants. "Touch her," I commanded Leon and he tugged her back against him by the hips before lowering his hand between her thighs. She gasped, leaning back against his shoulder as he rubbed his fingers over her clit, a teasing grin on his face.

I moved up close to her, taking my hardened length in my hand and rubbing up and down in firm strokes. Elise tilted forward to continue running her mouth over my chest and I groaned, dropping my head to watch her as I fucked my hand like a teenager and cursed Ryder over the deal for the millionth time.

"Get on the ground," Leon growled at me and I dropped down onto my back without a second's hesitation.

I watched as he pushed his fingers inside my girl, making her moan with every pump of his hand and pleasure built at the base of my cock in response.

He released her suddenly and shoved her down on top of me. She laughed headily as she knelt either side of my thighs, dropping her mouth to my ear and flicking her tongue around the shell. Electricity crashed through me in waves and she groaned as she felt it too, the air charging around us.

Leon knelt down behind her and I smirked at the sound of his fly dropping. Elise braced herself on my shoulders and her nails dug in as he entered her with a forceful thrust. I reached up to trace my thumb over her lips, jerking myself harder as my girl was fucked above me so I could almost imagine what it would be like to have her myself.

She raked her nails over my shoulders as she cried out with every powerful thrust of Leon's hips. I growled needily, letting go of my throbbing dick and taking hold of her hips instead, driving her back onto him and taking pleasure in the noises coming out of her mouth.

"Leon…Dante," she moaned. Then she took my hand, reaching between us and guiding my fist back onto myself. She kept her hand wrapped around mine, guiding my movements until my mind was blowing and I was building towards fucking heaven.

"Merda santa," I gasped as I leaned up to run my tongue across her collar bone, sending a wave of electricity into her skin.

Leon groaned as he felt it too and I lowered my free hand to the base of her stomach, letting electricity trickle down her skin to that sensitive place between her thighs.

"Fuck!" she cried, her hand tightening around mine and pleasure rocketed through my dick. "I'm so close."

"Me too," Leon said in a strained voice.

"Me three," I rasped just before I exploded and they both followed me a second later. I swore through my release and clutched Elise's hip, my fingers digging in as I stared up into her sea green eyes.

Elise cupped my cheek, a smile pulling at her lips and she panted heavily. "Happy birthday, Drago."

ELISE

CHAPTER TWENTY THREE

I was beginning to understand why Ryder called Nightshade *Nightmare*. I chewed on my bottom lip as I stalked across the grounds to my latest session with her which had been rearranged last minute, *again*.

I was starting to think that she was doing it on purpose to try and catch me in different emotional states, and the worst thing about that was that this time she damn well had. With such short notice, I hadn't been able to track down any of the Kings to overload me with lust before meeting her and had to head straight to my session instead.

I refused to use my Vampire speed though. If she was going to give me a ten minute warning of her schedule change then that wasn't my problem. My more than leisurely pace was the least she deserved.

While I walked, I tried to coax my brain to come up with lots of distracting thoughts. The memory of Leon and Dante sharing me at the party had given me plenty of fantasy ammo, but that had been a few days ago now and it wasn't keen enough to drown out my other emotions anymore.

Leon had gone home for the evening so I hadn't even been able to shoot around to his room for a few minutes of passion to distract me. And I couldn't even get started on Gabriel. He was still insisting that I was *going through a phase* that would pass as soon as we had our Divine Moment and I became his Elysian Mate. And though I was by no means against hooking up with him again, I wasn't looking to do it on monogamous terms. So I was leaving him to stew over his blue balls while he decided whether he liked me as I was or not.

As I drew closer to the corridor which held her room, Eugene suddenly rounded the corner, running towards me with his hands pressed to his face and tears staining his cheeks.

"Eugene?" I gasped, moving into his path to halt him. "What's wrong?"

"N-nothing," he hiccupped, trying to skirt around me.

"It's clearly something. Talk to me-"

"Honestly, it's okay. I've just been trying to figure some stuff out with Nightshade and it just all, well…people here are so *horrible*, you know. And sometimes I think that all I have to do is make it through my time here and I'll be free, but it's like she said…it's a big bad world out there full of Fae who will rip your head off just to gain an advantage and if I can't handle this, then how am I going to handle that?"

His eyes bored into mine with a desperate kind of fear as I tried to hunt for the right thing to say to that.

"Eugene…" I breathed, not even knowing where to begin. "I know that people can be assholes, but you're strong enough to face this. And everything else life has to throw at you too. You just have to-"

"Please don't tell me to Fae up, Elise. Because sometimes I don't feel like I'm Fae at all." A sob tore from his throat and before I could say anything else, he shifted into his Tiberian Rat form and scurried away, leaving a heap of clothes on the floor in front of me.

"Eugene!" I called, taking a step after him, but the sound of a door opening down the corridor halted me in my tracks.

"You're late, Miss Callisto, you don't want to lose rank points do you?" Nightshade's voice called. "Or worse, face expulsion?"

Fuck me, I hate this bitch.

I ground my teeth and headed down the hall to join her in the room, cooling my temper and glancing at the clock as I walked through the door, smirking to myself as I realised it was almost quarter past seven.

"Sorry I'm late," I said in a falsely polite tone as she waved me in towards the couch. "But you didn't give me much notice."

"Never mind, never mind, let's just hop straight into it, shall we? I'm pleased to say that you're not overloaded on lust for once, so perhaps we will be able to make some deeper progress with your issues today."

"Great," I muttered, crossing my legs beneath me as I tried to focus on my fantasies again.

"We were discussing the funeral in our last session," she reminded me as if I might have forgotten. I'd done a lot of work pretending that day had never happened and trying to scrub it from my memory, but of course she wanted to dredge through it and rake over it, stretching me through the emotional wringer. *Nosey bitch.*

"Mmm," I said noncommittally.

"You said there weren't many people in attendance?" Nightshade pushed.

By the stars, I hate you.

"Just me and my mom." We hadn't had the money for a funeral so it had been an open casket with no magical protection on it and a fifteen minute slot in the state run funeral parlour. As we couldn't afford the price of having him buried in a properly warded graveyard, we'd had to settle for cremation and a wooden plaque which would be displayed in the local graveyard entry hall for three years. After which, if I couldn't afford to pay for it to stay, it would be taken down and the spot given over to some other poor family. It would be like he'd never existed at all. Who knew there was an expiry date on grief?

"Open casket?" she asked.

"Yes," I replied tersely, the pain of that memory clawing at something raw and bleeding in my heart. I hadn't even been to visit that pathetic plaque since they'd put it up. Having his ashes in my closet didn't make me feel any less guilty either. I wanted to get him a proper headstone one day and scatter them there so that I could visit him regularly, in a proper resting place. But considering the price of a headstone and a plot in one of the warded graveyards, I didn't imagine that day would come any time soon.

"And how did it feel seeing him like that?" Nightshade pushed, her fucking Siren gifts nudging at me, feeding on my heartache and sorrow and urging me to tell her more.

I drew in a shuddering breath as that memory crashed over me and tears pricked the backs of my eyes. I could feel her influence slipping beneath the cracks in my defences, but in the face of this grief it was hard to reinforce my mental shields.

"Exactly how you'd imagine it felt," I snapped. "No one wants to see their flesh and blood like that. My brother deserved better than a fucking state funeral with no one there to mourn him. It was like he didn't even matter, like no one even gave a shit that his whole life was stolen from him!"

Nightshade stayed quiet for a long moment as my heart pounded with the agony of my loss and she sucked it in greedily.

She leaned forward slowly and I could feel her power increasing as she flexed her Order muscles. My tongue loosened and I found myself wondering why I hadn't trusted her with this before. Why I hadn't told her more of it, all of it? I should have let her pick my pain apart and stitch me back together anew. She was so kind and supportive, she only wanted what was best for me, she only wanted to *help*. And I needed help so badly that I could hardly breathe sometimes. This grief crushed me, drowned me, suffocated me and she could free me from it.

"*Elise*," Nightshade purred in a satin soft voice. "You said, *brother*. Do you want to tell me why you lied about it being your father before now?"

A tiny little voice in the back of my skull started screaming in panic for me not to trust her, but it was all too easy to ignore because it was wrong. So wrong. Nightshade was here to help me, to save me, I needed to tell her the truth. I *owed* her the truth.

"My brother," I said slowly, a tear slipping down my cheek. "Was the best person I've ever known. He was so *good*. He wanted to save me from the life I'd been born into. He was *going* to save me. We were going to run away from here and leave it all behind…but then he left me behind instead…"

"And how does that make you *feel*?" she urged, sucking on my sorrow and drawing my magic out of me alongside it. But I didn't mind. I wanted to give it to her. It was the least she deserved for helping me so much.

"Betrayed," I breathed the ugly truth which I'd never even admitted to myself before. "He promised he'd never leave me behind…" More tears spilled down my cheeks as the floodgates gave out and the pain consumed me. "He promised he'd never lie to me either but that wasn't true. He had so many secrets, so many deep, dark secrets…"

"Like what?" Nightshade asked, her grip on my emotions iron clad.

"He *knew*," I said. "He knew about the things happening in this academy."

"This academy?" Nightshade's surprise cut through her concentration and for a brief moment, my emotions were my own again. My fist snapped shut but before I could gather myself together, her influence increased.

Her grip on my emotions tightened instantly and I found myself wanting to answer every and any question she might ever have.

"Who was your brother, Elise?" Nightshade asked, forgetting to lace her voice with sugar in her desperation to know.

My lips parted, my brother's face sprang to mind and I was about to tell her everything she wanted to know. But as I pictured him, his brows pinched together and he started shouting at me. At first I couldn't hear the words, but then they cut through the clouds of bullshit she'd concocted.

Don't trust her!

I shot out of my seat with a snarl of rage, snatching a huge vase of flowers off of the table between us and smashing the whole thing over Nightshade's head.

It happened so quickly, I was pretty sure she didn't even see me coming.

She fell out of her chair with a crash that rattled the floorboards and I stared at her with my lips parted in shock.

I just attacked the school counsellor. Holy shit in a Christmas basket.

GABRIEL

CHAPTER TWENTY FOUR

I was pouring over a Numerology textbook in the library, lost to the words before me as I drowned myself in studying. It was only a few weeks until our end of year exams would begin and I wanted to be prepared. I might have been the most powerful Fae in the school, but that didn't mean shit unless I had the knowledge to back it up.

The page blurred before me and a powerful rush of feelings tore through my body out of nowhere. I lost sight of the book and a vision flared in front of my eyes of Elise gasping in fear, clawing at her hair as anxiety sliced through her body into mine. My gaze fell on the couch behind her then to a photo on the wall of Miss Nightshade collecting some certificate.

The vision faltered and I leapt out of my seat, startling several students around me.

My Atlas pinged and I snatched it from my pocket, eyeing the message.

Elise:
I need your help. I've done something bad. I'm in Nightshade's counselling room.

Please hurry. X

My heart pounded to a strange beat as I read that over. I'd been going to help her anyway but the fact that she'd actually asked me made me feel all kinds of things. Mainly, I was just relieved that she felt like she could call on me when she was in need of help, and that she trusted me enough to know I'd come.

I ran from the building, the librarian shouting after me as I went, but I didn't look back.

I sprinted to Altair Halls, bolting inside and racing up the staircase in the direction of Nightshade's room. I sped down the corridor, skidding to a halt outside the door.

Ryder frowned at me from a couch beside it. "Well if it isn't Big Bird on a day out from Sesame Street. What's the matter? Do you need to talk to someone about how Elmo's been touching you inappropriately?"

"Shut the fuck up, Draconis." I strode up to the door and he dove into my way, ramming his back against it.

"Go away, asshole. Elise is busy."

"Move. Aside," I snarled, raising a hand to cast magic at him. I didn't need this shit right now.

"Or what?" He smirked.

I snatched a fistful of his shirt, dragging him forward so he was nose to nose with me. "I don't have time for your bullshit." I threw him aside, but he rocked the ground beneath my feet so I couldn't make it to the door.

"Elise is in trouble!" I barked and his brows drew together.

"Well why didn't you fucking say that?!" He reached for the door handle and I knocked his hand away.

"You can fuck off, I'll help her," I commanded as his shoulder slammed into mine. If this had anything to do with Gareth, I couldn't let the snake in on it. I'd made a vow of trust with her.

"I'm not going anywhere," he hissed, bashing his palm against the door.

It opened suddenly and we stumbled forward into the room, coming face to face with an ashen-faced Elise.

My gaze fell on Miss Nightshade who was slumped on the floor in a heap beside a broken vase and I quickly shut the door behind me. "Holy shit."

"Yeah," Elise said, starting to pace as she clawed a hand through her lilac locks. "She started pulling on my emotions, she got under my skin and started making me tell her stuff I didn't want her to hear - and I just snapped."

"Fuck me, is she dead?" Ryder asked, not even trying to hide the hope in his voice.

"No," Elise said, looking to the woman on the floor.

"What did you tell her?" I asked seriously, throwing a look at Ryder. "Maybe Draconis should go…"

"I told you, I'm not going any-fucking-where and if you suggest it again, I'll carve my answer into your forehead," Ryder growled.

"It's fine," Elise said quickly. "Ryder can stay."

"What does she know about you, baby?" Ryder's voice softened to a tone I'd never heard come from his mouth before. He moved toward her with a frown and I stepped closer to her too, my neck prickling with irritation.

Elise dropped down onto the couch, pressing her face into her hands.

"You don't have to tell him," I said.

"Fuck you," Ryder hissed. "She can make up her own mind."

"He can know," she said at last. "Everything's fucked now anyway," she added, looking to Nightshade with an expression of defeat.

"We can figure this out," I promised.

She nodded, giving me a sad smile before looking to Ryder. I clenched my jaw, watching his expression as she opened her mouth to tell him the truth. It didn't sit right with me at all, but it was her decision. And I'd stand by her no matter the consequences.

"Do you remember Gareth Tempa? He was a Pegasus here at the

academy, he died in January."

"I remember," Ryder said in a low tone, lines appearing on his forehead as he waited for her to go on.

"Well...I'm his sister."

Ryder's expression gave nothing away but slowly, he nodded. "Why are you here?"

"To avenge him. The FIB said he died because of an accidental Killblaze overdose, but they're wrong. Gareth never would have taken drugs willingly. So I came here to find out who was responsible."

"So that's why you were trying to beat Harvey Bloom into telling you where the Killblaze comes from?" Ryder asked and I frowned. I hadn't known she'd done that.

"Yeah...I found out that Gareth was dealing it and I thought that maybe he was getting it from the person making it. He wouldn't have wanted anything to do with that stuff unless he was desperate...which I now know he was, but maybe he tried to get out of dealing and the person making it snapped or...I don't know." Elise shook her head, her brow furrowing with the unanswered questions that still haunted her.

"Why was he desperate?" Ryder asked, instantly latching on to the part of that explanation which pained her the most.

"He needed money to pay off our mom's debt. For me. To protect me. But if I'd known about it, I would have just paid the debt myself-"

"Don't ever say that," I growled. "You are no more responsible for that debt than Gareth was and he was right to protect you from what your mother tried to force you to do."

"So that's why he wanted to work for me," Ryder said thoughtfully as Elise looked up at him then his gaze hardened as he asked her another question. "What did your mom try and force you to do?"

"She was arranging for me to dance in the strip club where she worked as a way to pay her gambling debt...I had no idea."

Ryder hissed darkly and the anger that flashed in his gaze said he wanted to kill her mother for that. I'd never thought I'd agree with the snake on anything, but I guessed our contempt for Elise's mother was one thing we could wholeheartedly agree on.

"That doesn't matter now," Elise said dismissively even though it was obvious how much that hurt her. "The issue is that I think Nightshade has something to do with all of this and she almost found out who I am. I've seen her with the Fae responsible for killing that boy out in The Iron Wood, but whoever it is is using a powerful concealment spell to hide their identity."

I stepped closer to Ryder, squaring my shoulders. "I don't suppose you'd know anything about who they might be, huh Draconis?"

Ryder's eyes shifted to me, turning into reptilian slits as his glare intensified. I could feel him trying to force some hypnosis over me, but my mental shields were firm, keeping him out.

"And what exactly are you trying to suggest?" he spat, his right hand curling into a fist so the word *pain* stared up at me.

"I think you know," I said in a deadly tone.

Elise shot between us with a spurt of Vampire speed. "Can we please focus on the problem at hand? I don't think Ryder's responsible."

Ryder threw me a smirk and my jaw tightened. I took hold of Elise's arm, guiding her closer so I could speak in her ear.

"With all due respect, Elise, I don't think you can rule out the snake considering he's the most psychotic asshole on campus."

"If I killed someone, it would be a lot more painful than an overdose," Ryder added in an offhanded way like that was a good thing.

Elise shook me off, giving me a firm look. "I'm not asking you to believe me, but I'm telling you to drop it, Gabriel."

Ryder chuckled and I could have beat his smug face in for it.

"I know what to do," he said and Elise pulled away from me, turning to him hopefully.

Ryder folded his arms as his gaze fell to Nightshade. "I'll snap her neck, then we can roll her up in a carpet and leave her here until the middle of the night. When no one's around on campus, Big Bird can fly her down to The Weeping Well and I'll meet him there with a vat of acid. We'll toss her down there and I'll pour the acid over the body to make sure there's nothing left of her. That well is the perfect place to dispose of a corpse and the fact that every asshole on campus thinks it's haunted will stop anyone nosing around it too much anyway. Then, when the FIB come looking for her, me and Elise will tell them Nightshade didn't show up for our counselling sessions so we went back to my room and spent the night there fucking."

"Hold the fuck on, we aren't going to kill a member of faculty," I said in disbelief, looking to Elise.

She was gazing at Ryder with her lips parted and her cheeks flushed. Was she actually turned on by this fucking psycho??

"*Elise*," I snarled and she snapped around to look at me, her blush deepening.

"Yeah, right. Of course we're not going to murder Nightshade." She mock saluted me and I narrowed my eyes on her.

"Good," I said slowly. "So what *are* we going to do?"

Ryder released a grunt of annoyance, waiting for Elise to answer.

"Well…" She bit down on her lower lip then nodded as she thought of some plan. "We might as well interrogate her. Maybe she'll tell me who killed Gareth once and for all. And if the FIB come for me, then at least I'll have a chance to get to his killer first."

"I'm really fucking hard for you right now," Ryder commented and I glowered at him.

"She needs our help, asshole, so maybe keep your dick in your pants, yeah?"

He ignored me completely, his gaze fixed on Elise. "Don't worry about the FIB, baby, I can deal with Nightshade's memory. I've got an Elixir of

Memoria Deleo in my room and if she gets a good dose, she'll forget the past twenty four hours entirely."

"Really?" Elise gasped, hope shining from her eyes.

"There's side effects of a dose that strong, it's only meant for short term memories," I stepped in. "She'll be shitting her pants and hallucinating for two days straight and she'll know someone fucked with her head."

"But she won't know who," Elise said, arching her brows at me as she gave me the biggest doe eyes I'd ever seen.

"Yeah, and who cares if she shits her pants and sees Dumbo flying through her house for days?" Ryder snorted. "I personally see that as a bonus."

I pressed my tongue into my cheek then slowly nodded my agreement. It was the only way, and if it meant Elise could get answers then I was all for it.

"Alright." I strode toward Nightshade, scooping her up and placing her in her chair. Her chin rested against her chest as I pressed my hand to the wound on the back of her head. "I'll heal her when you're ready, Elise."

She moved to stand in front of her and Ryder stepped to her side with a wicked grin on his face. He was enjoying this way too fucking much in my opinion.

"I can hypnotise her before she gets her mental shields up," Ryder said and I had to admit that was a pretty good idea.

"Do it," Elise instructed me and I poured healing energy into Nightshade.

She groaned as she woke and Ryder stepped forward, catching hold of her chin and making sure he was the first thing she saw. She jerked violently then fell still and Ryder stepped back, looking to Elise whose eyes glazed as he put her under his spell too.

"Let your shields down," he commanded me and I pursed my lips, not wanting him inside my head. "Fine, go ahead and miss the show then."

"Wait," I said before he checked out to wherever he'd sent Nightshade and Elise. "Bring me with you."

Ryder smirked as I let my shields down, my heart thrashing in my chest as he caught me in his gaze. The world shifted around me and I found myself in a chamber with blood red walls and Nightshade lying at the heart of it on a steel table, looking unconscious. I guessed Ryder had her mind in his control now.

Elise was dressed in a tight leather dress with a whip in her hand and Ryder was eyeing her like a fucking piece of candy. His chest was bare and blood speckled his skin like he'd just finished murdering somebody.

I opened my mouth to rebuke him for Elise's outfit but all that came out was a honk. I gasped, realising something was horribly wrong. I gazed down at my arms which were coated in yellow feathers and two massive bird feet poked out beneath me.

"Hey Big Bird," Ryder said with a wide grin.

"*Ryder*," Elise barely controlled her laughter and I scowled, grabbing hold of his vision and forcing away his bullshit Sesame Street version of me.

"Very funny," I said dryly. "At least I'm not comical to look at in real life."

"The only thing amusing about my looks is your reflection in my eyes," Ryder tossed back.

"Enough. Cooperate or both of you can leave me with her to do this myself," Elise demanded, looking between us.

We both fell silent and Elise blew out a breath. "Wake her up."

Ryder straightened and the vision shifted until Nightshade was pinned to a huge metal X, standing upright before us. She awoke with a gasp, her eyes frantically searching our faces before settling on Elise.

"What have you done, you stupid girl?!" she yelled, but terror leaked into her expression.

"I need answers," Elise growled, moving closer. "And you're going to give them to me or we're going to hurt you."

Ryder smiled darkly as my pulse rose. I wanted this for Elise. I'd do what it took to get the truth for her, and at least in here none of the torture would be real. But sometimes I worried about the darkness which rose in her in her desperation for vengeance.

"Tell me who the cloaked Fae you work for is," Elise snarled, baring her fangs. I stepped to her side, flexing my fingers.

"How do you know about that?" Nightshade snapped.

"That wasn't the answer to the question she asked." Ryder lifted a hand and ropes appeared around Nightshade's wrists and ankles, starting to pull her limbs in opposing directions.

"Ah – stop!" she shrieked, but Ryder only intensified the torture, drinking in her pain with a sigh of delight.

"I don't know who they are!" Nightshade wailed as something popped in her shoulder. "I've never seen their true face!"

"Liar," I hissed and Nightshade looked to me with a glimmer of fear in her gaze. "Don't fall for that girl's lies, Mr Nox. There's something wrong with her. She's broken beyond repair!"

I strode forward in a rage, locking my hand around her throat and baring my teeth. "You talk about her like that again and I'll make sure Draconis leaves you in here for days, experiencing every kind of torture imaginable. And he's got a *really* good imagination." I glanced over my shoulder at him and he smirked at Nightshade, making her tremble beneath my touch. "So you answer anything Elise asks you, and I'll make sure he lets you out of here. If not…" I shrugged, stepping away from her and she gazed after me with her lower lip trembling.

"I'm telling the truth," she rasped. "I've never seen their face."

"Fine," Elise huffed. "Then what are they trying to achieve? What's with the creepy ass ritual and murdering of innocent Fae?" She slashed the whip in her hand and Nightshade flinched.

"Power of course," she blurted. "The Card Master can take Elemental power from each of the Fae who kills themselves on the full moon using dark magic."

"So what's your part in that?" I growled as Ryder made the ropes tighten even further so Nightshade yelped.

"The Card Master needs the sacrifices to be willing," she panted as sweat beaded on her brow. "I find candidates which are…suitable."

"What is that supposed to mean?" Ryder demanded and Nightshade screamed as he pulled her arms and legs even further.

"They're suicidal!" she cried. "The Killblaze pushes them over the edge, drowns them in those suicidal thoughts until one or two of the subjects are willing to give their lives and power to my master."

"Did you try to do that to Gareth Tempa? Did you force him to take Killblaze?" Elise demanded, her expression contorted. My heart twisted and I moved closer to her, wishing I could take away her pain.

Nightshade's brow pinched in confusion. "Tempa…no. I never sent him to the Card Master."

Elise nodded stiffly and a war of emotion broke out in her eyes.

Ryder blinked and the large X fell away, making Nightshade fall to her knees. She looked up through her hair, her shoulders shaking as she stared between us like she wasn't sure who to fear most.

"So what's your master's plan?" Elise hissed. "What do they want to do with all that power they're stealing?"

"The Card Master will one day rise against the Celestial Councillors when they're powerful enough, then they will defeat them and take over the whole of Solaria. And their loyal followers, the Black Card, will sit in the Court of Solaria alongside our master."

Ryder growled and electricity daggered down from the ceiling, tearing into Nightshade's body. She jerked violently under the flow of power and I glanced at him with a frown. She wasn't exactly withholding information, so was the torture really necessary? He definitely looked like he was getting off on it.

The electricity finally stopped and Nightshade lay wheezing, her fingers twitching as she tried to cast magic, but she wasn't in control here. Ryder had her fully captured in his mind.

"What will you do now that the Killblaze lab has been destroyed?" Elise asked with a smile twisting her lips up. She'd told me about how she'd found it beneath the toilet block and although I worried about how much she was pissing off these crazy assholes, I had to admit I was seriously impressed by the fact that she'd blown it up.

"You little bitch!" Nightshade snarled as she realised Elise must have been the culprit. "Do you have any idea what you've done?"

"Yes," Elise said brightly. "I've fucked up your pathetic plans, I've saved people from you and your asshole of a master. But that's not what I asked you." She strolled forward and stepped onto Nightshade's hand, making her shriek in pain as she pressed down her heel.

"We will have to make a new lab - but that will take time!" Nightshade gasped. "That's all I know – I swear!"

Elise gazed down her nose at her, driving her heel harder onto her hand. "If you're lying, I'll make sure you regret it."

Nightshade nodded several times, gazing up at Elise through teary eyes as she tried to get her hand free.

Elise turned and walked away, nodding to Ryder. "Make her spill everything she knows."

Ryder moved forward with a hungry glint in his gaze.

"There's nothing else, I swear," Nightshade vowed and I could see the truth in her eyes.

"Elise," I said quietly and she looked at Nightshade with a frown. "I think she's being honest."

Elise nodded and Nightshade slumped forward.

"Wh-what will you do with me now? I won't tell anyone this happened," she said in desperation.

"We all know that's not true," I said quietly, mostly to scare her shitless.

She shuddered, curling in on herself. "Please don't kill me."

"Knock her out," Elise whispered to Ryder and the hypnosis evaporated. Nightshade was asleep in her chair before us and I released a breath of relief.

"I'll fetch the Elixir to remove her memories," Ryder said, heading for the door and exiting.

Silence pressed in on me as I looked to Elise. "Are you alright?"

She moved toward me at speed, wrapping her arms around my waist and pressing her cheek to my chest. "I *know* Gareth is linked to this," she said and a sob broke free of her.

I clutched her tightly, holding her close as my heart ached for her. "We'll find out how," I swore.

"I just don't know where to look anymore. It feels like every lead I have is coming to nothing. Like doors are being shut in my face at every turn."

"The more we rule out, the closer we get," I said gently. "You're so strong, I know you'll find the truth, Elise. But I'm afraid of what it'll cost you to get it."

"I'd pay any price," she said bitterly.

"I know…that's what terrifies me. You're so very fucking precious to me, my little angel."

She lifted her chin up, her eyes asking for a kiss and I leaned down to give it to her. Her silence hurt me, because I knew I hadn't changed her mind at all. She would do whatever it took to get her answers, but I couldn't let her give her life for this. She had so much ahead of her, even if she couldn't see it right now.

Her mouth moved against mine as she clutched onto me, and it felt like the world came together right where our lips met.

Emotion spun through my body and I jolted as a vision swept me away from her arms. The Sight showed me the same guy I'd seen before with raven hair and dark eyes. But this time he was standing on a Pitball pitch, pumping his fist in the air. The name on the back of his shirt read *Orion* and recognition hit me at that name.

Lance Orion. He was Zodiac Academy's star player. He'd had photoshoots in magazines all over Solaria as they tipped him to be picked up by the Solarian Pitball League once he graduated. The image changed and Orion sat before me on a large bed with books spread out around him. The texts drew my gaze and I saw a hundred spells staring back at me. But they weren't things I'd ever learned. They were dark magic.

I jolted out of the vision, inhaling sharply and Elise's eyes widened.

"What is it?" she asked.

"I saw something. A guy. Lance Orion-"

"The Pitball player?" she questioned in confusion.

I nodded quickly. "He does dark magic."

Her lips parted in surprise. "Are you sure?"

"Yeah." I clutched her shoulders. "Elise, The Sight showed me him. So he must be important. Why else would my gifts show him to me now of all times?"

She nodded eagerly, hope filling her gaze. "Then we'll speak to him when we go to Zodiac Academy. Maybe he can help us figure out how to stop King."

I smiled as relief filled me, so glad I'd found some way to assist Elise in her hunt for her brother's killer at last.

She embraced me just as Ryder stepped back into the room with a small green bottle in his hand. His eyes studied the two of us wrapped together, but he said nothing, striding over to Nightshade and pouring the contents between her lips.

"She'll wake here and won't know anything," Ryder announced when he was done and Elise pulled away from me.

"Thank you." She looked between us. "I'd be lost without you both."

I shared a look with Ryder, wondering what it was she saw in him. All I ever saw was a heartless Fae with endless blood on his hands. But maybe there was more to him that I was missing. It didn't matter either way. The stars would bring Elise and I together eventually, and once we were Elysian Mates, she would never want anyone but me.

GARETH

CHAPTER TWENTY FIVE

ELEVEN MONTHS BEFORE THE SOLARID METEOR SHOWER…

"*Mr Tempa? We need you to come down to the station to answer a few questions.*"

I swallowed thickly as those words sank in, clutching my Atlas to my ear and tossing up a silencing bubble before I replied. I was walking through the Acrux Courtyard with the Lunar Brotherhood dominating the bleachers on my right and the Oscura Clan spilling all over the picnic benches to my left; I sure as shit didn't want either of them to know I was on the phone to the FIB.

"*Erm, can I ask what this is about…Officer?*" *I asked, my voice not coming out anywhere near as strong as I'd have liked it to.*

"*We are conducting an investigation into a professor at your Academy molesting one of the students there.*"

"*Oh?*" *I asked as casually as I could manage.*

"*Don't play dumb with us lad, we know you're the one who made the* recording we're using as our main source of evidence and we need your witness statement to add to the prosecution," the agent's voice was firm and unyielding as he spoke down to me like I was an idiot.

"I don't know anything about a recording," I tried as my heart thundered with panic.

I couldn't have my name linked to this case. If Ryder found out that I was the one who had filmed him then he'd kill me. Chop me up, grind me down, use me to fertilise some kind of psycho garden that he grew with his earth magic and let the worms shit out anything that was left over. Nope. I didn't want that future.

"Would you prefer me to send a team down there with a warrant for your arrest?"

"How can you arrest me? I haven't done anything!" I growled, finding my balls somewhere because I wasn't going to let them fuck this up for me. I needed both gang Kings on side and I needed to live. Not for me. But for Ella. She was counting on me to rise her up out of this life and to protect her from Old Sal even if she didn't realise it. I wouldn't let her down. Not for anything. Certainly not for some asshole FIB agent with an axe to grind and nothing better to do than ruin my fucking life over that goddamn recording.

"Like I said, we know you were there, we tracked the recording back to its original source. Dante Oscura may be the one who uploaded it online, but it only took us a moment to check the records on his Atlas interactions to find out that you were the one who sent it to him. We have a tap on his communications anyway. And once we checked your Atlas, it was clear that no one had sent it to you. Which means you're the one with the original copy. It will be no work for me to prove that if you want to go down the warrant route?"

"No!" I exclaimed, glancing around and damn near pissing myself as I found Ryder looking straight at me.

His gaze was distant though and my heart resumed beating as I realised he wasn't actually paying me any attention, just glaring off into the distance *as he no doubt imagined up new and terrifying ways to torture and kill people.*

I hurried out of the courtyard, wanting privacy for this conversation beyond the protection of my silencing bubble.

"Can you come down to the station now?" Agent Asshole asked.

"I have class-"

"I suggest you don't make this difficult."

"Fine. I'll cut class. It'll take me about an hour to get into town depending on the bus schedule." That would give me a bit of time to figure out what the hell I was supposed to do and maybe ask Dante for some help. He had plenty of experience dealing with the cops so I was sure he'd be able to get me out of this mess, even if I had to pay some price for his help.

"This is important. You're a Pegasus, right? So shift and fly here," Agent Asshole said lazily like the fact that he knew personal details about me wasn't terrifying as fuck. "I'll see you in fifteen minutes and if you're late, I might get sloppy with the details of this case the next time a member of the Brotherhood comes offering bribes..."

Shit on it.

"Okay, okay. I'll shift now and be there ASAP," I agreed, having no other choice.

"Good boy."

The line went dead and a wash of fear slipped over me.

It's okay. You can deal with this. Just take a deep breath and stay calm. They don't have anything on you. So what if you made that recording? You weren't the one fucking a teacher and there's no law against filming people from inside closets after breaking into their private rooms...

Fuck.

I started unbuttoning my school shirt as I jogged towards the Rigel Library and I quickly stuffed all of my clothes into my bag before shifting into my huge, black Pegasus form.

The elasticated strap on my bag stretched to accommodate my newly expanded size and I broke into a gallop as I stretched my wings then sprung up into the sky.

I beat my wings hard, flying straight up to the clouds and relaxing slightly as glitter tingled through my mane and my magic was replenished. But even the joy of stretching my Order muscles wasn't enough to banish the fear of my destination from my mind.

All too soon, I was gliding over the streets of downtown Alestria and I spotted the FIB station looming ahead like a big fucking monster standing in my path.

I tucked my wings, taking advantage of a red stop light to use the road as a landing strip while the cars were held at bay and trotted straight up to the station doors.

A shiver raced down my spine as I shifted back into my Fae form and I was too worried about this meeting to even care that I was standing in the street butt naked.

I yanked my bag over my neck and quickly threw my pants, shirt and shoes back on before jogging into the precinct.

An agent in uniform looked up at me with little interest from behind a huge desk as I walked in but before I could approach her, a door on my left buzzed electronically and swung open.

A short man strode out with dark red hair that was balding ever so slightly on top. He had mean eyes and a hard stare which he fixed on me as he beckoned me closer. "You made good time, Mr Tempa. Right this way please."

I swallowed thickly as I recognised Agent Asshole's voice and raised my chin as I strode towards him. I was a good foot taller than him so I shouldn't have been intimidated, but something about his wiry frame and confident attitude had me thinking that he outmatched me in pretty much every way Faely possible.

I stepped through the door into a long grey corridor and he pulled a pair of magic restricting cuffs from his pocket, offering them to me.

"Why do I need those?" I protested. *"I'm not under arrest, am I?"*

"Protocol," Agent Asshole replied flatly. *"All non-official personnel have to have their magic restricted while down here. You never know when some innocent looking kid might turn out to be a psycho with a thing for killing cops. I don't wanna find out that you're the bad guy by having the air ripped out of my lungs, do I?"*

I could tell there was no point in arguing with him so I accepted the cuffs and locked them around my wrists, trying to ignore the sick feeling I got as they cut off my connection to my magic. I didn't ask how he knew I was an air Elemental, he'd clearly done his research on me.

Agent Asshole, who obviously had no intention of offering me his real name, led the way down the corridor and I tried to ignore the cold feeling which seemed to press into me the further we walked.

He kept going until we reached a locked metal door which he unlocked with a combination of a heavy key, a code on the door and a flash of his magic.

My heart fell as he pulled the door wide and ushered me inside.

Professor King sat at a metal table in there, her wrists bound to it with thick chains and her eyes narrowing as she looked at me.

"I don't understand," I said, whirling back toward Agent Asshole just as he tossed the door shut in my face.

"Take a seat, Tempa," King ordered as if we were in class, not a fucking FIB interrogation room.

"What the hell is this about?" I demanded, staying by the door as I looked up at the camera in the top corner of the room which was capturing this little exchange.

"I've got an offer for you," she said, leaning back casually, as if she wasn't wearing an orange prison jumpsuit and her hands weren't chained to a fucking table at all.

"What?"

"The FIB have very kindly offered to reduce my sentence," she said like

we were chatting over brunch. "I won't even have to serve any time. I'll be power shamed of course but they'll let me go free, set me up with a new identity to start over in some city far away. I always liked the sound of Tucana…"

"What's that got to do with me?"

"Well that little deal comes with a price of course."

"So?"

"So…they want information on Ryder and the Lunar Brotherhood. I've given them all I can, but it's not enough to take him down. So I want you to get the evidence they need to seal his case." She smiled at me, licking her lips like she was thinking about biting me and I had to banish the mental image of her being fucked over a desk from my thoughts as I tried to understand what she was saying.

"Why would I give a shit about that?" I demanded. "Your conviction or Ryder's aren't my problem."

"That's where you're wrong, Tempa," Professor King purred seductively and a prickle of fear slid down my spine.

"Why?"

"Because I know your secret. You made that recording. What would Ryder do to you if he found out about that?"

I swallowed thickly, refusing to answer as a thousand different violent deaths flashed before my eyes. I knew all too well what Ryder did to people who betrayed him.

"So you're going to help me and I'll help you by keeping your dirty little secret."

"But…why are the FIB allowing this?" I knew it was the least of my problems, but I didn't understand how a law enforcement officer had just brought me in here to be blackmailed by a molesting criminal.

"They're not allowing anything. Just a casual chat between friends. Of course they can't take part in threats like the one I'm making against you. But they'll happily accept your assistance in my case once you hand over the *evidence they want."*

My mouth opened and closed like a fish dumped on dry land as my pulse pounded in my ears so hard that I couldn't even hear myself think.

"So what's it to be?" King asked with a wicked smile. "Will you help me take down the Lunar King? Or will I tell him what you did?"

My hands were trembling. Betraying Ryder like that would earn me more pain than I could even imagine, ending in my untimely demise. But I'd already betrayed him. She knew it. I knew it. Agent Asshole definitely knew it. This was my only option. Digging myself in deeper and betraying him even more in the process. It was no choice, but I had to make it. I had to keep doing everything I could to get Ella out of this city.

It wouldn't be long. Just a few more payments and I could rid myself of the debt hanging over her head and then I could start saving for our escape. Once we left Alestria and the gangs who ruled it far, far behind, it wouldn't matter what I'd done. They'd never find me. I just had to get through this first.

"Okay," I breathed. "What do you want me to do?"

ELISE

CHAPTER TWENTY SIX

"This is ridiculous," I muttered for the hundredth time as Leon practically dragged me down the stairs.

"Suck it up buttercup, this is happening. And don't kill my buzz, this is the best thing that's happened to me in a long, long time... aside from meeting you, little monster," he replied, winking at me.

It was only half six in the morning and the fact that Leon was even awake was a damn miracle in itself, but I guessed he really did care about this nonsense. It was Sunday and today was the day that the final decision was going to be made about who got to go on the exchange trip to Zodiac Academy, so whoever had their name in the top five positions on the leader board would be heading out for a week with the rich kids.

I'm sure they'll just love meeting a girl who was raised in a strip club, two gang leaders, a thief from the most notorious family of burglars in Solaria...and Gabriel.

I didn't know why Leon was so damn hyped about seeing his name up on the board. He knew he was in. He knew I was in. Greyshine was far too afraid of Dante to have reneged on their arrangement and yet Leon had still been so excited for this that he'd woken up early. Like, pre sunrise early. I'd only managed to make him hold off on coming down here for this long by sitting and brushing his hair for over an hour. Which I actually kinda loved doing – there was something achingly soothing about the deep purr he emitted while I worked the tangles out of his long blonde hair and I had to admit it was a bit of a turn on too. But when I'd suggested Leon make use of the fact that he'd banished Sasha and Amy from their room again he'd said no. *No.* Even when I'd started stripping, he'd just picked up my shirt and forced it over my head again. He *really* wanted to see the damn leader board.

I clearly wasn't going fast enough for him and Leon lunged for me, catching me around my waist and tossing me over his shoulder. I squealed in protest as I hung upside down and Leon gripped my ass, his fingers digging into my denim shorts to hold me in place.

He jogged down the stairs and ran across the Acrux Courtyard between the empty bleachers and abandoned picnic benches, heading straight for Altair Halls without even stopping for breakfast.

He elbowed the doors open and dropped me to my feet as he tipped his head back to look up at the ranks.

"Well?" I asked, my eyes on him instead of the board.

"We're going to Zodiac Academy, little monster!" Leon's smile was so big that I couldn't help but return it and he swept me into his arms, crushing me against the firm bulk of his muscles.

"Well done, Leo. You worked your ass off for this, you must be so proud of yourself," I teased.

"Don't mock me, little monster. I got in the exact way my family would have wanted me to."

"And how's that?" I asked as he released me.

"By stealing someone else's spot." He grinned like a Cheshire Cat and I couldn't help but join in.

"Hell yeah you did," I agreed, stepping closer to him and reaching up to press a kiss to his lips.

He growled against my mouth hungrily, catching my waist and driving me back against the wall. I giggled as he slammed me against the bottom of the leader board and he grabbed my thighs, hoisting my legs up around him.

"I'm gunna fuck you against this leader board," he growled. "Then it will be the owner of every dream I have at once."

I laughed again and he pushed his hand beneath my shirt, hoisting me higher as he dipped his head towards my body. I leaned back against the wall, closing my eyes for a moment as his mouth met with my stomach and he began marking a line towards my breast.

Leon's mouth moved over the thin material of my bra and I moaned as his teeth sought out my nipple through the fabric. He growled his approval as my nipple hardened at the attention and I gasped as he started to unbutton my shorts.

"*Leon*," I protested weakly. We were right in the middle of the hallway and despite the fact that it was a Sunday, people were fairly likely to walk by.

He growled playfully in response, his fingers skimming the top of my panties as he pushed his hand inside my denim shorts.

I moaned again, half forgetting what my complaints had been as he sucked on my nipple through my bra for a second time.

The sound of someone clearing their throat made my eyes snap open and I gasped as I spotted Professor Titan standing at the other end of the corridor by the stairs. He was clutching a thick book entitled *Mocravian Bullworms and their use in Potions* and a disposable coffee cup and he blinked more times than should have been legal before he found his voice.

"Perhaps you should relocate to somewhere a little more private?" Titan suggested in a voice that was way too flustered to sound authoritative. His cheeks were pinking and I couldn't help but laugh like a naughty kid who'd been caught stealing from the cookie jar as Leon slowly lowered my legs to the floor and stepped back.

"Sorry sir," I breathed as Leon damn near pouted.

I couldn't take another moment of the embarrassing interaction so I threw Professor Titan a salute then shot forward, grabbing Leon as I moved and hoisting him back up to his dorm in no time.

I dropped him to his feet and caught his wrist, slamming his hand to the door as he got his bearings before pushing him back inside.

"Who the fuck works on a Sunday?" Leon complained as I kicked the door closed. "He totally ruined my fantasy of branding the leader board with a print of your ass and making the halls echo with the sound of you screaming my name."

"Poor baby," I teased as I kicked my sneakers off and pushed my shorts down. "Whatever will you do now?"

His pout slowly turned into a smirk as he continued to watch me undress.

"I guess we have some time to kill before we leave for Zodiac this evening," he agreed as his gaze slid over me hungrily. "And maybe I can still make you scream loud enough to be heard in Altair Halls."

I grinned as I stepped out of my underwear and stalked towards him. "Let's hope so," I agreed.

To say that no expense had been spared on this trip was an understatement. I stood, staring around at the huge atrium where we were waiting to check in to our rooms, fighting the urge to let my mouth drop open.

Professor Mars was speaking to the woman behind the desk as he collected the keys to the rooms that had been organised for us. We were staying in south Tucana which was the closest town to the academy and it was clear that everything had been arranged to the highest spec. I just couldn't decide whether I was supposed to be impressed or if they were looking to rub our noses in their wealth.

Either way, I wasn't going to complain about it.

I wandered over to the huge fountain which sat in the centre of the white space and watched as the water shot from it in countless directions, only to return to the pool at the bottom again by way of some kind of magical tether.

"What a waste of time," Ryder commented as he came to stand beside me.

I rolled my eyes as I turned to look at him. "Oh yeah, why waste your time making something impressive in its beauty when you could just wander around with a scowl on your face, intimidating people to get out of your way?"

"Well I'm obviously not very good at that either, because you don't seem intimidated in the least."

"I am," I protested. "You're absolutely terrifying. I'm quivering in my boots."

Ryder's gaze slid over my blue and white striped sun dress before landing on my sandals. "You're not wearing boots. In fact, you look like the fetish version of a sailor."

"Do you want to practice your knot tying skills on me?" I teased, inching closer to him.

"I'm more interested in seeing what you look like all wet," he replied, moving closer and catching my waist.

I squealed in surprise as he swung me around and tipped me back so that I was hanging above the fountain. I grabbed his biceps, laughing as I clung to his arms. "You wouldn't."

"Is that a challenge?" Ryder released me for a moment before catching me again a few inches above the water.

"Please," I gasped, tightening my grip on him as I looked up into his dark green eyes which sparkled with amusement.

He leaned down to speak in my ear and my skin tingled as his lips brushed against my flesh.

"What will you give me to save you?"

"Anything," I swore. "Anything you want."

"Do you promise?"

"Yes!"

Ryder inched back to look into my eyes, offering me a smile for a brief moment before he swung me upright again, pulling me flush against him. "I'll hold you to that."

I laughed as I lingered in his arms a moment longer, but the sound of Professor Mars calling my name made me look around.

Gabriel, Dante and Leon were all watching us like they couldn't quite believe what they'd just witnessed and I could hazard a guess that they'd never seen Ryder do anything that light-hearted before.

Ryder's face had returned to its usual hard mask and his hands slid from my waist as he began to walk away from me, but I caught his hand before he could get far.

"Callisto, I'm giving you a room to yourself as you're the only girl in residence," Mars said, tossing a key at me. "Do you want me to put a magical lock on your door too to keep these scoundrels out?"

I bit down on a laugh and the urge to tell him that I didn't want to keep them out, shaking my head instead. "That's okay. I'm sure they can behave themselves."

Mars grunted like he didn't believe that for one second but if he'd been paying much attention at Pitball practice or in our Elemental Combat classes, I was going to guess he knew about the connection I had with the guys on this trip anyway.

He held out two more keys and I felt Ryder stiffen beside me even before Mars spoke. "You boys are sharing twin rooms, I don't care who's with who but-"

"I call dibs on Dante!" Leon shouted, leaping forward to snatch one of the keys from Mars as if Gabriel or Ryder might get there first.

"I'd sooner carve my own lungs from my chest than share with your precious Inferno anyway," Ryder muttered.

"I'll just find somewhere on the roof to sleep," Gabriel added, glancing up the huge staircase which led to the rooms as if he was planning on going to the roof right now.

"No need, Mr Nox. Your room has an easterly facing window and a lounge bed out on the balcony so that you can replenish your magic with the sunrise as required," Mars announced. "I suggest everyone heads straight to bed so that we can get a good night's sleep for the activities tomorrow."

He ushered us all towards the elevators and I fell into the middle of the group as we followed him.

Gabriel caught my arm to slow me down and I hesitated as he drew me to a halt.

"Is everything okay?" I asked him.

"I just had another vision about our new friend," he said in a low voice.

"Orion?"

"Yeah. I think he'll warm to us more quickly if you're friendly with him."

"Are you trying to pimp me out?" I asked teasingly and Gabriel growled beneath his breath.

"I think I've got more than enough competition for your attention already. But he's a Vampire and the two of you are going to be pushed into rivalry by your natures. I couldn't *see* any way around you coming to blows over it, but we need to make sure it doesn't happen for three days. After that, your friendship will survive past your altercation anyway."

"I'm not an idiot, Gabriel," I replied, rolling my eyes. "Lance Orion is from one of the most powerful families in Solaria. He has two Elements and is no doubt more powerful than me. Why would I fight him over dominance? I do know when to submit, you know."

"You really, really don't," he replied, shaking his head. "Anyway, the main thing is you play nice for three days while we butter him up. Got it?"

"Got it," I replied, offering him my most innocent smile and he snorted a laugh as we hurried to catch up to the group again.

Leon reached out to take my bag from me as I moved to his side and slung it over his shoulder with a smug grin.

"Look at you all chivalrous," I teased.

"Only for you," he replied proudly and I smirked to myself.

We rode the elevator all the way up to the top floor and I stood between the four Kings as Leon whistled loudly, ignoring the tension which hung between the rest of our group.

The doors slid open and Professor Mars led the way out into the corridor. He pointed at the three doors at the far end of the hall to direct us that way before moving into his own room opposite the elevator.

We walked up to our rooms and I moved forward to open mine as Dante unlocked the door beside it; Ryder headed to the one opposite mine and they both disappeared. Gabriel cast a look my way before following Ryder and I unlocked my room with Leon right on my heels.

My lips parted as I looked around at the enormous room. The apartment I'd grown up in with Gareth hadn't been as big as this place. There was a huge lounge area and beyond that sat a king sized bed with the fluffiest looking pillows I'd ever seen. I shot around the room to explore, groaning in excitement as I spotted the jacuzzi in the en-suite.

"This place is insane!" I exclaimed as I made it back to the main room just as Leon deposited my bag on the bed.

"Yeah, look at the bed," he said, grinning excitedly.

"We could definitely make use of that," I said suggestively, moving closer to him.

"Fuck yeah," he gushed. "I can't wait to go full star fish in mine! I'm gonna get the best night's sleep and then be bright as fuck for Zodiac tomorrow."

"That wasn't what I meant by-"

"Sweet dreams, little monster." He leaned forward to stamp his mouth to mine but he barely even caught the corner of my lips in his haste to leave.

He turned and jogged out of the room before I could protest, swinging the door shut behind him.

My mouth hung open in surprise for several seconds before I snorted a laugh. It was kinda cute how hyped he was about seeing Zodiac Academy. I just hoped it would live up to all his fantasies.

I strained my ears, wondering what the others might be doing and I instantly caught the sound of Ryder and Gabriel bickering about who got to sleep by the window. I decided to leave them to that and turned my attention to Dante instead. I could hear the shower running and the soft sound of Leon's snores came a moment later.

How the hell is he already asleep??

I sighed as I gave up on the idea of getting some time with any of my Kings and moved to my bag to hunt down my wash stuff before heading to brush my teeth.

My Atlas pinged as I returned to the room and I hooked it from the bed with a smirk as I spotted Dante's name.

Dante:

I'm bored, carina, the Lion is asleep already...

Elise:

That's a shame, I had been hoping the two of you might come over...

Dante:

I'll come if you want me to ;)

I pouted as I read that because it wasn't true. Dante wouldn't be able to do anything at all with me if he came over thanks to his stupid deal with Ryder.

But maybe there was something he *could* do from there.

I quickly opened up Faegle translate on my Atlas and checked a few phrases in his language before moving to lie down on the huge bed.

Once I'd committed them to memory, I called Dante.

It rang once before he answered and the deep purr of his voice had a shiver of longing racing down my spine.

"Ciao, amore mio."

My heart beat a little faster with the idea I'd had, but I wasn't going to back out through nerves. "Cosa indossi?" I asked him. *What are you wearing?*

Dante laughed darkly, the sound of it making my skin tingle.

"A towel," he replied, instantly agreeing to the game without me having to convince him.

"Are you all wet from your shower?" I asked slowly.

"Sì," Dante said. "There are beads of water all over my chest, sliding down my skin."

I bit my lip as I gave that image a bit of time to sink in.

"Are you lying down?"

"I'm in my bed," he replied. "Wishing you were in it with me. What are you wearing, bella?"

A heated smile tugged at my lips in response to the game and I glanced down at myself. "I'm still wearing my sun dress, but I'm taking it off now." I gripped the hem of my dress to act out what I was describing as I said it. "I'm pulling it up over my thighs and the material's brushing against my skin like I wish your hands could."

"I wish I could too, carina."

"I'm pulling it over my head now..."

"What kind of underwear have you got on?"

"White lace panties-"

"Because you're such an innocent girl?" he teased.

"And no bra," I continued with a smirk. "Because I'm not."

Dante groaned with longing and my grip tightened on my Atlas.

"Are you cold?"

"Yes," I breathed. "I wish you could come and warm me up. My nipples are hard and aching for you."

"Touch them," he commanded. "And think of me running my tongue over them, of my hands moving across your body and caressing them, of the electricity which would build in the room as my desire for you drove me to insanity."

I moaned softly as I did as he commanded, tugging lightly on my nipple as I pictured his mouth on my flesh.

"Is this turning you on?" I asked breathily.

"I'm so hard for you, I could burst, bella," Dante growled powerfully.

"Open your towel, and imagine I'm running my mouth down your body, moving lower and lower…"

"I've dreamed about your mouth on me far too often, amore mio. I want to taste the desire on your tongue and feel the fullness of your lips against mine."

"I want to feel the fullness of your desire in my mouth, Dante. Can't you picture how it would feel for me to wrap my lips around your shaft and draw you right in to the back of my throat?"

Dante growled again and an ache of need grew between my thighs.

"I want you so much, bella," he swore.

"Wrap your hand around your dick," I said, my chest rising and falling heavily as I pictured him doing just that.

"You wouldn't believe how hard I am right now," he groaned.

"I wish I could feel every inch of you inside me," I panted.

"Are you wet for me, bella? Can you feel it for me?"

"I'm pushing my fingers into my panties," I said, my thighs parting with a desperate need as I did exactly what I was describing. "And I'm sliding them lower…"

Dante groaned. "Tell me," he commanded.

I pushed my fingers down further, feeling exactly how much my flesh ached for his. I was soaking for him, my whole body alight with a desperate need which I wanted him to sate so badly it hurt.

"I'm so wet, Dante, I'm aching for you to be inside me. I want to feel you filling me, possessing me, consuming me."

"Push your fingers inside yourself," he commanded and I did, moaning loudly as I imagined it was him touching me instead. "Keep going, bella, don't stop."

I did as he asked, driving my fingers in and out as I gasped his name. "Are you touching yourself too?" I demanded, needing to know that we were doing this together.

"Yes," he growled. "I'm so hard that it's making my balls ache. My hand is moving up and down and I'm imagining it's the tight embrace of your body that I'm plunging into."

"Fuck, Dante, I wish I could feel that. I want every inch of you filling me," I moaned, moving my fingers faster as I started to circle my thumb against my clit.

"I want to know what you taste like, bella," Dante growled. "Put your fingers in your mouth and tell me you taste as sweet as cherries everywhere."

"I'm not sweet," I gasped as my body began to tighten.

"*Do it,*" he growled and I moaned in protest as I slid my fingers from my panties and pushed them into my mouth. "Can you taste your desire for me?"

"Yes," I groaned as I slid my hand back down my body, grazing my nails across my aching nipple for a moment before returning my hand to where I needed it most.

"I'm so hard for you, bella. I've never wanted a woman like I want you. I've dreamed of feeling myself inside you more times than I can count. My dick is straining with the need to feel your tightness around it."

"I'm so close, Dante," I panted as I pushed my fingers back into my panties and drove them inside myself again, imaging that it was him.

"Come for me, bella," he growled.

I gasped as I circled my thumb on my clit again and I could feel the orgasm building in me.

"Are you close?" I begged of him, wanting him to come with me.

"Yes, bella. Sono così eccitato da te che fa male. Riesco a malapena a trattenermi dal cadere a pezzi per te."

I moaned loudly as he spoke to me in his language and my back arched against the sheets as my body started trembling.

"Fuck," I hissed as I lingered on the brink of pleasure.

"Come for me, bella. Vieni per me."

I cried out as my body gave in to his demands and I tumbled into oblivion at the sound of his voice.

Dante groaned loudly as he spilled himself too, the sound of my orgasm finishing him.

A yelp of shock sounded from Leon in the room with him a second later. "Did you just electrocute me?" he demanded.

I laughed as I realised that Dante's pleasure must have translated into his gifts as he came, his electricity pouring from his body and hitting Leon.

"A bit. Go back to sleep," Dante commanded through a laugh of his own and Leon grumbled something before falling silent again.

My head fell back against my pillows as I panted heavily, trying to catch my breath as I grinned at nothing and everything.

"One day I'm going to do that to you for real," Dante swore breathlessly.

"I want that so badly," I whispered, wishing I could linger in his arms instead of laying alone in my bed.

"So do I. Sweet dreams, bella."

"They'll be about you," I replied, knowing it was true. I'd spend the night dreaming about the way it would feel to be with him for real and wake up aching with need once again.

"E il mio su di te."

"Goodnight," I breathed, a smile finding my lips as I ended the call and I let my eyes fall closed so that I could bathe myself in the picture we'd just painted all night long like I'd said.

LEON

CHAPTER TWENTY SEVEN

"Wake up!" I dove on top of Dante in his bed and he choked out a breath as I crushed him. I kissed him straight on the lips then smacked him across the cheek. "We're leaving in thirty minutes, dude! Get up!"

I leapt off of him, rushing to the mirror as I adjusted the Skylarks Pitball shirt I was wearing. The gold and black colours brought out the brilliance of my eyes and a deep purr emanated from my chest as I flattened the creases out of it.

I grabbed the top-of-the-range camera from my nightstand - I'd stolen it from a drunk Centaur back at Aurora - and hung it around my neck on the strap. *Purrrrfect.*

Dante headed past me into the bathroom, yawning broadly before stripping off with the door wide open and stepping into the shower.

"Meet you in the lobby," I called. "I'm gonna make sure everyone else is up. I'm not leaving one single second late."

"Good luck with that, mio amico," Dante laughed and I jogged to the door, energy bouncing through my veins as I headed into the corridor. I made a beeline for Gabriel and Ryder's room, hammering my fist on the door. "Twenty six minute warning! Don't spend too much time putting your make-up on, Ryder! You look beautiful as you are."

"Go fuck yourself, Mufasa," Ryder's voice came in response.

I pranced away to Elise's door, bashing my fist on it. "Are you up, little monster? Twenty five minutes and thirty five seconds to go."

The door opened and Elise stood there in a ripped denim skirt and a black halter-neck. Her hair looked freshly washed, hanging around her chin and feathering against her neck.

"You're ready," I said brightly, grabbing her waist and pulling her close to press my nose into her hair. It smelled like cherries of course.

"Yep," she said, placing a kiss on my cheek and I wondered if she'd made the effort to get up on time just for me.

"Ah, Mr Night, Miss Callisto," Mars called as he exited the elevator at the end of the corridor wearing a white shirt and a pair of cream chinos. "If you want breakfast, you'll need to head down to the buffet now. We're leaving soon."

"Yes, sir." I snatched Elise's hand, towing her toward the elevator and we headed downstairs to the huge atrium and through to the buffet.

Chandeliers glinted above us and enormous windows at one side of the dining room looked over sprawling grounds and a shimmering pond. It was immaculate, beautiful, fucking perfect.

"By the stars, I'm not going to be able to eat. I'm so nervous." I scooped up a plate, piling a stack of pancakes onto it with a topping of blueberries, strawberries, chopped banana, chocolate sauce and a waffle. I left the French toast and the ice cream. I just had no appetite at all.

We headed to a table by one of the windows and the sun pooled over us as we sat with our food. Elise ate a bagel with cream cheese, eyeing my breakfast with a look of amusement.

"Something funny?" I asked as I shovelled a forkful of pancake into my mouth.

"You're just so fucking cute sometimes, Leo."

"Sometimes?" I cocked a brow.

"Alright, always," she corrected with a grin.

A shadow moved in my periphery a second before Gabriel swooped down into the seat beside Elise like a fucking wraith.

"You're gonna give people a heart attack moving around like Casper the unfriendly ghost." I shook my head at him as he took a bite out of the apple in his hand. "Can you wear one of those cat collars that have a jingly bell?"

"Sure, shall I get one in pink or blue? I might have to order it to size too," Gabriel said and Elise released a laugh.

I raised a brow as a chuckle escaped me. Maybe Mr Boring Pants actually had a sense of humour.

Elise reached up to Gabriel's mouth, wiping a piece of apple from the corner of his lips. Gabriel watched her like a bird of prey about to strike and I realised I wouldn't mind participating in that particular show. In fact, it was getting me kind of hard. And I didn't need that sort of distraction today of all days.

I looked away from them and my gaze fell on Ryder at the back of the room, sitting alone with a bowl of porridge in front of him. I swear he didn't even have fucking milk on it. *Who eats dry-ass porridge oats? He's like a sad, starving little racoon. By choice.*

Dante was at the buffet and he moved over to join us with a plate of waffles and ice cream. I immediately swiped half his food onto my plate and he slammed a hand to my shoulder, sending a bolt of electricity through me.

"You snooze, you lose," I wheezed as my hair stood on end and I locked an arm around my plate protectively.

He barked a laugh, dropping into his seat and tucking into the remainder of his breakfast. "You must lose all the fucking time then, fratello."

Elise laughed and even Gabriel broke a small smile. Elise glanced over her shoulder, looking at Ryder and my heart tugged because I knew it upset her that he wanted nothing to do with her other boyfriends. I mean sure, this situation was kinda unconventional. But plenty of Orders had polyamorous lifestyles. Werewolves were totally into it before they found their true mate. And my Lion nature was to build a pride, I just hadn't expected it to consist of a hot ass Vampire chick and three other dudes. But if that made my little monster happy, then I was more than okay with Dante, Gabriel and Ryder being my little lionesses. *Better not tell them that if I want to keep my teeth though.*

I picked up a waffle, rising to my feet and launching it across the room. It smacked into the side of Ryder's head right on target. "Hey! Come join us."

A hiss slid between his teeth as he wiped ice cream from his temple and glowered at me. "I'd rather drink my own piss."

Elise frowned, glancing around at the three of us before getting up and moving to the buffet.

I pressed my lips together, discomfort stirring in my gut because I didn't know how to fix this rift between all of us. Even Gabriel looked like he was about to take flight now that he was left alone with me and Dante for half a second.

Elise headed over to Ryder's table with a bowl full of ice cream and a plate piled up with all kinds of breakfast foods. I watched as she proceeded to hand feed him bits and pieces of it all and he smiled like he wasn't the Tin Man. I'd shared Elise with him once, I'd seen the potential lying beneath his asshole façade. And I was determined to crack through it again. For her sake. But right then, I had other things to focus on.

I checked my watch, then snatched Gabriel's apple from his hand, stacked Dante's half eaten breakfast on top of my plate and hurried away to dump it on the buffet table before they came after me.

"We're leaving!" I shouted, heading out into the foyer where Mars was waiting. He had a fanny pack strapped around his muscular waist and a scowl on his face.

"Where's the rest of you?" he demanded.

I glanced over my shoulder and relaxed when Elise appeared, tugging Ryder along by the hand. Dante and Gabriel walked out after them and the glare that Gabriel shot me could have murdered a small village. *Jeez, it was just an apple, asshat.*

He promptly shifted his glare onto Ryder whose hand was still clutched in Elise's.

"Everyone ready?" Mars asked.

"Yes," I answered before anyone else could suggest they needed to go back to their room for anything. "Let's go."

I strode off towards the exit and Mars jogged to my side, taking out a pouch of stardust with the Zodiac Academy insignia printed on it. "Just a little pinch to save the cab fare today, eh?"

I winked at him. "Sounds good to me, sir. Can't we use it all week?"

"We mustn't get complacent," he said sternly and I rolled my eyes.

We headed out of the hotel onto the sidewalk and the morning sun fell over us, painting the street in golden tones. Cars zipped past us as Fae headed off on their morning commutes.

Mars turned to us as we grouped around him in a circle and I held my breath in excitement as he tossed stardust over us. The glittering powder swept us away, transporting us through the ether. A galaxy of stars spanned out around me; it was all I could see in every direction, a billion miles of endless light.

My feet hit the ground and I stumbled forward, completely unused to travelling this way. I crashed into Dante and forced him back into Gabriel. Someone caught me by the collar, yanking me back a step to stop the domino effect and I turned to find Ryder there with a look of irritation on his face.

"Thanks dude." I smirked and he scowled like I'd insulted his mother.

I gazed around at the quiet road we were standing on flanked by huge trees. Before us was a huge iron gate which blocked our view of the academy which laid just beyond it.

Mars checked his watch and a minute later, the gates slowly parted, making my pulse spike as I readied to live out one of my dreams.

A woman stood waiting for us with soft features and dark hair pulled up into a tight bun. But I didn't give one single shit about her. I gave all my shits to the guy beside her. He towered over her, his muscles stretching out the white T-shirt and jeans he wore. His raven hair was swept back and his cut-from-glass face made me shriek like a fucking school girl.

I ran forward and his eyes widened in alarm as I crashed into him, dragging him into a bone-crushing hug. Lance Orion was the best fucking Airsentry in all of the academies. He was tipped to be picked up by the Solarian Pitball League after he graduated. He might play for the fucking Skylarks one day. And I'd met him. I ran my tongue up one side of his face. And I'd licked him too. Which made him *mine*.

"By the stars." He tried to shove me off, but I held on tight, swivelling around and holding my camera up high to snap a picture of us together. His Vampire fangs had popped out and I almost considered letting him take a bite out of me so I could get a picture of that too.

I stepped back, grabbing his hand in mine. "I'm Leon Night. Captain of the Aurora Academy Pitball team and an ace fucking Fireguard."

"Great," he growled, rubbing the saliva from his face. "Lick me again though and I'll shove your tongue up your ass."

"Leon's tongue is already too far up *your* ass for you to get hold of it," Ryder commented and Orion barked a laugh.

"Ignore the snake, he only has two emotions," I said with a grin then I leaned towards Orion, not caring how much of an ass-licker he thought I was. He was my new best friend, he just didn't know it yet. "Will you sign my Pitball kit later?"

"Are you quite done harassing Mr Orion?" the woman asked sternly before he could reply, but there was a smile playing around her mouth.

I nodded, taking another step back. But the harassing was far from over. I was going to get Orion to show me the Pitball pitch of dreams soon enough and then I'd grill him for tactics.

The woman stepped forward, taking Mars's hand. "I'm Principal Nova, it's wonderful to have you all here." She shook everyone else's hands while I lifted my camera and took a hundred shots of Orion while he tried to ignore me, giving everyone the brooding simmer-eyes thing which was hot as fuck if I did say so myself. "Lance is going to give your pupils a tour of the school while I introduce you to the faculty and give you a little insight on how we run things around here."

Mars nodded, pushing his hand into his pockets. "Lead the way." Nova headed off and he marched after her, throwing a look at us over his shoulder. "Behave."

Elise mock saluted him and I gave him a thumbs up.

When they were out of sight, I hurried toward my girl. "Elise, get over here." I snatched her hand, shoving her into Orion's arms and lifting the camera again. Fuck yeah, the two of them looked hot together.

"Hi, I'm Elise," she said to Orion, looking up at him through her lashes. He gave her a slanted smile, sweeping a hand over his hair.

"Hey beautiful, do you play Pitball too?" His eyes dropped to her legs and a flash of movement in my periphery preceded Ryder swooping in on them and tugging Elise from his arms.

"She's taken," he said rudely and Orion's brows arched.

"Sorry man." Orion shrugged, still eyeing Elise like she was fair game.

Elise pulled out of Ryder's arms, throwing Orion an apologetic look.

"She's not taken by *you*, stronzo," Dante said, muscling his way past them and holding a hand out to Orion. "Dante Oscura."

"Oh you're the Storm Dragon, right?" Orion asked with a flicker of interest in his gaze.

I lowered the camera in surprise.

"Yeah, how'd you know that?" Dante asked, his eyes narrowing in suspicion.

"Because I know Lionel Acrux and he's mentioned you like three times, which is kind of a big deal for a guy with zero hobbies except world domination," Orion said lightly. "I'm friends with his son, Darius."

"Lionel as in the High Councillor asshole?" Dante asked and I frowned, unsure how much he should bad mouth one of the most powerful Fae in the world around here. Especially to a guy who knew him.

"That's exactly who I mean." Orion smirked, his eyes glittering and Dante smiled.

I liked Orion even more in that second, because that puffed up Dragon twit who was trying to poach my friend wasn't getting any respect from me. And clearly not from my new bestie either.

Orion stepped toward Ryder, holding out his hand and the snake looked at it like it was diseased. "And you are?"

"Bored out of my fucking mind," Ryder said with a glare.

"*Right.*" Orion turned his back on him, pointing at Gabriel. "I didn't catch your name."

"Gabriel Nox," he said, smiling. Actually fucking smiling. I didn't think the guy's lips moved in that direction. "And you're the guy all the papers won't shut up about right?"

"Yeah," Orion said with a slanted grin and his Vampire fangs showed. "But trust me, I wanna be in front of a camera about as much I wanna bite a fucking slug. My agent says it's the only way to gain sponsors though, so I'm pretty much topless and oiled up every weekend in front of a lens."

"That sounds like hell," Gabriel commented and Orion nodded in agreement.

"Is that the Starfire symbol?" Orion pointed to a tattoo on Gabriel's forearm which looked like a star consumed in a fiery blaze.

"Yeah, they're the best damn team in Solaria," Gabriel said, lifting his chin.

"Fuck yes they are," Orion said, splitting a grin.

"Yeah, second only to the Skylarks," I said with a lazy smile.

"Bullshit," Orion and Gabriel said at the exact same time.

I raised my brows, snorting a laugh. "I can give you a hundred reasons why the Skylarks are better."

"I can give you a thousand why they're not," Orion countered.

Elise moved to his side, linking her arm with his. "I'm more of a Blueshine fan myself, but maybe you can convince me." She stroked his arm, his motherfucking arm. It's. So. On. Threeway city with my hero.

"I bet I can convince you of a lot of things," Orion replied in a dark tone and Elise gave him a challenging glare.

"Go ahead," she said lightly and his gaze dropped to her mouth like he had a more filthy thought in mind besides convincing her of which Pitball team was better. I lifted my camera to snap a shot of them, but Elise knocked it aside at the last second with a playful smile.

Orion turned to lead the way forward and I moved to walk on his other side while Gabriel stepped up to walk beside Elise. If Orion cared about the fact that Ryder and Dante had staked a claim on her, he didn't show it. And weirdly, Gabriel didn't seem to mind it either.

We fell into a fierce discussion about our favourite teams in the League as Orion led us through a hilly area he called Earth Territory. Apparently they divided their students up into Elemental Houses here and the four quarters of the academy grounds had been wielded by powerful Fae to represent each Element.

Orion took us through Water Territory past a sparkling lake where Sirens were diving into the still water, their bodies transformed so they were covered in shining scales. We headed past an incredible waterfall where a couple of students were practising parting the torrential falls to reveal a beautiful lagoon beyond.

Where Water Territory bordered Fire, there was a hot springs where pools sat between smooth rocks and steam coiled up towards the sky. Beyond that, was Fire Territory with its desert-like landscape. A long canyon led us out to an enormous glass building which jutted up toward the sky in the shape of a star.

"This is Ignis House for fire Elementals," Orion explained.

"Woah," I cooed. "This is where I'd stay if I attended."

"You could always transfer," Orion said.

"Let's not pretend. Only the elite come here," I mocked and he inched closer.

"Well how good's your Pitball game? Maybe you can come on a scholarship," he suggested.

I glanced over my shoulder at Elise who was walking beside Dante. Ryder was trailing far behind the group, staring around at the landscape as if it didn't interest him in the slightest. I was surprised he'd bothered coming on the tour at all.

"Nah," I said, walking on. I wouldn't be leaving my home town, even if this place was amazing. Not unless I could uproot my little monster and bring her with me.

We headed into Air Territory which bordered a cliff overlooking an azure sea. Sweeping plains with long grass stretched out toward an immense tower that had a huge turbine spinning at the top of it.

"This is my House," Orion said proudly, twisting the air around us with his magic. "But I have two Elements." Rain tumbled from the sky and I laughed.

"We could make one hell of a storm together, mio amico," Dante called.

"We should head down to the beach later and try it out," Orion answered with a grin as he stopped the rain.

"Is this tour going to take all day, asshole? Because now I'm wet *and* bored shitless," Ryder asked from the back of the group, wiping raindrops from his cheeks.

"For fuck's sake, Ryder, why don't you try smiling for once?" I demanded.

He bared his teeth at me and a hiss escaped him.

"On second thought, maybe don't smile," I said and his eyes narrowed to slits.

"You can leave if you're bored." Orion folded his arms, giving him a challenging look.

Ryder's gaze slid to Elise then back to Orion. "Fine."

Elise turned, shooting to his side and threading her fingers between his before he could walk away. Orion eyed the two of them in confusion, looking to Gabriel who mouthed *don't ask.* He must have been confused as hell about who Elise was actually dating. And I wondered what he'd think if he knew the answer. Maybe he'd want a piece of that action. And *maybe* I'd be super okay with that and could totally make a sex tape to re-live it forever…

"Stay," Elise insisted and Ryder pursed his lips, but didn't make a move to leave again.

I stepped toward Orion, taking out my Atlas and pulling him in for a selfie with the view of the cliff behind us. Elise dove in at the last second and Orion cracked a grin as I took the picture.

I left them to talk as I stepped back, admiring the photograph as I uploaded it to FaeBook and tapped out a status.

Leon Night:

Check out the meat in my Lion and Vampire sandwich. Who wants a bite?
#liononorion#pitballpals#feastwithelise #doublesausagewithasideofhotsauce

Shirley Cuypers:

Oh my stars! Is that Lance Orion?? #hecanthrowmearoundanytime
#lanceme

Brittany Andriessen:

Move aside Callisto, I want to be the meat in a Night & Orion sandwich!
#myfrontandbackdoorareopen #thismindycanhandleit

Victoria Pauley:

You'll always be my one and only, Leon! #onesausagegirl

Mariane Bergen:

Come home Leon we miss you!! #thismindyneedsherlion

Erica Collins:

I want to play with those Pitballs #mypitiswideopen #mindy4life

Celia Marshall:

He can suck on my neck while I brush your hair #thismindywilldoit

I chuckled, scrolling through more comments as Orion led us back across Air Territory and through a thick forest that wound through the heart of campus. We arrived at a large ring of buildings which circled a massive golden dome at the heart of it with a building in the shape of a silver crescent beside it.

"This is The Orb and the Lunar Leisure building." He gestured to them in turn. "The Orb is our student hub where we grab food and hang out. It's basically a fancy ass cafeteria."

A group of girls caught my eye as they walked down the path toward us. They blushed as they spotted Orion then their eyes fell on us behind him and the heat in their cheeks intensified.

"Oh my stars, are they the exchange students?" I heard one of them whisper as they scampered past us.

"That was so much man meat at once, I couldn't cope," another said. "Did you see that girl with them? I'm *so* jealous."

"She better keep her paws off of Lance, he's *mine*."

"He doesn't even know your name, Dana!"

Orion walked on like he hadn't heard all of that with his bat ears and I shot a wink at Elise who was hiding a grin.

We headed off into Earth Territory again and my heart started to crumble as I worried we weren't going to be shown the Pitball pitch after all.

"Hey Lance-" I started then the words died in my throat as the massive stadium became visible through the trees.

I fucking squealed and raced forward through the woodland, charging out onto a huge field and tilting my head back to take in the circular exterior, the metal walls reaching high up above me and catching the sun.

Orion sprinted past me with his Order gifts, stopping by the entrance and producing a key.

"You wanna go in?" he taunted.

I ran forward, excitement racing through me as I hurried to his side and bounced on my heels as I waited for him to open it. I glanced back at the others and noticed even Ryder looked curious about the pitch. I wondered if he even watched Pitball. It was hard to know what he liked at all beyond the few references he gave to The Lion King. And after watching it with him, I wasn't entirely sure he even liked that.

Orion opened the door and I pushed my way past him with a moan which sounded like I'd just come in my pants. I tore along the gleaming corridors and past the locker room which I was definitely going to be taking a shower in later. But right then, I had something more pressing I needed to do.

I started pulling my clothes off, dumping them behind me as I ran up the ramp which led onto the pitch. Sunlight streamed down on me, my heart thumped with joy and my bare feet met soft grass.

I halted as I stood in the enormous space, gazing around at the stands which circled up above me. The pitch was split into four Elemental corners and at the heart of it was the huge Pit. It was immaculate, perfect, and sexy as hell.

I dropped my boxers and stepped out of them.

"No shifting on the pitch!" Orion commanded as he shot up behind me, but I wasn't about to shift.

I dropped to the ground, rolling across the grass and feeling its perfect little stalks rubbing against every inch of my naked skin. I pushed my fingers into its silky strands and tugged with delight before rolling across it once more.

"Not cool, asshole!" Orion called as I rolled all the way across the pitch. "Do you really have to – oh for fuck's sake."

I made it to the waterhole and stood up next to the tall metal pipe that would shoot out icy waterballs during a match. I leaned over and stuffed my head down it, running my tongue up the rim of it just like I swore I would. Metal and victory sat on my tongue and a grin nearly split my cheeks apart.

Elise and Dante's laughter carried to me as I sprinted across the pitch to the next hole, pushing my head into that one too.

Someone caught me by the arm before I licked it and Orion yanked me back a step. Amusement sparkled in his gaze, but his features were stern.

"Stop molesting my pitch," he demanded and I nodded, moving forward and wrapping my arms around him.

"Thank you for the best day of my life. And I'm sorry about my hard on."

ELISE

CHAPTER TWENTY EIGHT

Zodiac Academy was on a whole other level. It was impossible not to get sucked into the fantasy which had Leon spellbound as we sampled classes in buildings and arenas which were purposefully constructed with magic to create the perfect conditions for what was being taught. They even gave individually tailored lessons for each Element instead of the combined lesson we took at Aurora Academy.

I'd visited the incredible Earth Cavern which had been carved beneath the ground to create a network of caves and tunnels perfectly harmonised for channeling earth magic. I'd watched as even Ryder's eyes had lit up while we were down there and the magic he'd created within that beautiful space was some of the most impressive I'd ever seen from him. Gabriel had just as much success with his earth magic too and in the Water Elemental Class he'd created a stunning display of animals carved right out of liquid. For the Water Elemental Class, we'd been taken to a secret lagoon which felt like travelling through stardust to a tropical island filled with sandy beaches, stunning waterfalls and crystal blue water which was so warm it made me ache for another visit.

In the Fire Arena, Leon had challenged one of the top ranking students in the class to a fight and had managed to win (which was somewhat helped by the fact that he'd stolen the guy's Atlas before the match and kept playing a soppy message from his mom's voicemail on speaker for the whole class to laugh at). But when Leon had knocked that pretentious douche on his ass, I couldn't help but cheer with excitement for him.

We were still waiting to have an Air Elemental Class and I had to admit that I was pretty damn excited to see what I might be able to do with the help of the top rate Professors they had in this place. I planned on picking the air Elemental Professor's brain as thoroughly as I could during our brief stay and elevating my own skills as much as possible.

The excitement of the place did hold a certain sting to it though whenever I thought of my brother. Gareth would have loved it here. He adored books and learning and was always striving to make the most of his power so that he would have an advantage when it came time for us to escape Alestria.

He'd never been this far from our home town, but our dreams had been united in our need for escape and adventure. We'd had the same ache to travel and experience it all and though it made my heart sore to think of him missing out on this, I liked to think that I was doing it for him too. If I did manage to survive whatever it took to uncover the truth about what had happened to him, then I intended to do everything we'd always sworn we would. Which started with packing up my shit and getting the fuck out of Alestria. Away from the gang wars and crime and Old Sal and all the bad memories which haunted me there. I had plenty of good memories too, all of them involving my brother, but I could take those with me when I went. They were bound to my heart and I'd never let them go.

As my thoughts lingered on my brother, I knew that I couldn't just forget about my investigations while I was here. Zodiac Academy may have been amazing, but it was also my key to getting closer to the next piece of my puzzle.

I needed to find Professor King and I knew she was living in Tucana somewhere. I'd been biting my tongue around Ryder all day, aching to ask him for his help with locating her while feeling in my gut that he would refuse that request if I tried. But I didn't have any other way to find her. She'd sent Ryder messages, begging to see him on multiple occasions and I was willing to bet that all it would take was one quick reply from him to get a location.

As we ate our dinner in the stunning golden Orb where the Zodiac Academy students enjoyed their meals, I decided to try my luck anyway.

I'd chosen a seat beside Ryder today which meant that we were sitting to the far right of the room at a small table with Gabriel. Leon and Dante laughed loudly together on the far side of the room, impressing the Zodiac students with their banter and jokes while Leon surreptitiously robbed them blind. He'd emptied out his pockets in his hotel room last night and my mouth had fallen open as I took in the rolls of aura notes and handfuls of jewellery he'd lifted without even raising a single suspicion.

I picked at my food while Ryder and Gabriel ate in silence. There were no actual signs of bonding going on between the two of them, but I had noticed how they'd slowly started gravitating towards each other when we travelled between classes in our small group. I guessed it made sense for the two of them to form an alliance of sorts, what with Leon and Dante acting like they were half in love with each other most of the time. But I had to hide my smile at the idea of Gabriel and Ryder truly becoming something more than enemies.

The two of them were both such loners in such different ways, but the one thing they had in common was that they'd never let anyone get close enough to see the real them before. No one aside from me anyway. It seemed like such a lonely existence to me and I was sure that they could both use a friend or two.

"Didn't you say Professor King moved to Tucana after she got her new identity?" I asked casually, so casually that no one would ever suspect me of being up to anything.

"What are you after?" Ryder demanded instantly, narrowing his eyes on me as he hunted for the truth.

Dammit.

"Nothing," I replied innocently, raising my hands in surrender.

Ryder's narrowed gaze stayed locked on me like he could smell bullshit and I could feel Gabriel eyeing me suspiciously too.

"Okay, okay," I sighed, giving in because it was clear that he'd already figured me out. "I was wondering if you might want to go visit her?"

"Why the fuck would I want to go visit her? She's useless to me now. I have no reason to get caught up in her psycho behaviour ever again." Ryder turned away from me dismissively and I pouted.

"But I have a lead to follow with Gareth's case and-"

"I'm warning you, Elise. Stay away from that woman. She doesn't have the answers you're looking for and you shouldn't get yourself mixed up with her. She's like a fucking parasite. Once she gets her claws in you, you have to rip out a chunk of flesh to get her off again."

"But-" I began.

"No," Ryder growled.

Hurt flashed through me at that denial and he glanced at me as he felt it too. His brow pinched like he didn't like hurting me like that, but he didn't offer me her number either.

"If you knew what she was like, you'd know you're better off away from her, baby," he muttered into his meal.

I balked at that. I didn't need someone telling me what was best for me or trying to protect me by blocking my investigations into Gareth's death. If he hadn't figured out that finding these answers was the most important thing in the world to me yet then he clearly hadn't been paying enough attention.

I looked to Gabriel, hoping he might speak up on my side of the argument but his gaze was distant, fixed on some point of the wall beside me as he was lost to the power of a vision.

"Fine," I snapped, sounding like a petulant child and not giving one shit about it as I tossed my fork down with a clatter. "I don't need your help anyway and I won't be asking for it again."

"Elise…" Ryder reached out and caught my wrist before I could leave, drawing the pain of his refusal to the surface of my skin. "I'm telling you, you don't want to get involved with King. She'd left the school before your brother died. She can't be who you're looking for."

"Okay," I said in a voice that sounded as false as it felt. I'd already known that King had left before Gareth died, but that didn't rule her out. I needed to speak to her to do that and if Ryder wasn't going to help me then I'd help myself.

Ryder's expression became taut as he tried to keep me sitting there and the wash of emotions and hurt I felt over him not giving me what I needed fed his power.

His lips parted and I hesitated as I waited to see if he might change his mind. "I don't want to hurt you, baby," he growled in a low voice just for me. "But I've made my decision on this."

"Got it." I wrenched my arm out of his grip and shot away from him, crossing the huge room until I reached Leon and Dante.

Leon was lazing back in an armchair as his latest gaggle of Mindys delivered an array of deserts to the table before him and I dropped into his lap with a dramatic sigh.

"What's up, little monster?" he purred, his hand landing on my thigh and painting patterns across my jeans.

"It's Ryder," I pouted. "Will you help me with something, Leo?"

"Anything," he agreed earnestly as I reached up to brush my fingers through his golden hair.

"Steal his Atlas for me?" I asked.

Dante barked a laugh and I looked at him sitting opposite us. "Why do you need to steal from the snake, bella?" he asked excitedly.

"He's just got some information on there that I need and he won't give it to me willingly." I shrugged.

"Your wish is my command," Leon said, nuzzling into my neck and kissing the sensitive skin beneath my ear so that the brush of his stubble grazed against me deliciously. "You have to rub the lamp though," he added seriously, taking my hand and dropping it onto his crotch where I could feel the swell of him growing already.

"Get me what I want and I'll grant you a wish or two of your own," I promised, leaning in to brush my lips over his.

"Done." Leon shared a smirk with Dante and a tingle ran along my skin at the implications in their eyes.

We finished up our dinner and Professor Mars appeared to take us back to the hotel. We rode in a couple of cabs and Leon dropped into the back of one beside Ryder instantly.

I decided to ride in the other cab, not wanting Ryder to read my scheming from my expression and I found myself wedged between Dante and Gabriel as we took the short ride back to our hotel.

Gabriel had a smug kind of look on his face which I couldn't figure out and he didn't even complain when Dante started singing in Faetalian beside me.

We exited the cars and headed inside, making our way to the elevators but Leon caught my hand before I could get half way to them. He drew me to him, pressing a rough kiss to my lips and pushing me back against one of the pillars in the atrium with a groan of longing. His hand shifted to my waistband and I gasped in surprise a moment before he pushed something down the front of my jeans.

"Careful with that, little monster. If he gets a call, I'm pretty sure it's set to vibrate."

I laughed as I realised the thing in my pants was Ryder's Atlas and kissed Leon again to thank him for pulling through for me.

The hotel receptionist cleared his throat as we continued to linger in each other's arms and I giggled as I drew back.

We walked to the elevator and headed up in the empty space, the others having already gone on ahead.

"When do I get my wishes?" Leon demanded, prowling closer to me the moment the elevator doors closed.

"Later," I promised. "Just as soon as I've dealt with this problem."

"We'll be waiting," he replied and my smile widened at the way he automatically included Dante. He wasn't like the others. He didn't want to cage me. He saw the ache in me and wanted to heal it, give me what I needed and bathe in the happiness that provided.

He moved to place his hands against the wall on either side of me and I was struck with the strongest desire to brand his name onto my heart.

I reached out to brush my fingers along his jaw, losing myself in the golden depths of his eyes.

"*My Lion,*" I said possessively, like I was claiming him and he nodded his agreement, running his nose up the length of mine.

"*My little monster,*" he replied fiercely, claiming me right back.

I tilted my chin to catch his mouth. The kiss he gave me took my breath away as he drove me back against the elevator wall and the heat of his fire Element burned hot and fast beneath his skin. His tongue stroked mine, his lips punishing with his need and I rose to the challenge of that kiss with a fire of my own.

The doors opened on the top floor and Leon pulled away with a growl of frustration as a flustered bellhop scuttled into our little bubble of solitude.

We hurried down the corridor to our rooms and Leon paused at the door to his, pulling his Atlas from his pocket as I took out my key.

"What are you doing?" I asked curiously as my door swung open.

"Calling Ryder," he replied with a devilish grin and I gasped as Ryder's

Atlas began to vibrate against the thin fabric of my panties where it was still wedged down the front of my jeans.

"Asshole," I gasped as I fought to pull the Atlas back out again and Leon chuckled darkly.

"I'll see you later," he promised as I wrangled the Atlas free and I laughed as I headed into my own room and he joined Dante in theirs.

I kicked my door shut behind me and shot across the room to my bed, dropping down onto it and quickly unlocking Ryder's Atlas with his passcode. I wasn't an idiot and I'd been concerned that Ryder might not give me King's location easily, so I'd spent the last few days looking over his shoulder when he unlocked his Atlas for this very reason.

He still had the ridiculous bunny photo of the two of us saved as his screensaver and I grinned at it stupidly for a moment before getting back to my task.

I opened up his texts and paused as the app opened up onto a message he'd written. A message to me. It only had one word in it and he hadn't actually sent it, but I still felt my anger with him melting as I read it.

Sorry.

The fact that he actually cared enough to even consider apologising to me had my heart beating faster. I'd never heard him apologise for his actions before and though I was still sure he had no intention of changing his mind about helping me out with this, he clearly felt bad about disappointing me.

It only took me a moment to locate the messages from King and my lip curled back as I read through them. There was a lot of sexual content and over embellished descriptions of things she wanted to do to him and even a few photographs too. He hadn't replied to a single one, but that hadn't deterred her.

Desperate much??

I wrote out several messages to her, deleting them time and again as I tried to figure out what Ryder would even say before realising he would just keep it simple.

Ryder:

I'm in Tucana.

I chewed on my lip, wondering how long it would take her to reply and hoping that she did before Ryder realised his Atlas was missing. The moment he did, he'd figure out that it was me who had it and would be knocking down my door with murderous intentions.

Luckily for me, old desperate Debbie was right on it with her response and I received four messages in quick succession. Three were pictures of her restrained in various ways and laid out like some kind of fetish queen in leather underwear and the last was an actual response.

King:

I knew you'd come back to me! I'm awaiting my punishment keenly and will be ready for you whenever and however you want to take me.

Classy. Maybe I want to take you to the local dump and throw you out with the rest of the trash!

I gritted my teeth as I forced myself to reply like Ryder might.

Ryder:

Now. Where?

She instantly forwarded an address and I grinned in triumph as I got up to leave.

"Now what?" Gabriel's voice came from the balcony and I shrieked in surprise as my heart leapt half way up my throat.

"What the fuck are you doing?" I demanded as I stalked towards him. He was sitting on the railing which ringed the balcony with his chest bare and his gleaming black wings on display. He was just wearing a pair of black jeans and with his dark hair and tanned complexion he looked good enough to eat. Like a fallen angel come to corrupt me.

"I had a vision about your little hunt for Professor King," he said casually. "I saw how you would get around Ryder's refusal. And I know that there's no way to deter you from this search, so I'm just going to come with you."

"I don't need your help," I replied stubbornly, though in all honesty I wouldn't mind having him there for backup.

"Well you're getting it. Besides, I can fly us there and you won't even have to try and escape via the front door."

"Why would I need to escape?" I asked in confusion.

A fist suddenly started hammering at my door and I looked around in concern as Ryder started shouting.

"Open this fucking door, Elise! I know what you're doing!" he bellowed.

I looked back to Gabriel and found a smile tugging at his lips as he offered me his hand. He was enjoying this. And if I had to choose between a face off with an angry Basilisk who was spitting venom and a gorgeous Harpy offering to whisk me away to safety, then it was a pretty easy decision to make.

I took Gabriel's hand and he gave me a full smile as he tugged me into his arms.

He scooped me up against his chest and I wrapped my arms around his neck half a second before he launched himself into the sky with a beat of his powerful wings.

He didn't hold back for a second, shooting through the sky with a speed that could match mine as he tore towards our destination without even needing to ask for the address from me, which must have meant he'd *seen* it.

We dropped from the sky at an alarming pace and Gabriel came to land outside a small bungalow on the west side of town. I threw up a silencing bubble to hide us from King's Vampire ears and Gabriel slowly lowered me to my feet.

"We need to sneak up on her," he said thoughtfully. "We can't risk her getting the upper hand. We have to immobilise her magic before she gets a chance to-"

"I have an idea," I said with a grin, grabbing his hand and towing him down a little darkened alley between her house and the next.

I pressed Gabriel back against the wall in the small space as I pulled Ryder's Atlas from my pocket again. I quickly typed out a message, telling her to leave the door open and blindfold herself in preparation for his arrival. Gabriel snorted in amusement as he read what I wrote and I hit send.

"I don't suppose you *saw* anything about her having the answers I need, did you?" I whispered as we waited a little while in the shadows. Ryder wouldn't have been able to travel here as quickly as we had so I didn't want to alert her by moving too soon.

"The visions still won't cooperate like that," he replied bitterly.

"Why not?" I asked in a soft voice. I didn't think I'd ever actually questioned his gift before, but sometimes it seemed like he saw it as more of a curse than a blessing.

Gabriel frowned and I could see he was pushing aside his natural inclination to deflect from the question. He reached out and tucked a lock of my hair behind my ear with a sigh before he spoke.

"I'm not entirely sure. But I have a theory."

"Go on," I urged, moving closer to him.

"There are so many unanswered questions from my past which haunt me, but I do get flashes of memory from time to time. I think I can remember running through secret passages, the scent of smoke on the air and screams echoing behind me. I'm fairly sure I escaped something bad but... I just can't figure out any more than that. I know that there are people who want me dead,

I wasn't supposed to survive whatever happened that night. And I also know that someone saved me. Someone called Falling Star."

"The one who makes those payments to you," I said and he nodded.

"But I'm beginning to think that he did more than just give me a new identity to hide me. I think he might have put a block on my gifts too. I just don't know why. And the only way to break a block like this is either for the person who cast it to remove it or to somehow break through it myself. But all of my attempts have failed." He dropped his head in defeat and I reached out to catch his chin, making him meet my eyes.

"You'll break it, Gabriel," I growled. "You're one of the strongest people I know."

He looked into my eyes for a long moment and I was sure he was hunting for a lie, but he wouldn't find one. I meant every word.

A softness spilled into his gaze and he reached out to cup my jaw in his hand. "I can't wait until we're bonded by the stars, Elise. When they bring us together, I just know that everything will be alright somehow."

I frowned, unsure what to make of that declaration. I liked Gabriel, wanted him, hungered for him but not *just* him. And I didn't want some magical bond robbing me of the connection I had with the other Kings.

"Gabriel, I'm still not sure that-"

He caught my hand and pressed it to his bare chest right where the Libra tattoo was inked onto his skin. As our flesh met, he dropped the walls around his magic and the swirling tempest of his power rushed towards me in a flood as I instantly dropped mine too.

I gasped at the intensity of his strength as it poured through me, bathing in the depths of the deepest ocean and connecting to a pulse that beat within the bosom of the earth. The pleasure that washed through me at the connection was so intense that it was all I could do to cling to him and hope the world didn't tilt while I was lost in it.

Gabriel groaned in pleasure as he embraced the swell of my magic too and the combination of our power flowed between us.

When he finally pulled his magic back, I found myself panting in his arms, my body tingling with euphoria as I looked up into his dark eyes.

"I've never even come close to trusting someone enough to share my power with them," Gabriel breathed. "But my magic aches to be with yours. It recognises it. It knows that we're destined to be one."

I nodded, because I couldn't deny the way that had felt but it didn't lessen the other protests I had.

Gabriel kissed me and I wrapped my arms around him as I gave myself a moment to bow to the desires of my flesh for his.

He pulled back with a sigh and drew me into an embrace as I leaned against his chest. There were so many things I still needed to figure out about what had happened to my brother, but I was starting to think that with his help I really would get the answers I sought.

"Do you think Orion is ready to trust us yet?" I asked as he held me in his arms.

"Soon. I think I'll be able to get through to him at the party after the Pitball match," he replied and relief spilled through me at that. We could use whatever help we could get against the mysterious King I was hunting. The Card Master had been stealing power from suicidal Fae for the stars knew how long and I had to hope that Orion would be able to help us with something to counter that dark power when we went after them.

"We need to deal with Professor King. She could be who we're looking for or maybe Ryder's right and she's got nothing to do with any of this. But I need to hear it for myself," I said heavily, pulling back despite the fact that I ached to take so much more from him.

"Okay," Gabriel agreed, his hands lingering on my skin.

I smirked at him and stepped back more firmly then turned to approach King's house.

My silencing bubble hid our approach as we drew closer to the front door, but my heart pounded with anticipation all the same. King might be outnumbered but she was a fully trained Fae and a strong Vampire. I wasn't going to underestimate her.

The door swung open as I turned the handle and I smirked to myself at the brilliance of this plan.

A wide open living space greeted us as we entered and I fell still as I spotted King lying butt naked and spread eagled on her dining table with a thick black blindfold wrapped around her eyes as instructed.

My lip curled back in anger at the sheer audacity of this woman. She'd been Ryder's fucking teacher. And after what he'd told me he'd suffered through at the hands of Mariella, I had to wonder if Nightshade had had a point about King predating on him too. He was so much more than he showed to the outside world and the idea of her abusing him in any way made me want to rip her fucking pubes out. *It's called a hair removal spell, you fucking yeti!*

A snarl left my throat and I almost shot forward to attack her, but Gabriel caught my arm before I could do anything so stupid. He threw his hand out and vines shot over the table, wrapping their way around her and pinning her arms to her sides so that she couldn't use magic. She cried out but it sounded way too excited and I realised she obviously thought it was Ryder's earth magic containing her.

"I've let you down," she gasped. "I know. I'm ready to pay for it."

"Does the idea of being like that for him really turn you on?" Gabriel asked me in disgust, our voices still contained in the silencing bubble.

"He's never asked me to be submissive like that," I snapped in reply.

Yes Ryder liked to be in control, but I'd never gotten the impression he wanted me simpering or begging and I was pretty damn sure he got off on it when I fought back. Anyway, what we did or didn't do was up to *us*, not Gabriel.

"Whatever. You'll forget about him soon enough," he muttered in reply and I ground my teeth.

"Are you angry with me?" King whimpered and I glanced at Gabriel as I tried to figure out the best way to play this.

"I've got an idea," Gabriel said as he twisted his fingers in a complex pattern, weaving an illusion spell. "I can create an illusion of Ryder's voice. She'll think he was the one who came here, not us. If she finds out it was us she could call the FIB, but she can't admit to trying to contact Ryder or she'd be sent back to prison."

My lips parted at the brilliance of his plan. "How good is your Ryder impersonation?" I asked.

"I've spent enough time with him over the last few days to get a handle on it," Gabriel replied. "Shall I give it a go then?"

"Do it," I agreed.

Gabriel stepped outside of my silencing bubble, treading heavily towards King as she trembled on the table. He waved his hand to cast the magic and an illusion of Ryder's voice came a moment later. "I've got some questions for you."

King stilled, biting her lip at the sound of his voice. "*Anything* for you," she breathed.

"About Gareth Tempa." Ryder's voice came again at Gabriel's command.

King fell still and I could have sworn I detected a tremble in her limbs. "I...I'm sorry," she whispered. "I was afraid of going to Darkmore Penitentiary. When the FIB made me that deal I just panicked and took it, but-"

"Tell me about the deal," Ryder's voice snarled.

"They j-just wanted to know things about you. But I didn't know anything incriminating. That was why I got Tempa involved. *He* was the one who taped us in my office. *He's* the one who was trying to find enough evidence to put you away. I was hardly involved. The FIB just wanted me to be the one to put the pressure on him. But he was so soft, so nice, I knew you'd never let him close enough to get anything on you!"

I exchanged a concerned look with Gabriel. I had no idea that Gareth had been trying to collect evidence against Ryder for the FIB and I couldn't even imagine what the fuck he'd been doing lurking in a cupboard filming the two of them having sex. That would be more than enough motivation for the King of the Lunar Brotherhood to murder him, but I still didn't suspect Ryder somehow. I just couldn't believe that he would be lying to me about this.

"What evidence did Tempa get?" Ryder's voice demanded.

"Nothing good enough," she spat bitterly before quickly adjusting her tone. "I mean, he didn't get anything damning enough to convict you…so they abandoned the investigation and then I…"

"Then you went to prison anyway," Ryder's voice growled. "That must have made you pretty angry with Tempa."

"Well I certainly wasn't crying when I heard he'd given himself an overdose."

How fucking dare she discuss my brother's death in that flippant tone? A snarl of pure rage left me and I shot across the room, disbanding my silencing bubble and snatching hold of a fistful of her dark hair before slamming her head down on the table with the full force of my gifts.

"He was worth a thousand of you!" I snarled as she cried out in agony and I swung my fist back to punch her stupid fucking face in.

Gabriel lunged at me, locking his arms around my chest as he tried to heave me away. I snarled at him, baring my teeth as I prepared to fight him off of me if I had to. He threw a silencing bubble over us as King started crying out, demanding to know who else was here.

"She might be a callous, stupid bitch but you heard her. She didn't kill your brother," Gabriel growled as he locked his arms tight around me, using his weight to try and pin me down. I could have thrown him off with my gifts, but I hesitated as I considered his words and he barrelled on as he realised he was getting through to me. "Let's just get out of here before she realises that Ryder isn't even here and calls the FIB on us."

I clenched my jaw, battling against the bloodlust and the desire to vent some of my rage and grief on that piece of shit woman laying on the table.

"Fine," I gritted out eventually, clenching my fists to try and control myself.

I glanced at King; she was still blindfolded, still thought Ryder was here. I hadn't completely fucked up and Gabriel was right, it was better that she didn't know about me.

Gabriel held onto me for another long moment before slowly releasing me and dropping the silencing bubble.

"Take this as a warning," Ryder's voice snarled. "If you cross the Brotherhood again, we'll cut you into pieces and feed you to the fishes."

King whimpered as the vines holding her down slowly began to loosen under Gabriel's command.

He caught my hand and we strode from her house and he scooped me into his arms, taking off the moment we were outside.

"Feed you to the fishes?" I snorted a laugh as I clung to him. "You've been watching too many mafia movies."

"Sorry, I'm not used to the gang lifestyle you're becoming accustomed to," he replied, rolling his eyes.

"That's okay. I like you just how you are."

He smirked in response to that and we flew back to the hotel where I was going to have to explain myself to a really pissed off Basilisk. *Shit.*

RYDER

CHAPTER TWENTY NINE

I lay in Elise's bed in my snake form, no bigger than an arm's length as I hid beneath the covers, my clothes discarded around me. Rage coiled through my body and a hiss slid from my mouth. She was going to get the shock of her fucking life when she came back here. No one disobeyed me and got away with it.

I'd picked the lock to get in and made sure it was locked again so she wouldn't be able to tell I'd broken in here. I tried to ignore the sweetness of cherries around me, but my oversensitive tongue could taste it all. I was drowning in the scent of her flesh and it was the sort of bliss that might have doused my fury on any other day. But she was in trouble this time. So she was going to be reminded of exactly who I was.

The sound of the window opening made me fall still and anger burned hotter inside me as I heard Elise and Gabriel laughing and chatting together. It would be just my luck if they fell onto the bed and started fucking right on top of me. I would swallow that motherfucker whole if it happened.

"Thank you for coming with me," Elise said then the sound of them kissing reached my ears.

Fuck. This. Shit.

The punishment I'd had in mind went from a watered down version of hell to full blown hot pokers and brimstone.

"I'm going to take a shower," Elise said.

"I could join you…" Big Bird said suggestively and it took everything I had not to shift into my largest form and sink my teeth into him.

A long pause signalled Elise considering it and my heart crushed to dust.

"That's seriously tempting, but I'm only gonna have a quick shower then go talk to Ryder," she answered and Gabriel groaned as they kissed again.

"You can go talk to him after," he suggested. *Fuck no.*

"I can't Gabriel," she said, but she sounded like she really wanted to continue this. "Come see me later."

"Alright," he chuckled and I waited for the door to sound. And waited. And fucking waited.

How long does it take to leave a fucking room, asshole?

The sound of the door clicking shut made me relax. Elise was finally mine.

I gave her two more seconds, hearing a couple of items of clothing hit the floor as she stripped, then I shifted back into my Fae form. I cast a silencing bubble around me before I pulled the covers down, grinning as I found she had her back to me, humming softly as she tugged her tank top over her head.

I pulled my jeans on, sliding out of bed and moving up behind her as she reached around to undo her dark green lacy bra and I eyed her matching panties eagerly. I had to keep my lust firmly in check if this wasn't going to break the deal, but I could do it if I held onto this rage. And right then, that seemed easy.

I dropped my silencing bubble in a flash. "Need a hand?" I grabbed her fingers as they brushed her bra strap, clamping my hand over her mouth as she cried out in alarm. I dragged her back against my bare chest, casting a new silencing bubble around the whole room this time and releasing my palm from her mouth.

"Ryder!" she scolded me, trying to fight her way out of my hold, but she definitely wasn't trying that hard. "What the hell are you doing?"

I lowered my mouth to her ear, splaying my hand across her stomach to keep her in place. "You disobeyed me, Elise," I hissed. "Was it worth it?"

She shivered slightly, tipping her head back to rest on my shoulder as she turned to look at me. "You were right…King didn't know anything. But I needed to hear it myself."

"So my word means nothing to you?" I snarled, walking her forward and pushing her against the wall. I caged her in with my arms. She didn't even try to use magic to fight me off and I had the feeling she was enjoying this. But if she thought this was going to turn into a treat for her, she was really fucking wrong.

"It does," she said weakly.

"Clearly not," I spat, kicking her legs wide.

"Ryder," she said breathlessly. "What are you gonna do?" There was hope in her voice, but I was about to kill it. As far as the deal was concerned, I couldn't gain pleasure from hurting her. And I wasn't about to give her pleasure either.

I reached for my belt which was still unbuckled and tugged it free of the loops. At the sound of the buckle clinking, Elise glanced over her shoulder and her eyes widened.

"Turn around. Hands on the wall," I commanded.

She bit into her lower lip and I had to look away, forcing down the flicker of arousal that burned right to my cock.

I must not enjoy this.

I thought of Elise kissing Gabriel and my rage flared through me again, scorching away everything else.

I folded the belt around my hand then ran the leather down her spine, spreading goosebumps across her skin.

"Aren't you going to beg me not to?" I asked, pretty curious about why she hadn't said a word against this yet. I'd never whipped someone purely for punishment and not seen them tremble, beg and shatter before my eyes before I even struck the first blow. Pain delivered from me was merciless. I didn't stop until I drew blood.

"I don't beg anyone for anything," Elise said lightly, dropping her head as she raised her hands and spread them above her on the wall. "Besides, I've been bad, Ryder. So I'll take my punishment like a big girl."

I cracked the belt across the backs of her thighs and she gasped, looking up at the ceiling as red marks raised across her creamy legs.

"Are you sure about that, baby?" I growled. "Because I won't go easy on you."

"Life's not easy," she said breathlessly. "Sometimes you have to embrace the pain."

I whipped her again, this time striking her across her ass and making her back straighten sharply. I fed on her pain, drinking in every drop as I took my anger out on her and fuelled my magic reserves. I had to focus, because one slip of the mind was going to send me tumbling into oblivion. I'd fuck the life out of her before Dante could even get to this room and try to kill me for breaking the deal.

"Say sorry," I snarled.

"No," she replied immediately. "I'm not sorry."

I struck her again and a sharp crack splintered the air. She groaned as her pain washed into me and I devoured every drop of it.

"I'm...not...sorry," she panted.

I painted the back of her thighs in red stripes, so close to breaking the skin with every blow. But I knew some part of me was holding back.

"More," she demanded as I hesitated. "I deserve it."

I whipped her again, feeding on her pain and letting it soothe the rage in my heart.

One more strike would tear her flesh open, but I stayed my hand, dropping the belt and moving forward to heal her. I brushed my fingers over her thighs, the swell of her ass, taking away her pain and giving in to the lust that was clawing at the back of my skull.

She sagged forward, resting her head to the wall and I swallowed thickly, hoping I hadn't gone too far.

"Elise?"

She turned to me, a smile pulling at her mouth and tears swimming in her eyes. I frowned in confusion as she wrapped her arms around my neck and placed kisses along my jaw.

"You're the only one who gets it."

"Gets what?" I grunted, my dick swelling more and more with every kiss she gave me. She reached my ear then ran her mouth down to my neck and I groaned, fisting a hand in her hair and forcing her head back to look at me. "What do I get?"

"We both need pain to heal," she breathed. "I'm sorry I hurt you, but I'll always do what I have to to find out what happened to Gareth."

I nodded, seeing my reflection in her eyes and wondering how a girl like this could share a part of me I'd always thought was broken. Defected. But when I saw it in her, it didn't look like that at all. It was beautiful. And it was ours.

She pressed her hand to the X she'd inked on my chest, tracing it with her finger. My gaze raked over the curve of her lips, her long lashes and the flushed cherry colour of her cheeks. She was all of my broken, missing pieces. She was everything I needed and the only thing I wanted. She was sweet and pure and dark and twisted at once.

She tip-toed up, brushing her lips over mine in that feather-light almost kiss that drove me to madness. "Can you taste cherries?" she breathed against my mouth.

"No." I brushed a lock of hair behind her ear. "I can taste my own soul, because it's the exact same flavour as yours."

ELISE

CHAPTER THIRTY

"Wake up, little monster!" The hammering of a fist pounding on my door called to me from the corridor as I relaxed in my jacuzzi after our fourth day of exploring Zodiac Academy.

"The door's open," I called back lazily, not wanting to move away from the water jets which were currently doing an amazing job of working the knots out of my spine.

The door opened and Leon's footsteps drew closer as he hunted me down.

"I'm in the bathroom," I called.

"Oh, I thought you were asleep," he said as he strode straight in and stood looking down at me.

"It's like, ten past eight, Leo. You're the only one who goes to sleep this early," I pointed out.

The water was in constant motion and there were a lot of bubbles, but my breasts were peeking out above the surface and his gaze fixed on them for a long moment before he shook his head firmly to focus his thoughts.

"We're having a party…well, more of a gathering to watch the Supernovas vs the Moon Bulls match," he announced.

"Okay," I agreed easily. Kick off was at nine so I could enjoy my bubble bath for a while longer before it began.

"No. Not okay, we need to get this place looking right. Your room is the biggest and we need to make sure it's tidy and-"

"Are you saying my room isn't tidy?" I asked, arching a brow at him.

"It's…fine. It's just not Lance Orion fine," he replied, narrowing his eyes at a towel I'd tossed over the sink for when I got out.

"You invited him?" I asked in surprise.

That actually worked into mine and Gabriel's plans perfectly if we wanted to continue winning his trust, but it was also a little awkward. The more time I spent with Orion, the more the ache to challenge him pushed at me just like Gabriel had predicted. There was always the element of competition hanging in the air between Vampires unless they were mated and I had no intention of adding to the list of guys I was seeing. I had my hands full with all of the testosterone buzzing in the corridors as it was.

But maybe it didn't matter if me and Orion finally gave in to the desire to fight over dominance tonight. Gabriel only said I had to last three days and I'd managed four. I actually deserved a damn medal. And though I was almost certain that coming to blows with Orion would only end in me getting my ass kicked, the idea of it was more than a little exciting. Fighting with my own kind was a part of my nature and it had been a long time since I'd indulged in it. Besides, once we'd figured out which one of us took the top spot in the Vampire hierarchy, we wouldn't have this tension hanging between us anymore.

"Yeah I asked him. Twenty four times. Until he agreed. Which he just did." Leon pulled his Atlas from his pocket and waved a message from Orion at me with the biggest grin on his face. It was one word. *Fine.*

I snorted a laugh. "Why do I feel like I've got competition?" I teased.

"Don't worry, you're the only little monster for me. Although, if he wanted to join in with us, I'd be totally up for that too." He grinned at that idea, his gaze dropping to my hardened nipples again for a long moment.

"Well, if you want me ready on time, you should really help me to clean up," I suggested, plucking a sponge from the side of the huge bath and sitting up to give him a better view as I offered it to him.

Leon hesitated, a growl of desire coming from him before he shook his head firmly. "No time. I'll literally spend the whole night making you come after he's gone, but we need to get ready now. I've got Mindys out buying snacks and getting you something hot to wear but they're new, you know, untested. This could be a fucking shambles!"

"Did you just say you sent them to get me clothes?" I asked as I stood up, letting the water run down my naked body.

"Yeah…although this outfit is pretty fucking hot, so you could just stay like this," he said, inching closer.

"What's wrong with *my* clothes?" I asked as I got out of the bath and stalked towards him.

"Nothing. They're great. You know, for *normal* stuff. But this is a party with *Lance Orion.*"

"He's just some dude from another school," I pointed out as I picked up my towel and started drying myself.

"He's going to be famous. Like, Solarian Pitball League *famous.*"

"You're good enough to get picked up for the league too," I pointed out.

"*Fuck,* little monster, that's like…the hottest thing that's ever come out of your mouth." Leon growled.

I smirked at him just as a knock sounded at my door and he turned and ran back through to the room to answer it. I headed after him, wrapped in my towel and found a flock of Mindys rushing about laying out snacks and beers and cleaning my entire room. One of them handed Leon a big white box and he promptly walked towards me with it, flipping the lid to reveal a hand embroidered lilac dress and a pair of white stilettos.

"Isn't this a bit much?" I asked, pulling it out and holding it in front of me. It had thin straps and hung to my mid thigh and would have been perfect if we were going to a bar or a club, but I usually just watched the game in my sweats.

"It's purrrrfect," Leon said with a hungry look in his eyes.

"Fine," I laughed as I headed away from him to get changed while the Mindys finished off setting my room up.

By the time I emerged again, the Mindys were gone and Leon had collected Dante and Gabriel who he was in the process of assigning seats to.

"Lance needs to sit in the middle," he insisted, shoving Dante to make him move along on the couch. "And then you can have that armchair, Gabe."

"Don't call me Gabe," Gabriel muttered as he ignored Leon's commands and snagged himself a beer.

"Where's Ryder?" I asked and the three of them turned to me, their eyes dripping over my dress and making me flush.

"Sei incredibile," Dante murmured in a low voice.

"You look hot as fuck, little monster. But Scar didn't want to join in," Leon said, answering my question with a pout. "If you can convince him then please do."

"Or don't," Dante added.

"Play nice," I warned him.

"He won't come," Gabriel added. "He's in our room scowling at the ceiling."

"Can I have your room key?" I asked, moving into his personal space.

Gabriel sighed as he pulled it from his pocket and handed it over.

I flashed him a smile before shooting away to locate Ryder. I unlocked his door and headed inside without bothering to knock. Ryder was on the floor with his shirt off doing a set of press-ups and I wandered closer, watching the way his muscles swelled with appreciation.

"I thought you had a sad little party to attend?" he grunted as I got close enough for him to see my stilettos from his position on the ground.

"We're just watching the match. I want you to come."

"I don't like Pitball."

"Everyone likes Pitball," I countered.

"I don't. I don't even know the rules. I don't watch TV."

"I don't know which one of those statements is the most concerning. What do you mean, you don't watch TV?"

Ryder sighed and finished his set, pushing himself up onto his knees.

"You look fucking edible," he growled, reaching out to run his fingers up my leg, starting at my ankle and moving them higher steadily as I looked down at him.

"Well your silly rules say you can't eat me. So why not come hang out instead?"

"I don't hang out."

I pursed my lips. "Just because you've never done something before, doesn't mean you can't try it."

He hesitated with his hand beneath the hem of my skirt and slowly stood before me. "Do you want to change me because you don't like who I am?" he asked in a rough voice.

"I don't want to change you," I replied. "I want to free you."

He let out a long breath, his gaze searching mine like he was hunting down a lie. I reached up to cup his cheek in my hand.

"I'll explain the rules," I promised.

"Why do you even care?"

"I don't like you missing out. If you try to watch it with me this once and don't like it then I'll never ask you to watch it again." I painted a cross on my heart and his lips twitched in amusement.

"Fine," he grunted and I threw my arms around his neck, planting a kiss on his cheek. "I'm not wearing one of those fucking shirts like Simba though."

"No kit for you," I agreed, stepping back.

Ryder grabbed a black tank top from the floor and tugged it on before letting me lead him back to my room.

Leon cheered as we arrived while Dante growled, sending a flicker of electricity through the air and Gabriel just set his jaw, looking resigned.

I led Ryder to the empty armchair and nudged him to make him sit down before grabbing two bottles of beer and one of the pizza boxes the Mindys had delivered and dropping down on his lap.

Leon started pacing as the prematch discussion played on the screen and Dante and Gabriel fell into a heated debate about the starting line ups of the two teams who were about to play. I leaned in close to Ryder's ear to explain the rules of the game while no one was paying us any attention.

His gaze was on the screen as he took sips from his beer, but he nodded slightly now and again to let me know he understood.

"Who are we supporting?" he asked as I explained the difference between the teams.

"Well I prefer the Moon Bulls to the Supernovas," I said and Dante reached out to fist bump me without breaking his rant about Killian Dawn who he claimed had a weakness for water attacks. "But I'm a Blueshine fan when it comes to the overall League."

A knock sounded at the door five minutes before kick off and Leon practically sprinted to open it.

Orion looked into the room with his brows raising as he stepped inside. "I thought you said this was a party?" he asked mildly. "It looks more like the makings of a seriously sausage heavy orgy."

"Oh, errr, well I can get the Mindys to join us if you want a bigger crowd?" Leon offered, yanking his Atlas out of his pocket so fast that he sent it flying across the room.

"No, I prefer this. I'm not really much of a party person," Orion admitted. "Vampires are into solitude over company most of the time..." His gaze trailed to me in Ryder's lap and he frowned slightly like I wasn't acting very Vampirish. "Of course there are always misfits in every Order," he teased.

"All the best people are at least a little odd," I pointed out and he smirked.

"You certainly have varied tastes. Don't you ever mix with your own kind?"

Ryder hissed at the suggestion but I just laughed.

"Come sit down," Leon said, tugging him into the room and practically shoving him into the spot in the centre of the couch beside Dante. "Have a beer," he added, snatching one from the cooler and offering it to Orion.

"Oh, thanks man but I don't actually drink. Clean body and all that, I want to focus on my game and I can't afford to drink during the season if I want to go pro," Orion replied with a slanted smile.

"Oh yeah. Good idea. We wanna be on top form to destroy you on the pitch in the final," Leon agreed, throwing the beers he'd just grabbed back into the cooler then snatching mine, Ryder's and Dante's and tossing them back too.

"Hey!" I protested but he ignored me as he grabbed the entire cooler and strode out onto my balcony. I gasped as he tossed it over the edge and Orion's lips parted in surprise. A huge crash sounded from below as people started yelling and Leon quickly slammed the balcony door to shut out the noise.

"I wasn't trying to say that you guys can't drink, you fucking savage," Orion said with a laugh as Dante swore in his language.

"The Lion has a hard on for you," Ryder explained, rolling his eyes. "He won't fucking shut up about you."

I bit my lip on a giggle as Orion shifted in his seat.

"I'm not really into dudes," he said with a smirk. "But I guess with that long hair and a bit of imagination I could make it work."

"I don't entirely hate that idea," Leon joked as he dropped into the seat on Orion's other side and tossed his arm around the back of the sofa behind him. "I'm fifty kinds of hard for Elise, but I'm cool with watching her get it on with you if you like?"

"*Leon,*" I growled, flashing my fangs at him.

"I mean, if *she* likes. Obviously." Leon waved a hand and this time Gabriel, Ryder and Dante were the ones growling.

"I'm not a bag of pick and mix for you to offer about," I scolded.

"No. I know that. I didn't mean that," Leon said, glancing between me and the rest of the guys as Orion laughed.

"I'd sooner not have an audience of assholes who want to rip my throat out when I'm getting it on with a girl. But thanks for the super weird offer," Orion deadpanned.

We were saved from the awkwardness in the room by the match starting and everyone relaxed as they focused on the game. Ryder kept his attention fixed on the game throughout and I even caught him smirking as the rest of us screamed our support at the screen whenever the Moon Bulls made a pit. And when they won the match, I leapt up screaming with the rest of them and caught him actually smiling before he hid it again.

Leon snatched me into his arms and whirled me about in victory and my fangs started tingling as he drew me close to his skin. I gripped a fistful of his long hair and tugged his head aside with a growl of longing and sank my fangs straight into his neck, bathing in the fiery flavour of his magic as it washed over my tongue.

I drew back after a few long moments and he placed me on my feet with a grin.

I turned and found Orion watching us with a hungry glint in his eye and a hiss slid from my lips as his gaze landed on Gabriel like he thought he might bite him. I stepped between them and he raised an eyebrow at me.

"What's the deal with you guys?" Orion asked instead of challenging me, his gaze skipping between the others and landing on me like he couldn't figure it out. "If you were a Wolf pack I'd get it, but…"

"We're not a pack," Leon said, waving a hand dismissively. "We're a pride. But instead of a King with a bunch of lionesses we have a Queen with a bunch of Lions."

"I'm not a fucking Lion," Ryder disagreed.

"You are. You're Scar, Dante's Mufasa and I'm Simba and Gabe is… Zazu."

"Don't call me Gabe," Gabriel snapped. "And Elise isn't your fucking Queen, she's my Elysian Mate."

"Ignore the stronzo, he's deluded himself into believing that," Dante muttered.

"So you share her?" Orion asked, his eyebrows raising in surprise and for a moment I could have sworn he looked a bit impressed by me for claiming these four powerful beasts as my own.

Leon and Dante said yes while Ryder and Gabriel said no and I sighed.

"It's complicated." I shrugged.

"But you're a Dragon," Orion accused, pointing at Dante like he might not know what he was. "Dragons don't share things. Least of all mates. I should know, I once stole my mate Darius's french fries and he damn near burned my hand off with his Dragon Fire when he shifted over it."

"I'm a Dragon born of Wolves and the only thing I don't do is follow rules."

"Harpies don't share mates either," Orion added, raising an eyebrow at Gabriel.

"This is temporary," Gabriel said irritably.

Orion's eyes whipped to Ryder. "I don't know much about Basilisks, but you don't strike me as the live and let love type. More the I've pissed on it so it's mine type."

"You don't know shit about me or what I am," Ryder replied with a hiss.

"Well my extracurricular classes this term included Advanced Order

Biology so I know a bit about your kind and I'm pretty sure you aren't communal...and Vampires definitely aren't."

I rolled my eyes. "I don't fit into the standard Vampire cutout. So what?" I challenged. "They're *all* mine."

None of the guys objected to that at least.

Orion looked around for a long moment and a slow smile spread over his face at the challenge in my tone. "So they're all your Sources too?"

I pursed my lips. I'd only officially claimed Dante and Ryder as my blood Sources, but there was no fucking way I was going to let him sink his teeth into Gabriel or Leon either.

I bared my fangs at him as my Order pushed at my flesh, demanding I defend what was mine from this vulture.

"*Mine,*" I growled.

Orion's fangs snapped out and he growled right back in a clear challenge. "I'm stronger than you," he pointed out. "I can just take them."

"I dare you to try." A prickle ran down my spine as my fingers curled into fists in preparation for his attack. Gabriel had said this was inevitable and I'd begun to agree, but I'd never considered the idea of Orion trying to bite one of my Kings. There was no way I'd be allowing that. Which meant I actually had to win against him too.

Leon and Dante dropped back down to the couch to watch this play out and Ryder leaned forward in his chair eagerly.

"Make him bleed, baby," he purred.

"Who tastes the best?" Orion asked like a total cocky douchebag, licking his lips like he was already trying to decide between them for his feast.

"You won't be finding out," I promised him.

"Elise..." Gabriel warned, reaching out to catch my elbow. "He's got two Elements, is more powerful than you and he's four times the size of you."

"Then it will be all the more embarrassing when I kick his ass," I replied with a growl, tugging my arm out of his grip.

Dante laughed loudly and Ryder smirked in anticipation. This was what Vampires did. We couldn't be around each other for long without fighting for our spot in the hierarchy. And under normal circumstances I would have agreed with Gabriel; I wasn't strong enough to take on Orion. But I sure as shit wasn't letting him bite any of my Kings without a fight.

"As we're friends, I'll give you a fair shot," Orion taunted like he thought he'd already won. "No magic. Just Order skills. Winner takes all."

I smiled savagely at that offer because he'd just levelled the playing field. I might have been a lot smaller than him, but I was fast and I was ruthless and I'd fight tooth and nail to keep his fangs out of my Kings.

"On three then," Leon said excitedly, lifting his Atlas to film us.

Orion dropped into a fighting stance and I kicked my stilettos off.

"One, two-"

I shot forward in a blur of motion and sucker punched Orion straight in the gut before Leon said three then leapt aside again as he swung his fist straight for my ribs. His hit landed despite my attempt to avoid it, sending agony spearing through my bones as something crunched.

I hissed in pain and dove at him again, slamming my shoulder into his gut and trying to uproot him. He planted his feet and caught me around the waist, flipping me up over his head and tossing me to the ground behind him.

The side of my head smacked against the corner of the coffee table and I winced as blood spilled down the side of my face.

I hissed as pain poured through me and I swept my legs around, catching the back of his knees and taking him down. He twisted as he fell, grabbing my ankle as I tried to scramble away and dragging me back towards him.

I kicked out with my free foot, catching him in the face and busting his lip open so that his blood ran over my skin.

Orion growled, grabbing that foot too and shoving it aside before propelling himself on top of me and pinning me down with his weight.

I snarled like a wild cat, flailing beneath him as I started punching anywhere and everywhere I could reach. His face, his sides, his back. I threw every ounce of my gifted strength into the blows and I heard a few crunches come in response to my ferocity.

Orion hissed at me as he managed to catch one of my wrists and he slammed it down onto the carpet above my head.

I punched him in the side of the head with my free hand twice more before he caught that too and pinned me down.

"Yield," he demanded, baring his fangs.

I reared forward and slammed my forehead into his nose. A loud crack sounded and blood poured down his face onto me.

Ryder laughed loudly and Leon whooped in excitement but I couldn't spare any attention to look their way.

"*Fuck,*" Orion cursed, increasing the pressure on my chest as he transferred both of my wrists into one of his hands and slapped the other around my throat to pin me down.

Gabriel growled somewhere behind us as I continued to scramble beneath him despite the fact that he had me beaten.

"Yield," Orion demanded again, his grip tight enough to hold me but not enough to actually choke me out.

My heart thrashed against my ribs as I eyed his fangs and pictured him biting one of my Kings. Or all of them. The mere idea of it physically hurt me and a snarl of pure rage left me as I refused to give in to his demands. I came from Alestria where gangs ruled the city and blood ran in the streets every day. I'd learned a long time ago that you don't give up until you're dead. And my thundering pulse wasn't quitting any time soon. I might not have been a match for Orion in a fair fight, but I sure as shit knew how to fight dirty.

I went limp in his arms, panting heavily as I watched the triumph flashing in his gaze. He lifted his head, running his tongue across his fangs as he assessed the options available to him and tried to decide who he wanted to bite first.

The moment he lifted his hips an inch, I drove my knee up between his legs as hard as I fucking could. He gasped as he collapsed back onto me and the other guys all let out exclamations of pained sympathy in response.

I ripped my right hand free of his grip and slammed my fist into his kidney as hard as I could three times before kicking him off of me.

He rolled onto his back with a growl of anger and I dove at him, kneeing him in the balls for a second time before landing on his chest. I gripped a handful of his black hair and yanked on it as hard as I could as I forced him to sit up.

He lurched forward and caught me in his arms, tightening his hold on me until I couldn't move. I sank my fangs straight into his shoulder and the growl that left him was pure animal as I broke the Vampire Code. But I didn't give a shit about Vampire etiquette; he wasn't going to be getting his fangs into anyone in this room.

Orion released me, shoving me off of him as he leapt to his feet, but I was upright in the same moment and I slammed my knuckles straight into his throat.

Orion coughed as he stumbled back a step and I sped around him, leaping onto his back and locking him in a chokehold, using my weight to leverage him. I wasn't polite like he was and I didn't hold back as I tried my fucking hardest to choke him out.

He ran backwards, slamming me against the wall but I didn't relent despite the flare of agony that raced through my busted ribs and he cursed as he stumbled down to one knee.

"Fine," he hissed through my hold on him. "I yield."

I released him instantly and sprung up with an excited laugh. My dress was torn, my ribs were definitely broken and blood was pissing down the side of my face, but I didn't give a shit. Because I'd fucking won.

I pressed a trembling hand to my ribs to heal them, raising my other hand to point at my Kings who had all risen to their feet and didn't seem to know quite what to say.

"*Mine,*" I growled possessively, claiming each and every one of them in the same breath.

"Yeah," Orion said, snorting a laugh as he healed himself. "They're yours, psycho. And just so you know, you broke about eight of the rules in the Vampire Code then. Did you *really* have to go for my balls? *Twice?*"

"I fight to win," I replied, catching Ryder's eye as he smirked at me. "And it might be bloody and brutal and all kinds of fucked up. But I got what I wanted in the end. And that's all that really counts, isn't it?"

Orion looked at me for a long moment before finally nodding in agreement as he wiped the blood from his face with his shirt sleeve. "Well, thanks for the life lesson. I'll work on being more ruthless. And in the meantime I'm gonna say goodnight and go and find myself a nice willing girl to drink from."

Leon moved to show him out and I tipped my head back, closing my eyes and letting out a long breath as the adrenaline finally started to fade from my veins. I didn't know how the fuck I'd just managed that, but I couldn't have been more relieved that I had.

"You're so fucking incredible," Ryder growled and I opened my eyes again to find him standing right in front of me.

"I just got the shit beaten out of me for you," I teased.

"Yeah. And you look absolutely stunning." He reached up to touch the side of my face with two fingers where blood still slid over my skin from the wound to my forehead. I watched him as he painted two lines on each of my cheeks, a dark smile lighting his face as he admired his work. "My warrior."

I smirked at him, catching his wrist and turning his hand so that I could wipe my blood over his lips before leaning forward to press a kiss on top of it. He stilled at my touch and I growled as I pulled back, wishing that him and Dante would just let this fucking deal go for the thousandth time.

"Are you just gonna stand there staring at her, stronzo or will you heal her?" Dante demanded as he moved to stand before me too, knocking his shoulder against Ryder's aggressively before reaching out to heal the wound on my head.

"Always looking after me, Drago," I teased as I looked up at him.

"You don't need looking after, amore mio," he said fiercely. "I think you just proved that."

A rush of movement made me look up half a second before Leon barrelled into Dante and Ryder, forcing a spot into existence between them before snatching me into his arms and kissing me with all the heat of the sun.

"That was. So. Fucking. Hot," he exclaimed, kissing me between each word.

"No one's taking any of you away from me," I growled possessively. "Even the stars aren't allowed a say in that. And if they try, I'll beat their asses too."

DANTE

CHAPTER THIRTY ONE

Mars had informed us that we were all invited to a private party tonight to 'celebrate the union of our two academies'. Or some cazatte - *bullshit*. Tomorrow we were going to be playing Zodiac in Pitball and I wanted to be on top game. I didn't come all this way in the tournament and work my ass off in training not to win. Even though I knew it was unlikely as hell, maybe the stars would shoot us some good luck.

Mars had insisted we bring formal wear on this trip just in case we needed to make a good impression. More cazatte. The only impression I cared about giving right then was the one I'd leave in my bed after a good night's sleep.

"Elise is gonna be all over us," Leon said. He was standing in front of the mirror in a tux, adjusting the bright red bow tie he'd paired with it. His hair was pulled up into a topknot and his subtle spicy cologne tingled my senses.

"Dalle stelle," I sighed. "We can't afford distractions tonight, not with the game tomorrow."

"To be honest, I'm most excited about getting tackled on that pitch and leaving a mark in its luscious grass."

"You're the Captain, stronzo. You should be taking this more seriously."

"Oh my little Dragon." He turned to me as I struggled to tie my bow tie, moving forward and doing it for me. "Of course we're going to win," he said with a wide smile. "I've got the best fucking team they've ever seen. They just don't realise it yet. I have absolutely zero concerns. I could turn up as high as a Harpy on Killblaze tomorrow and we'd still win. One star player doesn't beat three."

"Orion isn't their only good playe-" Leon pressed his fingers to my mouth to shut me up.

"Shhh, let's have fun tonight."

I rolled my eyes, pushing him off of me and checking my bow tie in the mirror. My hair was swept back stylishly and I looked like a true mob boss in the fine clothes.

"Let's go see what our girl's wearing." Leon clapped a hand to my shoulder and my mood brightened by a mile. I pushed all thoughts of Pitball aside as we headed out the door and laid my faith in Leon. I could be nervous for the game when the party was over.

Ryder was standing outside Elise's room with his back to the wall. He hadn't bothered to put on the tux waistcoat and his bow tie was hanging loose around his open collar.

"You look like the end of the night not the start of one," Leon commented and Ryder's upper lip peeled back.

"You look like the asshole of a lion not the front of one," he tossed back.

"Touché," Leon laughed and I could have sworn Ryder almost smiled. "Do you need a hand tying that?" He nodded to the bowtie and Ryder clenched his jaw.

"No," he grunted.

I moved to the other side of the door, resting back against the wall and not offering Ryder any more attention. It was bad enough we had to spend this entire trip in close proximity, let alone having to go out and socialise with him.

A door opened across the hall and Gabriel stepped out, looking like a fucking model in his tux, his tattoos just peeking out below his sleeves and around his neck. He moved forward silently and folded his arms, gazing at Elise's door like we weren't there.

Tension spilled through the air and our group tightened as each of us inched closer and closer to the door, ready to pounce on Elise the moment she appeared. The only one who didn't seem tense was Leon who was casually taking selfies for FaeBook.

He turned around, moving across the hall. "Everyone get in." He held his Atlas up to take the picture.

"Press that button and I'll snap your fingers off one by one," Ryder hissed.

Gabriel casually floated out of shot, but Ryder remained stubbornly in place.

"Come on guys, don't be party poopers," Leon encouraged and I gave him a shake of the head which he could see in the camera, signalling him to stop.

The door opened and Leon almost dropped his Atlas as he swung around. I kicked away from the wall, twisting sideways to get a look at Elise and Ryder's shoulder crashed into mine.

She wore a dusky pink gown which was stunning beyond words, sweeping down to the floor around her feet in a tumble of silk. The sleeves sat off the shoulder and the necklace Ryder had given her sparkled against her collar bone, looking annoyingly perfect. Her lilac hair was twisted into a bun and a few loose strands hung around her neck. Her lips were cherry red and her eyes sparkled as she looked between us all in surprise.

"Sei più bella del sole," I breathed in awe.

"You look like the angel you are, Elise," Gabriel said.

"Fuck me on a toadstool," Leon sighed. "You look gorgeous, little monster."

Ryder made a strained noise, sweeping a hand over his closely cropped hair.

She blushed as she gazed between us all. "Oh thanks."

She stepped into the hall and I offered her my arm before anyone else could try it. She took it with a smile and Leon moved smoothly to her other side, linking his arm with hers too. *Perfetto.*

Ryder and Gabriel fell behind us as we moved toward the elevator and headed downstairs, the death glares they were giving us driving into the back of my skull. Mars was waiting in the lobby in a tux of his own, his broad chest looking like it was about to pop a button on his shirt.

"You look wonderful, Miss Callisto, I hope these boys aren't causing you any trouble?" Mars offered his arm to her and she slipped away from us with a grin, taking him as an escort instead.

"No trouble. They're all on their best behaviour."

"Well let's hope they stay that way." He gave us all a stern look over his shoulder before leading the way out onto the street.

An extravagant black Hydrummer limo was waiting for us and I snorted a laugh. "Are we really going to arrive on campus looking like stronzos?"

"We're not going to campus, Mr Oscura," Mars said as a valet opened the door for us.

"Where are we going then?" Elise asked.

"You'll see," Mars said, a note of excitement to his tone.

"I don't like surprises," Ryder growled as I followed Elise into the Hydrummer.

I could stand up inside the flashy space as I followed Elise down to the front and dropped onto a leather seat beside her. There was a bottle of champagne sitting in a cooler and Leon promptly snatched it up as he fell into the space on her other side. Mars and Gabriel sat in the middle of the long vehicle and Ryder remained right down the other end, looking like he'd rather be anywhere else.

Leon uncorked the champagne, pouring us all glasses as the driver took off down the road. Then he stood up with the final two glasses, moving down the limo toward Ryder. I frowned as I watched him hand him a glass and drop into the seat beside him. I'd never asked Leon to swear any allegiance to me or my gang. We were friends and I didn't want the business side of my lifestyle tainting that. The only problem was, that meant I couldn't hold him to any of my usual standards, like never hanging out with members of the Brotherhood. Especially not my mortal fucking enemy. I didn't have a right to be jealous or pissed, but I was.

Elise's hand dropped onto my knee and I looked to her, forgetting all about the sting in my gut. I placed my hand over hers, the gold rings on my fingers glinting under the spotlights.

The driver took a road out of Tucana and though we all questioned Mars, he wouldn't tell us where we were going. Ryder looked like he was about to start a knife fight by the time we pulled through two huge golden gates, clearly not liking being left in the dark.

An enormous manor house stood at the far end of the drive under the light of the moon, the grounds stretching out around us for miles into the darkness.

The limo pulled up outside the huge stately porch with doors so large they could easily have accommodated my Dragon form.

A frown knitted my brows as I spotted the golden knocker shaped like a Dragon head and my heart free fell in my chest.

"*No*," I snarled, looking to Mars. "Are you insane?"

"We had a personal invite," Mars said with a shrug. "I couldn't refuse a High Councillor."

"Which High Councillor?" Gabriel asked in surprise.

"Lord Lionel Acrux, the Dragon Master," Mars answered.

Elise turned to me with wide eyes. I'd told her he'd been trying to get me to visit him, but I'd refused his letters again and again.

Her fingers threaded with mine and a look of solidarity flared in her eyes.

My gut writhed as I stood up, knowing I had no fucking choice. And I had the awful feeling that this whole trip had been designed just for this purpose. Because no one said no to Lionel Acrux. He was practically a god in Solaria.

We trailed outside after the others and Leon shot me a concerned frown. I'd told him about Lionel and he'd told me I should accept his offer to come see him then rob him blind. Typical thief.

I pulled Elise closer before we left the car, whispering in her ear, "Stay with me."

"Of course," she promised, tip-toeing up to lay a kiss on my cheek. With my family miles and miles away, she was my instinctual kin in their place. I needed her presence, her strength. And together we'd face this Dragon bastardo.

We stepped out of the vehicle and I made sure we were at the back of the group as Mars approached the front doors, using the heavy knocker.

The doors opened a moment later and I trailed up the porch steps, gazing into the utter opulence that awaited us. Nearly everything was gold, from the stair banister to the glinting chandelier above. The wide staircase curved down before us and a butler ushered us to one side of it in a line. Mars was first, then Leon, Gabriel, Ryder, Elise then me.

My veins pumped with anger because this asshole had no right to force me here. I didn't want to join his little Dragon club or take a vow about the laws of our Order. I wasn't going to be held to anyone's rules but my own.

"Good evening," a booming voice sounded from the top of the stairs and I spotted a muscular man standing there with harsh features and soft blonde hair. The woman on his arm was presumably his wife, her tight green dress pushing up her fake tits and her smile painted on as thickly as her lipstick.

"May I introduce High Lord Lionel Acrux and his wife Catalina," the butler supplied before bowing his head.

They descended the stairs and moved along the line, shaking everyone's hands in turn. When Lionel Acrux reached me, his eyes roamed over my face with hunger in his dark gaze. He clutched my hand tightly and I clutched it back even tighter.

"Dante Oscura," I said. "But you already know that, don't you?"

Lionel chuckled but there was absolutely no humour in it. "You have our kind's spirit, I see. Come." He dropped an arm over my shoulders and steered me away from the group. I still had a tight hold on Elise's hand and dragged her along with me. Lionel shot her a look, but said nothing as I towed her after us.

"You must have canapés with us in the ballroom," Catalina said to the rest of the group. "The other Councillors and the Heirs are quite thrilled to be spending the evening with you."

The Heirs were here? Merda Santa. If Lionel thought schmoozing me with his son and the other pretentious next-in-line-to-the-throne assholes was going to work, he was going to be bitterly disappointed. I'd pretty much avoided the magazines which were full of photoshoots of the Heirs as they rose to fame and power, but I hadn't missed the fact they were going to be Awakened early. At fourteen, they'd have magic before any other Fae in their school year. They'd be way ahead of the game by the time they enrolled at Zodiac Academy when they were eighteen. It was completely unfair and totally typical of these aristocratic stronzos.

Lionel led us through to a large smoking room, releasing me and taking up a cigar box.

"Smoke?" He offered them to me, ignoring Elise entirely.

"No thanks," I said coolly.

"Perhaps you'd like to go and join the rest of the party, my dear?" Lionel asked Elise.

She swiped a cigar out of the box, clipping the end off and lighting it in a flash of Vampire speed. "I'm good. I love a cigar." She took a puff and blew it over Lionel's face. As the cloud cleared, pure rage simmered in his eyes.

I fought a smile as she dropped into one of the wing-backed chairs beside the fire.

"What an interesting choice of company you keep," Lionel said, his eyes swivelling to her then back to me.

"The best kind," I answered, a growl rumbling through my chest. "And she's not going anywhere, so if you have something to say you will say it in front of both of us."

Lionel's eyes narrowed. "Do not forget who I am, Mr Oscura."

"How could I forget?" I asked lightly, pushing my hands into my jacket pockets. "Is there something you'd like to talk to me about? I imagine you had to pull quite a few strings to get that student exchange from Aurora Academy, and I suppose you were the one who decided the top five students would attend?"

Lionel's face split into a pleasant smile. "You caught me." He gestured for me to sit and I slowly moved forward, dropping into the seat next to Elise.

Lionel sat across from us, stacking his hands in his lap. "I am sensing some animosity here, so I'd like to clear the air. As a fellow Dragon, I am simply extending an olive branch. I'd like us to be friends."

He picked up a bottle of whiskey from the table, pouring measures into the two crystal glasses beside it. Elise swiped one up before he could offer it to me and Lionel scowled before fetching another glass from a cabinet across the room. I smirked as he poured it then pushed it across the table and I reached into my jacket, taking out my chalice.

Lionel's brows arched as I tipped the contents of the whiskey into the golden cup and took a sip. It was oaky and tasted like burning money.

"You won't drink from my glass?" he asked, seeming offended.

"I have more enemies than you have scales in your Dragon form," I said lightly. "I don't drink from anyone's glass."

Lionel's eyes glinted as he inclined his head. "Well perhaps I can help you with that."

Elise sat up, puffing on her cigar as she eyed Lionel closer. She remained silent, sipping on the whiskey. I would have smiled if I didn't sense this stronzo was dangerous. Perhaps more dangerous than I'd realised.

"Just say the word and I'll have these enemies silenced," Lionel offered, casually swilling his drink in his glass. "And in return-"

"Ah, there it is," I cut over him. "The real reason I'm here. So what is it then, High Lord Acrux? What is it about me that keeps you up at night? I'm guessing it's not my ten inch dick."

Lionel scowled, his façade falling away in a moment. "You listen to me you arrogant little prick, you are in the house of one of the most powerful men in Solaria. If you think you can talk to me so crassly and get away with it, then you will soon discover that making an enemy out of me is a far greater problem for you than every other enemy you claim to have back in your hometown."

I clenched my jaw and Elise tensed beside me, the air in the room suddenly thicker, harder to breathe.

Power radiated from this man and I had no doubt he would keep to any death threat he made. I had the feeling that anyone who had opposed him in the past had been thoroughly silenced.

"What do you want?" I asked evenly, static energy beginning to build around me.

"Storm Dragons are exceedingly rare," Lionel said, his tone soft again like he hadn't just threatened me. "So rare in fact, that you are currently the only one in existence to my knowledge."

"So what? Do you want me to join your Dragon club so you can parade me around like some trophy wife?"

"He's already got one of those," Elise pointed out and Lionel cut her a sharp glare.

I squared my shoulders, sitting up in my seat, because he could point those furious eyes at me, but not her. And I was beginning to regret bringing her here.

Lionel licked his lips, contemplating us before answering. He leaned forward, resting his elbows on his knees. "I am offering you the world, Mr Oscura. You can have anything you ask; property, land, gold, protection. It's yours. And you can extend that to your family too."

He cocked his head and my heart twitched. He knew what my family meant to me and that could only mean one thing. He'd had someone watching me for who knew how long.

"And what do you want in return for all of that?" I asked, my hands tightening on the arms of my chair.

Lionel sat back in his seat, smoking his cigar for a long moment. "I want you to be a part of the Dragon Guild. I want you to take the oath of the Dragon laws and I want you to move to this part of Solaria. I will pay your tuition fees to Zodiac Academy and provide any and all provisions you need for your education. You can come and live here initially and I will buy you property once you've proved your loyalty to the Guild."

"To you, you mean," Elise stepped in and Lionel snarled, turning to her once more.

"This does not concern you."

Elise took my hand, sitting up straighter. "Well we're together, so yes it does."

Amusement flickered in Lionel's gaze and he nodded as if he accepted that fact. But I had the feeling he didn't.

"I don't want your answer today." Lionel stubbed out his cigar and rose to his feet. "But I will ask for it soon. Enjoy the ball, and remember what you'll be giving up if you refuse this offer, Mr Oscura. With the sort of life you live, you must lose family members all the time. That can end the moment you accept my deal." Lionel strode from the room and a heaviness weighed down on my shoulders. There was an undercurrent to his words that frightened me.

He knew where I lived, knew who my family were.

Elise stood up, dropping into my lap and combing her fingers through my hair, searching my eyes. "What are you thinking?"

I brushed my hands over her waist, a frown pulling at my brow. "You look worried, amore mio. Do you think I'll accept his offer?"

She chewed on her lower lip, running her thumb over my forehead to smooth out the creases there. "I don't think he'll let you refuse."

"I'm Dante Oscura, carina," I growled. "I can refuse the sun if I want to."

A smile spilled across her face and I groaned, longing to take a kiss from that mouth. She leaned in close to skate her lips across mine in the lightest of motions, but I felt it right through to my core. Electricity stirred the air around us, rising the hairs along my arms.

"Dalle stelle," I sighed. "You're the most tempting thing I've ever known."

She dipped her head as she smiled then slid off my lap and tugged me to my feet by one hand. "Come on, let's go cause havoc at Lionel's little party."

I wrapped my arm around her waist with a grin, guiding her from the room. "What are you going to do? Swing from the chandelier?"

"Maybe." Elise shrugged and my heart swelled to twice its size. *Cazzo*, I loved this girl.

We headed out into the large entrance hall and the butler directed us along a corridor and into an impressive ballroom. A huge mural pictured Dragons dancing in the air together, their massive forms taking up an entire wall. The place was full of guests in fine clothes, all simpering and drinking champagne like stronzos.

I spotted Leon's topknot and tugged Elise in his direction. As we pushed through the crowd, I realised he was talking to Orion. Beside him were four guys I knew from the media. The Heirs were dressed to the nines, all of them standing shoulder to shoulder. I recognised Lionel's son, Darius on the far end, his dark features nothing like his father's except for the cold look in his eyes. As a Dragon, he was growing fast, only a couple of inches shorter than me already. Beside him was Max Rigel with ebony skin, broad shoulders and eyes laced with mischief. Next was Seth Capella, a Werewolf who'd Emerged young like their Order usually did. He had unruly hair and a playful look about him as he joked with his friends. The final Heir was Caleb Altair who had dark blonde hair and model worthy features like the rest of them. He was looking at Elise as if he recognised her and immediately stepped forward from the group to greet us.

"You must be the Oscura Dragon," he said to me. "Who's your Vampire friend?"

"I'm Elise," she answered with a taut smile. "How could you tell I was a Vampire?"

"My family are all Vampires. And you look like a kid in a candy store." Caleb stepped closer with a cheeky grin, cupping one hand around his mouth. "Are you dreaming about sinking your fangs into everyone here? The power levels must be making you hungry as hell. I'll be a Vampire when I Emerge for sure. I can practically taste these suckers already."

Elise laughed and I smiled, warming to this particular Heir a little.

"Holy shit," Seth said, moving forward and reaching for Elise's hand. "Who are you, babe?" His eyes slid over her and though he was five years younger than my girl, the balls on this guy clearly weighed a ton.

"Elise Callisto," she said smoothly, extracting her hand from his before he could lay a kiss on it.

Seth ran a hand through his hair, flexing his muscles. "Do you wanna get a drink?"

"Are you offering it from the vein? Because if not, I'm not interested," Elise said lightly, brushing her fingers up my arm.

Seth grinned at her and Max slammed a hand onto his shoulder as he stepped forward. "I know you're about to say yes to that, bro, but if you spill blood on your shirt, your mother will have you castrated."

I chuckled and Elise curled a loose lock of her hair around her finger.

"I promise not to make a mess," she teased.

"He's not even Awakened, amore mio," I purred in her ear. "He won't taste nearly as good as me."

"One day I will," Seth countered with a smirk.

"You could never taste as good as a Storm Dragon," Elise said thoughtfully, running her fingers into my hair.

Leon moved closer to us to join the conversation and leaned in to speak in my ear. "I have so much fucking jewellery in my pockets right now."

I snorted a laugh as my eyes fell on Orion behind him. He and Darius were gravitating towards one another, talking together like old friends. The Dragon boy hadn't said a word to me yet, but I wanted to know if he was as much of a stronzo as his father so I extracted myself from Elise and Leon and moved towards him.

"Hey man," Orion said as I arrived. "Enjoying the party?" His tone said he knew how much this kind of party sucked and I offered him a shrug and half a smile.

"Lionel's offered me the whole world," I said. "So I can't complain."

Darius eyed me up like he was assessing me. "And you're going to accept and live like a king while Father uses you as another one of his little puppets, I guess?"

My brows lifted. Maybe Dragon Junior wasn't a carbon copy of his papà.

"No." I leaned closer conspiratorially. "I can't be bought with gold, little Dragon."

"Less of the little," he growled. "I'm almost your height."

"The key word is almost." I smirked.

"So you can't be bought with gold, but how about women?" Orion asked with a barely contained laugh, sipping from a beer before gesturing across the room.

I followed his gaze to a redhead who must have been in her late thirties in a tiny sparkly dress. Her boobs were pushed higher than Darius's mom's and she had so much makeup on I didn't know where she began and the fakeness ended. Lionel was talking in her ear and she was nodding keenly like she was taking instructions.

"Merda santa," I blew out a laugh as I turned back to them. "Is she for me?"

"Yeah, that's my cousin Juniper. And watch out, she's coming," Darius said with a snort.

I stiffened as a hand landed on my back and Juniper moved around to greet me, placing a sticky kiss on my cheek. She smelled like my Aunt Patrella – and that wasn't a compliment because she was eighty nine and wore enough perfume to drown a horse.

"Such a pleasure to meet you," she purred. "My my, aren't you a big boy?"

My balls jumped right up inside myself and I gave her a false smile. "Yeah, and this big boy needs a piss."

I nodded to Orion and Darius in goodbye, making a beeline for the exit before my dinner made a reappearance. *Al diavolo*, was that woman supposed to seduce me?

I didn't really need a piss so I wandered down the hall, glad to just be away from the place. A blur in my periphery announced Elise arriving and she grinned as she stopped in front of me, placing a hand on my chest. My heart beat unevenly as I gazed at this beautiful creature.

"Where are you going, Drago?" she purred.

"Anywhere but that ballroom," I said, a grin pulling at my lips.

"Want to have some fun?" she asked, her eyes glittering and luring me right in.

"Definitely."

"Let's find a bathroom, then grab as much toilet paper as we can and TP every room in the house," she suggested keenly.

I barked a laugh. "What if we get caught?" I lowered my voice to a whisper, though I had every intention of doing it anyway.

"Simple," she breathed, fisting her hand in my shirt and tugging me toward her. "We don't."

ELISE

CHAPTER THIRTY TWO

Dante and I could barely hide our laughter as we ran down the vaulted hallway back towards the pretentious party. A dining parlour, a games room and a bathroom had fallen prey to our TP skills before we'd decided to make a run for it and escape the scene of the crime.

"With a bit of luck, old Lionel will give up on trying to tame the savage once he realises what hard work you are," I teased as my fingers gripped his tightly and the sound of the party washed over us.

Dante tugged on my hand hard enough to halt me and I gasped in surprise as he pressed me back against the wall, his grip moving to my waist as he pinned me in place.

"Cosa farei senza di te, amore mio?" he purred, his mouth dropping to my neck where he brushed his nose across the sensitive skin beneath my ear. I could feel his breath feathering against my flesh and I ached for him to press his mouth to mine and mark me as his.

"I'm sure you only speak to me like that to turn me on," I breathed, placing a hand on his chest and running it down his fine suit until I was caressing the hard ridge of his dick through his pants.

"Everything you do turns me on, bella," he growled, pressing against me and making sure I could feel exactly how true his words were.

Heavy footsteps approached, interrupting us and Dante drew back with a growl of frustration as we turned to find none other than the Dragon Lord himself approaching us. He had a benign smile on his face as his gaze slid to me for a moment and then away again.

"You know, there are a lot of benefits to pure blooded breeding," Lionel said casually like we'd been in the middle of a conversation instead of him walking in on us dry humping against a wall. "Two powerful Dragons will almost certainly produce powerful Dragon Heirs, like my sons. But that doesn't mean there is no room for whatever other dalliances we may wish to indulge in. A wife only need bear you children, she isn't required to warm your bed at all times. There's plenty of room for more...*exotic* tastes." His gaze touched on me for a moment before locking on Dante again.

"If I choose to marry, it will be for love," Dante replied, narrowing his eyes. "And if my wife bore me children, I wouldn't disrespect her by bringing mistresses into our marriage bed. A morte e ritorno."

My gaze roamed over Dante's face as the passion he felt for his statement filled every inch of it.

"I'm afraid I'm not versed in your native tongue," Lionel replied.

"It means *to death and back*. It's my family motto and it means love, honour and sacrifice in all things for those who we name as kin."

Lionel's eyebrows rose. "Like honour among thieves?" he teased. "Well perhaps our morals aren't so far apart as you might think. I too would do *anything* for the strength of my family. When you join the fold, you'll soon find that out."

"I already have a family."

"Yes, of course. But you should be with others of your kind. It's only natural."

"I am a Storm Dragon born of Werewolves. I carved my own place in this world and I fit in it perfectly. There's nothing pure about my blood. I'm eighty percent Wolf, ten percent Manticore and ten percent every other Order you can imagine. Only a twist of fate made me a Dragon and by the mercy of the stars I cherish that gift, but it doesn't make me one of you."

"No," Lionel agreed with a soft sigh. "The transformation we will require to mould you into a suitable representative of our family will take time and hard work, but you're an intelligent boy, I'm sure you'll pick it up."

Dante's lip peeled back at the casual insult and static crackled through the air, making Lionel's perfectly quaffed hair stand on end.

"Think on what I've said, Dante," he added as he turned to head back to the party. "Everyone has a price. We're just entering into the negotiations."

I hissed at his back as he strode away from us, my hand moving to Dante's as I gripped it tightly.

"He's very determined," I said once I was sure he couldn't hear us anymore.

"Yes. I don't think I'll easily convince him to change his mind."

"Maybe not if you enter into *negotiations,*" I said, dipping my voice into an utterly hilarious impression of our host and drawing half a smile from Dante. "*But,* I bet we could convince him that he doesn't want you anymore…"

"How?" he asked, eyeing the dangerous glint in my eye.

"Well, look at this party. At all the fancy dinner guests and the pretentious music and the food that only comes in little cubes. I'm gonna bet he won't be too keen on it turning into a real party…"

Dante snorted a laugh. "You think that if I'm enough trouble, he will decide he doesn't want me?"

"Can't hurt to try," I pushed.

"Come on then, bella. Let's go get some shots."

I grinned at him as we headed back into the party and Dante led me straight towards a waiter in a penguin suit who was carrying a tray of champagne.

"I'll take that, mio amico," Dante announced, taking the tray from him and turning his back on the guy's startled expression.

We moved to the side of the room so that he could place the tray down on a table and I snagged a glass just as Dante did the same, pouring it into his chalice.

"To freedom," he said, holding it out to me.

"Freedom," I agreed, clinking my glass to his and draining it in one.

I laughed loudly as the champagne bubbled in my belly and several heads turned our way.

"What are you up to, babe?"

I looked around at the sound of Seth Capella's voice. The Celestial Heir walked towards us with the three other Heirs in tow behind him. They were all about fourteen, but their Orders meant that they were already tall and the Dragon kid, Darius, was bulking out with the signs of his inner Dragon already.

"I'm trying to win a bet, care to help?" I asked as I raised another glass. Dante caught my eye with a snort of amusement.

"How?" Seth asked, pushing a hand through his unruly dark hair.

"Dante here doesn't believe we can make this party fun. But I think that we can pull it back from the brink with enough effort. For a start, we're going to drink all of these." I pointed at the tray where around forty glasses stood waiting for our attention.

"You're going to get wasted?" Caleb asked, moving closer with a smirk that said he was tempted to join us.

Was I going to encourage a bunch of kids to get drunk? Hell no. Was I going to ban them from joining us? *Well I'm not their mom.* Was getting the four Celestial Heirs to join us in creating havoc at a fancy party run by their parents the best idea I'd ever had? Quite possibly.

"I want to have some real fun," I clarified.

Seth and Caleb seemed convinced and they both snatched glasses of their own before passing more to Darius and Max. They all looked more than a little nervous, casting looks out into the room where their parents were all talking business with other pretentious assholes.

"You're a bit young for drinking," I said, feeling like I should make some attempt to discourage them. "But you can have fun with us without getting wasted." I snagged another glass for myself and smirked in a challenge. "Unless you're too chicken shit, of course," I taunted before emptying my drink into my mouth.

Dante laughed darkly as he drained his own drink too and Leon appeared through the crowd as if he'd sniffed out the real party.

"Hell yes!" he announced as he instantly grabbed two glasses and drank them one after another.

The Heirs looked between the three of us then glanced at each other.

"It would certainly make this party more interesting," Caleb pointed out as he raised his glass to his lips.

"Fuck interesting," Dante growled, grabbing another drink and transferring it into his chalice. "I vote for carnage."

"I second that!" Leon announced as he tossed another drink back.

Caleb followed suit and the other Heirs instantly joined him.

"Father's gonna have a fucking aneurism over this," Darius muttered as he sank his third drink. He didn't seem inclined to hold back despite the fact that he knew this wasn't going to end well.

"Maybe a little less booze for the kids," I said, moving to stop them as they reached for more.

"Our parents don't care about us drinking," Seth shrugged. "But the carnage part of your plans might be a different matter."

"Fine by me," Dante said and I nodded my agreement.

As the drinks fizzed through my blood, I let out a giggle and looked around to the corner of the room where a dance floor had been set up and people were twirling around in choreographed moves I had zero chance of replicating to music provided by a string quartet.

Beyond it was a set of glass doors which opened onto the sweeping lawn outside the manor and the call of freedom was just too much to resist.

"Let's go," I said, snatching Leon's hand as he went in for his eighth drink and dragging him after me. Dante took my other hand and we carved a path through the overly pampered crowd surrounding us.

The Heirs followed and I smirked as we drew more than a few stares. Max stumbled as he walked, almost knocking Seth over and the two of them laughed loudly enough to catch their parents' attention.

Probably should have tried harder to stop them drinking...

We spilled across the dance floor, ruining the choreographed nonsense that was taking place before heading out through a door at the back of the room and onto the lawn.

It was a balmy evening and the scent of summer hung in the air as the cicadas sang.

Dizziness swept through me as I tried to count just how many drinks I'd had, but I shrugged off the question as my gaze fell on a balcony which jutted out over the lawn.

I released my Kings' hands and shot away from them, scaling the trellis that ran up the wall beside it and only breaking a few rungs on it as I went.

I leapt up onto the low wall which ringed the edge of it.

Leon let out a wolf whistle as they all looked up at me and I spread my arms wide like a bird.

"Dante, catch me!" I called as I fell forward with a whoop of laughter.

"Merda santa," he cursed, dropping his drink as he threw his hands out and I hit a cushion of his air magic a second before I could go splat on the lawn.

I laughed wildly as he flipped me up onto my feet then shot around to do it again.

"You're all crazy," Seth announced in a tone which said he liked it.

"We're just free," I countered from the edge of the balcony. "There's no one to tell me what I can do or not."

I leapt off of the roof again and this time Dante was ready, coiling his magic around me before I came to a halt on the lawn.

Leon had started to scale the trellis, breaking huge lumps off of it as he went and the Heirs grinned between each other as they all moved to follow him.

As Leon made it to the edge of the balcony, he threw his arms wide and belted out the chorus to the Circle of Life by Elton John before leaping straight over the edge.

I grinned as I rested a hand on Dante's arm and he caught him with his magic.

The Heirs all lined up to jump next, the wild look in their eyes letting me know that they didn't cut loose like this enough.

"If you let us die, you'll be throwing the future of Solaria into chaos," Max joked.

"Tempting," Dante replied with a laugh and the four of them dove off the edge, trusting him to catch them with his magic.

As they whooped in triumph, I shot around to jump again, this time climbing all the way up to the roof. I grinned as I backed up a few steps on the fancy tiles and started running for the edge. Dante was in the middle of all of the Heirs as they jumped on him, slapping him high fives and begging him to let them do it again.

"What the hell are you all doing?" Gabriel asked as he stepped out of the ballroom, looking up just as I dove over his head.

Dante cursed as the ground rushed towards me and he fought to extricate himself from the Heirs.

Panic gripped me as my heart leapt and I threw my hands out at the last second as a scream tore from my lips. Air blasted from my palms but in my panic and *slightly* inebriated state, I didn't judge it right and instead of making a cushion to land on, I created a pocket of air that was something like an elastic band.

I bounced backwards, flipped over and landed hard on my back in the middle of the lawn with an oomph of pain as my breath was driven from my lungs.

"Elise!" Dante yelled as he ran towards me with Leon right beside him.

Pain echoed through my battered body and I wheezed as I fought to catch my breath and arrange my muddled thoughts enough to heal myself.

Before Leon and Dante could reach me, a blast of water magic crashed into them, knocking them back and I found myself looking up at Gabriel's terrified face. He pressed his hands to my sides and the warm embrace of his magic swept beneath my skin, healing the damage I'd done.

"What the hell were you thinking?" he gasped, somewhere between terror and rage.

"Lighten up, Gabriel, we were just having fun," I said, rolling my eyes as I sat up.

He didn't back off, his hands moving to my arms as he gripped them tightly and drew me to my feet.

"What the fuck is wrong with you two, letting her jump like that?" he demanded, turning his rage on Leon and Dante as they stalked forward, dripping wet and looking like they weren't enjoying themselves so much anymore.

"Are you alright, little monster?" Leon asked with concern, ignoring Gabriel as the Heirs lurked awkwardly beside us.

"I'm fine," I said, waving off everyone's concern. "We should do it again!"

A snort of laughter came from behind me and I turned to find Ryder approaching us too. My heart lifted as I found myself surrounded by my Kings, but it fell again as I realised they weren't exactly glad to be in each other's company.

"I felt your pain and came to find out what was going on," Ryder explained, walking closer with a smile playing around his mouth. "I should have known you'd be jumping from rooftops."

I grinned at him, moving towards him as the only one of them who wasn't currently looking annoyed or worried, but Gabriel tightened his grip on me and yanked me back to his side again.

A deep rattle emanated from Ryder's chest and both Leon and Dante growled in a clear challenge, but Gabriel wasn't backing down.

"She could have fucking died!" he yelled, pointing at Dante like he was holding him personally responsible for this.

"I didn't tell her to jump, stronzo. She was just having fun. But I guess you wouldn't know much about that."

Gabriel snarled, throwing a fistful of ice in Dante's direction but Dante deflected it with a wave of his hand and it shot through the window of the ballroom instead, smashing the whole thing.

We all stared at it with our mouths hanging wide for a long moment as silence fell inside the party too.

"Shit, sorry guys but I'm out," Seth announced and the other Heirs laughed as they hurried away after him, running around the corner of the house just before Lionel Acrux stepped outside with a furious expression on his face.

"Sorry about that," I said, biting on my lip.

"It was my fault," Dante admitted and Lionel's brow furrowed in anger and maybe even disappointment.

"I'd blame Gabe, really," Leon put in and I really had to work hard not to burst out laughing.

"What the hell is this?" Professor Mars demanded as he appeared too.

"Not to worry," Lionel replied dismissively though his eyes blazed with fury. "Just a little high jinx with the excitement of the party. But perhaps it's best if you all head back to your hotel to ah…sleep off the champagne."

"That sounds perfect," I agreed.

"I'll see to it that they're punished for this," Mars said, bowing his head low in deference.

"Honestly, it's fine. I'm sure we'll be laughing about it the next time we see each other, won't we Dante?" Lionel asked, his eyes hard and the message clear. This little stunt didn't make the blindest bit of difference to him. He still wanted to get Dante into his clutches and he wasn't giving up any time soon.

"I'm sure we will," Dante agreed, his voice dark.

"Perhaps I can assist you in getting back to your hotel a little faster?" Lionel offered, handing a bag of stardust to Professor Mars like it was nothing. But it wasn't nothing. That stuff was worth a fortune and using it for a trip back to our hotel was beyond extravagant. Not that anyone pointed that out.

"Thank you, Mr Acrux," Mars said, bowing his head again. "I'll be sure to get them all back safely."

Lionel gave Dante one last, penetrating look before heading back into the party.

Mars looked like he was about to blow his lid but after several long seconds, he just huffed out a breath and beckoned for us to follow him. We walked around the colossal house and back down the drive until we had gotten far enough from the property's security shield to use the stardust. Mars narrowed his eyes on Dante and Leon's drenched clothes and waved a hand to remove the water from them with his magic. Once they were dry, he took a pinch of stardust from the pouch and tossed it over us. A moment later, the stars swept us away and we appeared in our hotel corridor, right outside our doors.

"Try to sober up and get some sleep before the match tomorrow," Mars said irritably before turning and striding away from us.

We all waited in silence as he walked away and I backed up towards my door.

Gabriel still looked mad enough to spank me and I was half tempted to ask him to do it, but I decided that poking the angry bear probably wasn't the best idea, so I opened my door instead.

All four Kings were looking at me like they weren't sure if I was going to invite them in or not and I smiled coyly before backing into the room and leaving the door wide open for them.

After a moment's hesitation, all four of them followed me and I smiled to myself, wondering how long they'd tolerate each other's company to stay in mine.

"That was pretty fucking funny though," Leon said, breaking the tension as he tossed the door shut behind him and I laughed as he took my hand and pressed his lips to the back of it.

"It was," I agreed. "We'll never forget the time I jumped from the roof of Acrux manor and nearly killed myself in front of the future rulers of our kingdom."

Ryder snorted a laugh with Leon and Dante cracked a smile too, though I could tell he still felt a bit guilty about not catching me.

I reached out to cup his cheek in my hand, giving him a warm smile and he returned it after a moment. "You can't really blame yourself for not catching me when I jumped without warning you," I teased. "Besides I'm all good now."

"Can the three of you just get the hell away from her?" Gabriel snapped and I looked around to find him pacing back and forth by the window.

"You don't own her, stronzo, so stop trying to control her," Dante snarled, turning towards Gabriel and putting himself between us.

"And you think *you* do?" Gabriel scoffed. "You don't even know her. The girl you think you've fallen for isn't even the real Elise."

Leon released his grip on my hand and turned to growl at Gabriel in warning beside Dante.

"You need to stop spouting that vision bullshit at us, Big Bird," Ryder snapped. "The girl I know doesn't have silver eyes. She isn't bonded to you. She's not your fucking Elysian Mate and until the day that happens, I'm not going anywhere."

"But you *will* leave when it does?" Gabriel demanded. "When you finally have the proof you need about what I've *seen,* you'll leave her to be with me?"

Silence hung thickly in the room until Leon broke it, ignoring that question and asking one of his own. "What do you mean we don't even know her? I spend more time with her than any of you assholes and I think I know her pretty fucking well."

My gut squirmed uncomfortably at his words as the lies that hung between us pushed at the base of my tongue, aching to be set loose. I'd gathered enough evidence to feel confident that none of the men in this room were directly responsible for Gareth's death now, so I didn't have any good reason to hold on to my lies. Especially with the way I was clearly beginning to feel about all of them...

"He's right," I said in a small voice before they could continue arguing. "I haven't been completely honest with all of you."

Suddenly, all eyes in the room were on me and I chewed my bottom lip nervously as I wondered how Dante and Leon would react when they found out who I really was.

"What are you talking about, little monster?" Leon asked in confusion.

I released a slow breath and forced myself to let my barriers down. They deserved the truth. All of it. No matter how ugly some of it was.

"Before I transferred to Aurora Academy, my brother was murdered," I said in a level voice, refusing to let my grief colour my words.

"Your brother?" Leon asked with a frown and Ryder nudged him roughly to shut him up.

"Yeah... Someone killed him by giving him a Killblaze overdose and the FIB won't believe that it was murder. But I *know* that it was. So I decided to find the piece of shit who stole him from me and dish out my own justice on them."

"But why would you-" This time, Dante was the one to shut Leon up and I barrelled on quickly, needing to get this all out.

"So I tracked down someone who I thought would know where I should start my search. And when I made him talk, he told me that one of the Kings of Aurora Academy was responsible for my brother's death…"

"You think one of *us* killed your brother?" Leon asked in confusion. "But I've never even met your brother! And I've never killed anyone either, not that you asked, but if you *had* I'd have just told you that-"

"My brother was Gareth Tempa."

Silence rang out as I waited for them to say something. *Anything.*

"Gareth?" Leon choked. "But…how…why…" He shook his head like he couldn't possibly have heard me right and I chewed on my bottom lip as I watched the hurt blossoming in his gaze. "So you've just been looking me in the eye and lying to me this whole time? Gareth was my friend! And you… you…" He shook his head again in denial and I tried to reach for him as tears pricked the back of my eyes.

"I'm sorry," I breathed. "I should have told you sooner, I just needed to keep my identity a secret. If anyone knows who I am then they might figure out what I'm looking for."

A dark growl ripped from Leon's throat. "Was any of it real?" he demanded. "Or was it all just lies so that you could get close to me? To *us?*"

Dante had gone very quiet and I could practically see him turning this information over and figuring out what to do with it.

"I never meant for anything to happen between me and any of you," I gasped. "All of that side of things is real, I swear. I just needed to find out what-"

"How am I supposed to believe that?" Leon snarled, his hands shaking with the desire to shift into his Order form as anger licked through him like wild fire.

"I'm sorry, Leon. I wish I hadn't had to lie to you, but-"

"So do I," he snarled, glaring at me for a long moment before turning and striding straight out of my room. He slammed the door so hard that the walls rattled and I flinched as pain splintered through my heart and my tears spilled over.

"Leon!" I called desperately, moving towards the door and meaning to follow him, but a hand locked around my arm, halting me before I could leave.

"I'll go calm Mufasa down," Ryder said in a low tone. "You stay here."

I was so shocked by him even offering to help that my feet remained rooted to the floor as he marched straight out of the room in search of Leon. I was struck with a sense of pure gratitude to him for doing that for me and I wondered if he'd ever gone to bat for anyone like that before in his life. I was fairly sure I knew the answer.

"Two down," Gabriel muttered. "One to go."

"Do you think this is funny?" I snarled, whirling on him.

Gabriel's face dropped and he shook his head in apology. "Maybe I should just leave you to explain the rest?"

"Fine," I replied dismissively, turning away from him. I was so sick of him trying to control me and it was past time for the truth to be spoken anyway. I just hoped it wasn't going to drive Leon and Dante away from me.

I waited for the door to click shut behind Gabriel and I looked up at Dante with nerves fluttering in my stomach. His family were everything to him. How was he going to react when he found out I'd played a part in his cousin's death?

"Why do you look so afraid, bella?" he asked me, reaching out to take my hand. The faint buzz of electricity reached me through that small point of contact and I took a little strength from it as I forced myself to speak.

"Before I came to the academy, I tracked down someone who I found out had been friends with my brother while he was alive…"

"Tell me," he said in a soft voice as I hesitated.

"I just wanted to find out what he knew, but he wouldn't tell me. My grief was so sharp it cut me open…" I took a deep breath, forcing myself to go on. "I dragged him into an alley and I beat him up to try and force him to speak, but he was off his face on Killblaze and he just kept rambling nonsense. He knew who I was looking for, but he wouldn't give me a name. Just said that they were the King of the academy and then he…killed himself." More tears slid down my cheeks as I tightened my grip on Dante's hand, hoping I could keep him here with me through pure force of will. "I swear I didn't know he'd do that. I didn't want anyone else to die, I just needed to know what had happened to Gareth."

Dante's eyes widened with understanding and my grip on his hand tightened further as I feared he might pull away.

"Lorenzo?" he asked in a low tone and I nodded.

"I promise I didn't want him dead, Dante. He killed himself to protect the identity of the person responsible for Gareth's death. He was terrified of them. Terrified enough to take that escape over offering me the truth."

Dante pulled his hand from mine and turned his back on me, pushing his hands into his dark hair as he strode away and static crackled through the room.

I waited for his anger, his wrath, his revenge. I'd take whatever punishment he thought I'd earned because I knew what it was to grieve a loved one and not know who had been responsible for their death.

"Lorenzo had been hooked on Killblaze for a long time," Dante said slowly, his back still to me. "And my family had done everything we could to try and help him shake it. But it had its claws in him too deeply. He wasn't the boy I grew up with anymore. And I wasn't even surprised when the FIB turned up on Mamma's doorstep to tell us he'd killed himself while he was high on that shit."

"But if I hadn't been there…" I breathed. "If I hadn't hurt him and demanded those answers from him-"

"Then I still believe this was how he would have died. He was a miserable soul and Killblaze caught its name from the suicidal desires it can raise in Fae." Dante turned back to face me with a sigh. "I don't believe you wanted him dead, bella."

"I'm so sorry, Dante," I whispered.

"I'm sorry for your loss too. Gareth was a good friend of mine for a while. I was devastated when he died."

Tears sprung from my eyes as my grief rose up unannounced and relief spilled through me. I'd always heard the saying *the truth will set you free* but I'd never realised until then just how true that statement was.

Dante reached for me and I moved into his arms, drowning myself in the feeling of him holding me and the current of electrical energy that passed from his body into mine.

He pulled me down onto the couch and I curled against him as I let myself cry and he wound his fingers through my hair.

"I'll always look after you, amore mio," he said.

"I'll always look after you too," I replied fiercely.

"Per sempre," Dante added softly.

"Forever," I agreed.

LEON

CHAPTER THIRTY THREE

I used magic to sober up, yanking off my shirt and tossing it across my room. *Fuck Elise.* How could she do this to me? Had she just wanted to earn my trust so she could figure out if I was her brother's motherfucking *killer*?

It had taken her this fucking long to admit it, so did that mean she'd thought it *all this time*?? Suspected I was capable of murdering Gareth like I was some piece of shit. He was my *friend*. And I already felt shitty enough about everything that had happened between us. I hadn't been there when he'd needed me. I hadn't fucking helped. And now his sister had wound herself into my heart, making me fall for her. Making me bleed over that wound again.

The door flew open and Ryder marched in with a scowl on his face. He kicked it shut behind him and I turned my back on him.

"Are you happy now? She's yours," I said coolly.

"Don't be such a pussy," he snapped and I spun back towards him with a snarl ripping from my throat.

"Excuse me? Did you not just hear what she said. Are your snake ears filled with sand?"

"I heard what she said. I've known for a while."

I started clapping slowly, laughing manically. "Oh of course you fucking have. Of course she told the psychotic Basilisk before she told me, because you're *clearly* so much less likely to have killed her brother than I am."

Ryder folded his arms, keeping his lips sealed.

"So I suppose you've been helping her with her investigation then, have you? Digging up dirt on me? Hunting for evidence?"

He still said nothing and fury tore through my chest. I moved to my bed, dropping down and heaving the whole thing over with a roar of anger.

"Fuck you!" I pointed at him. "Why don't you go back to her treacherous little arms and all have a great laugh about how she fucking deceived me."

I moved to the window, tearing the curtains down before slamming my foot against the window. A crack splintered up the centre of it and I snarled, snatching the vase off of my nightstand and launching it at the wall. Flowers, water and china cascaded everywhere and I turned to Ryder to see his reaction. Nothing. Not even a fucking flicker of concern in his gaze.

"What do you want?" I demanded. "Are you just here to drink in my pain, you asshole?" I stalked toward him, pushing my shoulders back in preparation for a fight. If the snake wanted pain, I'd gladly give it to him.

I swung at him and he was on me in a flash, throwing me back against the wall by the throat and pinning my arms to my sides with thick vines.

"You listen to me, Mufasa," he spat. "You're acting like a two year old who just got told he can't go to the playground because it's raining."

I twisted my hands out of the vines and fire flared in my palms, burning his earth magic away. Ryder jumped back to avoid the flash fire around me. I threw my hands into his chest for good measure and he grunted as I burned right through his shirt, revealing the artwork of scars across his chest. Guilt stirred in my gut for half a second before I squashed it right down. I didn't like seeing his scars. It made me see him as more than just a heartless shitbag with no morals. He'd been hurt more viciously than I could probably ever understand. And right then, I couldn't face it, because I needed to hate him.

"Just go back to her, Ryder." I stalked toward my bed, throwing it back upright and launching myself on it, burying my face in a pillow. "Go and initiate some new traitors into your Leon's A Fucking Idiot Club."

Silence rang out and I wondered if he'd slipped out the door, but a second later a weight pressed down the bed as he sat on the edge of it. "She cares about you, fuckwit. Only the stars know why, but she does. And if you hurt her, I'll peel your skin from your bones and make a fur coat out of you." A note of jesting to his tone made me lift my head. It was so subtle I barely heard it, but maybe everything about this guy was subtler than it seemed.

I rolled onto my side so I could look at him, pushing my tangled hair out of my face where it had come free from my bun.

"She thought I killed him," I rasped. "What if she still thinks that?"

"Do you really think Elise would spend a moment in your company if she did?" he asked in a low tone. "With any of us?"

I shrugged, because I didn't know anything anymore. I was cast adrift, lost without her and unsure how I could ever trust her again.

"Think about it, asshole." Ryder stood, moving to the door and exiting.

Yeah, I'd think about it. But the problem was, I kept coming back to the same answer. She'd lied to me. And now I questioned everything I knew about her. Except, when I really analysed it all, I realised I hardly knew her at all. All we ever did together was laugh, joke, fuck, and have fun. Which had been great up until this very fucking moment. I'd been a thirsty Lion, hunting the desert for water. I thought she'd been an oasis, but it turned out…she was just a mirage.

I stood in the guest locker room beneath the Zodiac Academy Pitball stadium, dressed in my dark purple and black kit, staring at the wall. Elise had tried to talk to me several times on our way here, but Dante had finally gotten her to back off. I couldn't find it in me to forgive her. I was blinded by rage. *Betrayal*. And now, before the most important game of my life, I was unable to focus.

"Right, listen up guys, we need to get our heads in the match," Mars called to us.

The rest of our team had arrived here early this morning in preparation for the game. And I'd been delivered some fucking awful news. One of our two Pit Keepers had been taken ill with Fae flu and Greyshine had elected a sub on a whim. A fucking whim.

Subs rarely even played Pitball. They basically signed up for extra credit and didn't show up for practise. And no one gave a shit about that fact because no one expected us to qualify let alone make it to the final. So who had he picked? The most useless Fae in the whole school. Who I'd forgotten was even on the substitute team, let alone played Pitball at all. Eugene motherfucking Dipper. He stood by Elise, pale faced and sweaty, but I couldn't stand to look at him for long.

"Zodiac might be strong, but this is the best team Aurora's ever had," Mars said, giving us all a firm nod. I didn't miss the concerned flash in his gaze as his eyes trailed over Eugene.

Fuck. My. Life.

"So we're gonna go out there and show them what we're made of!" Mars pumped his fist in the air and Eugene was the only one in the room to mimic him.

Mars strode over to me, slapping a hand to my shoulder. "Are you going to make your usual pre-game speech?"

"No," I grunted. I'd ripped up the piece of paper I'd written it on last night and flushed it down the toilet.

Mars frowned, sliding his arm further around my shoulders as he pulled me close for a chat. "What's going on with you, Night? We can't have these emotions out on the pitch today."

"I'm fine." I shrugged him off and he ran a hand down the back of his neck in concern.

A cheer went up from the stadium above us along with the clamour of applause.

"That's our cue," Mars said and he beckoned everyone after him as he headed out of the locker room.

I moved forward, grinding my jaw as I went, unable to shake even an ounce of this fury that was eating me up inside. Not only had I lost my girl, what should have been the best moment of my life was ruined.

A hand curled around mine and I snarled, twisting around to find Elise there.

"I'm sorry Leon," she whispered. "Please don't let this spoil today."

"It's too late for that." I yanked my hand free of her, stalking away ahead of the group and following Mars up the huge ramp that led onto the pitch. I didn't even feel nervous. I just felt broken.

The stands were full and rain was tumbling from the sky above, trickling over my skin and chilling my blood. The crowd were protected from it by a magical barrier, but Pitball was played in all weathers. It was up to us whether we wanted to waste magic shielding ourselves from rain or use it to attack the other players. Sidenote: using it to shield from rain was idiotic. And of course, Eugene was currently doing it with an umbrella made of leaves.

We couldn't recharge our magic until half time and that was only possible if our Orders allowed it within the confines of a locker room. As Eugene was a Tiberian Rat, he needed to make a nest and sleep for half a day in it before he'd recharge. So I was *extra* glad he was on our team today.

I stood at the far end of the line and Dante took the position beside me as Mars moved to the side of the pitch, passing through the shield which stopped any magic from hitting the crowd during the game. The two halves of the match were made up of an hour of five minute rounds. Only one ball would be in play during that time and if it didn't go in the Pit before the five minutes was up, it fucking exploded. We didn't usually practise with the exploding balls at Aurora as they were expensive to replace, but Zodiac's team would have. So we were already at a disadvantage. What made it extra difficult, was that if anyone dropped the ball during play they lost five points for their team. So if the countdown reached zero and someone was holding the ball, they sure as shit better hold onto it and let it explode in their face, because not losing five points was worth a few shattered teeth.

The Zodiac team jogged onto the pitch in their navy and silver colours and Orion stood opposite me, the clear captain of their team. He gave me a nod of acknowledgement, but everything about him said he was taking this game more seriously than a heart attack. And I should have been too. Except all I could think about was the fact that Elise had ripped my heart out, thrown it in a blender and made a smoothie out of it to share with her other boyfriends.

Principal Nova's voice rang around the stadium as she riled up the crowd and said some other shit I wasn't interested in listening to. My eyes fell on the purple section of the spectators at the far end of the pitch, supporting our team. It looked like half the school had come to watch us play, plus all of Dante's family were jumping up and down on their seats and waving Aurora flags. I hunted for my own family and spotted my three moms and Dad sitting together with my brother Roary beside Dante's mom. Of course my asshole brother was here. He was probably waiting for me to lose this game just to rub it in my face.

Ryder and Gabriel sat Pitside at the bottom of their group and I was surprised to find they were both wearing Aurora shirts. Probably to impress Elise, moving in on her now I'd freed up some space in our little harem. Professor Titan sat beside Principal Greyshine, the two of them waving little Aurora flags and wearing stupidly oversized hats and Elise smiled at our potions Professor like she actually gave a shit that he'd shown up.

I ground my jaw, setting my sights on Orion and concocting a plan. If I took out Zodiac's star player, we'd have a chance of winning. So no matter how much I liked him and admired his skill, today I was going to break his legs and make him eat mud after I smashed his perfect smile.

The Zodiac referee moved forward, holding out the first Pitball of the game. It was traditionally an airball which started the match which meant it was light as hell. After this first round, a ball would enter the game through one of the Elemental holes in each corner of the pitch. It was random and meant most rounds started with each player fanning out to their respective Elemental corners as they tried to predict which ball was going to be put into play. But for this round, it was a full out fight to get the first ball between the team captains. And I had more than enough rage inside me to be completely fine with that.

"Team Captains, step forward!" the ref called and me and Orion did as she asked, standing opposite each other as the rain pelted down on us.

"Good luck," Orion smirked.

"You're the one who'll need it," I snarled and his brows arched at the venom in my tone.

A challenge entered his eyes as he lowered into a fighting stance. No Order gifts were allowed on the pitch, so I only had his air and water magic to worry about. But I was going to pounce before he had time to use them.

The ref placed the ball on the ground between us then jogged back to the edge of the pitch. A huge glittering red timer lit up magically above us with five minutes on the clock and the crowd fell quiet in anticipation.

My heart pounded and my muscles bunched.

The ref blew the whistle and I lunged at Orion, throwing a fist at his gut. He took the blow but was running hard and threw his weight into me so I was knocked back a step. I swung for him again, but his fist connected with my jaw and he moved in a flash, snatching up the ball and racing away across the pitch.

The rest of the players tore after him and I took chase with a snarl, pounding across the pitch with him set in my sights. Dante took down a girl right in front of me who was casting a magical wall of air to keep some of my team back and a crack sounded as they hit the floor.

I sped up the pitch as Orion threw the ball to their Earthraider and she tore towards the Pit at the heart of the field.

"Stop that ball, Dipper, or you're dead!" I bellowed as Eugene quivered on the side of the Pit beside our other Pit Keeper, Lucy Fortnite. The two Zodiac Keepers were taken to the ground by an almighty blast of air and I spotted Elise in my periphery with her hands raised. Eugene tried to cast a wall of earth magic up to block the Pit, but all it did was knock him off of his own feet. *Useless.*

Orion circled back, knocking down every fucker on my team that he could with powerful tackles, leaving Harvey Bloom still in the mud alongside our Waterback, Georgia Rust.

"Get the fuck up!" I commanded them, but Orion held them down for the count, one hand on each of their chests and they were sent off the pitch, losing us two points. *Fuck.*

I took chase after Orion, rage scoring through me as I lifted my hands to take him out.

Fire flared in my palms as Orion made a beeline for Elise who was holding their Earthraider away from the Pit with a storm of air. She fled as he got too close and I released the fire in my hands, launching it at his back.

It burned through the material of his shirt, devouring his name and the Zodiac colours in a fiery blaze. He raised a hand with a yell of pain, immediately dousing the flames with a torrent of water from his palm and swivelled around in the mud to face me.

BUZZZZ.

Before he could strike back, someone Pitted the ball. I turned to find out who, my gut sinking as I saw the Zodiac Earthraider doing a victory dance beside Eugene's still body.

Dante had tackled three of their team so they were three points down, but their defence had taken out five of ours, leaving us down by four points already since they'd gotten a point for winning the round.

The next few rounds played out similarly. Orion was like a machine, knocking down our players and getting them sent off the pitch left, right and centre. Dante and the rest of our defence worked tirelessly to bring his team to their knees, while I tried to take Orion out before he could do as much damage.

By the fifth round I was fuming, unable to think straight as I moved to stand by Orion while we waited for the round to start. I was covered in mud and the rain was only increasing, making it harder and harder to run around the pitch. I occasionally used my fire magic to dry out the ground, but I didn't want to use it unless absolutely necessary.

"Zodiac cannot be beat, Aurora cannot take the heat!" a chant started up in the crowd and Orion smirked over at the cheerleaders who were doing a routine on the edge of the pitch.

I narrowed my eyes on him, flexing my fingers. This time, I was going to take him the fuck down.

"You know, you should really let some of that anger go. It's fucking up your game," Orion commented and I saw red, launching myself at him before the whistle blew and throwing him into the mud. He landed a solid punch to my gut, but not before I punched his damn beautiful face. He growled furiously, throwing me off of him and a shrill whistle sounded in my ear.

"Penalty to Zodiac and you're out of this round, Night!" the referee shouted and I scowled, stalking off of the pitch towards the seats reserved for the players. Elise threw me a concerned look and Dante called something after me about cooling down, but I shut him out as I dropped into the seat.

Orion was back on his feet, glaring at me like he was going to murder my first born and I welcomed the animosity. In the next round, I'd destroy him.

Aurora's game picked up in the following round and Elise grabbed the ball, tearing down the pitch toward the Pit. We were eight points behind

Zodiac, but we could bring it back. There was still time. And my girl was showing everyone it was possible. *Fuck*, not my girl.

I balled my hands into fists, refraining from standing up and cheering with the rest of the Aurora supporters as she blasted the Zodiac Pit Keepers aside and threw the ball into the Pit.

A smile tried to pull at my mouth, but I fought it back as the whole team rushed at her, lifting her into the air and chanting her name.

She looked my way and I folded my arms, staring anywhere else but at her.

I got to my feet, moving back onto the pitch for the next round and placing myself next to Orion again.

"If you start playing dirty, you're going to regret it, Night," he tossed at me, the lightness in his gaze gone.

"So make me regret it," I snarled and he clenched his jaw, his eyes narrowing on me.

"Fine by me."

The whistle blew and I dove at Orion the same time he came at me. He tackled me so hard, my back hit the ground and he knocked the wind out of me before I realised what had happened. I snarled, throwing fierce punches into his side and he stole the air from my lungs with his magic.

I grunted, bringing fire to life in my hands and slamming it down on his back, clutching him tight until he bellowed in pain. But he still didn't let go. The count sounded and the ref shouted, "You're out, Night!" and I roared in fury.

Orion stood up, offering me his hand, but I slapped it aside, stalking off of the pitch again as he raced after another member of my team to take them out.

I didn't sit down this time, I grabbed hold of one of the metal flip seats and wrenched it clean off of its fixings. I was half a second from throwing it onto the pitch when Mars's hand locked around my wrist. His eyes blazed with anger as I scowled back at him.

"You need a time out, Night," he snapped. "If you embarrass us here, they'll ban us from all future tournaments, is that what you want?"

I yanked my arm free, dropping the piece of the seat and hanging my head. "No," I mumbled.

"Good. Now sit the fuck down and get your head together or I'll sub you."

I nodded, taking a deep breath as I tried to collect my thoughts.

Elise soon scored another Pit and my heart twisted because I should have been sharing in her victory. Instead I was on the outskirts, unable to participate in anything to do with her except the pain she'd left me with.

I rejoined the match in the next round and tried to concentrate. I took down as many Zodiac players as I could, forgetting Orion as I tried to focus on the game. But I couldn't forget him for long as he raced past me, tearing toward Dante on my left. Orion grabbed hold of his throat, throwing him to the ground and an almighty thwack sounded as my friend hit the mud.

"Fuck!" Dante roared and Orion reared over him, still choking him as he tried to hold him down for the count.

I ran forward to throw him off and hit a solid fucking air shield, my nose breaking on impact. I hit the mud, flailing as I cupped my face, smearing mud and blood everywhere as I healed the injury. It was idiotic. I *knew* that fucking tactic, I just wasn't on point today.

The Zodiac crowd were laughing and jeering us. Our two best defensive players floored by one of theirs, it was a joke.

"Argh!" I cried in fury, hauling myself upright just as a BUZZZZ sounded Zodiac scoring another Pit.

When half time was called, we were minus eighteen points and half my team were healing themselves of injuries as we traipsed into the locker room.

We sat silently, muddy and defeated, listening to the Zodiac team cheering in the room across the hall.

I rested my elbows on my knees and buried my face in my hands.

This is the worst day of my life.

Mars gave everyone a pep talk and a little more enthusiasm returned to my team, but what they really needed was one of my epic speeches. I could have made even Eugene feel invincible out there if I was on top form. But I didn't have any scrap of positivity to call on.

"Leon," Elise said softly and I felt her take the seat beside me. "Please don't let this ruin the match. You've worked so hard to be here." Her hand gently rested on my back and a part of me longed to turn into her arms and drag her against me. But I couldn't find it in me to do it.

I lifted my head with an ache in my chest, casting a silencing bubble around us as Mars continued to talk tactics with the team. "How could you do this, Elise? I get that you lied at first, you didn't know me. But you've been at Aurora for *months*. Have you spent all this time with me trying to find out if I killed your brother? Do you really think I'd do something like that now that you know me?"

Her eyes shimmered with tears and she reached for my hand, but I shifted it out of her reach.

"I should have told you sooner," she choked out. "We just had so much fun together and I didn't want to ruin it. When I'm with you, I don't feel any of that pain anymore. You take it away."

"So I was just your distraction?" I asked bitterly, rising to my feet.

"Leo," she begged.

"That's not my name," I said sharply, disbanding the silencing bubble and walking away from her to sit alone. I didn't even want to be beside Dante, because it looked like he'd forgiven her without so much as a thought. I could have done that for her over anything else, but not this. Not now that I knew exactly what she'd thought of me and exactly what she'd used me for.

Music pounded up in the stadium and the Zodiac team were chanting together like soldiers about to go into battle.

I felt nothing as I trailed back out the door onto the pitch. It didn't matter what happened now.

We were going to lose. And the two dreams I'd ever had for myself were ruined.

ELISE

CHAPTER THIRTY FOUR

The second half of the match had gone from bad to worse, Leon's foul mood and determination to avoid me meant that the team wasn't functioning as a unit. Add Eugene Dipper to the mix with his fear of the goddamn balls and we were screwed.

I never gave up though. I kept playing at my best, racing around the pitch and using up every last drop of my magic in aid of the game. I scored pit after pit but it wasn't enough. Lance Orion took down members of our team like bowling down skittles and every time he knocked a player out for a round, we lost a point.

Most of the other players on our team had lost hope and with each bad pass or half assed tackle, the gap in the score widened. There was no chance of us pulling it back anymore. Only Dante and I had kept our focus. Leon was a total wild card, tackling members of the other team with a ferocity too savage even for Pitball. He was venting his rage on the game and ruining everything he'd worked so hard for, and it was all my fault.

As the final whistle blew, the ball shot out of the airhole and I raced for it, determined to end the game playing as well as I could despite the fact that we'd already lost.

I was down to my last bit of magic but that didn't matter, I'd give it all to score the final pit.

I sprinted full pelt towards the ball and leapt up to snatch it with a cry of victory.

I turned for the Pit, running hard as Orion charged to tackle me like a fucking bull. If he caught me I was done. But he had to catch me.

I directed the last scraps of my air magic at my back, pushing me to run faster and leaving him behind as both Dante and Leon raced to intercept him.

Orion snarled as he managed to outpace them, throwing his own air magic into my path to counter my speed.

I stumbled, cursing as I locked my gaze on the Pit ahead of me where the Pit Keepers stood ready to stop me.

"Eugene!" I roared as he lingered beside the keepers from the Zodiac team. "Take them out!"

His eyes widened and for a moment I thought he wasn't going to do it, but then he threw his hands at them and vines shot from the ground to entangle them and knock them out of my way. Eugene's eyes lit up with victory and I gave him a huge smile as I kept running.

I could feel Orion right behind me and with a cry of effort, I threw the ball as hard as I could, propelling it on with the very last bit of my magic. Orion collided with me a second later and I hit the mud hard as he pinned me beneath him.

But it didn't matter, the ball sailed into the Pit and the whistle blared to sound the end of the game. I'd scored. And they'd won.

I twisted beneath Orion and he grinned broadly as he held me down in the mud for another second.

"Good game, Callisto," he said.

"Better for you," I replied as the reality of our loss washed through me. The Zodiac Academy supporters were screaming their excitement at their win and the sound of it echoed around me like a thousand taunting voices.

"Yeah." Orion pushed himself upright and offered me a hand, wrenching me up to stand beside him. "Leon needs to keep his head on the game."

"It's not his fault. He's angry at me for something I did."

Orion frowned. "Well I'm sure you can fix it. You're pretty resourceful." He winked then clapped me on the shoulder before turning to run a victory lap of the pitch.

My body was battered, I was covered in mud and I was completely out of magic. Worse than that, I'd finally had the chance to live out one of Gareth's dreams for him and I'd failed at it.

My gaze slid over the crowd for a long moment as the disappointment of what had just happened washed over me. I'd let him down.

A tear slid from my eye and I dropped my gaze, hunting for Leon on instinct, wanting to bathe in the comfort of his company as my grief reached out to wrap itself around me. But as I spotted him trudging away from the pitch, I realised that he was feeling a hundred times worse than me. I might have been trying to bring Gareth's dream to life, but this had been Leon's. And he'd ruined it all because of me.

I bit my lip as guilt twisted up my insides and threatened to drown me. He was right to be angry with me. I *had* used him. Not intentionally, but by only ever giving him the light sides of me I'd denied him the opportunity to find out about the dark. I'd given him a half version of myself. A false version. And perhaps now that he'd seen that there was so much more to me, so much that was hard and bitter and dark and broken, he wouldn't want me anymore. If that was the case then I'd have to accept it, but I'd never even given him the chance to prove whether or not that was true.

I swallowed my self pity and raised my chin as I shot after him with a burst of Vampire speed.

He'd almost reached the locker room by the time I made it to him and I reached out to place a hand on his chest to halt him.

"Talk to me," I begged.

Leon's gaze was dark, his brow furrowed and none of the light I loved so much shimmered in his eyes.

"We lost. What do you want me to say?"

"I'm sorry, Leon. Really. I know that this is all my fault and I wish I could just go back and tell you sooner, but-"

"But you didn't. Because I'm just good for fun, for a laugh, right? You told Ryder though, because clearly a psychotic gang leader can understand you so much better than I could. Not that you gave me the chance to find out," he said bitterly.

"I-"

"Save it. It's all fucked now anyway so what's the point?" he snarled, shoving past me and heading into the locker room.

I chased after him as he grabbed his kit bag from his hook and he turned to leave again without another word.

I stood in front of the doorway, spreading my arms to stop him from walking out on me. I couldn't bear to see the hurt in his eyes and know I'd caused it. I needed to fix this like I needed to feel the sun on my skin.

"*Please,*" I begged.

"There's nothing to say, Elise. You're a liar and a fake and you just cost me my fucking dream too. I thought I knew you but it was all just bullshit. You're bullshit. And I'm done." He walked straight at me, knocking my arm aside as he headed back out to the pitch and my heart splintered at the venom in his words.

"This wasn't just *your* dream you know," I said, chocking back a sob. "This game meant something to all of us. To Gareth."

Leon whirled on me, his eyes flaring with rage and his inner Lion glaring out at me, poised to kill.

"Don't you dare use him as a weapon against me," he snarled, pointing a finger straight at me. "He was my friend. Do you think I don't know that he should have been out there on the pitch with me? *You're* the one wearing his shirt. *You're* the one standing in his place. Maybe if he was still here we'd have won and as a bonus I never would have met you either. And I wouldn't know what it felt like to be destroyed by you."

He twisted away from me and stormed outside, leaving me reeling from his words with tears painting lines through the mud on my face.

I almost didn't follow him. I almost let him go. But the thought of this being the end of us cut me in two.

I ran after him, my heart pounding painfully as I spotted him on the far side of the pitch, standing with his family with a solemn expression on his face.

I crossed the pitch with my fists clenched at my sides and the pain in me shifting to rage as I thought over what he'd just said. Did he really think I'd wanted to take Gareth's place in this match? I would have traded everything I had to be out there in the stands now, watching my brother playing in my place.

Leon's brother, Roary, spotted me coming and pointed me out, an amused smile tugging at the corner of his mouth. I strained my ears to hear what he said as he nudged his brother's arm.

"Looks like your girl is pissed at you for fucking up the match," he teased.

Leon growled, his eyes narrowing as he looked at me and all of a sudden I was struck by the feeling of his Charisma washing over me as he called on his Order gifts.

Girls all around him in the stands looked around suddenly, zeroing in on Leon with slack jawed expressions and doe eyes.

They all ran towards him and I frowned as he was engulfed by the swarm of Mindys.

"Keep that girl away from me," he commanded, his eyes meeting mine for a moment before he was swallowed by the crowd.

"What the fuck?" I demanded as the Mindys all turned to glare at me, blocking my way on and casting magic in their hands as they prepared to keep me back if I tried to get around them. "Leon!" I shouted. "Are you seriously doing this to me?"

He didn't reply but I caught sight of him storming away beyond the crowd of Mindys, ripping his Pitball shirt off and throwing it down in the mud as he went.

"Leon!" I shouted again. I knew he could hear me, but he just kept walking.

Dante turned at the sound of my voice, extracting himself from the embrace of his family members as he came to stand beside me.

"He's gone full Lion tantrum then," he said, his jaw ticking.

"He told me he wishes he'd never met me."

Dante growled angrily. "I'll make him eat his words and then I'll make him apologise," he swore. "Nessuno fa male al mio amore."

"Who's hurt your love?" a voice interrupted us and I turned to find a young girl smirking at us. I remembered her vaguely from Dante's birthday party but there had been so many Oscuras there for me to meet that I couldn't quite remember if she was a sister or a cousin. She had long, black hair and was wearing an Aurora Academy Pitball shirt which she'd fashioned into a crop top so that the name *Dante Oscura* could be seen where she'd painted it onto her stomach. "And more importantly, who *is* your love?"

"For the love of the stars Rosa, you're so nosey," Dante muttered, glancing at me apologetically.

"Well if you won't tell me things then I have to find them out for myself. I thought you were the girl who's been making my cousin all moony, but he tried to fob me off saying you're with Leon," she said, smirking like she'd just caught him out.

Dante cleared his throat, scrubbing a palm over his face like he was embarrassed and I managed half a smile.

"I'm Elise."

"Rosalie Oscura, Dante's favourite cousin," she replied proudly, gripping my hand surprisingly tightly for a fourteen year old.

"And what do you mean by moony?" I asked her, glad of the distraction from my issues with Leon.

"Oh you know, he comes home and sits by the window, looking up at the moon and batting his eyelashes," she said. "And in his sleep he keeps murmuring *amore mio* and puckering up his lips like he's dreaming about kissing you." She started doing a good impression of fish lips completed with really loud sucking, kissy noises and I snorted a laugh as Dante took a swipe for her.

"Ti appenderò dal tetto per le caviglie!" he said jokingly as he tried to grab her.

"You have to catch me first Dolce Drago," Rosalie taunted, darting behind me and using me as a shield.

"She has a point, Dante," I said, laughing as he tried to wrap his arms around me and snatch her. "You do make those weird kissing noises in your sleep."

Rosalie barked a laugh and Dante joined in as he gave up on catching her.

"Well maybe he's just dreaming about me," Roary's voice joined our conversation and I turned to look up at him as he offered Dante a wide smile. His mane of dark hair was half pulled back into a topknot and he was wearing a black leather jacket which bulged around his muscular frame.

Dante smiled widely as he saw him and pulled him in for a hug, smearing his clothes with mud from his filthy kit. Roary laughed as he released him and used his water magic to clean his jacket off again.

"Nice to see you again, Elise," he said easily, as if the last time I'd seen him he hadn't caught me starting on a three way with Dante and his brother. Actually, he'd never mentioned anything about chasing me down the street in his Lion form and threatening to rip my head off for helping Leon steal his car either. "You'll forgive me for not hugging you. I'd rather keep all of my possessions today."

I smirked at him, quietly impressed that he could joke about something which had clearly enraged him at the time.

Rosalie had fallen strangely silent and as I looked around at her, I found her staring up at Roary with a blush lining her cheeks while she nervously chewed her bottom lip.

Dante followed my gaze to his cousin and grinned wickedly as he pulled her under his arm. "Funnily enough, little Rosa here was just talking about you, mio amico," he said to Roary as Rosalie fought to get out from under his arm.

"I was *not,*" she protested, shoving him as she tried to escape and her blush deepened.

"Sure you were," Dante said. "You were saying how you're all moony for him."

Roary laughed as he glanced at Rosalie dismissively. "Don't worry little pup, all the girls get moony over me. It's just my Charisma."

"I'm not moony over you!" Rosalie spluttered, turning the colour of a beetroot.

"Yeah Roary, not *all* of the girls are sucked in by your Charisma, just the weak ones. And I don't think Rosalie is the weak willed type," I pointed out, trying to come to Rosalie's aid as her cousin embarrassed her.

Dante however seemed quite content to keep on mortifying her. "I don't think it's your Charisma either, mio amico," he said. "I think she's just straight up obsessed with you. I found this little diary in her room once and it was full of-"

Rosalie snarled in rage and punched Dante in the kidney as hard as she could. He let out an oomph of pain, releasing her as she cursed at him.

"Per me sei morto, Dante! Ti odio!" she snarled before turning and running away from us as fast as she could.

Dante laughed and I swatted him on the arm. "Asshole," I chastised. "What did she just say to you anyway?"

"That I'm dead to her and she hates me," he replied with amusement and Roary laughed too.

"Poor kid," Roary joked. "Don't you remember what it was like to have your first crush, Dante?"

"I feel like that most of the time at the moment," he replied, giving me a heated look.

"Is that why my brother is off pouting?" Roary asked, looking at me. "Because you dumped him for a Dragon?"

"Elise is more than able to handle both of us," Dante assured him, saving me from answering. "And Leon's quite happy to share her, his issue is something a little more complicated."

"I was hoping you might be able to talk some sense into him, Dante?" I asked. "He won't listen to me right now."

"Qualsiasi cosa per te, amore mio," he replied, brushing his hand along my jaw. "Go and enjoy the after party and I'll work my magic on our Lion friend."

"Good luck with that," Roary snorted. "When he gets in a mood like this it can go on for weeks."

"No one's as stubborn as a Dragon," Dante said dismissively, offering me a smile before striding away to find Leon.

I gave Roary an awkward smile, not really sure what to say to him now that we were alone.

"You really care about little Leonidas, don't you?" he asked, the corner of his mouth twitching like he was pleased about that.

"What's the deal with you two?" I asked, unable to help myself. "You act like you don't even like each other but you're brothers, surely you should make more effort to get along with each other."

Roary smiled, giving me a half shrug. "We tease each other a lot but that's just Lion rivalry. It's in our nature to try and rise up, claim the best lionesses, assert our position over each other. It doesn't mean I don't love him."

"I'm not sure he sees it that way," I muttered, knowing how much Roary got under Leon's skin.

Roary frowned at my words, pushing a tongue into his cheek as he mulled them over. "He knows how much I care about him. I don't just turn up at Academy Pitball matches for the hell of it. And I travel back home for dinner whenever I know he's coming. I don't need to say it."

My heart twisted as I read the sincerity of those words in his eyes and I thought about what Leon had said about him. He thought Roary only showed up to taunt and tease him. He had no idea his brother just enjoyed his company.

"Maybe you should say that to him then," I said, wondering if my words might go any way towards helping bridge the gap between them.

Roary shrugged, letting me know he wouldn't and I caught his arm before he could walk away from me.

"I mean it," I pressed. "I lost my brother and I'll never get him back. It hurts me to think of Leon missing out on that bond with you while you're right here."

Roary looked at me for a long moment. "I'll talk to him then," he agreed finally and I managed a genuine smile at his words. "You know, I can see what he sees in you now," he added.

"Is that so?"

"Well, aside from the obvious." His gaze slid over me appreciatively and I felt his Charisma pushing at my will for a moment before he withdrew it again when he couldn't claim any influence over me.

"Ass," I muttered, rolling my eyes.

"Catch you later, little Vampire." Roary winked at me then strode away to find his family.

I sighed as I turned away from him, wondering if I could get away with ditching the after party even though I didn't actually have anywhere else to go.

"Wanna find somewhere quiet where you can tear my throat open and I can work around these fucking rules to put a smile back on your face, baby?" Ryder spoke in my ear and I turned to him with my pulse spiking in surprise.

"How did you know I needed to escape?" I asked, eyeing the vein in his throat with an ache of longing.

"Same way I know everything about you. I'm always paying attention." He offered me his hand and I bit my lip as I let him pull me away from the crowded stadium. I'd probably have to show my face at the after party eventually, but for now, escaping with him sounded like bliss.

RYDER

CHAPTER THIRTY FIVE

I sat in a corner of the party, sipping a beer and thinking about calling a cab. The only thing keeping me there was watching Elise dancing and enjoying herself, even though she wasn't dancing with anyone. She didn't seem to care. She raised her arms above her, swaying to the music, her black dress swinging around her thighs.

I fell prey to a thousand filthy daydreams as I watched her. I was usually the one to hypnotise Fae with my power, but she was the only one who'd ever managed to do it back. I was transfixed by the movements of her body and it took me a long moment to realise she was looking right at me.

She beckoned me over and I shook my head, turning away as I sipped on my beer. I didn't do dancing.

After the Lion asshole had continued to ignore her this evening, I was glad to see her smiling again.

I spotted Gabriel approaching her through the crowd and my chest tightened as he closed in on her. Before he made it, he bumped into Orion and they started chatting together, making my shoulders relax. I sank back into my chair to watch her again, but she started moving toward me, pretending to reel herself closer with an imaginary rope.

"Come dance with me," she demanded, snatching my hand and leaning backwards to try and heave me up. It didn't work.

"I don't dance," I growled, tugging sharply so she fell into my lap. I laid my hand on her thigh and my dick twitched happily as the sweet cherry scent of her surrounded me.

She leaned in close with a mischievous grin, brushing her mouth over my ear and sending an electrical current right down to my balls. "I could teach you."

"If you think I'm going to make an idiot of myself in front of all these people-"

"I don't," she cut me off. "Let's go somewhere private."

A smirk pulled at my mouth. "I like the sound of that."

"To dance," she reiterated and my smile darkened.

"Sure, baby," I lied. Because fuck if anyone was going to make me dance. Even her.

She guided me through the crowd and I had to admit it felt good being with her in front of all these people. She had chosen to spend time with me instead of them and that made me feel fucking incredible. Even if I didn't understand why she had. I must have been the most miserable fucker in here.

She led me outside and the music carried to us through the golden walls of The Orb. She continued to tug me along as the summer breeze tangled around us, lifting up her skirt a little and making me growl with desire.

She could have led me anywhere right then and I would have followed. To swim in an alligator-infested swamp, to jump off a cliff, to a children's fucking puppet show. Wherever it was, I'd be all in.

I eyed her delicate neck as she walked ahead of me, her hair pulled up on top of her head to keep her cool.

I reached out to skate my knuckles down it, pressing the word *lust* to her skin and she shivered keenly.

She led me between the shadow of two trees beside the path and turned, wrapping her arms around my neck. She started to sway and I stood rigidly, my arms limp at my sides.

She laughed softly, reaching down to take my hands and place them on her waist. "It's not hard, you just have to hold onto me and turn in circles."

I swallowed thickly, feeling awkward as fuck. "Elise..."

"Please," she begged, tip toeing up to brush her nose against mine. Something about that action made my resolve turn to dust.

I clutched her waist, clearing my throat and looking down at our feet, unsure what to do.

"Just rock side to side and turn." She started to move and I shifted my feet away from hers as she did so, meaning we turned in a slow circle.

She grinned so widely, it brought a small smile to my lips too. *Fuck it.*

The thumping music changed to a slow song and Bob Marley's Three Little Birds started playing. We were suddenly moving in perfect time to it and I didn't feel so stupid anymore.

Elise tightened her grip on me, but stopped guiding the movements, letting me lead her instead. It felt divine.

"You're a good dancer, you should take up salsa lessons," she teased.

"Don't push it," I said and she chuckled. I leaned forward to rest my forehead to hers and her lips parted as she looked up at me.

I wanted to be brave enough to tell her how I felt about her, but I wasn't sure of those feelings. How could someone like me be capable of loving someone after all these years of feeling nothing but pain and lust? How had she begun to heal me with nothing but her presence, her laugh, her smile? She brought out a side to me I'd never seen before, and reawakened a part that I'd only known as a child.

"What are you thinking?" she breathed, brushing her fingers up and down the back of my neck.

"I'm thinking...that you helped me remember that I can feel more than the words painted on my knuckles."

Her brows lifted and warmth spread through her eyes. "I want you to feel everything, Ryder. The good, the bad. That's what living is."

I skated my thumb down her cheek with a frown. "You've experienced too much of the bad."

"So have you," she whispered, her eyes glimmering for a moment.

We spun in circles until I was sure we'd mark the ground forever as song after song played.

"Do you want to go back to the hotel?" she asked eventually, her throat bobbing as she gazed up at me with a dark promise in her eyes.

I nodded as desire rushed through me, claiming me. I wanted Elise alone and I'd find a way to make her pant my name before midnight.

Her fingers threaded between mine as we walked back down the path and we were soon heading off campus to catch a cab back to the hotel.

She sat right next to me in the back of the car, tracing her hand up and down my thigh until I was going mad with how much I wanted her. My balls ached and my cock was throbbing. I didn't think I was going to last much longer within the terms of this fucking deal. I needed to bury myself inside her. I needed to feel her come while she raked her nails down my skin and made me bleed. It was driving me to fucking insanity.

I caught her hand before I started to get ideas about breaking the deal and dipped my fingers under her skirt instead. She gasped and buried her face against my shoulder as the cab driver gave us a look in the mirror. I gave him a stone cold look in response and he quickly turned back to face the road as I inched my hand higher up her silky smooth thigh and reached a layer of lace.

She parted her legs and I skated my fingers up the centre of her, feeling her heat. Her body flexed against me and she bit down on my shirt with a moan, making a grin pull at my mouth.

"We're here," the driver said sternly and I tossed him a handful of auras before dragging Elise out of the cab and placing her on her feet.

She gave me a heady look full of need and I hounded after her into the hotel, the two of us hurrying into the elevator together. The doors closed and Elise moved in front of me, lowering her hand to squeeze my throbbing dick through my jeans.

"Fuck," I sighed. "I can't stand this anymore."

She groaned, tipping her head back in frustration and releasing me. The doors slid open and I spotted Dante down the hall, sitting outside his room with his back to the wall.

I grunted in annoyance as Elise slipped away, hurrying toward him and I drifted after her.

"What are you doing here?" she asked him.

He looked up from his Atlas with a frown. "Leon's got about fifty Mindys in there pandering to his every need."

Elise rolled her eyes. "He needs to get over this. Did you tell him how much I care about him? He won't listen to me."

"He just needs time, amore mio." He rose to his feet, shooting me a scowl over her shoulder.

Elise glanced between us with a huff. "Could you two at least *try* to get along?"

"No," we answered at the same time.

She tutted, moving to her room and unlocking the door. "Well if you did, you could break off that stupid deal and both of you could come in here and the three of us could have some fun." She opened the door, turning and resting her shoulder against the doorway. "But you're both too stubborn for that, aren't you?"

Neither of us answered and she sighed, moving into her room. "Goodnight then."

She shut the door and I glowered at Dante. He'd cost me a night with Elise just because he was standing here in this hallway. It was so fucking infuriating.

"I'm sick of this deal," Dante snapped then descended into angry Faetalian as he stepped away from me.

"Well you heard her. There's only one way out of it, and I'd rather keep your dick away from her than do that, thanks."

"Yours would be there too, stronzo." He rolled his eyes, glancing at his door as if wondering if it was worth facing all the Mindys over me.

"Oh so you wanna fuck her while I'm there too?" I laughed coldly. "And how would our gangs repay us for that?"

He blew out a breath. "I don't want to do anything with you, but I'm getting fucking desperate here." He looked at her door like he was really considering this. "Maybe she wants some company…" He stepped forward and I grabbed hold of his shoulder, forcing him back a step.

"You're not going near her," I snarled and he shrugged me off.

A tense beat of silence passed between us and I could see the cogs working behind his eyes.

"What?" I demanded.

He shrugged. "Never mind."

"Say it, Inferno."

He turned to me with his brows lifting. "I was just thinking you're too much of a pussy to go through with it."

"I'm not a fucking pussy," I snarled.

Silence stretched out once more.

All it would take was us agreeing to end the deal and the stars would deem it so. We could do whatever we wanted with her, whenever we wanted. But was I really considering that?

He pressed his tongue into his cheek, glancing at Elise's door again. "So let's share her. It'll be one night only. We break the deal, then never mention this night again once we're back at Aurora. No one would have to know."

A rush of emotions flooded me. My first reaction was that it was a fucked up idea. As if I'd ever share Elise with my mortal enemy. But the second was that this was my *only* fucking chance to have her. And I was losing my mind.

And I'd lose my balls too if I didn't take her soon. They would literally fall the fuck off.

"I knew you were too much of a pussy," he said lightly, turning toward his room again.

I caught him by the collar and shoved him towards Elise's door.

"One night only," the words spilled from my mouth before I could stop them. I didn't even feel like myself right then. It felt like I'd lost my fucking mind over this girl.

Dante's eyes widened like he couldn't believe I was agreeing then he slapped his hand into mine.

"I agree to break the deal between us," he blurted.

I hesitated for a long second, trying not to think of how this was a betrayal to the Brotherhood. How they would have me gutted if they knew I was standing here with our arch nemesis agreeing to be with the same woman. Even if it was only one night, it still wasn't something we could ever come back from.

But for Elise…it had to be worth it.

"I agree to break it too," I rasped and a flash flared between our hands then flickered up our arms, the magic that bound us dissolving away.

I dropped his hand and we stared at each other for a long moment. Finally, he moved, lifting his hand to knock on Elise's door. I stepped up beside him and clenched my jaw.

It went entirely against my nature to share a woman. I was possessive and I wanted her all to myself. But if this was the only way I could have her, then suddenly it seemed like the perfect answer. Even though it was the most fucked up thing I'd ever considered doing. And of all the Fae in the world, why did it have to be with *him*?

I pushed all of that doubt away and focused on the pounding of my heart and the ache in my chest that was about to be sated at long last. I was going to have my girl. And it didn't matter if Inferno was there too, because I was the only one she was going to remember once I was through with her.

ELISE

CHAPTER THIRTY SIX

My heart pounded as I moved back to the door, my fingers curling around the handle as I hesitated for a long moment. It was just possible that one of my dirtiest, most forbidden fantasies lay waiting for me on the other side of this door. Just possible enough to send a surge of heat racing between my thighs at the mere thought of it.

I released a slow breath and arranged my features into a neutral expression before I gave away what I'd just been considering with parted lips and panting breaths. The idea of having Dante and Ryder together was practically blasphemy. It was a fantasy that got me hot at night in part because I knew it bore no reflection of reality. There was no way that they would be able to put their differences aside and come together over me. Was there?

I pulled the door wide and there they stood, shoulder to shoulder, towering over me and exuding the kind of auras that nice girls ran from. But I wasn't a nice girl. And I'd been dreaming about sinning with them for far too long.

"Can we come in, bella?" Dante purred.

"Together?" I asked in a rough voice, my gaze skipping between them as a dark hope began to build in me.

"We decided to set aside our deal," Dante said, his gaze dripping over me and making my nipples harden with the mere thought of what that meant. "Which means there are no more rules if you say there aren't."

I bit my lip, admiring the way his shoulders filled out every inch of his shirt before skimming to Ryder and imagining those huge arms wrapped around my naked flesh.

"No more rules," I agreed, unable to hide my smile.

Ryder stepped forward instantly, smacking his shoulder into Dante with enough force to knock him back a step before he grabbed a fistful of my hair and drove his lips against mine.

I gasped in surprise and his tongue pushed straight into my mouth, raking against mine in a way that was so filthy, I couldn't help but imagine how it would feel between my thighs. His piercing rolled across my tongue and I groaned as I grasped his shoulders, dragging him closer. His free hand gripped my ass hard enough to bruise me as he forced my body flush with his, making sure I could feel exactly how hard he was inside his pants.

The door slammed shut with a bang that seemed to seal this fate and Dante caught my arm, tearing me away from Ryder's kiss, growling hungrily. I turned to him and his mouth met with mine a moment later, electricity spilling over my lips as he kissed me.

Ryder was forced to let me move back an inch and he released his grip on my hair to catch the strap of my black dress in his grip and tug it off of my shoulder. He kept tugging until a rip sounded and I gasped into Dante's mouth as my breast was freed and Ryder bent low to capture my nipple between his lips.

His cold tongue had me moaning within moments as he rolled his stud over the peaked flesh before tugging it between his teeth hard enough to hurt.

Dante growled with lust as he pushed his tongue further into my mouth and his hand moved to the hem of my dress. His fingers slid up my inner thigh, crackling with electricity as he closed in on the centre of me, promising me the sweetest of oblivions with barely a touch.

His fingers made it to my panties and I parted my legs eagerly, aching to feel every part of his body against every part of mine.

I had a hand on each of their chests and my fingers fumbled over buttons as I tried to focus on removing their clothes while they both tried their hardest to steal my attention from each other.

Dante groaned as his fingers shifted beneath my panties and he felt how wet I was for him. For both of them. I wanted to fall prey to these predators. I wanted them to take me and use me and ruin me and more than all of that, I wanted them to want me like I wanted them. I needed them to need this like I did and in that moment, it was clear that they did. Even the divide which split them apart, the war they waged on each other every day of their lives couldn't keep them from this. From me. They were mine and I was theirs and though that should have been wrong, it wasn't. It was right. So right that I couldn't even breathe with their flesh against mine, let alone think straight.

Dante's fingers slid back and forth beneath my panties, circling against the perfect spot at the apex of my thighs. A current of electricity shuddered through me which had me crying out against his lips.

Ryder growled, his hand shifting to hook my skirt up too before he found the top of my panties and pushed his fingers beneath them.

The two of them growled in warning at each other as their hands collided and I broke my kiss with Dante as a desperate moan left my lips.

"Please," I gasped, rocking my hips against their hands as their hesitation to work together held my pleasure at bay.

They both turned from glaring at each other to looking at me instead as I panted between them.

"You're so greedy, baby," Ryder purred. "You want it all at once, don't you?"

"Yes," I begged. "I need you. Both of you."

They exchanged a glance for the briefest of seconds and I gasped as they both shifted their hands lower at the same moment. The cool touch of Ryder's flesh and the electric warmth of Dante's had my head spinning as they both teased their fingers through the wetness which awaited them.

"Noi siamo i tuoi schiavi, amore mio," Dante purred. But before I could ask what that meant, they both pushed two fingers inside me.

Ryder groaned hungrily as they fell into a torturous rhythm, his other hand moving to grip a fistful of my hair again and knotting it through his fingers.

"This is everything I've ever dreamed of with you and everything I ever feared at once," he growled in my ear. "Do you enjoy torturing me, baby?"

I could only whimper in response as my body tightened around the two of them and my back arched in anticipation of the pleasure I could feel building in me.

I gripped Dante's bicep in my right hand and Ryder's in my left as I gave up on undressing them and focused all of my attention on not collapsing beneath the power of what they were doing to me.

They kept going, working together for the first time ever just so that they could destroy me, pumping their fingers in and out of me in perfect synchronisation until I came, screaming my pleasure to the ceiling as Dante sent a shot of electricity ripping right through me to prolong the ecstasy.

Ryder's grip in my hair tightened painfully and he pulled me towards him, claiming my mouth once more as they both pulled their hands back out of my underwear.

His teeth caught my bottom lip and he bit me hard, groaning as my pain slid beneath his skin and he drove the solid ridge of his dick against my hip urgently.

I fought against the trembling in my muscles as I caught his shirt in my grip and ripped it open with a flash of my gifted strength, sending buttons flying in my haste to feel his skin against mine.

A gust of wind knocked into us and I stumbled back a step as we were forced apart and Dante spun me to face him instead.

He caught my face between his hands and tipped my bruised lips up to meet his as I unhooked his shirt buttons with a desperate ache in my body. I needed this. Needed to see them, all of them, here, before me. No rules, no work arounds, no deals, just the freedom to indulge in the fantasies we'd all been denying ourselves for far too long.

I shoved his shirt over his broad shoulders and he rolled them back so that it fell to the floor.

Dante cursed as he was pulled off of me again and I groaned with need as I spotted the vines which Ryder had wrapped around his arms to drag him away.

Dante snapped the vines with a sharp yank and a growl escaped him as they both stalked towards me with intent.

"Stop," I demanded, panting with need as I reached out to place a hand on both of their chests.

I increased the pressure and started walking, turning them and making them back up until they knocked against the bed. "I want *both* of you."

They didn't seem entirely sure how to give me that so I decided to show them.

I moved closer slowly and they both watched me as I slid my hands down their bare chests, tracing the swell of their muscles and the scars which marked Ryder's flesh.

I made it to their waistbands and they both watched me as I unbuckled their belts and slid their zippers down.

Ryder groaned with desire and Dante released a flare of electricity which made the lights flicker overhead and my nipples hardened even further.

I looked between Ryder's dark green eyes and Dante's deep brown ones as I pushed my hands into their boxers and took both of them into my palms at once. I moaned as I felt the silky smooth skin, the solid length of them, both begging for release. My left thumb skimmed over Ryder's piercing and I felt him shudder as I pumped my hands up and down slowly, exploring them both, enjoying this moment of finally getting to feel them after so long denying how much we needed this.

Their restraint snapped in the same moment and they both reached for me, their hands exploring my body through my dress and trying to draw me closer so that I could kiss them again.

I drew my hands back suddenly and shoved them with a surge of my Vampire strength so that they both fell back onto the bed beneath me, their sides pressed together. They made no move to shift apart, both of them watching me in desperation and seeming to forget each other for a moment.

I smiled wickedly as I pulled my dress off, dropping it to the floor so that I stood before them in my black panties and stilettos. I kicked the shoes off then placed a knee between each of their legs as I crawled up over their bodies, half straddling them both and resting my hands on each of their chests.

I looked between them, trying to decide what I wanted to do with them next and wondering if I could really handle these two monsters at once.

"Non ho mai desiderato nessuno come te," Dante said and I bit my lip as I wondered what he was saying. Whatever it was had heat spinning through my body and I leaned down to steal a kiss from him, caressing Ryder's dick at the same time.

Their hands moved to roam my skin and I moaned as they slid their fingers across my breasts, toying with my nipples and driving me wild with need.

I lingered in the kiss with Dante and Ryder grew impatient, his hand striking my ass hard enough to leave a print.

"*Fuck,*" I hissed against Dante's lips and he did it again, harder. "More," I begged and a flash of electricity crashed through my body, echoing through every point where my flesh met Dante's and passing on into Ryder too.

Ryder groaned and I could tell that he'd liked that just as much as I had even if he wouldn't admit it.

Dante claimed my mouth again, pushing his hands into my hair as he filled that kiss with all the promises he'd given me when this hadn't been allowed.

I pulled back and moved to kiss Ryder, but his lips barely brushed mine before he gripped my jaw and angled me back towards Dante again.

"We can both kiss you at once, baby," he said and Dante instantly leaned up to reclaim my mouth for his own, kissing me with a passion so fierce I was afraid I might burn up in it.

Ryder shifted down the mattress, lifting my leg off of him as he moved to kneel at the foot of the bed.

He gripped my hips and lifted my ass into the air, spanking me again as I resisted slightly.

"Do as you're told," he commanded darkly and I couldn't help but moan into Dante's mouth as Ryder slowly rolled my panties down, lifting my knees one by one to remove them from me.

He parted my thighs, stroking his thumb straight down the centre of me and making me pant as he dropped his mouth to my inner knee. Ryder ran his cold tongue up the inside of my thigh, his stud sending a shiver of anticipation tumbling through me as he reached the very highest point of my leg.

He drew back and I groaned, expecting his mouth to land on the centre of me at any moment but instead, his teeth bit into my ass with a bite of pain that made me yelp.

Ryder laughed darkly and I gasped as my fangs snapped out, aching for *me* to be the one doing the biting.

Dante tipped his chin back obligingly as his hands found my breasts and he began to tease my nipples in a way that almost had me coming apart on its own.

I panted heavily and Ryder's mouth suddenly landed exactly where I needed him, his piercing rolling right over my clit as he gripped my ass and pushed it higher to give him the angle he wanted.

I moaned as Ryder twisted his tongue against me and I reached out to grip Dante's throat, pinning him down as I sank my teeth straight into his neck.

The electricity of his blood washed into me as Ryder flicked his tongue between my thighs, his piercing finding the perfect spot with every move he made.

My body started shaking as he took control of my flesh and before I knew it, I found myself bathing in ecstasy all over again, my cries muffled as my mouth remained locked to Dante's neck. Ryder kept licking and teasing me, wringing every drop of pleasure from me before he finally pulled back and spanked me once more.

My heart leapt in time with the strike against my ass and I pulled my fangs free of Dante's flesh as a string of curses left my lips.

Ryder stepped back and Dante caught my arms, flipping me beneath him as he reared upright and pushed his pants off, freeing the full, hard length of him. I lay panting beneath him, wondering if I could seriously keep up with the two of them long enough to return this pleasure they were bathing me in.

Dante dropped over me, catching my wrists in his grip and holding them on either side of me, pinning me down as the tip of his cock ground against my entrance.

"Mio Vampira," he growled possessively as I looked up into his dark eyes and he claimed my body with a powerful thrust of his hips which was punctuated by a shock of electricity flooding my veins.

I cried out as I got used to the fullness of my body, every hardened inch of him driving me wild. I wound my legs around his waist as he fucked me hard, his pace punishing and my screams echoing off of the walls. I wanted to reach for him, touch and caress him but he kept me pinned down, something utterly Wolf about him in that moment.

The sound of Ryder's pants hitting the floor stole my attention for a moment and I managed to turn my head, taking in the hard length of his cock and the silver stud which adorned it as he moved closer to us.

Ryder hissed impatiently as my body tightened around the thick length of Dante's dick and I looked up at him with a plea in my gaze.

"You're mine, bella," Dante growled, his lips stamping to mine in a clear demand for me to yield before he pulled back. He released his grip on my wrist and caught my jaw in his large hand, turning my face so that I was looking at Ryder while he continued to fuck me. "And you're his too."

"Yes," I gasped as something broke apart inside me at that admission. That I could belong to both of them. All of them. And that we could all share in this together without any need for us to choose.

Dante released his grip on my chin, kissing me once more before he pulled back out of me and stood at the foot of the bed.

He caught my waist and flipped me over, positioning me on my hands and knees before gripping my hips and driving himself into me once more.

I cried out as the new position allowed Dante to fill me even more, pounding deeper with each powerful thrust of his hips.

Ryder closed in on me with a dark hunger in his eyes and his cock straining with need. He stood before me, looking into my eyes as Dante continued to fuck me right in front of him and I begged for more.

"Open your mouth, baby," Ryder commanded, reaching out with his right hand to grasp a handful of my lilac hair and knotting it around the word *pain* on his knuckles.

I did as he said, aching to feel him inside me too, to touch him, taste him, have him be a part of this. Of us. Together.

He wasn't gentle with me, but I wouldn't have wanted him to be. His dick slid straight between my lips and to the back of my throat with one hard thrust. The moment I moaned my encouragement, he pulled back before driving into me again.

I gasped at the fullness of the two of them inside me, rolling my tongue around Ryder's cock piercing as I tasted his lust in my mouth and felt Dante building another wave of pleasure within my flesh.

Ryder's grip in my hair was unyielding, painful as he fucked my mouth with a rhythm that met the rocking of my body from Dante's thrusts.

Dante growled and the electricity in the room grew more potent as he thickened inside me, nearing his end and mine all at once. I cried out around Ryder's thick shaft as my body fell apart again and Dante swore in his language as he came with me. A sharp jolt of electricity shot through my body as he finished, setting every nerve ending on fire and transferring it to Ryder where my lips were still wrapped firmly around his dick.

My whole world fell apart and Ryder growled hungrily as he suddenly pulled himself back out of my mouth.

Dante fell back on the bed with a satisfied groan, but the look in Ryder's eyes let me know that this was the moment he'd been waiting for.

He caught my wrists and dragged me up onto my knees so that he could kiss me, groaning with pure pleasure as I wrapped my hand around his hard cock.

"You taste like me and cherries," he growled against my lips as his hands encircled my wrists and vines crept out to lock them together.

Ryder kept hold of the end of the vine and gave a sharp yank to make me follow him as he stood. He fastened the vines to the top of the four poster bed with his magic, tightening them until I had to stand on my tiptoes before him.

"I'm gonna need some pain to finish me, baby," Ryder growled as he stepped forward, nudging my thighs apart with his knee and stepping between them with a look in his eye that said he wanted to devour me. "So make sure you bite me. And don't hold back."

My fangs tingled hungrily at that offer and Ryder caught my right knee in his grip, hooking it over his elbow before plunging inside me.

I gasped as his piercing rolled right through the centre of me, drawing a line of burning pleasure all the way to my core which was so intense that for a moment I couldn't breathe.

He didn't give me any time to adjust, his fingers biting into my leg as he thrust his hips at a merciless pace, slamming my spine into the bed post as he took what he needed from my flesh.

I cried out again and again, my head tilting back as I absorbed the feeling of his body owning mine.

Ryder's chest pressed to mine, the rough skin of his scars grazing against my nipples in a way that set my flesh on fire.

I gasped as warm hands slid across my stomach and I turned my head to look at Dante just as he pressed his electrically charged fingers to my clit.

My body was shattered and re-broken, it had been flooded with pleasure so many times since they walked into my room that I couldn't quite believe they were going to draw even more from me.

"Bite me," Ryder commanded, his gaze catching mine with a desperate need and I snarled at him, baring my teeth a moment before I drove them into his flesh.

I wasn't careful, I made no effort to be gentle, I just ripped into his veins and drank from the deep well of darkness that resided there.

Ryder started fucking me even harder and I could only cling to him as I tightened again, his blood, Dante's fingers and the thick length of him driving my body haywire.

I tipped my head back and screamed as my orgasm ripped through me, blood dripping from my lips as I felt Ryder emptying himself inside me at the same moment.

The three of us stayed there for what felt like forever, panting with the most thorough sense of satisfaction after months of fighting what our bodies craved.

Ryder pressed his forehead to mine and Dante kissed my neck tenderly, lovingly.

"You're everything I could ever want, bella," Dante breathed.

"You're more than I ever could have imagined," Ryder added.

"Good," I replied. "Because I'm never letting any of you go."

Ryder sighed like that statement had soothed something in his soul and the vines holding me up fell away.

The three of us dropped back onto my bed and I found myself sandwiched between the two of them with my body aching in the best possible way.

"Stay here tonight," I breathed as my eyes fluttered shut and their arms wound around me.

"I was planning on it, baby," Ryder whispered in my ear as Dante flicked out the lights. "And then in the morning, we're going to do that to you all over again."

"Twice," Dante added with a soft laugh and I bit my lip in excitement.

That was the kind of wake up call I could get used to.

GABRIEL

CHAPTER THIRTY SEVEN

"Hey congrats on the match today," I said to Orion.

"Thanks man," he said. "You wouldn't believe how many girls offered me blood afterwards. I don't think I've ever had this much magic in my veins." He pushed a hand into his hair with a smirk.

I sipped my beer, a grin pulling at my mouth. "My favourite part of the match was when you took out Dante and Leon within two seconds of each other." The way the two of them had flailed on the ground had probably been the highlight of my entire trip.

Orion barked a laugh. "What's the deal? You don't like those guys?"

"You could say that. I know Elise and I are meant to be together, but they keep getting in the way," I said and he frowned.

"That sucks man," he said. "It was pretty funny when I tackled her too though, right? She screamed real good." He grinned, mischief lighting his gaze and I pressed my lips together.

"That wasn't funny," I said seriously and he tried to stop smiling but completely failed. Part of me wanted to punch him for it, but I knew I had to make friends with him. If The Sight was anything to go by, and it usually was, Orion was vital to helping us with King. Besides, apart from his obvious interest in Elise, I couldn't deny there was something about him that I liked.

"Is there somewhere quiet we can go for a chat?" I asked, figuring now was a good time to get him alone. I couldn't see Elise anywhere and I had the feeling she'd left with Ryder. But instead of dwelling on how that cut me up inside, I was going to focus on what we'd come here to do instead. Even if I had to do it alone.

"You're not really my type." Orion smirked, sipping from his glass of water. He looked about as comfortable at this party as I felt. But as he'd won Player of the Match, he'd spent most of the evening being grabbed by various groups to be congratulated and forced to socialise.

"Maybe I can convince you," I jibed and he laughed, moving ahead to lead me toward the exit and leaving his glass down on a table. A couple of girls wrestled over it like a dog with a bone and I wrinkled my nose as I dropped my empty beer bottle in the trash.

We headed out into the warm summer air and took off down the path.

"How fast can you move in your Harpy form?" Orion asked, a challenge in his gaze.

"Faster than you," I replied with a grin.

"Wanna bet?"

I shed my shirt, stuffing it in the back of my pants and releasing my wings. They stretched out on either side of me and I heard a few girls giggling somewhere behind us.

Orion's gaze fell to my tattoos, looking mildly intrigued. "Ready?" he asked, preparing to run.

"Ready."

He shot away from me in a blur and I took off into the sky, spotting the rush of movement up ahead and racing after him. The world sped past me as I soared overhead, keeping pace with him as he travelled north across campus into Earth Territory.

A grin pulled at my mouth as I pushed myself harder. I couldn't remember the last time I'd flown just for fun. It felt incredible.

Orion shot toward the Pitball stadium and I laughed as he headed inside. *Now I'm gonna win.*

I sailed over the top of the open roof, plummeting down inside it to sit on one of the seats in the top of the stands. Orion appeared half a second later, dropping into the seat beside mine with a huff.

"Cheat," he accused.

"You never said I had to take the same route as you," I taunted, leaning back in my chair and propping one elbow on the edge of it.

"It was implied," he laughed then reached into his jacket pocket and took out a packet of biscuits. "Oreo?" he offered, holding out the pack.

I snorted a laugh. "Why are you carrying them around?"

"Some chick gave them to me." He shrugged. "And I don't get to eat sugar half as much as I want to." He crunched down on one of the Oreos and I took one too, toying with it in my hand.

"I don't either," I agreed. Half the time, I was too distracted to even remember to eat all of my meals. I was usually watching Elise across the Cafaeteria during meal times while she flirted with one of the assholes, or thinking about my past and trying to unravel it through the few clues I had.

"By the stars, you're hot," Orion breathed, leaning in closer with a dark expression on his face. "I bet you have a big dick too."

"What?" I balked, leaning away from him as he reached out to cup my cheek.

"All those muscles look like they need some attention," he growled, taking my hand as I slid down into another seat. "Stop running away, Noxy, let me make you feel good. No one can see us here."

"I'm not into guys, dude." I slid further away and his eyes sparkled with a reddish glow.

My gaze fell on the Oreo packet discarded on the ground and I inhaled sharply, tossing away the one in my hand. "You've been drugged with a lust potion, idiot." I reached for the packet, but Orion shot into my way with a blur of Vampire speed, stamping his mouth to mine.

"Hey!" I shoved him back and his eyes widened with hurt.

"Don't you want this?" He ran his hand down my chest, desire pouring from his gaze.

I figured I had to play along if I was going to get him anywhere near an antidote for this, but fuck if I was going to let him kiss me again.

"Yeah sure, of course I do. But not here." I stood up and he reached for my belt buckle.

"Why not?" he purred, his eyes hooded. "I want you right here moaning my name, Noxy."

"Right yeah, me too. But let's go somewhere else," I said firmly, pulling him forward and lifting him into my arms. He was a heavy fucker, but I managed it and took off into the sky.

He didn't even react to being held high up above the ground, instead he tried to kiss me again and I couldn't do much to stop him pressing his mouth to my cheek then my jaw, my neck.

"Lance!" I snapped and he tipped his head back with a frown.

"What's wrong, baby?"

I tried not to laugh but shit, having this beast of a Pitball player giving me his bed eyes was kind of hilarious.

"Where's your potions lab?" I asked as his hands roamed over my biceps.

"To the east of The Orb," he said vaguely then sucked on his lower lip. "I bet you'd look real good beneath me."

I ignored his stream of dirty talk as I flew us to the lab, dropping down in front of the tall building with red brick walls. I lowered Orion to his feet and he brushed his fingers over my chest, lingering on the Libra tattoo.

"You have my star sign on you," he growled, clutching the back of my neck as he tried to pull me in for a kiss. "It's fate."

"Wait -not yet." I threw him off of me again, guiding him into the potions lab and moving into the first classroom I found, retracting my wings as I went. I pushed Orion down into a seat as I headed to the supply cupboard, using my power to undo the magical locks on it. Luckily, I'd made the antidote for this potion last year in Professor Titan's class after there'd been an outbreak of lust potions being put in the Cafaeteria food. The girl responsible had been expelled for it, but not before several students had tried to screw anything and anyone in their general vicinity over the course of a week.

I took out what I needed and moved to the desk beside Orion with a cauldron.

"What are you doing, Noxy?" he purred, rising from his seat as I started placing the ingredients into it.

"I'm making you a special drink."

He growled appreciatively then started unbuttoning his shirt to reveal his muscular chest, letting it drop to the floor as he pushed a hand into his hair. "Are we gonna do it over a desk? Is that your filthy fantasy? I like being in control." He moved behind me, wrapping his hands around my waist and grinding his hard dick into my ass.

I straightened in surprise and turned to him, pushing him back a step and raising my palm. I used my earth magic to bind his wrists in front of him which he seemed even more excited by. So I tethered him to a desk a few feet away from me and his fangs extended as he gazed at me.

"Do you like it rough?" he asked in a low voice and I snorted a laugh as I returned to the potion while he started describing several filthy positions he wanted me in and how he was gonna bite me until I screamed.

I soon had a cup of the antidote ready and moved toward him with a frown. "Drink this for me." I held it up to his lips, but he didn't drink.

"What is it?" he asked suspiciously.

"It's a cocktail," I said with a shrug.

His eyes narrowed and he shook his head. "I don't drink alcohol."

Dammit. Why would he remember that right now?

I pressed my hand to his chest and faked a seductive smile. "Lie back on the desk."

He smirked, doing as I said and I leaned over him, pinning him in place and pushing one hand into his hair. I knotted my fingers in it and yanked hard, making him gasp. The second his mouth opened, I poured the antidote down his throat and clamped my hand over his mouth. He thrashed beneath me, but my vines held him in place and slowly, his body relaxed.

His eyes widened with realisation, then horror, anger, then shame.

I took my hand away from his mouth and climbed off of him, folding my arms. "Better?"

"Oh fuck." He shut his eyes. "What the hell happened?"

I released him from the binds and he sat on the desk, running his hand over his face with a pained noise.

"You were given a lust potion," I said and he groaned.

"Shit," he breathed. "Coach told me not to accept gifts from anyone. But it was just a pack of Oreos…" He shook his head. "Katie Episcopo is so dead for doing this to me." He looked to me with an awkward expression. "Sorry about…you know."

"It was pretty fucking funny until you rubbed your dick against my ass," I said, a laugh tearing from my throat.

"Fucking hell." He jumped from the desk, fishing up his shirt and pulling it on. "Thanks for bringing me here and making that antidote. If I'd been left on my own like that, I'd probably have fucked a tree or something."

"No problem." I shrugged. "It was either that or lose myself to a night of passion with you."

He laughed and I couldn't help but feel a strange kind of pull toward him. Certainly not one that had anything to do with lust, but more like friendship.

And that wasn't something I was used to.

"So um…this might sound kinda messed up. But I had a vision about you before I came here," I told him, leaning back on the edge of a desk.

"You've got The Sight?" he asked, looking intrigued as he finished buttoning his shirt.

"Yeah, I mean, it doesn't work half the time but when it does it's pretty accurate."

"So what did you see?" He frowned and I raised a hand to cast a silencing bubble around us.

"Well…I saw that you might be able to help us." I knew I was placing a lot of faith in this guy, but I could rely on my visions. And if Orion did do dark magic, then we needed him. And it didn't mean he was bad exactly. Just that he was breaking the law.

"Help you?" he questioned. "Why, what's wrong?"

I drew in a deep breath, because this was going to sound seriously screwed up. He might run a mile, but I had the feeling he wouldn't. "People are being killed in Alestria in some really fucked up way," I started. "And me and Elise have been trying to figure out who's doing it."

His brows arched, but he said nothing as he waited for me to continue.

"We interrogated one of the people who we know is working for them and she told us about the ritual the murderer is performing when he kills them."

"He?" Orion questioned.

"Well we don't know for sure, but whoever it is is calling themselves King."

"Shit," Orion breathed. "So what's the ritual?"

"It's dark magic," I said, searching his eyes as a flicker of trepidation filled his gaze. "But I don't know anything about dark magic, I don't know how this spell works or whether it can be undone…"

"What's the spell?" he asked thickly.

"When King kills his victims…they sacrifice themselves willingly and

497

he takes their Elemental magic," I breathed and tension spanned through the air between us.

His adam's apple bobbed and his eyes widened.

"You know about dark magic," I said, stepping forward and he glanced at the door behind him nervously. "I've *seen* it. And I need you to help me with this."

He laughed nervously. "I dunno what you think you saw in your vision-"

"I know what I saw," I said firmly. "And I'm not judging you for it. Frankly, I don't care what reasons you have for doing it and I'd never breathe a word of it to anyone. So please…can you help us? Does that ritual sound familiar to you?"

Orion ran a hand through his hair, anxiety pouring from him. "Not here," he said firmly. "Come on, we'll go to my room." He turned and headed out of the classroom and I disbanded my silencing bubble before heading after him.

He didn't say a word as we walked through the thick forest that ran through campus and headed into Air Territory. He guided me up to the huge tower which housed the air Elemental students and lifted his hand to cast magic at a triangular symbol above the door.

It opened and we headed inside, taking a huge winding stairway nearly all the way to the top of the tower. He led me down a dark corridor and moved into a room. I followed him, finding myself in an enormous bedroom with a massive king sized bed at the heart of it. There were Pitball posters on the walls and a bunch of trophies lining a shelf above his bed. To my right was a enormous bookshelf that took up nearly an entire wall and was filled with all kinds of textbooks and tomes.

Orion cast a silencing bubble as he moved to a closet at the back of the room and opened the slatted door. He walked inside and appeared a moment later with a huge leather-bound book.

"Before I tell you anything, we need to make a deal that you never breathe a word about the magic I do to anyone outside of the people who are helping you catch this killer."

I nodded, moving forward and extending my hand willingly. "I swear it."

He took my palm and we shook, a clap of magic ringing between us and binding the deal.

Orion relaxed slightly as he dropped onto the end of his bed and opened the book, flipping through the pages until he found something. He patted the space beside him and I cocked a brow.

"You're not going to try and fuck me again are you?"

He laughed. "In your dreams, Noxy."

A grin pulled at my mouth. "Only in yours, Orion. Or should I call you *Orio?*"

He snorted, shifting the book toward me so I could see the page he was showing me. "This is a spell called magic transference. It can be done through the bones of dead Fae, but the Element you take from each bone only lasts in the host's body for a short amount of time."

"Have you tried that?" I asked in alarm.

Orion shifted next to me and I realised Zodiac's golden boy wasn't that golden at all. "Yeah. But there's a higher magic to this which is far more complex. This book talks about it a bit, but the kind of scriptures containing that information are probably long destroyed or if there are any texts remaining on it they'd be kept well hidden by whoever has them. Basically the theory goes that an Element can be taken from a living Fae in the final moments of their life. But they have to die willingly to pass it on…" He pointed out a passage in the book and I leaned forward to read it.

Death opens a gateway to a Fae's Elemental magic for a brief moment of time. However, to harness this magic the subject would have to lower their magical barriers at the very moment of death. This has only been observed to happen in suicidal Fae, making it near impossible to orchestrate.

My mouth became overly dry and my heart beat unevenly. "The murderer is using a drug called Killblaze which amplifies Fae's emotions. The woman we interrogated was a councillor who's been finding suicidal patients for King to use in his rituals. He gives them Killblaze and gets them to kill themselves."

"Fuck," Orion breathed. "Why haven't you gone to the FIB?"

I frowned. "The FIB are pretty useless in Alestria. Besides, Elise doesn't trust them and proving this stuff is pretty difficult when we have no solid evidence. Plus King is covering their tracks well."

"I see," he said, closing the book.

"Is there any way to remove the Elemental magic King has taken? I don't wanna put this on your shoulders, but the bastard is going to take on the Celestial Councillors when he has enough power. He wants to rule over Solaria and who knows what kind of kingdom this would be with someone as ruthless as that on the throne. We have to stop him."

Fear flashed across Orion's eyes and he nodded quickly. "I'll look into it for you. My mom has more books I can gain access to. I'll be going home this weekend with my sister." He took out his Atlas. "Give me your number."

"Sure, just don't get any ideas about trying to sext me." I smirked, taking the Atlas and keying it in.

He chuckled. "I prefer my girls with a little less muscle."

"Have you got a girlfriend?" I asked, tossing his Atlas back to him.

"Nah…I don't really have time for anything long-term. I have to focus on my game. Besides, Vampires are solitary anyway. Unless I find my perfect match, I'll probably stay solo. I can't really imagine meeting a girl I'd want to be around twenty four seven."

"I felt that way before I met Elise," I said, the words tumbling from my lips. Something about Orion made me innately trust him, even though opening up to other Fae was something I rarely did. "Do you think her being a Vampire is why she can't settle down with one guy?"

He arched his brows, mulling that over. "Maybe. I mean, I always believed that if it's right it will just work out, you know? So do you really think she's the one for you?"

"I've *seen* it," I said in a low voice. "I've seen both of us with silver rings around our eyes."

"You're Elysian Mates?" he asked in awe. "Man, if that's true, then you've got nothing to worry about. The stars will bring you together."

"Yeah, that's what I'm banking on. But seeing her with other guys is kinda killing me."

He clapped a hand to my shoulder, his brows pulling together. "Hang in there. No Fae can fight fate."

"Yeah, I guess you're right." I broke a smile. "It's just a matter of time."

GARETH

CHAPTER THIRTY EIGHT

TEN MONTHS BEFORE THE SOLARID METEOR SHOWER...

*G*etting information on Ryder Draconis for the FIB was about the scariest thing I'd ever done. And that was saying something considering the shit I'd been getting myself into lately.

The first step in my plan was to try and get more work from Ryder. And as terrifying as it was, I had to hope that that work involved watching him doing something illegal. Preferably not murdering someone in the woods. Again. But something I could gather intel about. I wasn't going to risk taking another video of him because if he did end up arrested, I was not going to have any physical way for someone to trace it back to me. Lesson learned.

Approaching Ryder during school hours was a no go. I couldn't risk the Oscuras seeing me with him, so I had to wait until after classes to make my move.

I'd heard a rumour that the Lunars were heading out to the lakeshore tonight for some event. And though I'd missed the details, I had the feeling it wasn't to frolic in the water like school girls.

I waited until it was dark then made my way toward Lake Tempest, stuffing my hands in my pockets as I moved at a casual pace. Plenty of unallied were heading that way so I started to relax about the Oscuras. It was my right to go along, I wasn't allied to them.

The sound of shouts and cheers carried to me as I walked through The Iron Wood toward the beach and I upped my pace as curiosity got the better of me.

I soon broke through the tree line and the milky glow of the half moon above highlighted the crowd before me. I was higher up the shore than them so I could see right down to the centre of the gathered Fae who were standing in a large circle. Ryder stood at the heart of them, blood coating his hands and flecking his bare chest as he threw savage punches into the gut of his opponent in what looked like a bare knuckle fight. The unlucky Fae soon hit the ground and Bryce Corvus rushed forward, lifting Ryder's arm into the air.

"Our undefeated King!" he roared. "Who dares take him on next?"

A huge guy called Hagen stepped from the crowd. He was a Cerberus and built like the huge beast that lived within his flesh. He had nearly half a foot on Ryder and the Lunar King wasn't short by any stretch of the imagination.

I hurried down the beach, my heart pounding as I pushed through the crowd.

"Place your bets!" Bryce called and everyone raised their hands, sending a spiral of glittering magic out from their fingers. The magic collected in a peaked hat that Bryce waved in the air then he flipped it over onto his head and turned to watch the fight. I managed to elbow my way to the front – alright, slither like a slug to the front – and crossed my arms as I waited for the fight to break out.

Ryder spat blood on the ground, his face a mess of bruises and his left eye swollen to hell. The most terrifying thing was the smile on his face as he fed on his own pain, filling his magic reserves. But it didn't look like magic was being used in these brawls anyway.

"What a fun game! I volunteer to play!" Lorenzo appeared at my side and I tried to catch his arm a second before he stumbled into the ring. His eyes were red with the high he was currently riding and he was soaking wet like he'd just come straight out of the lake.

"Lorenzo!" I hissed, but Ryder set him in his sights with a snarl.

"Get the fuck out of here before I break your Oscura neck," he growled and the look in his eyes told me he'd really do it.

Lorenzo started laughing wildly, pointing at Ryder and clutching his side. "That tree is talking. And oh look how frowny its bark is. What an angry tree!"

Ryder's fist connected with his nose and he toppled backwards with a manic laugh. "Ouch, it hit me. Did you see that? Its big branch swung right at my face!"

I rushed forward, dragging Lorenzo to his feet and the Lunars started heckling and shouting abuse at him.

"Get out of here," I said seriously, pushing him toward the crowd as blood spilled out from his nose.

"Red is my favourite taste, what's yours, Garfield?" he asked as he licked his lips, falling apart into manic laughter again.

Someone yanked him from my arms and the Lunars split apart as they shoved him out of the crowd.

"Get out of here!" a girl kicked a bunch of pebbles at him and Lorenzo snatched them up, gathering them in his pockets.

"So many sweeties, all for me," he said in glee.

My heart twisted as a few more of the Brotherhood ran toward him and I was relieved when he raced away, his laughter carrying back to us as he darted into the woods.

"Fucking Blazer," Ryder spat and I turned my attention back to him to watch the fight.

Hagen shed his shirt, rolling his massive shoulders back and looking to

Ryder with a challenge in his gaze.

Ryder cracked his neck, looking bored as he waited for Bryce to call the start of the match.

"Three-" he started and the crowd picked up the chant. "Two, one – fight!"

Hagen moved first, throwing a huge fist out and slamming it into Ryder's gut. The Lunar King growled like a beast, snatching hold of his wrist and twisting so hard a crack sounded in response.

The Cerberus roared in pain and Ryder laughed, the manic sound carrying all the way up to the moon. Hagen lunged again but Ryder was faster, moving behind him in a flash and slamming his knuckles into Hagen's side. Blood poured and I realised he had razor blades lodged between his knuckles. It was dirty and brutal, but he clearly didn't care. And maybe those were the rules anyway because Hagen instantly took something from his pocket and flipped out a switch blade.

He slashed it at Ryder with impossible speed and Ryder jerked backwards as the blade sliced his chest open. Blood poured over his skin and he grinned like a psycho, making Hagen balk as Ryder didn't falter, racing forward and punching his gut until he bled and bled.

Ryder kicked out his legs and Hagen toppled, crying out as he raised his hands to try and stop his attacker. But Ryder was like a starved animal, falling on top of him and cutting him to shreds with every blow he struck. There was a nothingness in his eyes that made me retreat into the crowd. I'd come here to talk to this guy. This fucking lunatic.

Ryder only stopped when Hagen ceased to move, climbing off of him and rising to his feet. Bryce hurried forward to lift his arm into the air and a bunch of the Lunars ran forward to heal Hagen and drag him off of the blood-stained pebbles.

Ryder shook Bryce off, muttering something in his ear and Bryce nodded, moving into the crowd and passing out people's winnings as he went.

Ryder turned and marched toward the crowd, all of them splitting apart in an instant to let him through. He strode between them down the beach and headed straight into the lake, walking in up to his neck as blood pooled out around him.

I steeled myself as the crowd dispersed around me, waiting for Ryder to return from the water. He stayed there for a long time, staring out toward the opposite shore, as still as a crocodile. And just as lethal.

Music started up in the woods and I guessed everyone was heading to the Lunar Pit for a party. It was just me and Ryder left there and I suddenly felt like I should announce I was here before he accused me of spying on him or some shit.

I cleared my throat, but he didn't give me any response at all.

"Um...Ryder?" I called.

He turned his head just enough to see who dared bother him and I swallowed the hard ball in my throat, taking a step toward the water's edge.

Ryder turned, walking back out of the lake with water streaming off of him. He'd healed his wounds and the blood was gone, but it did nothing to take away from the imposing aura he gave off.

He didn't spare me a glance, walking straight past me up the shore towards the trees.

Fuck. Shit. Craptarts.

I hurried after him, moving to his side and leaving a decent foot of space between us. "I just wanted to see if you have any more jobs for me?"

He grunted.

"So...?" My question hung in the air as we walked and I finally started to accept I wasn't going to get an answer at all.

Ryder swung toward me suddenly, pinning me in his icy gaze. "You want work, pony boy?" he growled and I nodded. He raised a hand, casting a silencing bubble around us and my skin prickled as the magic settled over me. "I already gave you a job," he hissed. "Hand me the fucker who recorded me with King."

"I'm looking for them," I promised, forcing my voice not to shake. Shit shit shit.

"Then look harder," he snarled, stepping toward me and I winced full bodily, expecting an attack. He lowered his voice, lifting a hand to rest it on my shoulder and looking at me intently. *"The Brotherhood will lose faith in me if I don't find this little piece of shit. So if you can't find out who did it, I'm going to need a fall guy. And my gang are going to watch me rip his innocent spine out of his innocent throat."*

I trembled as the pressure of his hand on my shoulder increased.

"Maybe I'll pick someone with an angelic face like yours and glitter in his hair." He clapped the side of my head and glitter tumbled around me, drawing a whinny of fear from my throat. *"Or maybe you're worth keeping around and I just haven't seen any evidence of it yet."*

I nodded quickly. "I'm worth keeping around," I swore because fuck a fucking duck on a truck, I did not want my spine ripped out of my throat by this guy. And I knew he'd actually do it. It wasn't just some idle threat. *"I promise."*

I held out my hand and Ryder's brows raised as he stepped back to look at my outstretched palm.

"You've got big balls for a Pegasus," he commented. *"I'll have some more work sent your way in the next few days."*

Thank fuck for that. Then I can find something incriminating to give to the FIB.

I raised my hand higher, forcing myself to look him in the eyes. Finally, he took it and his cold, hard skin met with mine.

"Swear you'll work out who took that recording," Ryder snarled and relief rang through my body like a gong.

"I swear it." I nodded and magic flashed between our palms.

He dropped my hand and stalked away into the darkness, leaving me sagging with relief in the aftermath of his company. I wasn't at risk of bad luck from the stars, because I'd already worked out who took that recording. He never made me promise to tell him who.

A tingling along my spine made me look around and I stared into the thick shadows between the trees with the awful feeling of being watched.

I'm just being paranoid.

I took a heavy breath, turning and heading in the direction of the Empyrean Fields. I was going to head back to my room and try to forget about seeing Ryder slice open a Cerberus who could have crushed me in his fist. And in the next few days, I'd face whatever work Ryder sent my way. Then screw over that scary asshole and hand him to FIB. I just hoped they locked him up in Darkmore Penitentiary and threw away the key. Because if he ever got out, he'd come for me. And the spine ripping would commence.

I knew something was wrong the moment I awoke in the dark to the feeling of magic brushing over my skin.

I jerked upright in my bunk and several hands grabbed hold of me, dragging me onto the floor. I shouted out in alarm as I realised their faces were masked by a shadow spell.

I looked to Leon across the room in his bed. "Hey! Wake up!"

Knuckles slammed into my cheek and I slumped backwards, my thoughts scattering as I tried to rise again. The hands locked around me once more and I yelled at the sleeping bodies in my dorm, but none of them stirred. I realised with a jolt that a silencing bubble must have surrounded me and my attackers and fear coiled around my heart like a serpent. The window was wide open; they must have come up the freaking fire escape to break in.

"Who are you – what do you want?!" *I demanded, kicking out as they hauled me upright.*

One of them stuffed a hessian sack over my head and cast ice over my
hands to block my magic.

I was dragged along, panic sliding down my spine and near paralysing
me.

Ryder must have found out what I did. He must have suspected
something. I must have given it away!

My thoughts clashed together as I begged my captors for answers, but
they said nothing as they hauled me along out of the Vega Dorms.

My feet pounded across concrete as I breathed heavily, the space
around my face heating up fast and making me feel like I was suffocating.

Come on, think Gareth. You've got to be ready to talk your way out
of this.

I could tell Ryder about the FIB, that I was forced to do it. But what
difference would it make? He'd kill me anyway for being a fucking snitch.
And what if he didn't stop there? What if his rage extended to Ella and
Mom? What if he made everyone I loved pay in blood for my betrayal and all
of this hell had only caused far more horrors than I was trying to prevent?

Eventually, I was forced to my knees and the impact sent another
wave of fear through me. Energy crackled along my skin and made the hairs
rise all across my body. It was familiar, but in my panic I couldn't place it.

The hood was dragged off of me and I found myself looking up at
Dante Oscura in the Acrux Courtyard. I stilled, momentarily blindsided. But
my fear came tumbling back in response to the look on his face. His jaw was
locked tight and lightning flashed in his eyes. A storm was brewing around
us, the air wild and the clouds knitting together above.

I glanced behind me, expecting to find the entirety of the Oscura Clan
but only Dante's beta, Tabitha, and his cousin Renaldo stand there as they
removed the shadow spell from their features.

I turned back to Dante as he took something from his pocket and
tossed it toward me. A crumpled photograph tumbled in the wind, landing

beneath my nose.

My heart stopped beating. My lungs stopped labouring. The photo must have been taken just last night in The Iron Wood. My hand was clasped with Ryder's and a flash of magic glowed between our palms.

Had Dante had me followed?

I took a shuddering breath as the world started turning again, tilting my chin up to look at Dante. In my wild terror of Ryder, I'd forgotten to fear the Storm Dragon. The guy who always seemed so nice, who I'd come to think of as a friend. But where Ryder wore his monster on the outside, Dante wore it on the inside. It was just as violent, just as dangerous. And the fact that it was sleeping most of the time, meant it was easy to forget.

"I can explain," I blurted a second before Dante's boot slammed into my jaw.

I hit the ground, my head impacting with stone and I groaned as pain resounded through my skull.

"Traditore," he snarled and I had the feeling I knew what that word meant. Traitor.

"Let me explain," I slurred, my mind still reeling from the might of his kick.

"This photograph explains it all, bastardo." His foot collided with my gut, then again and again.

He aimed for my ribs next, kicking until a crack sated his rage and he started pacing around me instead. Pain spiked through my body and I wheezed against the pressure of broken bones pushing against my lungs.

"Dante," I rasped.

He leaned down, snatching me by the collar and yanking me to my feet so I was eye to eye with him.

"Do you take me for a fool, cavallo? Did you think I wouldn't find out?" he snarled, his eyes spitting venom as lightning flashed in the sky above.

"I don't work for him," I forced out the lie and he tossed me to the ground.

His two Wolves howled excitedly and I tried to crawl away as Dante approached. The ice on my hands had almost melted away and I brought air to my palms, forcing my way through the last of it. A second before Dante kicked me again, I through up an air shield and his foot bounced off of it.

He released a dark laugh, lifting his hands and casting a storm of air around me, increasing the pressure as he unleashed his superior power on me. I yelled out as I used every ounce of strength I had to keep my shield in place, but it popped like a bubble of gum as he finally broke through it and he stamped his foot down on my chest, keeping it there to pin me in place.

"Lie to me again," he demanded. "I dare you." Lightning slammed into the ground near my head and I whinnied in terror as rubble cascaded over me.

"The FIB are blackmailing me!" I wailed before he could bring down a strike on me.

He stilled, his eyes narrowing.

"They traced that video of Ryder and King back to me," I stammered. "King told me if I didn't help the FIB get something on Ryder to convict him, she'd tell Ryder I recorded the video." I was one second from pissing myself as I stared up at Dante's cold eyes, but a sliver of hope filled me as he removed his foot from my chest.

"Prove it," he growled and I tried to think of something I had as proof.

I didn't have a letter, an email. All I had was the record of the phone call from the agent and some unknown number wasn't proof.

"I can't," I breathed, the strength going out of my body. "They brought me down to the station."

Dante raised a hand in some signal and his cousin Renaldo appeared at his side. "Search his memory for a meeting with the FIB," he directed and fear gripped me again as Renaldo's two eyes pulled together and merged into one large entity. He wasn't a Wolf after all, he was a Cyclops, a mind reader. And if he hunted too deep, he could unveil all of my darkest secrets. But if he was only looking for the FIB agent, he wouldn't see anything else. I *just prayed Dante didn't ask him to claw his way through my mind. It wasn't honourable. And I'd always believed Dante was honourable to his core. I just had to hope I was right about that.*

Renaldo stepped forward, kneeling down before me with a sneer. "This will hurt more if you fight it."

I nodded, trying to get myself to relax as he reached out and pressed two fingers to my forehead.

Pain speared through my mind and I was dragged down into oblivion before I could even try to resist his power.

I awoke a second later and my stomach churned violently. Cyclops interrogation was the most invasive kind of Order gift and it left you sick and weak. I lurched over sideways, vomiting up the contents of my stomach as Renaldo and Dante moved away from me.

I wiped my mouth, wincing against the pain hammering through my body. There wasn't an inch of me that didn't hurt as I laid back against the cold stone and stared up at the clouds. They began to part, revealing the night sky above, a thousand tiny lights staring down at me as they contemplated my fate.

It took me a second to realise that if the clouds were evaporating, then Dante's foul mood must have been too.

He appeared a moment later, kneeling at my side and pushing his hands beneath my shirt to cast healing magic into my skin.

I sighed heavily as the pain ebbed away, unable to look Dante in the eyes. He took my hand when I was healed, pulling me to my feet and dragging me into a firm hug. He clapped me on the back and muttered, "A morte e ritorno, mio amico." He released me, patting my cheek. "I never should have doubted you, cavallo. But the evidence was hard to ignore."

"You could have interrogated me first," I said in anger.

"Forgive me," he begged, holding his hands together in a prayer. "I will repay you. I will help you hand Draconis to the FIB." His smile widened

and I found myself smiling slightly in return.

One beating was worth another day out of trouble. But with the tangled web I was weaving, it was starting to seem like trouble was going to follow me wherever I went. I just had to keep outpacing it.

ELISE

CHAPTER THIRTY NINE

Arriving back at Aurora Academy felt like stepping into an alternate reality. Leon still wouldn't speak to me and suddenly I was without my most constant companion on campus. We'd only been back a day and I already felt his absence like a missing limb. I wasn't smiling as much and I certainly wasn't laughing. In fact, my heart just felt even heavier now that I had lost him too.

I wanted to fix it. I wanted it so much that it hurt. But I had to respect his wishes. He'd made it clear he didn't want me near him and there were only so many times that I could hear that before I had to listen.

The end of the deal between Dante and Ryder had obviously changed things dramatically too. I was free to be with both of them as much and as often as we wanted but that came with it's own ties. My relationships with them couldn't be open. No one could find out that I was seeing them both or my life and theirs would be in danger from their gangs.

Gabriel still wasn't happy with me seeing the other guys and that was keeping us apart too. I got the feeling he was just waiting me out, expecting me to wake up one day and realise that I didn't want the others. But that was never going to happen. And this distance he was building between us only served to isolate me more.

The week that we'd spent at Zodiac Academy had left Ryder and Dante with a lot of things to deal with in their gangs so despite the fact that I could technically go to either of them, I didn't. I was sitting on the steps outside the Rigel Library, looking over the exam schedule that had been waiting for me upon my return.

The end of the year was fast approaching and I needed to pass all of my exams to keep my place here. And as I still hadn't solved the mystery behind Gareth's murder, that was even more important than ever.

I blew out a breath as I tried to focus on a Numerology equation but my heart wasn't in it. I was pining. For Leon, my brother, the girl I'd been before my world had been ripped away from me. Sometimes I felt like I was growing into someone new. Someone braver, stronger, tougher. But then that idea cut me apart. Because if I wasn't the girl who Gareth had loved anymore then who was I?

My Atlas pinged and I hooked it from my pocket with a sigh of relief, wondering who had decided to save me from my pity party.

Gabriel:
I've been looking over the footage from Nightshade's office while we were away. Can you meet me on the roof?

I shot from my perch on the steps and raced up the Vega Dorms' fire escape ladder before coming to a halt beside Gabriel where he was sitting in his tent.

"This is a funny way to ask for a hook up," I teased as he turned to look at me.

"Why do you think I'm after a hook up?" Gabriel asked, his gaze sliding over my hot pants and crop top combo as I blew a bubble with my gum.

"Because that often seems to be the deal with us. You call me up here, get all serious on me then rip my clothes off." I shrugged as I reached out to brush my fingers over his black wing and his gaze heated.

"I really do have something to say," he protested, tucking a lock of my hair behind my ear.

"Go on then," I replied, trailing my fingers down the inside of his silken wing and marvelling at the beauty of his feathers.

Gabriel cleared his throat as he tried to focus his thoughts.

"Well, I had to piece this together from several phone calls she made, but I'm pretty sure they performed another successful ceremony during the full moon that occurred while we were away."

"Shit," I cursed. I'd known it was unlikely that I'd destroyed the entire stock of Killblaze in that explosion, but I'd been hoping I might have.

"She mentioned something about building a new lab too," he said in a low voice. "Though it sounded like that would take some time."

"So now we only have to worry about whether or not they have any more Killblaze stored?" I asked. "If they don't then we might have bought ourselves some time-"

"She said that there was enough stock for one more month," Gabriel replied darkly. "So we can assume that the ritual will take place again on the next full moon."

I groaned, leaning my head against Gabriel's shoulder. "So we need to do everything we can to be ready for then," I said, concerns warring through my mind at the idea of that. "We keep trying to uncover King, hope Orion can come up with some way for us to undo this spell they've used to bind the stolen magic to them and ideally kill that son of a bitch before the full moon rises next month."

"We should probably get in some study for our exams too," Gabriel teased and I snorted a laugh.

"Easy," I agreed.

Gabriel sighed, pressing his lips to the top of my head. "Is this the part where you run off and leave me alone again?" he asked, half joking, half not.

I pulled away from him, turning and cupping his cheek in my jaw. "I don't enjoy running from you, Gabriel," I said, holding his gaze to make sure he could see how much I meant that.

He looked back at me for a long moment before pressing his lips to mine and I sighed as I fell into his kiss.

"Why do I always feel like I'm half in a fight with you?" I growled as I shifted forward keenly, moving to straddle him.

I kissed him again, pressing my lips to his more firmly as his hands moved to cup my ass and he rocked my hips against the swell in his pants.

I moaned as I traced my fingers down his bare chest, painting the lines of his tattoos hungrily before dropping my mouth to the Libra tattoo which always seemed to burn hot just for me.

"Because we always are," Gabriel replied with a humourless laugh as he leaned back to give me more access.

He shifted his hands up my sides slipping them beneath my crop top and groaning as he found no bra there. His thumbs rocked against my nipples and I moaned with need as I tried to focus on what he'd just said to me.

"That's because you want to cage me," I gasped as he continued his torture on my nipples.

I ground my hips back and forth, the denim of my shorts and his jeans chafing together where they separated us and rubbing against me in the most delicious way.

"I'm just waiting for you to get bored of them, my angel," he growled firmly and I hissed as he stopped my movements in his lap and tugged his hands back out from beneath my shirt.

"Did it ever occur to you that when you tell me you don't like the fact that you have to share me, you're telling me that you don't like one of the core parts of my personality?" I growled, my lust fading fast in favour of my anger at this stupid fucking argument coming up again.

"I like everything about you," he protested firmly, looking right into my eyes. "I just don't see how sleeping around is a core part of your personality."

Nice.

"Did you ever think to ask me *why* I don't want to be tied to one guy or are you just so set on the idea that what *you* want is so much more important than my desires that it doesn't even matter to you how I feel about that?" I asked.

Gabriel stared at me for a long moment and I could tell he never had considered that.

"You think I'm just so obsessed with dick that I need four to keep me satisfied?" I demanded, pursing my lips. "Because you do understand that there's a whole lot more to my relationships with Ryder, Dante and Leon than just sex, right?"

"I don't know what to think of your relationships with them," he admitted. "It doesn't make sense to me that you want them. I only want *you.* Nothing else, no one else. *You.*"

I sighed as I reached out to trail my fingers down the side of his face. "And I want *you,* Gabriel," I swore. "I just want them too."

His brow furrowed and I could tell he just didn't understand. Like he couldn't. Or maybe wouldn't. But if I wanted to build what I had with him into something more solid, it was important that I try and explain this to him in a way that he might understand.

"I hate that it hurts you to see me with them," I breathed. "And maybe it's selfish of me to want so much with so many… Or maybe it's selfish of *you* to expect me to give the others up for you. Would you ask me to give up my friends? My hobbies? My family to be with you?"

"Of course not."

"So why is this any different?"

"When we get called beneath the stars and come together as Elysian

Mates then you won't want any of them anymore anyway," he said, refusing to even consider what I was saying.

"So you're just counting on the stars to change who I am as a person?" I balked. "You're putting your faith in them stamping out an integral part of my personality because that would suit you better? Am I not good enough for you as I am?"

Gabriel's face paled and his grip tightened on my waist. "Of course you are. You're all I want, all I think about, all I need-"

"Just not as I am, right?" I asked bitterly. "You've fallen for some fantasy version of me who only wants you. Did it ever occur to you that I might *like* who I am? That I don't want the stars to steal anything or anyone from me?"

"It won't feel like that," Gabriel insisted. "Once we're bonded, your love for me will just make your feelings for them seem small, irrelevant."

"But they aren't irrelevant," I growled. "They're important to me. Part of me. And if you don't like that then what you're really saying is that you don't like *me*."

"That's ridiculous. You're so much more than a girl who likes to date multiple men," Gabriel scoffed.

"Yeah I am. And each of the men I'm with are perfectly suited to the different parts of me. When Gareth died, the girl I used to be was shattered, broken, split apart into pieces I could never imagine reuniting again. But somehow I've started to heal. And the different parts of me have only managed that through finding their kindred spirits. Would you rather let the rest of me wither and fade away than let me have what I have with them?"

Gabriel's lips parted as he looked into my eyes and he released a long breath. "I don't want that," he replied slowly. "All I want is you. I just don't want a share of you. I want it all."

"You can have it all. Sharing me doesn't mean you have any less," I protested. "You can have every single piece of me as often as you want it. But if you're asking me to cut the other Kings out of my heart then you're asking me to discard a huge part of myself with them. Which means you don't want all of me at all."

Gabriel's brow pinched and I could tell he needed time to think about that. I leaned forward and kissed him hungrily, showing him just how much I needed him and wanted him too.

"Think about it," I breathed against his lips.

"Okay," he agreed and the look in his eyes said he really meant that. He really would try and see my side of this. I sighed softly, brushing my lips against his one final time then got up and shot away from him.

He wouldn't be able to think about my words with my body pressed to his and I didn't want to force him into deciding on anything that he wasn't happy with any more than I wanted him to force me to change either.

As I passed the Rigel Library, I spotted Cindy Lou leaning against the wall as she spoke to a guy in a black tank top and a baseball cap. His head turned my way as I approached them and my eyebrows rose as I recognised Bryce. Cindy's eyes narrowed on me as I kept walking and Bryce tossed a silencing bubble up around the two of them so that I couldn't listen in on what they were saying.

I had no idea what the Dragon whore drama queen and Ryder's little bitch had in common, but they clearly didn't want me to know.

My skin crept with the feeling of eyes on me as I walked away from them and I glanced back to find the two of them glaring my way. I hoped they hadn't banded together to form an *I Hate Elise Club*. That would be too damn pathetic.

I arrived down in the Acrux Courtyard and found Dante holding court amongst the picnic benches with his Wolves. The Brotherhood weren't currently in residence on the bleachers, but the blazing sunshine had obviously tempted the Oscura Clan out to sunbathe. Most of them were half naked, catching some rays and I eyed Dante's ripped torso as more than a few of the female Wolves tried to snare his attention.

He noticed me and a slow smile slid over his face as he casually got up and walked away from his pack, muttering some excuse as they whimpered their disappointment. He nodded towards the Cafaeteria as he headed that way and my lips twitched as I kept walking toward Altair Halls. I couldn't kiss him in front of his pack or they'd expect me to sign up to the Clan, so we had to find moments together in private.

I headed inside and as soon as I was sure no one was around, I put on a burst of speed, racing to the main entrance and speeding around the building, taking the long route back to the Cafaeteria.

I made it there before Dante thanks to my speed and I waited for him to appear on the path, catching his eye before I backed up around the corner of the building where no one would be able to see us.

A small patch of grass was hidden around here creating the perfect sun trap. I closed my eyes as I felt the sun's rays washing over me, bathing in the feeling of it.

"Why did you look so concerned back there, amore mio?" Dante asked as he rounded the corner and found me waiting for him.

"I've been talking to Gabriel about King...amongst other things." I shrugged, not wanting to go over all of it again. "Long story short, we're going to try and lay a trap for them on the next full moon."

"I'm in," Dante agreed fiercely without me even having to ask. He was always so certain, no hesitation, no prolonged consideration, he decided on his course of action and stuck to it. And I fucking loved that about him.

I reached out and caught the waistband of his shorts and tugged him towards me.

"You said something to me once before," I purred in a low voice as he leaned his hands against the wall either side of my head, caging me in with his huge body.

"Did I?" he asked casually, like he had no idea what I was referring to.

"Yes," I replied firmly. "And sometimes I want to say it back to you."

Dante smiled widely for a moment before leaning down so that his lips were inches from mine. "Well don't," he replied darkly.

"Don't?" I asked in surprise, pressing my palms back against the wall behind me.

"Only say it when you want to say it all the time. Not sometimes," he inched closer to me and I gasped as electricity crackled between us.

I tilted my chin up, hungry for his mouth but he hesitated just shy of touching his lips to mine.

"Ti amo," he growled before closing the distance between us and devouring the gasp of surprise that left me at his words.

He kissed me deeply, his tongue stroking mine and his passion making me weak at the knees as he showed me just how much he meant that. He loved me. This beautiful, powerful, dangerous creature loved me. Even though I was broken and grieving and had lied to him, he loved me still and my heart pounded with the aching need for me to say it back to him.

But I wasn't sure I could. It wasn't that I didn't want to. It was more that I wasn't convinced that I was healed enough to feel it. Not truly. Not fully. Not in the way he deserved. And until I could give him that kind of love, it didn't seem fair to let the words pass my lips. So instead of labelling it, I showed him how I felt with that kiss, I gave him every piece of me, even the broken, ruined parts and laid them bare before him.

"I thought you couldn't kiss her?" Leon's voice interrupted us and Dante pulled back, breaking our kiss as he turned to face his friend.

Leon's gaze was dark, his expression unreadable as his gaze skipped between us and I chewed my bottom lip, all the words I wanted to speak to him catching in my throat.

"Ryder and I decided to end the deal," Dante explained, his hand sliding into mine.

Leon nodded, his brow furrowing as he processed that. "And how exactly did you convince him to do that?"

"We both decided that it was worse not having her than letting each other have her as well. So the three of us just stopped fighting it and did what we'd been aching to for the last few months."

Leon's eyes narrowed at that. "The three of you? *Together?*"

My lips parted with the need to say something to ease the pain in his voice, but I didn't know how.

"It wasn't planned, mio amico," Dante said placatingly. "You know I'd rather share her with you any day-"

"But you didn't, did you? After all the times I helped you to get around that stupid fucking deal, the first time you didn't have to follow those rules, you were with her with *Draconis.*"

"Leon," I tried, inching towards him. "You know how much I want you too. Please can't we just talk about everything? And if you want to, then the three of us can-"

"Psh, I don't want a pity three way," he snapped. "It's not like you need me now anyway, is it?"

"Just talk to her," Dante demanded, reaching out for his friend with a pained look on his face. "We belong together. We need you."

"You looked like you were doing just fine without me a minute ago."

My heart fell as Leon walked away from us again and I sighed as Dante pulled me into his arms.

"Don't worry, bella, he'll come around," he promised.

I didn't reply because I wasn't so sure. I'd hurt Leon with my lies and even if he heard me out, I wasn't sure if I could make up for it. The only thing I was sure of was that, if he gave me the chance, then I'd try as hard as I could to convince him to come back to me.

DANTE

CHAPTER FORTY

I sat in the Voyant Sports Hall, rows of desks spreading out around me as I finished up my written Astrology exam. With everything that was going on lately, I was distracted as fuck. I kept mixing up my Cardinal Qualities with my Mutable Qualities and had to keep going back to change them. I couldn't afford to fail this year. Even *I* wasn't immune to losing my place at this academy. I couldn't blackmail Greyshine into keeping me here if my grades sucked. The school board went above him.

I forced away my worries about Leon, how Elise was feeling, the plans we were making for the full moon to catch a murderer, and the underlying anxiety I always had about my uncle Felix, and finished up my paper.

Professor Rayburn finally called time on the exam and although my essay looked *terribile*, I was pretty sure I'd swapped all of my Mutables for Cardinals. *Let's fucking hope so.*

I filed out of the sports hall with the rest of the students, heading into the afternoon sun. It was my last exam of the day and I was free to do what I wanted now. But instead of lazing in the sunshine, I was going to head to the library to get in some revision for tomorrow's exams.

Gabriel rushed ahead of me, tugging off his blazer and unbuttoning his shirt and I frowned, wondering where he was running off to.

"Hey stronzo!" I called and he glanced back at me.

His lips became tight for a moment, but then he beckoned me over and I jogged to his side. He cast a silencing bubble around us and the serious expression on his face made me frown.

"What's going on?" I asked.

"Orion's coming to meet me by stardust in the city," he said. "He's got something to help us with King."

"Merda," I breathed, my heart beating harder with hope. "I'm coming with you."

"It's fine, I can go on my own."

"It wasn't a request," I growled and he gave me an icy look before nodding and dropping the pack from his shoulder.

"It'll be quicker if we fly. Put your clothes in here." He opened the bag, stuffing his blazer inside and I shed my clothes, receiving a few wolf whistles as I got completely naked in broad daylight.

Gabriel shouldered the pack and I turned away from him, leaping forward and shifting into my navy Dragon form, making students scatter around me in alarm as my huge claws slammed onto the path.

I looked to Gabriel and he smirked, releasing his wings from his back. "Keep up."

He launched himself into the sky and I flexed my wings, taking off after him and locking him in my sights. He was fast, racing through the sky and twisting through the clouds like a damn pixie, but I had sheer power behind me and the wind at my back so there was no chance he'd out-fly me today.

I tore after him over the Campus gates, following him as he wound over the streets of Alestria far below, searching for something. After a few minutes longer, he dropped out of the sky and I lowered my nose, diving after him.

I shifted before I hit the ground, landing on my feet beside Gabriel on a quiet road with nothing but an old abandoned house at the end. He tossed me my clothes and I pulled them on as he looked around, waiting for Orion to appear.

It wasn't long before glitter danced in the air across the road and Orion appeared a second later via stardust, standing beneath a large oak tree wearing a dark hoodie. We hurried over to meet him and cast a silencing bubble around us.

"Hey," he said in a tense voice. "So…I haven't found what you need to bring down King unfortunately. I hunted my mom's library, but there wasn't anything there."

I folded my arms. "So why are you here?"

"To give you this." Orion reached into the sports bag he was carrying, taking out a black, cylindrical object which was about a foot long and shimmered with silver engravings. They looked like runes, but none that I'd ever seen in Arcane Arts.

"This is a Shroud," Orion explained. "It's a powerful shield which will protect the one who holds it from dark magic. That should include the additional magic your King has stolen in their dark rituals." Gabriel held out his hand for it but Orion pulled it out of reach, his brows pulling together. "It's made from blackthorn and enchanted with powerful blood magic. The shield it creates is projected from the confines of this vessel, but the magic is volatile and wants to escape."

"You make it sound like it's alive," I said with a grimace.

"Dark magic is different to Elemental magic," Orion said in a low tone, his eyes glimmering. "It's made of shadow and it wants to be free."

My gut coiled. I'd traded dark objects before in my line of work, but I'd never used them. This Shroud was not only illegal enough to earn a life sentence in Darkmore Penitentiary, it was probably worth a hell of a lot on the black market too.

"So how do we keep the magic contained?" Gabriel asked.

"Simple," Orion said. "It must *never* touch the ground or the magic will be absorbed into the earth and the Shroud will be useless. Otherwise, it will remain intact." He held it out to Gabriel who swiftly placed it into his bag.

"Noted," Gabriel said with a nod then pulled Orion in for a hug and clapped him on the shoulder. "Thank you for this. It means a great deal."

Orion stepped back with a frown. "I'll keep trying to find more texts that can help. My family have a few connections with Fae who trade in these kinds of things."

"Be careful not to get caught," I said seriously. "You're fucked if the FIB find you with stuff like that, Vampira."

"I know." Orion smirked. "But I've been playing this game a long time. No one's going to catch me."

"I did," Gabriel pointed out with a taunting smile and Orion shoved him playfully.

"Well neither of you two will hand me to the cops or I'll drag your asses to Darkmore with me."

I laughed, clapping a hand to his arm. "Grazi, amico."

"Be careful," he warned, then threw a handful of stardust into the air and disappeared into the ether.

We headed back to campus and were soon standing in the Acrux Courtyard together while I pulled my clothes on.

Gabriel moved to walk away and I caught his arm, tugging him back to look at me. "Don't drop that thing, stronzo. Maybe you should give it to me?"

He scowled. "Do you really think I'd let anything happen to it? It can protect Elise."

I gripped his arm tighter, my lips pressing together into a firm line. "I'd still rather be the one to look after it."

"Tough shit." He yanked away from me and took off into the air.

I glared after him, releasing a huff as I headed out of the courtyard.

My Atlas rang as I walked down the path toward the library and I took it out of my pocket, answering it and automatically putting up a silencing bubble around me.

"Ciao, Dolce Drago," Mamma said, a heaviness to her voice.

"What's wrong, Mamma?" I asked immediately.

"We've found where Felix is hiding out."

My heart pounded and I stopped walking suddenly, nearly taking out a freshmen as she crashed into my back and scampered away.

"That's grande news," I said, excitement rushing through me. "Why do you sound so worried?"

"Because, amore mio, I know you'll go after him. And I already lost your father, I am not strong enough to lose you too. Il mio cuore non si riprenderà mai." *My heart will never recover.*

"Mamma, I'm a Storm Dragon and an Alpha of the strongest pack in Solaria. You won't lose me. I'm coming home." I hung up, turning back the way I'd come and hurrying back toward the Vega Dorms.

I needed a change of clothes, my car key and a plan.

I'm coming for you Felix, il mio nemico. Tonight is your last night in this world.

I stormed into my family home where chaos was breaking out. The Oscuras were howling and pacing, chatting frantically to their cousins, uncles, aunts, mothers, sisters, friends.

I whistled to catch their attention and held up a hand to halt the dog pile which was about to fall on me.

"Mamma?"

She appeared from the crowd, her dark hair having half fallen out of its braid and her cheeks flushed.

"Mossa." She snapped her fingers. "Everyone come stand in front of your Alpha. Children, go to bed."

My brothers and sisters groaned along with a bunch of my younger cousins. They headed up the stairs, trailing their feet and I waited in silence until they were gone. I didn't spot one girl in particular with them and frowned as I looked around for Rosalie, failing to find her. She was normally at the heart of any excitement, so I was sure she wasn't far away.

Everyone else had lined up and I swept my eyes over the large group of my family, moving down the line and pointing at those I wanted to come with me. I chose fourteen in total. It was a small enough group to move undetected if we split up, but I'd picked the strongest magically of our pack. Barring Mamma, who I refused to put in danger.

"Who found his location?" I asked and Uncle Gino stepped forward. I'd already chosen him to come with us; he was a beast of a man with more Lunar deaths to his name than most Fae in this room.

"I did, Alpha," he said in a gravelly tone. "I tracked him out to the Letterman farm. Looks like him and the other traitors killed the Letterman family and are holing up there. It's got four exits out of the house but only one main gate onto the land. The fence ringing the property is charged with a magical detection spell, but I figured one good lightning strike should take it down." He smirked and I smirked right back, moving forward to kiss him on both cheeks.

"Bravo, Uncle." I turned to the group. "Load up two vans and cast a shadow spell on them. We'll take different routes down the back roads to be sure we're not spotted."

The pack I'd chosen for the job rushed past me out the front door and Mamma moved forward to embrace me with watery eyes. "Be careful, Dolce Drago."

"I will, Mamma. After tonight, you'll be able to sleep comfortably in your bed. Felix will be done."

She nodded firmly, setting her jaw. "Do your father proud."

534

"Always. Ti amo, Mamma." I kissed her cheeks then moved to the door, stepping outside to find a girl dropping down from the top of the porch to land in front of me.

Rosalie was dressed in all black with a fierce look in her eyes and a backpack hanging from her shoulder.

"Ah, there you are." I moved down the steps, eyeing her bag. "You need to stay inside and look after Mamma."

"No, I'm coming with you." She started striding toward the vans and I rushed forward, catching her arm in an iron hold.

"You're staying here, Rosa."

"I won't be any trouble," she swore. "I just want to watch. I want to see Felix's face when he realises he's beat." She didn't even call him Father anymore. Rosalie had shown more allegiance to my pack than anyone by disowning her bastardo of a sperm donor. At least one good thing had come out of his existence. And he was a fool for never cherishing his children.

"Don't be ridiculous. You're not even Awakened." I turned her around, pushing her back towards the house.

"Don't be boring, Dante," she huffed.

"I'm protecting you," I snarled, letting my Alpha tone drip into my voice until she was forced to bow her head. "Go back inside."

She growled under her breath but moved back to the porch steps, dragging her feet as she headed up them.

"Ti amo, Rosalie," I called. Just in case.

She glanced back at me, her eyes widening as she realised why I was saying it.

I strode away before she could answer, moving to the passenger side of one of the vans while the Wolves piled into the back of both vehicles.

Gino got in the driver's seat and took off down the drive. I took my medallion from beneath my shirt, twisting it between my fingers and drawing a little power from the gold.

535

We headed off of the Oscura property and made our way into the hills through winding roads. There were no streetlights here and the darkness pressed in thickly all around us. The shadow spell surrounding the van meant we had to pull over whenever we saw another car. It would keep us hidden on one side of the road, but a hulking shadow moving down the street was pretty suspicious. Fortunately, we only met two cars on the journey and soon arrived in the woodland that bordered the Letterman farm. Gino took us up a dirt track into the trees, parking a few feet from the outer fence which bordered the farm.

It wasn't long before the second van joined us and I jumped out, moving through the trees and approaching the wire fence. I could sense the energy humming from it, the magical barrier stopping anyone from passing this way without alerting Felix.

I dropped to a crouch, assessing the wire and lifting my hand. I let electricity build in my palm, circling in a storm of energy as I gathered it into a ball of power. I unleashed the powerful shot of lightning and it slammed into the wire. Blue energy raced out along the wires in both directions, shooting around the farm in a flash. It died just as quickly and the magical barrier dissolved.

I stood up, turning and smiling at my family. "Hoods up," I commanded and they did as I said.

I pulled mine up too then directed Jaco forward. He clipped the wires with his earth magic, making a path for us.

"Fan out," I ordered everyone. "Stay in pairs. We storm the house at exactly eight o'clock." I checked my watch and everyone nodded, moving forward to sync their watches with mine.

I directed everyone ahead of me in twos, patting their shoulders as they slipped through the gap in the fence then took off across the farmland.

There was one person left as the seventh pair headed on and I frowned in confusion as the girl stepped forward, pushing her hood back.

"*Rosa*," I hissed, my heart jolting. "What the fuck are you doing here?

I gave you a direct order."

"I crawled under the van and held on," she said innocently, showing me her reddened palms.

"Idiota." I moved forward, healing her hands and pointing to the vans. "Stay here."

"No, I want to see," she said fiercely. "I'll be no trouble. I'll stay in your shadow."

I surveyed her for a long moment, seeing so much of myself in her that it hurt me. I wanted to protect her from making the same mistakes I'd made at her age. I'd been manipulated by Felix, turned into a killer. I didn't want her to enter this brutal life too soon. But she had that same spark, that determination that made her feel the need to be included in every mission. She had the makings of becoming a true Alpha.

"Oh cucciolo di lupo," I sighed, reaching out to cup her cheek and she batted my hand away.

"I'm not a pup anymore," she insisted. "I'll never challenge you, cugino, but let me see what it takes to be an Alpha. I have to see." There was an ache in her eyes which I knew so well. I'd felt it too. It burned and burned until it forced you to act. And she would do so one day, no matter if she promised not to. We were destined to clash. But I would not stand in her way. If her path led her to challenge me, then so be it. I'd face that fight with honour and pride. And if she beat me, I'd fall gracefully to the better Wolf.

"Come then," I said in a growl. "Stay close, never walk past me."

"I swear it," she breathed, moving to walk at my back as I turned to step through the broken fence.

I cast a silencing bubble around us as we started to run. I took the most direct route to the house as we'd wasted time talking, circling around the large barn and slipping into the shadowy courtyard which stood before the farmhouse. There were several lights on inside and I moved into a crouch as I reached the outer wall. We slinked along in silence as I glanced in windows.

All of the rooms I checked were empty and I began to grow impatient.

I spotted Katy and Lewina under the front porch and nodded to them as we headed past it. I checked the next room and stilled as I spotted Felix's pack inside, all of them sitting around in a large lounge. His ranks had swelled to over thirty Oscura traitors. But none were as powerful as the Wolves I'd chosen to bring here. And once I shifted, this whole place would be flattened by my storm.

I checked my watch, finding we had two minutes until we attacked. My heart beat harder, but not with fear, with exhilaration. I was ready to bring my treacherous uncle to his knees.

The door opened at the far end of the room and I frowned as Felix appeared with a cloaked figure at his back. More and more cloaked Fae filed into the room and a chill ran through my bones as I recognised what they were.

"Who are they?" Rosalie breathed.

"The Black Card," I rasped, fear twisting through me as the ringleader of their group moved to the head of the room and turned his face to the crowd. Except they were only male for a moment, before they were female, young then old, thin then fat. This was the King Elise had described. The killer she was looking for.

More of the Black Card flashed into existence via stardust and my throat tightened at the sight. If they had access to that, they could move around the city with ease. They continued to appear in the room until there were over a hundred Fae in the space. Far more than the sixteen of us could take on.

"Fuck," I hissed, turning to Katy and Lewina and lifting my hands together to make an X as a signal to stop the attack. They nodded, turning to whoever was beyond them and making the same signal.

"Run around the house, Rosa," I commanded. "Make sure everyone receives the signal. And stay low."

She nodded, her expression serious as she darted away in the opposite direction to Katy and Lewina.

I gazed into the room and pressed my fingers to the very base of the window, shutting my eyes in concentration as I cast an amplifying spell. The voices in the room rushed out to meet me and I thanked the stars that they hadn't cast a silencing bubble. And why would they? Felix wouldn't suspect anyone being out here to listen.

"How kind of you to welcome me into your home," King spoke, their voice changing constantly so I couldn't get a true read on it.

"Sure," Felix said in his gruff tone. "My Wolves are happy to have you here, aren't you?" A clamour of howls filled the room and Felix grinned, turning to King. "Of course, we'll need a little reassurance from you if you want this deal to go smoothly. What are we gonna get for helping you?"

My mouth dried out.

"Alestria is yours," King said. "Just as soon as you help me and my followers take over Solaria. Your numbers are growing every day and I can see the power you are starting to hold in the city. Even the infamous Dante Oscura is shaken by you."

Felix smirked and rage simmered under my skin, begging to be unleashed. But even as a Dragon, I couldn't take on so many Fae. Especially not without knowing the level of power that flowed in their veins.

"Yeah but my little nipote is a stubborn bastardo. He won't stop coming at us," Felix growled.

"I offer you the strength of the Black Card," King said, their currently female face grinning conspiratorially. "Use them to seize the city. Recruit every Oscura Wolf you can and kill the rest. Strike fear into the heart of Alestria and make every Fae here bow to your will."

Felix nodded excitedly, throwing his head back as he howled, bringing on a chorus from the rest of his pack.

Someone caught me by the scruff of the neck and I lurched around, raising my hands to fight them a moment before I saw Rosa there. She dragged me under the porch and a moment later footsteps pounded this way, hammering up the steps above us. I looked to Rosalie with my lips parted, gratitude pouring from me. With the amplifying spell directing our enemies' voices into my ears, I hadn't been able to hear anything behind me.

The Fae headed inside and their shout carried to us. "Alpha, the magical barrier is down!"

"Merda santa," I growled. "We've got to go."

I lifted my head and whistled to signal the other Wolves to run then led the way from under the porch, tearing across the courtyard with three of my pack in tow. We made it into the shadow beside the barn a second before the front door flew open.

I kept my hand locked around Rosalie's as we raced into the darkness, tearing towards the farmland. It was so exposed, I was terrified of taking us out there in the open, but we had no choice.

"Let me show you what I can do!" King's changing voice boomed behind me as I cast a thick air shield around me and Rosa as Katy and Lewina tore off across the field ahead of us.

Energy crackled around me as I called on my storm powers and rain started pelting the ground.

"I know you're here Dante!" Felix called, howling to his pack like a madman.

"Shift, Rosa!" I commanded and she leapt forward without hesitation, tearing through her clothes and hitting the ground on all fours in her silver wolf form.

A horrifying shriek sounded to my left and I spotted Katy tumbling to the ground in a net of vines. Lewina staggered to a halt to help her, but vines wrapped around her too. A huge fire fell on them a moment later, consuming them in moments and a howl left my lips as pain tore through my chest at their deaths.

I turned to face the culprit, finding King standing on the edge of the field, their cloak billowing around them in the storm I'd created.

I raised my hands with a roar of exertion, willing the heavens down on them and lightning tore from the sky. Eight bolts of lightning slammed into an air shield surrounding the bastardo and they raised their hands higher, laughing as the electricity flickered out of existence.

Fear sizzled through my veins. Hardly any Fae in the world were powerful enough to withstand a strike like that. It should have cut through their shield like a knife through butter.

Felix bounded past King in his ruddy brown wolf form and a snarl ripped from my throat. I aimed a lightning strike at him, but King moved their hands, shielding my uncle in an instant.

The ground suddenly trembled beneath me and though King's face continued to change, the darkness in their eyes never did as they directed their power onto the earth around me.

"Alpha!" Uncle Gino bellowed up ahead and I turned, running away as the ground crumbled beneath my feet.

I hated that I was forced to flee, despised that I was made a coward. But the only thing which awaited me here today was death. And if I couldn't spend my death in taking down one of these stronzos, then I wasn't going to waste the value of it.

Gino sped toward me, having circled back and I shook my head at him, pointing the other way.

"Run, Uncle!" I demanded, an Alpha command in my voice. But he didn't listen. He dove forward with a tremendous fireball ripping from his hands and shooting up above me a moment before a colossal storm of ice shards cascaded down around me. The fire burned away the ice directed at me, but the shards pinned Gino to the ground, killing him instantly. His eyes were glassy, but his smile was still tilted up in victory.

Pain ripped at my heart as I sprinted on, having no choice but to abandon his body there as the ground fell away around me. His death would not be forgotten. He was a hero.

I made it to the trees, racing through the gap in the fence and moving to the back of the nearest van. I directed Wolf after Wolf inside, raising my hand to cast the strongest air shield I could around us.

Ten made it. The rest were gone. Lost.

I dove into the driver's seat of one of the vans, finding Rosa in the footwell of the passenger seat in her Wolf form, her eyes wide and mournful as she looked up at me.

I kicked the engine into gear, taking off down the road at high speed.

Rage and grief nearly tore me apart as we put more and more distance between us and our enemies. I punched the dashboard as my anger spilled over and Rosa tipped her head back to release a pained howl which was echoed from our kin in the back of the van.

"I swear on all that I am, I'll kill them. All of them," I hissed, lifting my medallion and kissing our family symbol. "A morte e ritorno."

ELISE

CHAPTER FORTY ONE

One month was not the longest time in the world to try and catch a mysterious killer who was an expert at hiding their identity and covering their tracks. Especially when that time was packed full of revision and exams. By the morning of the next full moon, the exams were over, the academy was getting ready to break up for the summer and I was background wondering where the fuck I'd be spending the next eight weeks.

I had no home, no family, no idea where I'd even want to go if I did and no idea how I was going to entertain myself. Sal's was the only real option I'd been given and I was constantly yo-yoing over whether or not I wanted to go back there. I'd almost brought it up with the Kings a bunch of times, but every time I imagined how that conversation would go I could only hear myself coming off as pathetic and needy, begging for a place to stay when I hadn't been invited. *No thanks.*

Besides, Leon still wasn't talking to me so he was an obvious no go. Dante and Ryder couldn't openly admit to seeing me so they clearly couldn't invite me to stay in their homes. And even though I was fairly sure Gabriel was due to be spending the summer alone like me, I just hadn't been able to ask if I could tag along.

It was mortifying and pathetic and in all honesty I had been mostly trying to block out the idea of the summer altogether anyway. That had always been the time I spent with Gareth. Day after day in each other's company, living in each other's pockets and driving each other up the wall while laughing, joking, getting into trouble and generally partaking in far too much mayhem to stay within the confines of the law at all times. So no matter what other plans I made for this summer, they weren't going to compare to that. And it didn't seem fair to force my moping self onto someone who hadn't even invited me.

I had a fair bit of money saved up from the jobs I'd done for the Kiplings recently and I was pretty sure that it would cover the cost of an average motel for the eight week duration. Okay, a shitty motel. And I'd probably have to get some kind of summer job if I was planning on eating...

Tomorrow's problem, Elise. Let's just focus on not dying tonight first.

The fact that we now knew King had teamed up with Felix only made the prospect of going up against them more terrifying, but we didn't have a choice. I wasn't going to let that bastard kill again.

Somehow, I'd made it through all of my exams without flunking a single one despite the distractions that were plaguing me, and I was on my way down to the end of year assembly while running mildly late.

I could have shot down there but in all honesty, sitting through one of Greyshine's godawful speeches just didn't appeal to me on any level. So I was content to meander down at the slow ass pace I was currently managing.

The grounds were quiet as I crossed them but just as I made it to the Acrux Courtyard, Leon arrived too.

We both fell still, my gut twisting as we looked at each other for a long, drawn out moment.

"Hey," he said eventually, his gaze sliding over me slowly. That was the only word he'd spoken to me since he'd caught me kissing Dante last month and my bottom lip trembled as I fought the urge to shoot towards him and throw myself into his arms.

"Hey," I breathed, not moving one inch.

Leon pushed his tongue into his cheek like he was considering saying something else before turning and continuing his walk down to the assembly.

I hesitated, not wanting to walk two paces behind him the whole rest of the way while not feeling like I'd been invited to join him either.

Eventually, I took the chicken shit way out and shot past him, racing to the assembly with unshed tears blurring my vision.

I almost didn't see the figure stepping out of the assembly room door and I stumbled to a halt as I half crashed into Miss Nightshade.

"Good heavens, Elise!" she exclaimed, reaching out to grasp my arm to steady me.

Her Siren gifts slammed into my mental shields at the touch of her hand and I scrambled to keep them up as fear, hatred and suspicion filled me in reaction to her proximity.

Nightshade's eyes narrowed like she'd felt all of it and I stammered an apology before shooting away again in a panic.

I sped straight to the back row of the assembly, dropping into an empty seat beside Gabriel and almost falling into his lap in my haste.

"What's wrong?" he gasped, tossing a silencing bubble around us before I'd even managed to regain my balance.

"Nothing," I breathed as he took my hand and I drew more than a little strength from the feeling of his fingers surrounding mine. "At least, I hope it's nothing. I just bumped into Nightshade unexpectedly and I was a bit flustered from seeing Leon and... I dunno, she might have caught a good whiff of my emotions. You know, suspicion, mistrust, that kind of shit. But that doesn't matter, right?"

Gabriel stayed silent just long enough for my heart to start racing again.

"Hopefully it was nothing. I mean, she can't have figured out our plans for tonight from that, so..."

"So we just carry on as planned?" I confirmed.

Ryder had agreed to help me try and catch King tonight too so I was hoping between the four of us and the Shroud Orion had sent us which could shield us from the effects of dark magic, we were in with a good chance of stopping this creep once and for all. We had been hoping that Orion might find a way to undo the magic King had used to steal power from other Fae, but unfortunately we'd had no such luck. He was still looking into it for us but we couldn't wait. We had to strike now and hope that our combined power could match King's.

I still didn't know if they were the one directly responsible for Gareth's death or not, but I had enough evidence to say that they'd had some kind of connection to him. Besides, now that they'd aligned themselves with Felix, they were a threat to Dante and Ryder too. And that was good enough for me. I'd beat the truth out of them once we had them at our mercy, and if I found out that it *had* been them who had stolen my brother from me, then death would be the least they had to fear tonight.

Gabriel's grip on my fingers tightened. "Are you okay?" he breathed.

"Yeah," I replied, shrugging off his concern. "I just need to get on with this. Tonight we're going to catch ourselves a murderer and hopefully find out what happened to my brother at the same time. So long as it goes as we hope it will, I'll be more than fine."

Gabriel nodded in agreement. "I keep trying to *see* what will happen," he murmured as he painted circles on the back of my hand with his thumb. "But it's like The Sight only becomes harder to use the more I try to focus it."

"It's okay," I said soothingly, turning to lean against his shoulder.

"It's not," he breathed as his fingers drifted up my arm and he held me close. "If I could only control the visions then I could *see* how this would go. We could be sure we were making all the right decisions and-"

I cut him off with a kiss, leaning into him as he groaned softly beneath his breath. We'd spent a lot of time together recently planning out how things were going to go tonight, but he hadn't brought up our conversation about what he expected from me since the day that we'd last discussed our positions on things. I knew what that silence meant though. He was still waiting on our Divine Moment to save him from having to decide if he really could deal with sharing me long term. And I was starting to fear that happening with at least as much conviction as he was anticipating it. I didn't want the stars to tear my other Kings away from me. I didn't want my heart to be forced to make a choice I didn't want to make.

"I just couldn't bear to lose you," Gabriel breathed as I pulled back.

"I'm right here," I reminded him. "And I don't plan on going anywhere."

The concern in his eyes didn't fade and all I could offer him was a tight smile. We both knew I'd be going in tonight all guns blazing. I might have had more to live for now than I did in the weeks directly following Gareth's death, but I'd still pay for his justice with my life if that was what it took. Gabriel knew me well enough to know that and he also knew me well enough to know not to ask me not to do it. I needed to do this. My life would never truly be able to move on until I knew that Gareth's killer had paid for what they'd done.

I was his kid sister, his avenging monster and his little angel all in one. He may have put me up on a pedestal to try and keep me out of harm's way, but it was far past the point at which he could protect me. I might have been his angel once. But even angels fall…

I spent the rest of the day in a state of anxiety and when the sun finally made its slow ass way below the horizon, I practically jumped for joy. We might have been trying to go up against something totally unpredictable, but I was so relieved to be acting on all of this information at last that I could have cried.

Dante and Ryder obviously couldn't be seen together so we'd agreed to meet at a spot directly between the Oscura Haunt and the Lunar Pit out in

The Iron Wood at sun down. The others had left before me but with my speed, there had been no point in me setting off until now.

I glanced in the mirror as I pulled a black baseball cap down over my hair to cover the recognisable lilac colour and gritted my teeth as I tried to focus my energy on what I needed to do tonight.

I was wearing a black sweater and leggings to help me blend in out there and I'd been practicing my concealment spells too. If all went to plan, King wouldn't see us coming before it was far too late to stop us.

I shot out of my room and raced down the stairs and across campus at full speed as I ran out to the meeting point in the woods. It was dark beneath the trees and my heightened senses picked up the sound of every single creature hiding around me.

So far, I couldn't detect any signs of the Black Card or their mysterious master in the trees, but I was sure it wouldn't be long before they appeared.

I came to a halt exactly where we'd planned to meet and my heart leapt as I found not three, but four Kings waiting for me in the clearing.

"Leon?" I gasped as I spotted him.

I hadn't known that he was coming. After everything that had been going on between us, or not going on, I'd just assumed he wouldn't be here. His golden hair was loose around his shoulders and his black shirt hugged his muscular frame and for a moment he looked like *my Leo*. But the tension in his posture told me he was still tangled up in the hurt I'd caused him with my lies, and my heart ached with the knowledge that I'd dampened his flame.

"Dante told me what you're planning. I'm here for Gareth," he muttered, not meeting my gaze.

I shot forwards as tears sprang to my eyes and threw my arms around him before I could overthink it.

"Thank you," I breathed as I crushed him against me and his arms slowly closed around me as well.

"And I'm here for *you*, too," he admitted in a low voice, just for me.

A sob caught in the back of my throat as I squeezed him so hard I was probably in danger of breaking ribs.

"As much as we're all jumping for joy at the return of The Lion King, I think we should be focusing on the plan," Ryder muttered behind us and I stifled a laugh as I forced myself to release my hold on Leon.

His hands slid from my body a little reluctantly, but he didn't say anything else as he waited to hear what I had to say.

"Okay…" I had to force my thoughts to refocus, but I'd gone over the plan so many damn times this month that it was on the tip of my tongue with barely a thought. "So, the plan is simple. We head to the cabin and set ourselves up hiding around it, cloaked in shadows and spelled to keep our presence undetected. When the ceremony starts, we close in. If the victims they've brought with them seem likely to actually kill themselves then I'll snatch them and run them to safety away from here. But aside from that, we all go hard at King and Gabriel uses the Shroud Orion gave us to shield us from their magic and we try to trap them."

"What if you come with me, carina?" Dante suggested slowly. "I could transform, we could hide in the clouds until King is here and-"

"That's a great idea," Gabriel chipped in and Leon nodded. Ryder didn't object which was as good as a goddamn flashing sign lighting up above his head to say that he was in on this bullshit too.

I bristled as I looked between them. I knew they just wanted to keep me safe, but the only way for them to do that was for them to help me in this. If not, I'd still go after King alone.

"Is there a point during the time in which you have known me that you got the impression that I was some kind of damsel in distress? Or that I required saving?" I demanded in a hard voice.

The four of them looked at me with concern in their eyes, but none of them could claim I'd ever been either of those things.

"Good." I growled. "Because I'm not some soldier in this war. I'm your goddamn commander, your ruler, your fucking *queen*. So we will stick to the plan the way that I laid it out and you'll all listen to me when I give you commands, or you might as well fuck off back to your dorms right now. This isn't a negotiation. We're here because of *my* brother. And we're doing this *my* way."

There was a beat of silence then Ryder's lips twitched with amusement. "Yes, your majesty," he said teasingly, bowing his head to me. And I had to admit that though it was an act, I didn't totally hate the idea of dominating him.

"Good," I growled. "Then let's go catch ourselves a King."

There were no more objections as I led the way into the woods and as we approached the cabin, each of them leaned in to press a kiss to my lips before they headed off to take up their own positions. Leon just grasped my fingers in his for a moment before stalking away from me, but that was even better than a kiss. It was a start. A tiny, near invisible crack in his resolve to stay away from me and I intended to burrow my way right back inside his heart using it.

The woods were cold as we waited and I remained perched in a tree with a view of the cabin for more than long enough for my ass to be numb by the time the sound of footsteps reached me.

I held my breath despite the silencing, concealment and deflection spells I'd placed on myself and I watched as the door to the cabin opened and a crowd of people dressed in black robes flooded out of it.

I frowned in confusion, wondering how the fuck they'd gotten in there only to realise there must be some sort of tunnel beneath it. But me and Gabriel had searched that place from top to bottom and I'd never found any kind of sign that there had been a secret way out through it.

I wished I could see my Kings, but obviously they were as well hidden as me so it was impossible. But something about hiding in this tree while the Black Card all filed out of the ground like a bunch of fucking creepy ass cult weirdo ants had me aching for the reassuring presence of them near me.

Around fifty members of the cult arranged themselves outside the cabin and as one, they broke the silence and started chanting.

My heart pounded in time with the beat of their words and my grip on the tree trunk tightened as I waited for King to show themselves.

The mumbling words of someone who wasn't joining in with the chanting reached my ears and I craned my neck to look as two more hooded figures strode through the trees, dragging a boy between them.

"I'm a little nervous of the dark," he muttered. "And I can see shadows in the shadows! They have long claws and hooked beaks."

My heart stilled as they passed beneath my hiding place and I caught sight of the latest sacrifice Nightshade had selected for King. A shock of white hair and pasty skin caught my eye along with the pinched features of the unfortunate boy I'd chosen to befriend.

Eugene Dipper.

I almost bit straight through my tongue as I forced myself to remain where I was. Eugene's pupils were too wide and he kept muttering about the shadows as the Killblaze they'd given him kept him firmly within its influence.

As soon as he was deposited on the wooden veranda before the cabin, the doors opened again and King stepped out. It looked like they only had one victim lined up for tonight and they sure as shit wouldn't be claiming him.

My breath caught in my throat as I looked at King, their figure shifting in height and weight so much that I couldn't get a single solid read on their appearance. It was so fucking infuriating it was untrue. But it wouldn't help them now. Little did they know that they were surrounded by predators and we were poised for the kill.

Eugene started begging on the porch like even in his fucked up state he knew to be afraid.

This was it, the moment we'd been waiting for.

My muscles tensed as King approached Eugene and each passing second had my heart climbing further and further up into my throat.

They asked if he wanted to die and my heart crumbled a little as Eugene squeaked out a terrified *no*.

But King wasn't satisfied with that for a response and I gasped in horror as they pulled a new tube of Killblaze from their pocket, shaking it fiercely to turn the crystals into smoke.

If Eugene took a second hit, he was done for. Suicide or not, he wouldn't survive that. The kid was a hundred pounds when wet at most. No way he could handle a dose that size.

What the hell is taking so long, Dante??

Lightning tore through the sky and I leapt from the tree at the signal. Air magic cushioned my fall and I bared my teeth as I raced towards Eugene.

I shot between members of the Black Card and leapt up onto the porch, wrapping my arms around Eugene's waist just as King uncorked the Killblaze and shoved the tube right at him.

I caught the full hit of it in my face, my eyes widening as I inhaled it before I could stop myself.

Fuck, fuck, fuck, FUCK!!

I heaved Eugene into my arms and started running as fast as I could with my Vampire speed, but the world was already twisting around me.

A cry of rage went up behind me, but it was instantly met with a blast of lightning.

My heart leapt with panic for my Kings, but I couldn't focus on them yet. I had to get Eugene away from here. I had to make sure he was safe.

But as the colours of the world began to warp and twist around me and my heart started beating way too fast, I began to wonder if I would even manage to do that much.

RYDER

CHAPTER FORTY TWO

The second Elise was safely out of sight I dropped from the tree, death calling the name of the fucker below me. I rammed into him full force, taking him to the ground and stabbing stabbing, stabbing with the blade I'd fashioned from wood with my magic.

Cries of pain sounded around the clearing and the Black Card split apart as death descended on them from everywhere. Inferno, Mufasa and Big Bird carved through the edge of the group before King even realised what was happening. The motherfucker called out for their followers to attack and a swarm of black cloaks raced toward me. This wasn't a group of whipped little school kid cult members, this must have been the fully fledged. The trained version of the cult. And they were as dead set on killing us as they were on serving their psychotic master. But unluckily for them, no one was as psychotic as me.

Gabriel had the Shroud, so we had to get him close to King to halt their power and gut the bastard like a fish.

"Fuck – Ryder!" Big Bird called my name and I swivelled around, slamming my fist into the face of the nearest asshole.

Gabriel was being overwhelmed, his magic exploding from him in waves, but it wasn't enough to stop the cult from storming him with magic of their own, trying to force him to his knees. And if that Shroud touched the earth, we were fucked. The magic would flee into the ground and the gift from Orion would be useless.

"Here!" I called and the Shroud came sailing toward me through the air. I leapt upwards, kicking a cloaked fucker in the chest as I used him to propel myself higher.

I snatched it and slammed to the ground, keeping the cylindrical object raised above my head. Fire seared my back and I swivelled around with a roar of pure rage, casting vines with my free hand and skewering the culprit like barbecued chicken. Pain licked up my spine and I smiled as I fed on my own wounds.

I turned my attention to King, happy to be the one to take the fucker down. King raised their hands and magic poured over the crowd of the Black Card, multiplying their numbers twofold.

What the fuck??

I swung my fist at the nearest bastard and my hand sailed through vapour as they evaporated. The illusion spell was more powerful than I'd ever seen and it was confusing as fuck. I swung left and right, my fists slamming into faces, some real, some not.

A vine snared my arm and I was jerked back a step as I clutched harder onto the Shroud in that hand. I used my own earth magic to sever the vine and dropped to one knee, placing my free hand on the ground. Sharp stakes of wood tore up around me in a circle and every unlucky sucker close to me met their end while the mirages twisted away on the wind.

The cult closed ranks on me and I took in faces old and young. No one I recognised from Aurora; these fuckers were from the city and their eyes were set on the Shroud in my grip like they knew what it was. But with the wall of stakes raised around me, they couldn't get close.

A shout of pain sounded and my gut tugged as I stood, raising myself up on a platform of earth as I hunted for the source of the noise. Mufasa was burning away blades of ice as they were shot toward him again and again. His arm and neck were bleeding badly and despite the fire blazing out from his palms, there were too many Black Card coming at him to hold them all off. It was only a matter of time until one landed a fatal hit.

Vines whipped around me as the Black Card tried to shoot me with fireballs and daggers of wood, but there was none too strong amongst the assholes whose attention fell on me. I deflected everything they threw, but their sheer numbers were the problem.

King's eyes locked on Leon and as their face changed from old to childishly young, the freak raised their palms and impossibly powerful water magic blasted toward Leon.

"Catch, Mufasa!" I bellowed and his eyes locked with mine half a second before I tossed the Shroud.

He jumped into the air with a yell of exertion, catching it like a Pitball and tumbling to the ground as he hugged it to his chest. King's water magic was deflected as if Leon stood in a bubble of solid steel, arcing over him like a wave breaking on a rock. The Lion smirked, raising a palm full of flames, trying to keep the cult off as their assault started again. The Shroud might have stopped King's stolen magic, but it did nothing against the natural Elemental power of their followers.

Dante was brewing a storm beyond him, cut off from the Lion by rows and rows of the Black Card. He directed lightning strikes at them again and again, but it looked like half of the fuckers were made of nothing. He soon cut through their ranks and raced to Leon's side, snatching his hand in his grip. The second they shared power, the game changed. Leon's fire flared and Dante fed it with pure oxygen that twisted around and around until a huge firenado reached up into the trees above. It spun through the crowd and the cult fled, their shouts of pain bringing a grin to my face as I fed on every drop in the air.

Gabriel caught my eye, swooping overhead with his wings outstretched as he made a beeline for King.

"Here!" he called to Leon and the Lion tossed the Shroud into the air.

Panic tore through me as a vine whipped after it from King, the asshole knocking it off course and sending it careening toward the dirt. I leapt over the barrier I'd built around me with a yell of determination, blasting up huge pillars in the ground to run across. I raced over the crowd, jumping from one to the other as fast I could. I locked the Shroud in my sights and dove through the air with my fingers outstretched. It hit my hand and I wrapped my fingers around it with a grunt of satisfaction, falling on top of several members of the Black Card and crushing them beneath me.

I tucked the Shroud into the back of my jeans and went to town smashing in faces and feeding my magic with their pain. Blood spewed and tears were shed as they tried to fight me off, but I was a machine built to destroy and they stood no chance against me.

"Fuck!" Gabriel's voice reached me and I looked up, finding him being forced back into a tree by a net of vines cast by King. He was nearly thirty feet above the cult and the vines wrapped around his arms, chest and neck, pinning him there and choking the life out of him. He fought wildly, but I could see how close he was to death already. It looked like he only had a little longer before he was royally fucked.

I clenched my jaw, rising to my feet and bouldering my way through the crowd, splitting the earth apart to get the freaks out of my way. I knocked into Dante and nearly crashed to my knees, but he caught me by the arm and yanked me upright.

Sweat was beading on his brow as he concentrated on feeding the fiery tornado which was still blasting through the fuckers.

"Throw me up there." I pointed to Gabriel and Dante's eyes widened as he spotted him. "Now Inferno!" I yelled and he dropped his concentration on the tornado, forcing his air magic beneath my feet and propelling me toward the tree at high speed.

A powerful blast of air pressed down on me and I snarled as King tried to force me off course.

I created two wooden blades in my hands as I readied for the collision with the tree trunk ahead of me instead then rammed them into the bark. I got a good grip then willed the tree to listen to my command, its bark shifting to make hand and footholds for me to climb with.

I powered my way up to the top of the tree as Gabriel gasped for air, dragging myself up onto the branch below him. I took the Shroud from my pocket and raised my arm and the dark shield ripped through the power of King's vines around Gabriel, making them fall away to dust. I laughed manically, looking to King standing on the porch of the cabin, their many faces twisted in rage.

Gabriel crashed down onto my shoulders and the wind was knocked out of me as I hit the branch. He kept falling and I snatched his hand in my grip a second before he was bird meat and hauled his unconscious ass up beside me with a yell of effort.

Dante and Leon distracted King from us, sending the firenado their way and leaving a flaming trail of death in its wake.

I pressed my hand to Gabriel's bare chest and sent healing magic beneath his skin. I gritted my teeth as I focused, feeling the depths of his wounds and drinking away his pain as I gave him more and more of my power.

"Wake up you stupid peacock," I demanded. "If you die here, Elise will have my balls for it."

He grunted and his eyes flickered open. "Elise…got to…"

"What?" I growled, pushing him upright.

"Got to get to King." He blinked awake and he held out his hand for the Shroud.

I glanced over my shoulder to check we weren't being watched by King, then fashioned a fake Shroud from wood which looked pretty similar from afar.

"Here." I handed him the real one.

"I'll distract the fucker and you fly down and go bald eagle on his ass."

His lips pulled up at the corner. "Not a bad plan, asshole." He clapped me on the shoulder then took off into the tree canopy.

I stood up on the branch and pushed two fingers into my mouth. I tasted blood and death and it was my favourite flavour in the whole wide world. Second to Elise's pussy.

"Hey fuckers!" I waved the decoy as eyes turned to me and King snarled in fury.

I flipped them the finger for good measure as I raised my free hand then cast a vine into existence, hanging from a branch out ahead of me. I placed the stick between my teeth then ran forward, leaping off of the branch and grabbing the vine, tarzaning my way over the heads of the cult.

I slid down it at high speed aiming for King as I let go and I fell toward him like a fucking death-bound soldier on his final mission. I spat the stick from my mouth and King's eyes widened as it hit the ground.

I landed before the shitbag on the porch steps and yelled, "Fuck!" like I'd just ruined our chances.

King smirked, raising their hands and with all of their attention on me they didn't see Gabriel dropping onto the porch roof and ninjaing his way under it, landing silently behind them.

Nothing appeared in King's hands and the freak frowned at the decoy on the ground.

"Looking for this?" Gabriel smashed the Shroud into the side of King's head and I lunged forward with a wooden blade in my grip. I was going to make this fucker bleed. I'd take every drop of their soul and devour their pain until I was full and they were an empty hollow *nothing*.

Gabriel threw an ice covered fist into King's head then kicked the bastard toward me. I stabbed with my knife, but King twisted fast and fire tore out around him, making me fall back while Gabriel was shielded by the Shroud.

King eyed the object in Gabriel's hand with realisation then a hurricane of air built in the asshole's palms. I gasped as the Shroud did nothing to stop it, and I knew this was King's true Elemental magic. King blasted Gabriel with the storm and sent him flying away through the trees. I lunged forward with my palms raised, but my head felt like it was about to explode as air magic burst away from King once more. I was thrown at high speed across the clearing, my head spinning and rage clinging to every fibre of my being.

At the last second, I remembered to cushion my fall with a bed of moss.

I scrambled to my feet but I was a hundred fucking feet away from the cult now and as I raced back toward them, they fled into the cabin. I couldn't spot King and my heart pounded frantically as I powered forward as fast as I could, desperate to reach the fucker and destroy them for Elise.

The cabin door swung shut and fire blazed to life in a circle around it. I clenched my jaw and dove through it, my skin blistering as I landed on the other side and sprinted up the steps. I kicked the door down and raced inside only to find the cabin completely empty.

"King!" I bellowed, my throat rubbing raw. "Your death is mine!"

ELISE

CHAPTER FORTY THREE

The trees loomed around me like monstrous creatures laying in wait to gobble me up.

There was something warm and heavy in my arms. Something that flapped like a fish and stank like a rat.

"Gracious!" Eugene mumbled. "The world flipped downside up!"

I started laughing. *Who the fuck says gracious?*

The tree monsters didn't like it when I laughed. They glared at me with angry eyes and gnashed their branchy teeth.

I gasped as I ran on, my legs staggering and stumbling as I shot between the trunks of the carnivorous conifers with my heart racing in panic.

"They're going to eat us!" I cried as my laughter fell away.

"Eat her!" Eugene shrieked in panic. "Rats carry diseases! You don't want me!"

A purple badger appeared on the path ahead of us and I screamed, launching Eugene off of my shoulder and throwing him straight at it.

"Every man for himself!" he cried as he tumbled across the dead leaves and the badger disappeared in a puff of smoke. I almost agreed with him, almost turned and fled to save my own skin but something stopped me. A little voice, screaming in the back of my skull that I wasn't meant to be throwing him away, I was meant to be saving him.

"I am Sir Lancelot and you are my moley grail," I growled, pointing at Eugene.

His eyes widened as I stalked towards him and he stumbled to his feet with a scream.

"Don't eat me!" he cried as he started to run from me and he was so fast I couldn't keep up.

I chased him through the trees, hooting like an owl as I ran after the speedy little mouse.

How is he so fast?

Eugene was almost out of sight before I realised that I wasn't moving at all. I was rubbing my face against the bark of a tree and it felt. So. Fucking. *Good*.

"I'll be back for you, my love," I whispered to the silver birch before shooting away from it to catch my little rat.

Eugene shrieked like a choir boy who'd seen a ghost as he saw me coming for him but I didn't slow. I collided with him, tossing him over my shoulder again and racing back to the big building with all the books. So many books. Books on reading and writing and singing a song, books for building and burning until they were gone.

I started laughing again. That crazy, creepy psycho laugh which went all *mwahahaha*, echoing through the trees and scaring them away from me. There were monsters in these woods but I was their queen. I just needed a crown made of my victims' bones…

We shot out of the wood and raced towards the book kingdom where I was going to start my bonfire. But the books didn't want me to burn them and they turned the ground to quicksand to stop me from completing my quest.

I cried out, dropping Eugene as I tried to claw my way out of the sticky mud but as my palms met with the ground, all I found was bricks beneath me.

This isn't right. Something is wrong, so very, very wrong.

I tried to fight the fog in my brain, tried to remember why I was here and what I was doing.

My monsters need me.

I gasped as I remembered, the King in the woods, my Dragon roaring, my men fighting. Fighting for me.

"I have to go back!" I shouted, searching all around until I spotted Eugene where he was in the process of pulling his shirt off and rubbing his nipples across the wall of The Rigel Library.

"What's wrong?" he asked as I crawled towards him.

"You need to get help," I growled, clinging to reality with an iron fist. I had to remember. Remember the…the…

"Yes," Eugene hissed, reaching up and tugging my baseball cap off of my head before stuffing it down the front of his pants. *What the fuck? I don't ever want that back.* "They wanted me to kill myself."

"Who did?" I asked, tears pricking my eyes at the thought of something so sad.

"The no face," he replied with a shudder. "I'll go get help!"

"Okay." I was nodding and nodding and nodding.

Eugene disappeared with a squeak and I screamed as a rat ran out of his clothes, scuttling along with a black baseball cap hanging over its ass. I leapt to my feet and tried to kick it but it just scampered away, losing the hat as it ran from my stampy feet.

He's getting help!

I sighed as I realised the little voice was right. The rat was my friend.

I watched as it scurried away, running and running until it reached the doors to the Rigel Library where it shifted into a pasty skinned boy.

His skin was so pale that it blinded me and I cried out as I covered my eyes. "I'm moon blind!"

"Please kind sir, we need your help!" Eugene gasped and I peeled my eyes open to see who he'd found to help us. Because we definitely needed help. There was something I was supposed to be doing. Somewhere I should be...

Eugene was telling the door to the library all about him being kidnapped, but the door didn't care. It didn't even smile.

"Help us!" I yelled at the door, as Eugene told it about the figure in the woods.

"I knew you were up to something," a cold voice purred in the dark and for a moment I wasn't sure it was real.

Nightshade stepped in front of me and I screamed in terror. She was bad. All bad.

Eugene turned my way in fright, his dick flapping in the moonlight and blinding me again a moment before he transformed back into a rat and raced away.

"You foolish, insolent girl!" Nightshade growled, reaching out to grab my arm. "You stole the Card Master's sacrifice."

"Fuck you, you shrivelled old ball sack," I snarled, swinging my fist at her. But before I could land the blow, a wash of unfamiliar emotions flooded me. I didn't want to hurt her, I wanted to do whatever she asked of me. Anything. Everything. And she didn't look like a ball sack at all. She looked like...well actually she did look like a ball sack and that was fucking hilarious.

"Ball sack!" I started laughing and she growled as she tugged me along.

"I knew there was something off with you from the very first moment we met," Nightshade hissed. "What else have you done to upset the King's plans?"

I opened my mouth to tell her to go suck a hairy nut but the feeling of trust and love for her was overwhelming. She deserved the truth. All of the truth.

"I blew the Killblaze lab up," I said with a wide smile. *"Bang!"*

I started laughing again and Nightshade slapped me. My head wheeled sideways and I lunged back at her instantly, slamming my forehead into her nose.

She shrieked as it shattered and blood pissed down her face onto her fancy pants shirt which was a kinda vomit yellow colour anyway so I'd actually done her a favour.

She snatched my other arm into her grip and her gifts washed over me again as she made me feel the most hopeless kind of fear. I was blinded by panic, my heart thundered. I was trapped in an icy vault of pure terror where only her voice could find me.

"What else have you done?" she demanded, releasing me from the fear so that I could function well enough to speak, lifting her hand to heal her ball sack of a face.

"Everything! I went to your office in the city and poured coffee all over your computer. I would have fucked Ryder on your expensive ergonomic chair too if we hadn't been bound by the deal." I started laughing again and the fear slammed into me once more.

I gasped as she started to make me walk, but I couldn't focus on where we were going, only the utter panic which had me aching to run as far away from here as I could get and never ever look back.

My ass hit something solid and as she withdrew her influence on my emotions, I found myself pressed up against the creepy fucking ghost well. The one with the dead boy at the bottom. I could hear him now, wailing, crying, begging and screaming as he died.

"Ryder Draconis is in on this with you?" Nightshade questioned and at the mention of his name, I remembered something. He'd made me a gift. A gift that could save me.

"Yes," I hissed as I reached up to brush my fingers along my throat where the necklace he'd made me sat.

"Why?" Nightshade demanded. "What made you start looking into any of this?"

She pressed her influence over me and I wanted to tell her everything, I trusted her implicitly. She wanted to help.

"I think your King killed my brother," I said, choking on a sob as I gripped the chain of thorny roses which hung around my neck.

Nightshade flinched like she was afraid of something. "Who was your brother?" she demanded.

For a moment I could see him, laughing and joking and holding me in the dark. And I could hear him, shouting at me to buck the fuck up and do something about what was happening to me.

I gritted my teeth and tightened my grip on the necklace Ryder had made for me so that its thorns pierced my flesh and his antivenom washed into my bloodstream.

"My brother was Gareth Tempa," I snarled. "And I want to know what happened to him."

Nightshade's face paled, her grip on me tightening as she stared into my face. My thoughts were slowly realigning, my memories coming back as the antivenom burned the Killblaze from my blood. My monsters were out there in the woods, facing King without me. I had to get to them, I had to help.

"Well you'll be seeing him again soon, so you can ask him yourself," Nightshade hissed.

My fangs snapped out as I regained full control of my body and the bloodlust rose in me sharply. Nightshade screamed as I lunged at her, meaning to tear her motherfucking throat right out with my teeth alone.

She threw her hands up and a blast of earth magic slammed into my chest in a column of dirt.

I was thrown back, my legs flipping up over my head as I tumbled straight over the edge of the well where I plunged down, down, down into the darkness. I screamed as I fell, my voice echoing around the walls as I tried to figure out which way was up so that I could use my air magic to save me.

Before I could manage it, I slammed into the thick sludge at the bottom of the well and the air was driven from my lungs as agony swept through my body.

I stared up at the starlit sky above me as Nightshade peered down into the well.

"Get up, Elise," she called. "You're going to want to run."

GABRIEL

CHAPTER FORTY FOUR

I was lost to a dark abyss in my mind. I was vaguely aware that I'd caught myself in a net of vines when King had blasted me away. Then everything had fallen dark and I could feel Elise's fear everywhere. She was so close, her screams echoing around me as the vision failed to offer me anything but her terror.

Strong hands hauled me up into a sitting position, but I couldn't escape the trap I'd fallen into in my head.

"Wake up!" Dante snapped and a bolt of electricity sliced through to my core.

"Fuck!" I roared, jolted out of my nightmare. But I knew it wasn't a dream. It was real. Elise was in danger, but I couldn't break through the block on my powers to see her.

"*Elise*," I gasped and Leon and Ryder moved forward to flank Dante, frowning down at me.

"What is it, stronzo? What did you see?" Dante hauled me to my feet and Leon inhaled sharply, looking to the ground beneath me.

I glanced down, finding the Shroud laying on the earth, its powers gone.

But I didn't have time to worry about that as I clawed a hand into my hair and shut my eyes, desperately trying to pull on the vision that was evading me. I could see it like it stood beyond a wall of frosted glass, the figures shadowed and murky.

Please stars, let me see her. Let me know where she is. Let me save her.

Dante shoved me in the chest and my eyes flew open once more. "What's going on?" he growled.

"She's in trouble," I revealed. "But I can't *see* her. There's a block on my powers."

Ryder muscled past Dante with a threat in his gaze. "You better break that block or I'll start breaking bones."

Leon caught his arm as he moved forward too. "That's not going to help, Ryder." He gave me an intense look. "You need to focus."

I nodded, starting to pace again as I tried to let my mind drift into that space inside me that could foretell the future. But even the few scraps I'd received about Elise seemed distant now.

Panic scored through my chest as I tried to force my gift to work. I had to go to her, had to help her. If I didn't, it would destroy me.

"Well?" Ryder demanded a minute later and I twisted around to glare at him.

"It's not that simple!" I snapped, furious with myself, the stars, and whoever had put this lock on my powers. I needed them to work now more than ever before. I needed it more than I needed the sun to rise tomorrow. "I've never had control of The Sight. Someone powerful has shielded it from me. I can see snippets from time to time, but I can't make it do what I want."

"Here." Leon strode forward, clutching my arm and staring into my eyes. "Maybe you just need more power to get a glimpse of her." His shirt had been burned away in the fight and blood smeared his skin from recently healed wounds. I didn't know how much magic he had left, but I'd take anything he had to give.

I nodded, focusing on his magic pushing up against my skin as I tried to drop my barriers to let him in. I didn't know Leon that well, but I held enough animosity toward him to make this difficult as fuck. He'd kept Elise from me too many nights and watching them together had made my heart fucking ache. But for the sake of saving her, I could do anything.

I hissed as I forced my barriers down and his magic burned under my flesh like a forest fire.

He gasped at the same time as I did, our power washing together and making my mind instantly sharpen.

I locked my jaw and focused on The Sight, channelling all of our power at it as I tried to force it to work for me.

Elise's screams twisted through my head and made my heart hurt. Her fear rushed back into me once more, but I still couldn't see anything.

"More," I rasped. "I need *more*."

"*Dante*," Leon barked and the Storm Dragon moved forward, placing his hand on my other arm. It was even more difficult to let him in. We'd held contempt for each other long before Elise had walked into our lives and since he'd laid a claim on her, I'd found my hatred for him growing. But maybe it wasn't hate exactly, more envy. Resentment for every moment they spent together.

"Let me in, stronzo," he growled and Leon knocked his shoulder against his in warning.

Dante growled, looking to me and I took a deep breath.

"For Elise," I said firmly and the anger went out of his eyes. He nodded seriously and we both focused on letting down our barriers between each other.

The moment his power washed into my veins felt like a hurricane colliding with a sea shore. I groaned as the full force of his and Leon's power rolled through me, combining with mine and warping into something magnificent.

I threw all of it at the block around my mind and begged for a vision to slip through.

Let me see her. I have to see her.

Flickers of light moved on the edges of my mind. I saw a tunnel, dark walls, the sound of water dripping. Then it stuttered out and I was left gasping.

"*Elise,*" I groaned in desperation. "I can't reach her."

"Ryder," Leon demanded and the snake moved forward to join us, his eyes hesitant as he laid his hand on my shoulder.

"I can't," he grunted.

"You have to," Leon snarled, glaring at him. "Or do you want her to die? Because if we can't find her, that could happen, Ryder. Do you really want to be responsible for that?"

Ryder's expression twisted into something pained. His trust of us was so little, I didn't think he'd be able to do it, but I could see he was trying.

"We're all doing this for our girl," Leon said and though I hated hearing him claim her, I knew I couldn't deny what she felt for these three other men. I had to let them help.

"She needs us," I said to Ryder and a deep V formed between his brows as he focused.

Her screams grew louder in my ears and I winced as pain tore me apart. Ryder breathed in sharply as he felt it and suddenly his walls crashed down. The cold, dark power of his magic ran into me like venom, but as it rushed in harder it felt less like a poison and more like a drug I wanted more and more of.

Our four power sources surged together and we groaned collectively with the pleasure of it as the full force of our magic swam between us like pure starlight.

I directed it toward the block in my mind once more and I tipped my head back as I hunted for Elise beyond the veil of my mind.

"Show her to me!" I demanded of the sky. "Show me Elise!"

Something splintered in my head, like a huge fissure ripping up the centre of my mind. Our combined power poured into the crack and peeled it wider and wider. Images flooded my head. A thousand things at once, more than I could handle.

Endless tunnels, twisting and turning, a girl with silver eyes brighter than the moon, a stream of tarot cards then a pair of fiery wings that twisted up into the sky. A necklace of thorns then a girl with lilac hair covered in mud. A huge palace reached above me then a Dragon with jade green scales landed on its roof, two babies lying in a cot, then two dark haired twin girls clutching hands at the bottom of a darkened pit.

"Gabriel!" someone was shouting and I tried to wrangle my thoughts.

The intense power inside me receded and I found myself down on my knees, staring up at the three other guys who surrounded me in a circle.

My mind felt free, light, malleable. I pushed it towards Elise and it moved in that direction as easily as the wind. The block on my mind was gone, broken. Somehow, the four of us had been strong enough to destroy it. I released a breath of disbelief, unable to accept it was gone after all these years.

Elise appeared in my mind at The Weeping Well beside Nightshade a second before that witch of a councillor pushed her in. Panic gripped my heart in an iron fist and determination took hold of me.

"I know where she is." I rose to my feet and flexed my wings. "We have to hurry."

Elise

CHAPTER FORTY FIVE

I groaned as the pain of my injuries washed through me and I pressed my hand to my side. The warmth of my magic slid beneath my skin, healing away my wounds just as the sound of a wailing shriek reached me from somewhere to my left.

I scrambled up onto my knees, my hand sliding through the mud and clamping onto something long and hard which I found within it. I hefted the makeshift weapon into my hands as the shriek came again, closer this time. It was beyond the wall beside me, and I strained my gifted eyes in the dark as I tried to reassure myself that there was nothing but brickwork there. Whatever was on the other side of it couldn't get to me down here.

I tossed a globe of orange Faelight up so that I could see more clearly, even my gifts not letting my sight fully penetrate the darkness which surrounded me.

The light dissolved the shadows and I gasped in horror as I spotted the lifeless eyes of a corpse staring up at me from the mud a few feet away.

I leapt up, backing away so fast that I tripped over something and fell back down again. I screamed as I rolled over, finding yet another body beneath me as I stared into the dead eyes of the boy I'd seen murdered in the woods a few months ago. It was so cold down here that his remains were still recognisable despite the time that had passed. My heart thundered at the thought that it could have so easily been me in his place.

A deep growl came from the spot behind the bricks and I leapt up again, swinging the weapon I'd found in front of me before releasing it with a scream of horror as I realised it was a bone. A big fucking bone like the kind that came out of someone's thigh.

I looked down at my feet, the orange glow of my Faelight revealing limbs and bones all around me. I was in a fucking tomb. A tomb filled with King's victims.

Why the hell had I thought I could go up against this creep?

I looked up at the sky far above me and tried to focus so that I could lift myself out of here with air magic but as I called on my power, I found it almost entirely gone. The Killblaze had burned through it while it ran in my blood and I was left with barely enough magic to maintain my light and not nearly enough to get me out of here.

The sound of stone grinding on stone reached me and I whipped around as a door began to open in the bricks behind me.

A foul stench washed out of the dark tunnel which was revealed and I recoiled until my spine was pressed to the stone wall behind me.

An ominous snarl came from the depths of the shadows ahead of me and I was struck with the most certain knowledge that I did *not* want to go in there.

I tipped my head back, looking up at the slick walls of the well and hoping I might find a handhold to let me climb out of here.

I cupped my hands around my mouth, wondering if there was any chance Eugene was still nearby. Or even if one of the guys might have come looking for me. I'd been gone too long now. I'd promised to go straight back to them. But what if they'd gone up against King without me and gotten hurt?

"Help!" I yelled, my heart pounding as I strained my ears to listen for any sign that someone had heard me.

A dark growl came from within the tunnel ahead of me at the sound of my voice and I instantly dropped my hands. Whatever the fuck was in there didn't need my help to find me. And I had the most definite feeling that it was looking, searching, hunting…

The dark tunnel seemed to whisper my name and I drew in a shuddering breath as I surveyed the space ahead of me. I didn't want to go in there. No fucking way. But it wasn't just a tunnel to nowhere. There had to be a way out in there. A way back to the surface. And if I just stayed here then all I was doing was waiting for *it* to come to *me*.

I wasn't some quivering mouse waiting for the cat to pounce. I was the falcon who would strike before anyone even knew I was there.

I thought of my Kings out in the woods, fighting for me, needing me. I couldn't just stay down here and wait for fate to find me. I chose my own destiny. And I was going to face this threat with my chin held high and my fangs bared for blood.

I squelched across the sludge at the bottom of the well, turning my mind from the things that caught on the toes of my boots as I stepped up into the tunnel.

My Faelight followed me as I moved further into the dank passage and I shivered as the cold intensified. My clothes were drenched and clinging to me. Even my hair dripped mud to the floor.

My boots painted footsteps along the dark stone which created this passage and I wondered if I'd find something following that trail right to me before long.

The walls of the tunnel were carved from black stone which shone wetly beneath the orange glow of my Faelight. They almost seemed natural, but there was no way that could be so. Someone had created this passage. And I had the horrible feeling that that someone was King.

I banished that thought and upped my speed.

The sound of stone grinding on stone found me a moment later and I spun back just in time to see the door at the foot of the well closing again.

Well I'm in this now whether I like it or not.

I rolled my shoulders back and decided to spare a scrap of my magic on tossing a silencing bubble up around me. I probably should have banished my Faelight too, but if I did that I was pretty sure I might just piss my pants. Being alone in this dank tunnel with whatever the fuck was making those screeching, groaning noises was one thing, but doing it in the pitch black was unthinkable.

I'd sooner see my death coming and stand a chance at fighting it off.

I may have been scraping the bottom of the barrel as far as my magic was concerned, but I was no helpless girl. The stars had gifted me with the power of my Order and the darkness of the bloodlust and I knew how to use them both well enough to face down monsters in the shadows.

I took a deep breath and shot forward, wanting to get out of here as fast as I fucking could. Ideally without finding the source of those noises.

Before long, I came upon a crossroads and skidded to a halt, my heavy breaths echoing off of the stone walls as I strained my ears to listen for a sign of anything approaching me.

A frenzied shriek echoed around the tunnels and I was almost certain it came from my right so I shot left.

I kept running at full speed, finding more and more forks in my path and choosing my turns at random as I grew certain that something was chasing me.

A whimper of fear escaped me as I sped on, knowing my Faelight would only be drawing them after me.

At the next turn, I exerted my will into the light and sent it down the left hand path while I took the right and plunged into the dark.

I ran on and on, almost blind and barely making out the turns until I was upon them. I skidded to a halt as a dead end loomed before me and I stopped, pressing my back to the cold stone wall as I listened for the sound of whatever the hell was down here with me.

My breath feathered in and out, a lock of my hair fluttering before my eyes as the sound of pounding footsteps echoed to me through the darkness.

I froze as they drew nearer, not knowing if I was better to hide or run.

A low snarl sounded somewhere far too close for comfort and I shot forward, aiming for a turn half way along the pitch black tunnel. Just as I made it to the turn, a figure leapt around the corner ahead of me, screaming with desperation as it spotted me.

I took in a curtain of filthy white hair, eyes filled with an aching hunger and fangs as sharp as mine before I shot away again with a scream of fear.

I ran at full speed with the stench of their breath washing over the back of my neck and their footsteps pounding right behind mine.

Terror gripped me and fuelled my limbs as I raced on. I couldn't stop, couldn't slow. One hesitation and it would have me in its clutches. One wrong move and I'd be dead.

DANTE

CHAPTER FORTY SIX

Gabriel reached The Weeping Well before any of us because of his Order gifts, but me and Leon made it barely a minute later out of sheer determination. The serpente had taken a moment to bury the corpses of the dead Black Card members deep underground so that there was no evidence linking us to their deaths. But he was hot on our heels now, clearly used to hiding evidence fast. *Stronzo*.

My magic reserves were bordering on empty after giving what I had to Gabriel and I suspected everyone else was in the same boat. But Elise needed us and I could still shift if I had to. Plus I still had the power of electricity.

"She's down here!" Gabriel called as we ran to his side.

I leaned over the edge of the well, gazing down into the darkness below with my heart in my throat. "We're coming amore mio!" I called.

"No." Gabriel shook his head with a grave look on his face. "She's not at the bottom. I saw a tunnel. There's a way into some passages down there." His brows knitted together as he focused and his dark eyes took on the glassy quality they got when a vision stole him away. "There's something down there with her," he rasped, terror skewing his features.

"Come on then," Ryder snarled, moving to the edge of the well.

"How are we going to get down? I'm nearly tapped out," Gabriel said in concern.

"Me too," Leon agreed.

I nodded and Ryder glanced between us all with a scowl.

"I'm almost out too," he growled then he swung his fist at Leon who was gazing into the well and he stumbled back from the blow with a yell.

I grabbed Ryder's arm, yanking him back with a snarl ripping from my throat. "What the fuck, stronzo?"

"I can recharge with pain," he said, shaking me off with a hiss passing between his teeth.

"Fuck, he's right." Leon stood up straight and puffed out his chest. "Do it again."

Ryder stepped forward, throwing a fist into his gut without hesitation and drinking in his pain as Leon hunched over. "Motherfucker," he wheezed.

"We don't have time for this." Gabriel swung his legs over the edge of the well. "We have to go after her."

"Wait." Leon eyed the well. "I never told anyone this before, but Gareth went down there once. He said he saw something. A monster."

"We don't have time for fairytales, asshole." Ryder took a razor blade from his pocket, slashing open his arm without a thought and blood rushed down to his hand, dripping from his fingers. I wrinkled my nose, moving to the edge of the well and leaning forward to get a look at the darkness below.

I glanced at Leon as he inched forward. "We don't have a choice, fratello. Monster or not."

"I'm not afraid for me," he growled fiercely. "I'm afraid for her."

I nodded, drawing on the power of the gold I was wearing, but I wasn't going to recharge fast enough. I needed a whole pile to restore quickly and there wasn't time to waste. I lifted my hand, casting a Faelight down into the well for us to see by, putting what little magic I had left to good use.

Ryder stepped to the edge of the well and cast a vine into existence that hung from the wooden awning covering the top of it.

Gabriel grabbed hold of it, locking his leg around it and sliding down it without a word. I jumped up onto the wall next, but Ryder's shoulder crashed into mine in the same moment.

"For fuck's sake, Draconis," I snapped and he glared back at me with a demon in his eyes.

Ryder jumped past me, sliding down the vine before I could move and electricity tumbled off of my body.

"Watch it," Leon muttered, moving up behind me.

He pressed a hand to my shoulder and I shared a brief look with him, his eyes telling me to focus.

"The serpente is asking for it," I growled before taking hold of the vine and shimmying my way down it. Darkness closed in around me, the Faelight below not nearly bright enough to light up the walls of the well all the way down. But I'd go into the darkest abyss in the universe to get my girl back.

I continued on and on before finally landing in an inch of sludge and rubbing shoulders with the others in the small space. Leon dropped down beside me and I grimaced as I looked around.

"Now what?" Ryder growled.

Gabriel moved forward, pressing his hands to the walls as his eyes glazed over and my gaze drifted to the ground. Bones and twisted bodies stuck out of the sludge and my nose wrinkled as the smell of death clawed at my senses.

"Merda santa," I breathed and Leon followed my gaze.

"The legend's true," he gasped.

"This isn't some legend about a bullied boy, mio amico," I muttered. "This is a body pit."

"What do you mean?" He frowned.

"A place for a killer to hide the evidence," Ryder supplied and I shared a look with him that said we'd both used places like this in our lives.

"Here," Gabriel gasped and I lifted my head, spotting him pressing his hand to the glistening bricks. "I've *seen* a way through. We have to…scream."

"What?" Ryder grunted.

"It's how the door is opened," Gabriel explained, pointing out a faded symbol on the wall that kind of looked like a tongue.

Leon tipped his head back and screamed to high heaven and Ryder rammed his knuckles into his gut a few seconds later, making him cough and splutter.

"*Why?*" Leon rasped.

"Couldn't resist," Ryder replied dryly.

Leon growled and my skin crackled with electricity as I glared at Ryder. "Why don't you go wait up top, stronzo? No one wants you here."

"We work better together," Leon said despite the fact that he was still clutching his stomach.

"He's acting like a-" I started.

"Shut the fuck up," Gabriel snapped and we all fell silent. The sound of stone grinding against stone reached my ears and my breathing quickened.

I forgot our feud in a heartbeat as I gazed into the dark tunnel that stretched out ahead of us. A yawning, groaning noise sounded from the depths of the pitch black cavern and I sent my Faelight forward to light the way, a shiver running down my spine.

"Move," Ryder hissed behind me and we moved forward together.

Elise was in here somewhere. And from what Gabriel had said, it sounded like she wasn't alone.

The door shut behind us the moment we were all inside the dark passage and I quickened my pace, my heart hammering as I thought of her lost in here.

"Which way?" I asked Gabriel, moving to his side.

He drew in a long breath as he used his Sight to find her. Then he broke into a run, making my heart jolt as I raced after him.

"This way!" he demanded and for the first time ever, none of us argued.

ELISE

CHAPTER FORTY SEVEN

A vampire. A motherfucking, half starved, half crazed, deep in the bloodlust and far beyond sanity, *Vampire*. I was built to be stronger and faster than every single Order in their Fae form but my own.

Fuck!!!

I ran on and on but I was starting to think that I was going around in fucking circles.

I couldn't keep this up forever. My Order gifts wore me out and running like this for extended periods of time just wasn't possible.

Fingernails scraped down my spine and I screamed as I leapt forward. He was too close. Too fucking close. And I had no way of knowing which of us was the stronger of our kind. Maybe I could take him. But maybe I couldn't. And that desperate look in his half starved eyes had told me all I needed to know about just how lost he was to the thirst.

I tossed a globe of Faelight up above my head again, needing to see where the fuck I was going so that I could keep ahead of him.

The Vampire behind me shrieked in response to the light and I chanced a look over my shoulder as he recoiled.

How long has he been down here?

He looked emaciated, anaemic, half goddamn dead and the other half, really, really hungry.

Shit, shit, shit, shit!

I charged away from him, knowing that the light wouldn't keep him back for long as I took turn after turn down the black passages.

I took a left and suddenly my feet were pounding up a sharp incline. A sob of relief left me as I spotted a doorway up ahead and I raced towards it like the fires of hell were up my ass.

I ran on, the sound of footsteps chasing me again as I tore towards the freedom I imagined beyond that door.

But as I closed in on it, my heart fell. There was a symbol painted on the thick wood. One which I recognised from Gareth's journal. I could only pass through it without any magic in my body.

My heart pounded at the idea of burning through the last of my power, but I had no choice. I *had* to get through that door. But more than that, I had to stop the Vampire who hunted me from following me. Which meant one thing: I had to let him drink my blood.

If he stole the last of my magic then I'd be able to pass through and he wouldn't. I just had to hope that I'd be able to fight him off before he ripped my fucking throat out.

The path beneath my feet crunched with loose chips of the black stone and I trained my eyes on the ground before me as I ran, hunting and hunting until I spotted a piece large enough to use as a weapon.

I lunged forward, grabbing the sharp hunk of rock from the ground before racing on but in the second it cost me to do it, the Vampire pounced.

I screamed as his weight fell against me and I was slammed face first into the wooden door.

His teeth drove straight through my sweater and pierced my shoulder as he bit me and a curse of rage spilled from my lips.

Within two deep swallows, my power was stolen from me and I felt my silencing bubble wink out of existence half a second before we were plunged into darkness as my Faelight died too.

The door I was crushed against sprang open as my magic was lost and we fell forward into an open room which seemed like little more than a cave.

My heart sank as I realised it wasn't the way out then rose again as a new plan formed in my mind. He had my magic. If I could just fight him off then I could escape this room while he remained trapped in here.

I tried to struggle as the desperate Vampire continued to bleed me dry despite the fact that he'd already taken every drop of my magic.

His weight crushed me and his fingers bit into my sides as he pinned me down, snarling like some feral dog as he lost himself to the sensation of my blood passing over his lips.

My limbs felt weak as the power of his venom immobilised me and I growled in frustration as I struggled pathetically beneath him.

My vision blurred as he continued to drain my blood and I almost gave in to the inevitability of this moment. I'd always known the hunt for Gareth's killer could end me. I'd even quietly hoped for it once or twice.

But I wasn't that girl anymore. I wasn't so broken that I couldn't find enough hope to go on. I had things in my life worth fighting for. People who would be broken by my death.

My mind fixed on the faces of the four Kings who had given me so much while demanding so little in return. They'd brought me back from the brink even when they hadn't known what they'd been doing. And the least I owed them for that was the fight of my life.

With a snarl of determination, I twisted my arm over my shoulder and slashed the sharpened rock at the creature on my back.

He shrieked in pain as I found my mark and the hot spill of his blood fell against my skin. The moment his fangs left my flesh, the strength of my Order returned to me and I threw my elbow back into his face, knocking him off of me before leaping to my feet.

I spun around and screamed a challenge as he leapt at me again. I kicked out as hard as I could, catching him in the stomach and sending him flying back against the wall at the far side of the open space.

I shot back towards the door which sprung open at my touch and flung it shut behind me as I leapt back into the tunnel.

It clunked into place and a moment later, the sound of him colliding with the other side of it echoed through the tunnel.

I backed up quickly, my heart pounding as my limbs trembled and he continued to batter the door. It didn't matter though. He couldn't get through while my magic thrummed in his veins.

I was safe.

I continued to back away as I tried to figure out how the fuck I was supposed to get out of here. This system of tunnels had been designed like a fucking maze and I had no idea how far they went.

As I continued to retreat from the door, the sound of something crunching on the ground startled me and I spun around just in time to see Nightshade throwing a net of vines at me.

I cursed as they snared me in their hold, binding me tightly and knocking me off of my feet.

"You've caused a lot of trouble for me, Elise," Nightshade growled as the feeling of her Siren spell washed over me and I found myself closing my eyes and drifting towards sleep. "It's time I ended that."

She stalked towards me as I fought the leaden feeling in my eyes but it was no use. I was too weak after my fight with the feral Vampire and I had no magic left in me to protect myself from her spell.

My eyes fell shut as darkness captured me and I found myself apologising to the Kings I was letting down and praying I'd get to see them all again.

RYDER

CHAPTER FORTY EIGHT

We were running in circles and I was five seconds from using every last scrap of my magic and blasting holes in the walls to find Elise. But if she was in trouble, I had to save it to help her. Fuck if I was used to this kind of restraint though.

"Where the fuck is she?" I grabbed hold of Gabriel's arm, yanking him to a halt. "You're taking us nowhere."

"The visions keep changing," he growled, his brow creasing with frustration and worry. "The future isn't set in stone, I can't see which path she's going to take. Every time we move closer, she seems to move further away."

"That's it, I'm taking the lead," Dante said, shoving past us and my back hit the wall behind me.

"Wait," Leon hissed. "What's that noise?"

We all stilled and the sound of grinding stone reached my ears. I frowned, raising my hands in anticipation of something happening. The wall behind me swung backwards and I stumbled into another chamber. The secret door kept turning, slamming shut the moment the other's tried to follow and darkness swallowed me whole.

"Fuck." I cast an orange Faelight into existence and ran forward, placing my palm on the wall to try and break back through it.

"Ryder?!" Leon shouted from the other side, actually sounding like he gave a fuck about whether I was alive or dead. Which didn't make a bit of sense to me.

"I'm here!" I called. I didn't want to waste my magic, but splitting up didn't seem like the best idea, even if going it alone was more my thing.

I pressed my palm to the wall and sent out a blast of earth magic. The moment it hit the bricks, I was thrown backwards, slamming onto my back in the dark tunnel with a grunt. Pain ricocheted through me and I fed on every drop.

"Are you alright?" Leon called frantically. By the fucking stars, why was he getting frantic over me?

"I'm fine, asshole. The pain helped replenish my magic stores. This door isn't gonna open again."

"Go find her!" Gabriel suddenly shouted. "I can *see* you finding her."

"See ya, fuckwits." I turned around, letting my orange Faelight float ahead of me as I started running down the dank tunnel. My heart felt like it was clamped in a spiky vice, bleeding with every pump it gave out. And it wouldn't feel right again until I had Elise in my arms. My girl. My fucking salvation.

I ran on into the maze of passages, following my gut as I had nothing else to go on but that.

A noise reached me from somewhere up ahead, the *click click click shhhuck* making me frown.

I quickened my pace, casting a silencing bubble around myself to conceal my movements as I approached. I'd been in too many ambushes in my life not to be cautious. That noise could either be to do with Elise, or it could be a fucking monster waiting to devour me. It wasn't worth the risk of approaching loudly.

I reached the next corner and pressed my back to the wall, throwing a glance around into the passage.

A shadow moved out of sight at the far end of the tunnel and I frowned, moving forward to hurry after it. I reached the archway where it had disappeared and chanced a look through it.

A large cavern stretched out before me with huge stalagmites reaching up from the cave floor. Walking across it was Nightmare in high heels and her fucking office clothes. Elise was wrapped in vines, being dragging along behind her.

A venomous rage took hold of me as I took in Elise's still expression and for one horrible moment, I feared she was dead. Her brow pinched in sleep and the clamp around my heart eased a little.

Nightmare was dead. Pure and simple. The second she'd laid a hand on my girl, she'd sealed her fate.

I moved into the cavern, raising my palms and setting Nightmare in my sights. This vile woman who'd dug into the depths of my soul and sifted through my memories. Who was she to lay judgment on me? Who was she to say whether I was broken or whole? She was just a woman who abused her Order gifts, who used them to rip and tear rather than heal and mend. And now she'd used them against Elise. So she was F.U.C.K.E.D.

I sent a vine spearing through the air and it latched around Nightmare's throat. She choked on her gasp as she was yanked backwards, her strangled scream bringing a dark smile to my lips.

I forced her to her knees, pouring what little magic I had left into killing her. I fed on her pain as I tried to crush her windpipe and her eyes lit with horror as she looked up at me.

She reached out a hand and I tried to catch it with another vine a second too late. The cave roof shuddered and I glanced up, spotting razor sharp stalactites spearing toward me. Adrenaline tangled in my chest as I leapt aside, forcing roots from the ground to cage me within them as the rock hard minerals crashed down over my head.

"You worthless *runt!*" Nightmare snapped, her voice raspy from how close I'd come to choking the life out of her. Not nearly close enough.

My magic waned and my mental shields fell as I tried to hold onto my powers, but I couldn't. I had to shift, but before I could manage it Nightmare latched onto the weakness she found in my mind, pouring her Order gifts into my head.

The cage of roots dissolved around me and I blinked, unsteady as I rose to my feet, trying to force her out of my mind.

Nightmare twisted one hand and Elise was thrown against the wall, pinned there by the vines. Her eyes flickered open and my heart lurched as her gaze fell on me. I'd failed her. I'd had one chance and I'd fucked it.

"You found me," Elise breathed, her eyes burning with intensity.

Nightmare's influence washed over me, my own feelings of failure multiplying tenfold until it echoed through every inch of my skin.

"I'm sorry," I told Elise. "I'm so fucking sorry."

"Did you really think you could save her?" Nightshade scoffed and I suddenly felt small. As small as the boy who'd been left behind when his father died. The boy who'd been taken into Mariella's home and broken down piece by piece.

I bowed my head. How could I have thought I was capable of doing this alone? I'd never been able to save anyone I loved.

Nightmare's shrill laughter rang around me. "How pathetic you are. You *love* the girl, don't you? I can feel it everywhere in you."

A ball rose in my throat and I looked to Elise. Her eyes were wide, but she said nothing. Why would she?

Nightmare moved closer until her shadow fell over me, cast by the orange glow of her Faelight behind her. "Do you know why Mariella hurt you, Ryder? She wasn't trying to break you. You were always this way. She was trying to *fix* you."

"Ryder!" Elise's voice echoed from somewhere but it seemed so far away somehow. "She's lying!"

"You're worthless," Nightmare hissed, leaning down into my face. "Always have been. Always will be."

"Ryder!" Elise screamed again, but I couldn't look at her. I couldn't face her. I was so ashamed of coming here, for thinking I could really help anyone. All I ever did was deliver pain and feed on it like a leech.

"Do you really think anyone could love you?" Nightmare breathed. "Even a little slut like *her*?"

Rage tore through my gut at this bitch calling Elise that, but more and more weakness rushed into my body until I could feel myself dropping to my knees.

"No," I breathed, my tone hollow and empty just like my soul. No one could love an insignificant creature like me. Especially not someone like Elise.

"I love you!" Elise's pained cry reached me in the darkness of my mind. "I love you Ryder! You're mine and I'm yours."

I lifted my chin as her beautiful words rang through my skull. But Nightmare locked me in her gaze, a smile skewing her lips as she reached out to cup my jaw in a gentle caress. The moment her skin touched mine, I lost all control.

I was useless, worthless, *nothing*.

And I couldn't save anyone. Not even the girl I loved.

ELISE

CHAPTER FORTY NINE

I cried out as Nightshade forced Ryder to his knees, the sense of despair, loneliness, heartache and unworthiness filling up the cavern we stood in so thickly that I could hardly breathe. Her rusty brown scales glimmered with the magic of her Order form as they rushed up to coat her body, peaking out beneath her collar and covering her bare arms and legs as she focused on driving those feelings into the King of the Lunar Brotherhood, preying on his insecurities, abusing all the knowledge she'd gained on him during their sessions together.

Vines whipped from her palm and latched around his neck, tightening as she closed her fist with a flash of excitement in her eyes.

Rage burned through my blood like hot lava and my fangs pierced my bottom lip as I snarled my rage at her. He was fighting it but the vines which she'd conjured to choke him were tightening their hold and tearing him down.

The pain and despair the two of us were feeling only served to feed her magic as she sucked power from the air, draining Ryder of all he had. But while his heartache and mine fed her magic, the pain of it was strengthening him too.

Nightshade groaned as she pressed her hands to Ryder's face, drawing even more of his emotions to the surface of his skin.

She was drinking in his pain just as surely as he was and though his teeth were gritted in a firm line, I could see the war of emotions taking place within his dark green eyes.

"Ryder," I gasped, choking on my own terror as Nightshade fed herself on all of the terrible things that had ever been done to my poor, abused serpent. "She might be able to feel your pain but that doesn't change anything. It's your strength that makes you who you are. It's the way you survived and how you keep surviving that made me take notice of you. That's the man I see when I look at you, or when I feel the scars which mark your flesh, not a victim, a survivor, a warrior, a fucking *King.*"

Ryder's jaw tightened and a snarl parted his lips as he fought back with more strength than before. Nightshade growled in rage as his eyes darkened and the agony in them was pushed back.

"Why would you trust the words of a girl who used you?" Nightshade demanded as she threw a hand out at me and more vines sprung from her palms, driving me back against the cavern wall so forcefully that one of the enormous stalactites which hung from the cave roof came crashing down. It slammed to the floor right before me and I screamed as fragments of razor sharp rock were blasted over me, cutting into my flesh and burrowing into the vines which held me.

The sound of stone grinding on stone reached my heightened sense of hearing and I gasped as I turned towards a doorway on my right.

For a moment there was nothing to see through the darkened arch and then a deep roar sounded in the shadows, echoing off of the walls of the cave and reverberating around the wide space so that it sounded like a hundred beasts surrounded us.

An enormous golden Lion leapt into the room, charging for Nightshade with his teeth bared and his mane billowing around him.

Nightshade screamed, leaping away from Ryder and throwing her hands up so that the ground beneath Leon's paws bucked and trembled before splitting apart as a huge chasm ripped through the centre of the room.

I cried out a desperate warning as Leon twisted and leapt aside and he was forced to run as Nightshade's earthquake chased him.

Ryder was knocked back by the trembling earth and I lost sight of him as he fell behind a pillar of stone which jutted from the ground.

Nightshade bared her teeth as the cave continued to buck and quake as she fought to make the ground swallow my Lion.

I snarled in rage, fighting against the bonds which held me with all of my might and growling in triumph as one of the vines snapped. The shards of stalactite which had struck me had severed some of them and I gritted my teeth with determination as I used the extra inch of space that gave me to work at breaking the rest.

Lightning slammed into the cave wall right behind Nightshade just as Dante and Gabriel raced into the room and she screamed as she built a shield from the rocks at her feet to block the next strike.

The moment Gabriel made it into the wide cavern, he called on his Order form, fully transforming so that his black wings sprung from his back and glimmering silver scales coated his flesh like armour as he leapt into the air.

Nightshade cursed as she threw her influence into the foundations of the cave itself, wielding the stalactites so that razor sharp spines sprouted from them where they hung from the roof. They raced after Gabriel, cutting into his flesh as he tried to soar between them and forced him back time and again.

Dante fixed his eyes on me and started running straight for me as Leon raced around the far side of the cave, outpacing the huge crevice that had formed through the centre of the room as Nightshade was forced to concentrate on holding Gabriel off.

None of them were using magic and that was enough to let me know that they were all as tapped out as me. But between the power of their Order forms, Nightshade was forced to retreat.

She scrambled between the stalagmites which jutted up from the cave floor, using them to shield her from the lightning which crackled through the cavern while concentrating on keeping Gabriel at bay.

"I'm coming, amore mio!" Dante called as he sprinted over the uneven floor which rocked and bucked beneath him as I continued to fight against my bonds.

"Don't worry about me," I snarled. "Just take her out!"

Gabriel shot overhead, nothing more than a blur of motion as he dove straight for Nightshade with a battle cry.

He caught her in his grasp, his speed too much for her to predict as he wrenched her off of the ground and up into the air. She kicked and cursed, throwing her hands out in panic and a razor sharp chunk of rock snapped off of the closest stalactite, spearing towards him like an arrow.

"Gabriel!" I screamed, my heart thundering in panic as the rock slammed into him, piercing his left wing and driving straight through it into his spine.

Nightshade slammed her hands into his chest, knocking him back with palms coated in wooden spikes which sliced through the tattoos covering his skin and destroying the Libra brand which tied him to me.

Blood poured down like rain as Gabriel's bellow of pain tore through the room and he fell from the air like a puppet with its strings cut. He slammed into one of the huge shards of rock that jutted from the ground, an awful snapping sound ricocheting off of the cavern walls as his wing broke.

I screamed as my heart was ripped in two and Gabriel's blood ran freely from his body, pooling around his still form as he lay dying on the floor, his body twisted at an unnatural angle.

An agony ripped through my core so sharp and pure that I was sure my soul was tearing in two. It felt like the world was caving in and the sky was falling down on my head. Like a vital part of me had just been snuffed out, burned alive, destroyed and all that remained in its place was pain.

Nightshade barked a relieved laugh as she fell against the ground which she'd softened with her earth magic to save her. I saw red as I tore my gaze from Gabriel's broken form. And though my grief for my mate threatened to overwhelm me, one thing remained utterly clear in my mind as the bloodlust rose to take control of my limbs. *Nightshade will die.*

Leon roared a challenge as he pounded around the outer edge of the cavern, shaking his mane out and baring his teeth in a snarl.

He leapt up onto a boulder before diving over the huge chasm she'd created to keep him away and racing straight for her.

Dante was running at her too, his family motto spilling from his lips as electricity crackled through the room and crashed into the cave wall behind her as she fought to shield herself with lumps of stone.

Leon charged her down, his teeth bared for the kill as she threw her hands up at him and the ground beneath his feet suddenly fell away, forming a huge abyss.

Dante yelled out and a bolt of lightning crashed through the room, finally striking her and sending her flying beyond a shelf of rock as Leon tumbled out of sight with a roar that echoed through the dark pit which swallowed him.

A shriek of terror left my lips and with a snarl of pure, animal rage, I snapped the vines containing me.

I shot towards the hole where Leon had fallen but as I made it to the edge of the abyss, my heart stilled as I spotted him hanging suspended in a net of vines.

Ryder grunted with the effort of wielding the magic as he scrambled to the opposite edge of the hole.

"Shift back you ten ton pussy cat," he snarled as the vines creaked and groaned with the effort of holding Leon's weight.

With a growl of defiance, Leon shifted back into his Fae form, catching the vines as he began to heave himself out of the pit and Ryder reached out for his hand to yank him up.

Dante's yells stole my attention and I shot away from the abyss as I turned in search of my Storm Dragon.

Lightning flared beyond the rock shelf where Nightshade had disappeared and I raced towards it with fear in my bones.

"Merda!" Dante's cry of panic sounded as the lightning flashed one final time before stopping abruptly.

I leapt over a stone precipice and landed hard on the far side as I shot around the rocky outcrop and found Nightshade standing over Dante. Vines tightened around his neck and he fought desperately to prise them free.

I raced towards Nightshade at full speed, slamming into her and knocking her from her feet.

Nightshade fell back, skidding across the ground and back out towards the abyss where she'd attempted to throw Leon.

I chased after her but the ground beneath my feet bucked and trembled wildly, knocking me over as she fought to keep me away.

Sharp spikes of wood speared up from the rocks beneath me and I cried out as they pierced my flesh.

An echoing roar sounded and Leon suddenly appeared, diving over my head.

A snarl of utter fury left his lips and his gigantic paws collided with Nightshade's chest, knocking her back to the ground with a sickening thump.

She shrieked in panic as he lowered his jaws to rip her head clean off and threw her hands up with a flash of magic.

Two spears of wood shot from her palms and straight into Leon's chest, impaling him and drawing a heartbreaking cry of pain from his feline lips. He slammed into the wall on the far side of the abyss as blood spilled over his golden coat and a roar of agony left him before he fell terrifyingly still.

"Leon!" I cried, panic and fear clawing its way through my chest and snaring my heart in iron talons.

I shot to my feet as Nightshade scrambled upright, huge claw marks torn through her shirt and her chest coated in blood. I raced towards my Lion with a desperate cry as I tried to reach him and the sound of his laboured heartbeats rang in my ears. I focused all of my gifts onto listening to that sound. The thump, thump, thump which told me he still lived, could still be saved.

I charged to the left, trying to circle the abyss but vines twisted and tangled across my path as Nightshade directed her magic at me.

They snared my legs and tightened, knocking me to the ground as I fought to get to my Lion.

"Leon!" I roared, agony spilling through me as the sound of his heartbeats faltered and he fell deathly still. The silence which sat in the space that should of held his next heartbeat destroyed something in me and I felt it fracture with a bolt of grief which crippled me.

My lips parted in horror and I shook my head in a desperate kind of denial as I strained to hear the familiar thump of his big heart. There couldn't be a world without my Leo. I refused to believe that the sun would rise again without him to bathe in its rays. There was no good in a world that didn't hold him, no light, no laughter, no joy at all.

The vines were tightening on me as Nightshade drew in for the kill and for a moment I didn't even fight them. I didn't want to. I couldn't live on without my Lion. I'd already lost too much. So much. The pain of losing him too would destroy me.

"And I thought Nemean Lions were supposed to be difficult to kill," Nightshade mocked.

My ears rang with her words and I tore my gaze away from my beautiful Lion whose golden fur was stained with so much red. Because of *her.*

A murderous snarl tore from my lips and with a surge of my gifted strength, I ripped myself free of the vines which trapped me and sprang to my feet. Her death was mine. For Leon. I'd fucking gut her.

I ran for her, more and more vines springing into existence between us, tripping me up and catching me as she fought to keep me back.

"I'm going to rip your fucking heart out!" I snarled at her, my fangs aching for blood and vengeance as I fought against her magic with everything I had.

"When my King gets here, he'll destroy you and the last of the men you've cast under your spell," Nightshade hissed in response. "And I'll laugh as I watch him devouring your souls!"

She changed up her attack suddenly, throwing her Siren gifts at me and assaulting me with a wave of grief so pure that I couldn't breathe. I stumbled to a halt as my love for my brother threatened to consume me, images of him laying still and pale in his coffin punctuated by the sight of Gabriel falling from the air and laying broken on the ground. Then all I could see was Leon, his blood spreading beneath him as he lay lifeless on the cold cave floor because of me.

They'll all die because of YOU. Nightshade's voice echoed through my skull. A sob tore free of my chest as my gaze slid to Gabriel who lay to my left, his black wings broken and glistening with far too much blood. And to Dante who had managed to rip the vines from his throat, but was now battling a hundred more as Nightshade directed them to destroy him. Electricity crackled around him, frying some of the vines but it was barely even sparking as exhaustion clawed at him from using his Order gifts so much.

The fear of their deaths and my grief over Leon's and Gareth's paralysed me as I was trapped in a never ending well of despair.

I couldn't live without them. I couldn't go on. I had nothing if I didn't have them, my life held no meaning and certainly no joy.

I was a broken, stupid girl who'd come here to seek vengeance and caused so much more pain instead. I never should have come. Why had I thought that I might have been able to do this? All I ever did was make things worse. Gareth would still be alive if it wasn't for me. Everything he'd done came back to me.

All of the bad choices he'd made, the debt he'd taken on, all of it, every part, was because he'd felt the need to save me. To protect me. And now my Kings had sacrificed themselves for me too. They'd come here for me. Followed me into the dark and chased after monsters far beyond anything that any of us could match.

It was my fault Gabriel was dying. It was my fault Leon was dead. It was all my fault…

The grief and self loathing retreated like a wave pulling back from the shore of my mind and I suddenly found myself gasping for breath as I stood before Nightshade whose jaw was slack and her eyes wide with terror.

"I've got her, baby," Ryder snarled and I whirled around to find his green eyes burning with the power of his hypnosis as he trapped Nightshade in the terrors of her own mind. "She's in more pain than anyone could ever survive," he snarled viciously. "Now finish her."

A snarl ripped from my throat and I whipped back around to face Nightshade as a whimper of horror slid between her lips.

I shot forward with my fangs out and the bloodlust burning through my veins like the sweetest, purest drug in the world.

I snatched a fistful of her short brown hair into my grasp and wrenched her head back to bare her throat.

Ryder released her from his hypnosis half a second before I lunged and a scream of terror escaped her as she found herself in the arms of a monster.

My fangs ripped into her throat and her blood and magic poured into me in a rush as I tore her veins open. She flailed in my arms weakly, a desperate sense of realisation filling her as I bathed in her blood for a long moment before wrenching my fangs free again.

I shoved her away from me with a snarl and she shrieked to high heaven as she found herself in Ryder's arms. His gaze lit with fury as he locked his hands on either side of her head.

"You never should have touched my girl," he growled and with a sharp twist of his grip, he snapped her neck.

Silence rang out for a long second as he dropped Nightshade's broken body to the ground and I was overwhelmed by the finality of that act. It was over. She was gone.

I whirled around as reality came crashing in on me, my gaze catching on Dante for a moment as he fought to catch his breath now that Nightshade's vines had fallen still. I looked at Leon, his eyes closed with a finality so severe it cut me in two. I couldn't bear the tide of grief which was drowning me with his death. I couldn't begin to process the idea of never feeling the heat of his kiss on my lips again or bathing in the warmth of his company. I tore my eyes away from him with a sob of agony, searching the cavern for someone I *could* save.

Across the cave, I could just make out one of Gabriel's broken wings and the pain that the sight of it caused me almost shattered what little resolve I had left.

I shot towards him in a blur of motion, my heart racing as a pained groan left his lips.

I dropped down over him, choking on a sob as my fingers fluttered over his silken wing, and a hiss escaped his lips.

"It's okay," I breathed. "I'm here. I've got you."

Gabriel had promised me eternity at his side and I'd scoffed at his predictions. But now that that future had almost been stolen, all I could think was that we hadn't even had our time. We'd never even had a chance. And I wasn't going to let it go now.

"Elise," he groaned, his fingers catching mine as he looked up at me. "You need to go before King gets here."

"I'll never abandon you," I growled fiercely, pressing my hand to his chest and throwing every drop of the magic I'd stolen from Nightshade into healing him.

Gabriel growled through the pain, his hands shifting over my wrists as he drew me close and I leaned down to press my forehead to his.

My magic stuttered out and I sobbed as blood slid beneath my palms, but the flesh I was touching was whole, healed, restored.

Gabriel sighed in relief, retreating back into his Fae form as his wings disappeared and the silver armour evaporated from his skin, revealing his tattoos to me.

I sagged forward with a sob as his arms closed around me and the tears I'd been fighting back finally broke free.

"I thought I lost you," I cried, pressing my lips to the Libra tattoo on his chest as his strong arms wound around me. I clung to him like he was a life raft and I was floating away into the depths of the darkest ocean. Which I was. Because I might have saved my dark angel but my heart was still tearing in two for my Lion.

Grief drowned me, choked me, threatened to destroy me.

Leon had offered himself to me wholeheartedly, unconditionally, honestly and I'd broken his trust with lies and deceit. I'd wanted to make it up to him, I'd been aching and hurting every moment that this rift had stood between us, but I hadn't found the words to express to him just how much I regretted hurting him. And just how much he meant to me.

I was a coward who had been too afraid of rejection to face him with the truth that lived in my heart. I loved him. But I'd never told him. And now it was too late.

DANTE

CHAPTER FIFTY

I knelt beside Leon, pressing my fingers into his golden fur as grief struck a chord in my heart that would ring on forever.

"Ritorna da me, caro amico," I begged. I wanted him back, I wasn't prepared to lose him. Surely the stars wouldn't dare take such a bright light from this world?

"We need to go," Ryder said seriously and I shot him a glare.

"Not yet," I hissed. "Let us say goodbye."

He nodded and I kissed my knuckles, pressing them to Leon's forehead as I fought back the pain splitting my heart in two.

A choked sob sounded behind me and I turned, finding my girl, my beautiful amore standing beside Gabriel like the world was falling down around her.

I stood, moving toward her and she rushed to meet me, our shared grief over Leon needing to join and spill over. I wrapped my arms around her and she pressed her face to my shoulder, sobs racking through her body and making me ache. Electricity rolled off of my skin in waves, threading through the air as I nearly lost control of my power.

"I didn't tell him," Elise said through choked breaths. "He didn't know I loved him."

"He knew, carina," I said softly, stroking her hair. "He'll feel your love right through to the afterlife. A morte e ritorno."

"It's not enough," she rasped. "I can't bear to lose him. I won't survive it."

"I'll make sure you do," I growled fiercely.

"We all will," Gabriel said in a low voice and she glanced over her shoulder at him. "I'm sorry, Elise," he said seriously, bowing his head. "I know…I understand how much he meant to you now."

Elise nodded, choking out a thank you before falling back into my arms.

"I wish we had more time, but we need to say goodbye now," I said gently, fearing how long we had before King arrived, but this was too important to ignore. "We have a way of doing so in my family…I'd like to give that to him, if you're okay with that?"

She nodded and I lay my arm around her shoulders, guiding her back towards Leon where Ryder was now kneeling. He didn't say a word as we dropped down beside him, but his brow was taut and I wondered if it was possible that the Lunar King had felt something for Leon Night.

Gabriel moved to kneel at my side and I pulled my medallion free from my shirt, pressing my lips to the symbol of my family. Leon had always been a brother to me. *Mio fratello leone.*

I took the medallion from around my neck, lifting his large paw and wrapping it around it.

"It's a tradition to give a gift in death, a token of our love," I murmured and Elise nodded, releasing a shaky breath as she reached into her pocket and took a silver coin from its depths. The word *Leo* was etched into it with an image of a lion shining proudly at the centre of it.

My throat thickened as she laid it under his paw. Gabriel reached forward, laying a black feather at his side and I shared a look with him, sensing the weight of his pain.

The electricity around my body was growing more potent and I had to focus to pull it back, closing my eyes. When I opened them, I found Ryder cutting open his own palm with a razor blade then reaching forward to press his hand to Leon's shoulder, leaving a bloody handprint there.

Elise leaned in to kiss his cheek and a sad smile pulled at my lips. In Leon's death, I felt the four of us pulling tighter together, a thread of gold binding us all as one. Even Ryder.

"Goodbye Leon," I breathed. "Until we meet again beyond the veil…"

Elise fell against me once more as she cried and my own grief tore me apart, cutting away a fundamental part of me as I tried to let my friend go, but it felt *impossibile.*

I leaned forward, resting my hand on his side as tears burned the backs of my eyes. Electricity poured from me and I let it rush into Leon's body instead of hurting everyone around me, hoping he could feel me calling to him in the afterlife.

"*Fuck*," Ryder growled and I lifted my head in alarm at his tone.

Elise gasped and lurched forward, pushing me aside and resting her ear to his chest. "His heart's beating!"

"You jumpstarted it, Inferno," Ryder said in realisation, his dark eyes brightening. "And it hurt like a bitch."

Leon stirred and I shook my head in disbelief as his golden eyes opened, falling on me. He released a growl that sounded a lot like *ow* and Ryder set to work healing him while I dove forward and locked my arms around his huge neck.

"Meraviglioso bastardo!" I laughed, half choking him as he ran his rough tongue up the side of my face. "Don't ever leave me again."

LEON

CHAPTER FIFTY ONE

I gazed at Dante then Elise then Gabriel and Ryder, relieved to find they were all okay and confused as crap to what had just happened. The fuss they were making over me meant I'd definitely almost badassed my way outta this life, and shit if I wasn't over the moon about staying here. Solidly alive.

Dante headed away to fetch my clothes and I shifted back into my Fae form. The second I did, Elise fell on top of me, pressing a kiss to my mouth as tears ran down her cheeks. All of the rage I'd felt toward her faded away like a fog over glass. Because how could I stay mad with my little monster when she looked so terrified about losing me? She must have wanted me all along. And maybe I'd just been too stubborn and too stupid not to realise that until now.

"Did we kill the crusty old Siren bitch?" I asked and she nodded against my shoulder.

"Don't ever leave me again, Leon," she demanded, drawing back and emotion burned from her eyes. I wanted to say it was love, but maybe I wasn't *quite* that lucky.

"Leo," I corrected in a low tone, running my thumb over her cheek to wipe away her tears. "And can I not even leave you when I need a piss?" I joked and her face split into a grin.

"Not even when you need a shit," she tossed back and I roared a laugh.

"That's gonna be awkward, but if you're sure, little monster." I smirked.

"Hate to break up the reunion." Ryder kicked me in the side which was probably affection in his language. Or maybe I was just hopeful it was. "But if we don't get our asses out of here before King shows up, we're fucked."

Dante tossed me my pants and sneakers and I dragged them on, finding a pile of items lying beside me as I moved to get up. I scooped them into my hand, recognising the Oscura tradition of tokens for the dead. At least they'd sent me off nice, but had they been planning on leaving me down here or carrying a ten ton Lion back up to the surface? Also, where the fuck was my Ryder token?

I pocketed the lot with a smirk then glanced down at my shoulder which was marked with a red handprint. *Oh there it is.*

I looked to Ryder with a grin and he scowled like I'd kicked him in the dick. *I know you love me, Rydikins. Your secret is out.*

"I want that medallion back, fratello." Dante grabbed my hand, tugging me to my feet and my smile widened.

"It was a gift."

"Because you died," he said in frustration, reaching toward my pocket.

I batted his hand away then dragged him in for a hug and he went slack in my arms. "Merda santa, I'm glad you're back."

"Me too," I sighed. "Being dead would be so boring."

"Move," Ryder snarled, shoving his way between us and forcing us apart.

He snatched Elise's hand, tugging her toward the passageway we'd come from. I shared a nod with Gabriel and though he said nothing, I could see the relief in his eyes. Did Gabe like me? Definitely did. Which meant I'd just won the Elise's Harem Boys Bingo.

I hurried after the others and Elise kept glancing back at me like she thought I was going to vanish.

"I'm not going anywhere," I promised and she broke a smile.

We quickened our pace as we made it out of the cavern and darkness surrounded us.

"Fuck going back through those tunnels," Ryder said, slowing to a halt. "I fed on enough pain in the last hour to fill me up." He turned his head to the cave roof and started wielding the earth above us, creating an enormous staircase out of the soil as he tore through the mud with absolute skill.

My mind went hazy and I blinked, suddenly finding myself half way up the stairs with Dante still at my side. The others were ahead of me and I rubbed my eyes, wondering how I'd just lost track of time like that.

Another blink and I found myself above ground in The Iron Wood, staring up at the sky between the branches, my jaw going slack. There was something pulsing through the air, wrapping around the essence of my being and begging me to answer its call.

"What's going on…" I murmured and Dante frowned, clutching my arm as he looked at me.

"Are you okay, fratello?"

I pulled away from him suddenly, a desperate need burning through me as I strode along.

I turned away from the others and walked between the trees as the leaves were blown off of the path before me and some strange magic guided me on. My heart was beating to a heady rhythm which seemed to pulse from the very fabric of the world around me.

My skin was tingling and my heart pounding as I followed the strange path through the trees and the others scurried after me. They were asking questions, calling out in confusion but I couldn't give their words any attention. They didn't matter. This wasn't about them. There was something I had to do and it was more important than all the stars in the sky. I didn't know where my feet were leading me but there wasn't a force of nature which would keep me from my destination.

Something was whispering sweet promises in my ears and the taste on the air held the sweetest scent of destiny.

There was a string pulling at my heart, tugging me forward and a gust of warm air billowed around me like a mini tornado, though I couldn't feel it. It was like I'd wandered into the eye of the storm and my feet stopped moving as I suddenly found myself standing before Elise between two enormous trees. A frown creased her brow and her lips parted as if she was as confused as I was and I was filled with the certainty that the same magic had led her here too.

"What are you doing?" Gabriel demanded. "We need to go." He strode toward Elise but a powerful energy burst out around us and he, Dante and Ryder were thrown away to the ground.

I gasped, my head drawn to the sky as the trees parted above us, creating a perfect circle for us to gaze upon the stars. Two constellations burned next to each other in the sky, just like I'd seen in Astrology. But this was real. Actually happening.

Leo and Libra glittered down at us, united in the heavens despite the fact that they usually sat far away from one another. The night sky was rearranging itself just for us.

"Elise," I breathed, the word locking in my throat as I accepted what was happening.

This was our Divine Moment. The stars had decided to bring us together as Elysian Mates tonight of all nights. My little monster and me bound together for all eternity. And nothing in the world, not King, not anything that had happened, or the three guys around us could make a single doubt flit into my mind.

I was hers the day she walked into this academy. And she was mine the first time she called me Leo. I wanted her more with every passing moment and this was my chance to have her in every single one that would follow.

But with that decision came a ball of terror rolling up my throat. If she chose me, it meant rejecting the three other men her heart beat for. If we became Elysian Mates, her heart would want no one but me. But if she didn't, we'd be Star Crossed forever, doomed to an eternity of pining for each other while never being able to fulfil our desires as the stars forced us apart.

So what would my little monster rather? A life with me alone, or a life with the three who could satisfy the parts of her I couldn't?

I'd never tried to smother that need for them which lived in her like an undying flame. I'd encouraged it, stoked it until it roared. Perhaps that had been a test all along to show how I could do anything for her, but wasn't it cruel to make her feel like she could have us all only to be told she must choose? Maybe the stars had always intended for us to be together though. Because I embraced that side of her when the others couldn't.

And if that was true, then I'd have to be a better man to fulfil everything she needed. I'd have to be *more*. And by the stars, if she chose me, I'd spend the rest of my days trying to be enough.

ELISE

CHAPTER FIFTY TWO

I stood looking at Leon with my lips parted and my heart hammering to the beat of his name. I'd just lost him. The tears I'd cried over his death were sitting dry on my cheeks. I'd gone from contemplating a lifetime without him in it to being offered one with him beside me forever more.

"You just told me you never want to leave my side," he teased, taking a hesitant step closer to me.

"I didn't mean…" I looked all around us at the strange dome of space we appeared to be locked within. The world beyond this little bubble of peace seemed blurry, obscured, like here and there were somehow so far apart that even the stars didn't care about the laws of physics anymore.

Three hazy figures stood outside this moment but my mind couldn't stay focused on them long enough to worry about them. This wasn't about them. It was about me and Leon.

My gaze strayed to the dark sky above us where our constellations sat peering down at us. Watching. Waiting.

"I know it's not what you would have chosen," Leon said in a low voice, slowly raising his hand in offering to me as I looked back down from the heavens and met his golden eyes. "But the stars think we're perfect for each other, Elise. And I think I might just agree with them."

My lips twitched as he used my name. I loved being his little monster but the way he'd just said that sounded so pure, so real, like my name meant so much more to him than just something to call me by.

"I didn't hit my head down in that tunnel did I?" I asked teasingly as my brain tried to catch up with what was happening.

"Probably," Leon replied, his mouth hooking up at the corner. "But I'm pretty sure that this is real all the same."

"I just thought that if this happened it would be with…" I trailed off, not sure where I'd even been going with that thought because there wasn't a thing about this that seemed wrong. It was just how it should be, me and my Lion.

The smile slipped from Leon's face and he lowered his hand like he thought that was some kind of rejection. I shot forward and snatched his fingers into my grasp before he could let that thought take up any space in his mind.

"It's okay," he said, wetting his lips. "I mean, he kept going on about it and I'm just the fun one after all, so-"

"You're not *just* anything, Leo," I growled, reaching up to cup his jaw in my hand. "You're the one person who could make me smile even when I thought that I was broken beyond repair. You're the one who saw exactly who I was and what I needed and never questioned it or judged me for it. You're the one who was designed to be a selfish creature, but has gone out of his way to care for me and provide for me time and again in ways that I didn't even know I needed. When you look at me, you don't see a broken girl just trying to tread water before she drowns. And the way you look at me makes me want to *be* the girl you see."

"You're all I think I could ever want for myself, little monster," he murmured. "I've stolen more treasures than I can count in my lifetime, but you're the only thing I've ever tried to *earn*. I just hope that I can be enough for you…"

"You're more than enough for me," I growled fiercely. "You're *my* Lion. And there isn't a universe in which I'd ever say no to you."

I pushed up on my tiptoes and Leon dragged me against him as his mouth claimed mine, our kiss marking our decision to be together, to accept the bond the stars were offering us and allowing our souls to be joined irrevocably.

My lips tingled and heat pooled through my body as I pushed my fingers into Leon's hair and he groaned with desire, kissing me like he never wanted to stop.

The world seemed to spin around us, a million stars racing by on an endless journey filled with so many possibilities that it would have been impossible to count them even if I spent a lifetime doing so. Because that's what they were gifting us. A lifetime. Eternity with our souls bound to one another and our hearts in each other's grasp.

My pulse was pounding so fast that it was the only sound I could hear alongside Leon's, and the powerful rhythm our hearts created had every inch of me aching to climb up to the top of the nearest tree and scream loud enough for the world to know that he was mine and I was his.

The balmy summer air tumbled over us suddenly and I was forced to remember that the world existed outside of the magic of the stars.

"What the fuck was that?" Ryder growled and I broke away from Leon, turning to my right where he, Dante and Gabriel stood staring at us like they couldn't quite believe what they'd just witnessed.

"No," Gabriel gasped, his gaze locking with mine as he shook his head in horror. "It can't be…I couldn't have made a mistake like that…"

"Alla luce delle stelle," Dante murmured, his gaze skipping between me and Leon like he couldn't believe what he was seeing.

Leon's hand stayed locked around mine, not possessively, more defensively, like he wanted to place himself between me and the others to protect me from them.

I looked up at him and as he returned my gaze I gasped, reaching up to cup his cheek as I looked into his golden eyes which were now rimmed with a line of purest silver. Like starlight given life. The stars had marked him as mine and from the way his gaze was fixed on my eyes, I knew that I'd been branded as his too.

"Well you were going to have to pick at some point," Ryder growled darkly, his glare cutting into me and making my heart bleed for him.

"What?" I breathed as I turned back to look at the others again.

"Un vero amore," Dante breathed. "You only get one mate."

I started shaking my head just as the sound of sirens reached us.

"Someone called the FIB," Ryder growled, reaching over his shoulder and yanking his T-shirt off. Something cracked in his eyes, a fundamental piece of him seeming to crumble to dust.

"Wait," I said, stepping towards him as he started unbuckling his pants.

"You'd better run if you don't want your name linked to Nightshade's disappearance." He dropped his clothes to the ground and used his Earth magic to bury them deep beneath the soil where they couldn't be found to be used as evidence.

"Ryder-"

"Goodbye Elise," he replied coldly with a finality that echoed into the depths of my soul. Before I could say anything else to stop him, he shifted into his Basilisk form and slithered away into the trees.

Gabriel was staring at me like I'd just dug his heart out of his chest with my fingernails and tossed it at his feet. I looked between him and Dante, not knowing what to say, aching to tell them that me choosing Leon didn't mean I'd rejected *them*. But the look in their eyes said they'd already come to their own conclusions about that.

"Get her out of here, mio amico," Dante said to Leon, avoiding my gaze as he pulled a pouch of stardust from his pocket and took a pinch for himself. He tossed the rest of the pouch to Leon who caught it automatically, seeming confused by what was happening right now.

"Where are we going?" Leon asked. "We need to talk about-"

"There's nothing else to say," Dante replied firmly, a wall in place behind his eyes as his jaw locked tightly. "The stars have spoken. Take her home. She's meant for you, not me, not any of us."

"Meant for?" I asked, his words stinging like a rejection. Like suddenly, I wasn't allowed to make up my own mind about what I wanted. Or *who* I wanted.

"Sarei stato tuo in un'altra vita, amore mio," he said to me in a rough voice and though I had no idea what it meant it sounded horribly like he was letting me go.

"Dante, please," I breathed, but as the sound of the FIB drawing closer called through the trees, he tossed the stardust over his head and disappeared without another word.

My gaze fell to Gabriel last and my heart pounded at the look of utter despair in his eyes. He'd seen this for the two of us. Or so he'd thought. He'd claimed me like the stars had already offered me up when in fact they'd just been playing a cruel prank on him. He'd been alone for so long, he deserved so much more than to have the one thing he'd pinned his hopes on snatched away from him like this.

My lips parted to say something as his wings sprang from his back and with a sharp beat of them, he took off into the sky and shot away from us. From me.

The cries of the FIB were even closer now and I looked up at Leon with my heart breaking in despair.

"What can I do to fix this?" I begged of him. I didn't regret my choice for one moment. As I looked into his golden eyes, the silver ring which haloed them seemed so right that the knowledge of it bled into my soul. But I couldn't bear the pain it had caused my other Kings.

He shook his head, having no more answers than I did. "I don't know," he breathed, reaching into the pouch Dante had given us and taking the stardust from it. "But right now we have to run, little monster."

"But-"

"We have to *run,*" Leon growled more firmly. "Are you with me?"

He took my hand and the answer that sprang to my lips had a ring of truth to it that I couldn't deny. Because despite whatever else this might mean for me and my Kings, there was absolutely one thing that I *was* sure of in all of it. I was destined to be with Leon Night and the rest we would figure out together.

"Are you with me?" Leon demanded again.

"Always," I replied fiercely.

He pressed his lips to mine just as he threw the stardust over us and we were yanked away from our place in the world to travel through the stars side by side. Exactly where we belonged.

GABRIEL

CHAPTER FIFTY THREE

I left my heart behind me in the clearing, torn clean from my chest by fate itself.

I didn't know who had betrayed me more; Elise or the stars. But as pain merged with rage inside me, splicing into something fierce and unrecognisable, I realised I blamed them both.

The visions I'd received had never shown *us* as mates, I'd just seen us both with silver rings in our eyes and made the assumption. So it all meant nothing. And now I had real access to The Sight, I realised how fragile every outcome was. There were endless choices, decisions and circumstances which could sway fate. Very few paths were set in stone. But there was one which was as hard and as irreversible as sediment turned to coal: Elise and I could never be together.

I clearly had an Elysian Mate somewhere in this world. But it wasn't her. And who knew if I'd ever find them? Who even cared? The only girl that mattered, the only one I wanted was Elise Callisto.

I flew hard and fast across the treetops, racing toward the city as the wailing sirens of the FIB followed me. I decided on abandoning everything in my dorm for the rest of the summer. I wouldn't be coming back here until term restarted and I wouldn't see Elise until then either. And by that time, I vowed to be free of her, body and soul. I had to purge myself of her. Had to slice her out of me no matter what that meant for my future. Because this *was* going to break me. Stripping her from my life wasn't something I'd survive in one piece. And I had a feeling that the parts that remained would be the darkest, most blackened lumps of my being, useless for nothing but hate and bitterness.

I swept across the high rise buildings, heading for my apartment on the Lunar side of the city. I needed to be alone. Somewhere quiet where I could let my heart break.

I swooped down to land on the skylight atop the tall building, using my magic to gain access, dropping inside and standing in the pool of moonlight that fell over me. I turned my head to the stars, cursing each and every one of them for deceiving me. Laughing at me.

I shoved the skylight shut and strode across the open plan space, but as I walked the stars gifted me more torture. I was dragged away into a sea of visions. Elise wrapped in Leon's arms, them kissing, fucking, adoring each other. It was a blinding summer of heat, passion and love and I held no part in it. The two of them were tangled up in awe of one another, having found their one true match. And I was pushed to the wayside, forgotten and abandoned. Elise would hardly remember my name, let alone recall that she'd ever cared for me.

The visions shifted onto my own future and all that awaited me was a void of loneliness. A hopelessness that resounded through my bones.

I'd retreat into the life I'd led before I met her. I'd focus on the only thing which had ever mattered to me before she'd come along. But somehow, the mysteries of my past didn't call to me like they once had. Because, for a moment there, I'd thought I'd had a future which could offer me so much more than the lost secrets of my childhood. I'd had something to live for.

Something to walk toward instead of forever turning back. And now I was trapped in purgatory in a life that wouldn't move in either direction. And for that, I was going to make the world pay.

ALSO BY

CAROLINE PECKHAM

&

SUSANNE VALENTI

Brutal Boys of Everlake Prep

(Complete Reverse Harem Bully Romance Contemporary Series)

Kings of Quarantine

Kings of Lockdown

Kings of Anarchy

Queen of Quarentine

Dead Men Walking

(Reverse Harem Dark Romance Contemporary Series)

The Death Club

Society of Psychos

**

The Harlequin Crew

(Reverse Harem Mafia Romance Contemporary Series)

Sinners Playground

Dead Man's Isle

Carnival Hill

Paradise Lagoon

Harlequinn Crew Novellas

Devil's Pass

**

Dark Empire

(Dark Mafia Contemporary Standalones)

Beautiful Carnage

Beautiful Savage

**

The Ruthless Boys of the Zodiac

(Reverse Harem Paranormal Romance Series - Set in the world of Solaria)

Dark Fae

Savage Fae

Vicious Fae

Broken Fae

Warrior Fae

Zodiac Academy

(M/F Bully Romance Series- Set in the world of Solaria, five years after Dark

Fae)

The Awakening

Ruthless Fae

The Reckoning

Shadow Princess

Cursed Fates

Fated Thrones

Heartless Sky

The Awakening - As told by the Boys

Zodiac Academy Novellas

Origins of an Academy Bully

The Big A.S.S. Party

Darkmore Penitentiary

(Reverse Harem Paranormal Romance Series - Set in the world of Solaria,
ten years after Dark Fae)

Caged Wolf

Alpha Wolf

Feral Wolf

**

The Age of Vampires

(Complete M/F Paranormal Romance/Dystopian Series)

Eternal Reign

Eternal Shade

Eternal Curse

Eternal Vow

Eternal Night

Eternal Love

**

Cage of Lies

(M/F Dystopian Series)

Rebel Rising

**

Tainted Earth

(M/F Dystopian Series)

Afflicted

Altered

Adapted

Advanced

**

The Vampire Games

(Complete M/F Paranormal Romance Trilogy)

V Games

V Games: Fresh From The Grave

V Games: Dead Before Dawn

*

The Vampire Games: Season Two

(Complete M/F Paranormal Romance Trilogy)

Wolf Games

Wolf Games: Island of Shade

Wolf Games: Severed Fates

*

The Vampire Games: Season Three

Hunter Trials

*

The Vampire Games Novellas

A Game of Vampires

**

The Rise of Issac

(Complete YA Fantasy Series)

Creeping Shadow

Bleeding Snow

Turning Tide

Weeping Sky

Failing Light

Milton Keynes UK
Ingram Content Group UK Ltd.
UKHW010818020524
442115UK00001B/93